THE WATERS BETWEEN

HARDSCRABBLE BOOKS Fiction of New England

Other Books by Joseph Bruchac

The Boy Who Lived with the Bears

Bowman's Store, an autobiography

Children of the Longhouse, a novel

The Circle of Thanks

Dog People: Native Dog Stories

Eagle Song

The Faithful Hunter

Flying with the Eagle

Four Ancestors: Stories, Songs and Poems

The Girl Who Married the Moon
    (with G. Ross)

Iroquois Stories

Keepers of the Animals (with M. Caduto)

Keepers of the Earth (with M. Caduto)

Keepers of Life (with M. Caduto)

Keepers of the Night (with M. Caduto)

*Lasting Echoes: An Oral History of Native
    American People*

*Many Nations: An Alphabet of Native
    America*

Native American Animal Stories

Native American Gardening

Native American Stories

Native Plant Stories

Return of the Sun

Roots of Survival: Essays on Storytelling

& the Sacred

Tell Me a Tale: A Book about Storytelling

Thirteen Moons on Turtle's Back (with
    J. London)

Turtle Meat and Other Stories

The Wind Eagle

Books for Young Adults

Dawn Land, a novel

Long River, a novel

The Native American Sweat Lodge

Native Wisdom

Picture Books

A Boy Called Slow

Between Earth and Sky

The Earth Under Sky Bear's Feet

The First Strawberries

Fox Song

Gluskabe and the Four Wishes

The Great Ball Game

Makiawisug: Gift of the Little People
    (with Melissa Fawcett)

The Maple Thanksgiving

The Story of the Milky Way

THE WATERS BETWEEN

□ □ □ □ □ □ □ □

A NOVEL OF THE DAWN LAND

JOSEPH BRUCHAC

UNIVERSITY PRESS OF NEW ENGLAND

HANOVER AND LONDON

UNIVERSITY PRESS OF NEW ENGLAND
publishes books under its own imprint and is the publisher for Brandeis University
Press, Dartmouth College, Middlebury College Press, University of New Hamp-
shire, Tufts University Press, and Wesleyan University Press.

Published by University Press of New England, Hanover, NH 03755
© 1998 by Joseph Bruchac
Printed in the United States of America   5   4   3   2   1

Library of Congress Cataloging-in-Publication Data
Bruchac, Joseph, 1942–
    The waters between : a novel of the dawn land / Joseph Bruchac.
    p.   cm. — (Hardscrabble books)
    ISBN 0–87451–881–4 (cloth : alk. paper)
    1. Abenaki Indians—History—Fiction.   2. Indians of North America—New
York (State)—Adirondack Mountains Region—Fiction.   3. Indians of North
America—Vermont—Green Mountains Region—Fiction.   I. Title. II. Series.
PS3552.R794W37   1998   98–6225
813'.54—dc21

This book is dedicated to my wife, Carol,
who has always stood beside me —
with the exception of those times
when she has been in front
waiting for me to catch up.

CONTENTS

ACKNOWLEDGMENTS

"Two Lodges" (Chapter Fourteen) first appeared in Volume 25, Fall 1997, of *Paintbrush, a Journal of Poetry and Translation.*

I need to say a special word of thanks to those who have worked so hard to preserve and pass on Western Abenaki language and traditions. Two of them have now followed the Sky Trail from the top of Wawnbi Wadzoak—Maurice Dennis and Grandmother Doris Minkler. I miss them, but they will never be forgotten.

Among those friends, colleagues, and teachers still with us who have provided far more help and encouragement to me over the years than I have deserved are Cheryl Bluto, Jeanne Brink, Stephen Laurent, John Moody, Donna Roberts, and Cecile Wawanolett. Ktsi wliwini, nidobak.

Lastly—for those who teach us are not always older than us in years—I have to thank my younger sister Margaret for her tireless work as a researcher, my son Jim for continuing to follow the trails with the Ndakinna Wilderness Project, and my son Jesse for hearing our language with such open ears.

INTRODUCTION

Petonbowk. "The Waters Between." That is the old Abenaki name for the long lake that fills the deep northern valley between the present-day states of New York and Vermont. It lies there between the high peaks of the Adirondack Mountains to the west and the Green Mountains to the east. A boundary water.

It is a place of many stories, some of them as ancient as the shaping of this land. Ten thousand years ago it was salt water, an inland arm of the sea. Then, as the land rose when the incalculable weight of the mountains of glacial ice melted away, it became cut off from the sea. Within those waters of that new great lake were such large marine animals as beluga whales, dolphins, walruses, seals, sharks, and, perhaps, other creatures less well known.

The Waters Between takes place not long after that lake's geological creation. It is the third novel I have placed in that time and location. As in my earlier novels *Dawn Land* and *Long River*, the story revolves around the extended family and friends of an Abenaki man known as Young Hunter. It is based on Abenaki traditions, Algonquin material culture, and my own brief lifetime of encounters with the place and the Native peoples of that part of *Ndakinna*, "Our Land." It is also deeply informed by the stories that I have been told are our oldest Abenaki stories and by the living Abenaki language, which shapes a good deal of what is said here, even in English. And it is rooted in dreams.

The Waters Between continues the stories of such characters as Young Hunter and his wife Willow Woman, his grandparents Sweetgrass Woman and Rabbit Stick, his friends Red Hawk and Blue

Hawk, and Young Hunter's loyal dogs. However, it is written to stand on its own, not just to be a sequel. It is a complete story and can be read without knowing the two previous books.

Two elements of the tale, however, might need some discussion. The first is the great being beneath the waters of Petonbowk. Those familiar with either cyrptozoology or contemporary Vermont popular culture have heard of "Champ," the sea serpent of Lake Champlain. A friend and neighbor of mine, Joseph Zarzynski, wrote a book about Champ over a decade ago. But sightings of a "Lake Champlain Monster" are no new thing. They go back hundreds of years among Europeans and much longer than that among the Abenaki. It is no frivolous thing to speak of that one we call *Padoskoks*. I have attempted to do so in a respectful way. To this day, most Abenaki people will not speak the name of the "bigger-than-big snake" when they are anywhere near the lake.

The second is the subject of rivalry, even to the point of murder, between *mteowlins*. Although the character in this story known as Watches Darkness is an extreme example, contests between "conjurers" or "shamans," as Europeans have called our deep-seeing people, have always taken place. Such rivalry is even to be found in *Old John Neptune and Other Maine Indian Shamans*, (Portland, 1945) by Fannie Hardy Eckstrom. There are always people whose hearts are good and people whose minds are twisted by grief or anger, selfish ambition, or jealousy. We find them at every time of history and among every people.

The things done by the various *mteowlins* or "deep-seers" in this novel are not, to my mind, unusual or unbelievable. One reason why Carlos Castaneda's ersatz "nonfiction" books about the "Yaqui shaman" Don Juan and the equally questionable books of Lynn Andrews and her ilk have enjoyed such popularity is that they present a reality, a body of mysteries that most European-minded people have failed to see. It is a simple truth that too many today have become divorced from the spiritual. Then, when they are made aware of its existence in a New Age or "pop Native American" context, it blows them away. They do not realize that they are often in the same position as the blind person who places trust in a one-eyed con artist.

To the Native people of the Americas, that world of the spirit is as everyday as eating and sleeping. It is not something to be bought or sold. It is a given. A gift like the gift of breath, which still remains the greatest mystery to me. So, again, I have tried to show respect to the gift.

Anhaldam mawi kassipalilawalan. That is the old New Year's greeting in Abenaki, the thing to say to your family, friends, and neighbors when the new cycle of seasons begins soon after the shortest days of winter. *Anhaldam mawi kassipalilawalan.* "Forgive me for any wrong I may have done you." I say it now at the start of this novel. Any mistakes here are my own and they were not intended. Anything in these pages that is informed by the truth, touched by the spirit, shaped by the beloved land and our old ones who will never be forgotten is not my own. Think of it instead as a gift to me that I was meant to share.

THE WATERS BETWEEN

1 ▣ DEEP WATER

Young Hunter dipped the cup deeply into the still waters of the lake. The cup, which his grandfather Rabbit Stick had carved for him, was made of basswood. Its handle, held lightly between his first finger and his thumb, was in the shape of an owl's head. The cat-owl, those birds that were the guardians of their thirteen villages. At night the cat-owls would sit in the cedars at the edge of each village. If any dangerous person or creature approached, they would call in a certain way. So the cat-owl carved onto Young Hunter's drinking cup had a meaning. Watch, it meant. Be vigilant.

He lifted the cup to his lips and sipped. Its taste, though not as strong as that of a medicine spring, was still faintly salty. He shook the last drops of water from the cup. Then he hooked the toggle, which hung from a short rawhide cord on the handle, under his belt. The stars that swam above him, following their great chief, the Night Traveler, were reflected in the smooth surface of Petonbowk.

Perhaps, Young Hunter thought, if I walk forward I will not sink into the lake. I will walk instead up into those stars. That is how it was long ago, when the three hunters chased the Great Bear. He remembered when he heard that story for the first time. He was so small that his head did not yet reach his grandfather's belt. Together he and Rabbit Stick stood outside the wigwam on a cold night in midwinter. They were both barefooted, for they did not intend to walk far, only far enough to relieve themselves before sleeping.

* * *

"There," Rabbit Stick had said, pointing with his lips to the shape of stars. "Those four stars are the great bear. The three behind are the hunters. They are Gray Jay and Chickadee and Robin. Chickadee is carrying his cooking pot with him and Gray Jay has a load of wood on his back to make their cooking fire. The last one in line is Robin, the lazy one. All he is carrying is his spear. He will pretend his foot was hurt so that his brothers will carry him. His two brothers are so determined to get that bear—it has been threatening their people for a long time, killing all the game—that they will tell him to sit on his spear. Then each of them will grab one end of that spear and they will carry him between them. They know he is the one who would strike that bear with his spear. It has always been that way before. When the bear runs up a great hill that is sparkling with frost, they will run up after it."

Rabbit Stick paused then and looked down at his grandson to see if he was listening.

"Unh-hunh," Young Hunter said, his eyes in the stars.

"So they will keep on," Rabbit Stick continued, "not knowing they have chased the bear up Wawnbi Wadzo, the great white moun-tain. Not knowing that they have begun to follow the road of stars. And when it seems they can run no further, Robin, the lazy brother, will tell them to put him down. His foot feels better, he will say."

Young Hunter laughed. "He tricked them, didn't he?"

"Unh-hunh. And because he is rested, just as always, he will run ahead and kill the bear with his spear. Its blood will fall from the sky and turn the leaves of the trees red. Some of that blood will get on Robin's chest. Gray Jay will make the fire. Chickadee will use his cooking pot. But as the hunters rest, eating some of the meat from that bear, it will come back to life and begin to run again. So they will follow it. And every year, just as before, Robin will kill the bear."

"And the leaves turn red again," Young Hunter said.

"Unh-hunh," Rabbit Stick said, placing his hand on his grand-son's shoulder. "And now we must go back into the wigwam before our feet freeze to the earth."

"Could we walk upon that road into the stars?" Young Hunter said.

"We might do so if we do not go inside now," Rabbit Stick said. "No, I am joking, Grandson. Come inside. Maybe you will be allowed to climb the sky road in your dreams."

Young Hunter carefully placed his foot on the calm surface of the lake. "There are those," Bear Talker told him once," who walk so lightly on the water that they do not sink." Young Hunter felt the coolness of the water spread over the sole of his foot. He pressed down gently. . . and his foot went beneath the surface. It did not stop until it touched the bottom and his leg was knee deep in the water. He took an equally slow step with his other leg and now he was hip deep, the reflected stars rippling gently about him.

A deep, throaty growl came from close behind him. Young Hunter turned to look at the big dog that had come down to the water's edge.

"Agwedjiman," Young Hunter said. "Do you not want to walk into the stars with me?"

Agwedjiman growled again. A low warning sound.

"Kina?" Young Hunter said. "What is it?" He held his hand back toward the dog. Agwedjiman leaned forward and placed his head beneath Young Hunter's hand. Then he, too, stepped into the water. But he did not go as deep as Young Hunter had gone. His back legs remained on the shore and he reached up to grasp Young Hunter's woven basswood belt firmly between his strong teeth. He pulled back. The stars vanished in the many ripples that broke the surface around them as Agwedjiman moved back, step by step, dragging the young man with him.

Young Hunter did not resist. A part of himself was amused. Yet he also trusted the stronger senses of this dog, who was the most faithful and protective of companions. As he moved back step by step he narrowed his eyes to scan the calm, starlit expanse of Petonbowk, the Waters Between. It was so bright that he could clearly see the mountain tops just beyond the far shore. What was it that Agwedjiman, his guardian and friend, had seen or heard, scented or sensed in some deeper way? What might be out there? There beneath the calm surface.

Step by step, Young Hunter allowed himself to be pulled back. Out of the lake. But that was not far enough. His feet grinding in the gravel, Agwedjiman continued to draw him away from the water. Up from the sand and drying water plants, up from the small white shells and pieces of wave-smoothed driftwood that came carried by the wind from the sunset direction.

At last, when they reached the soft green grasses, a spear's throw from water's edge, Agwedjiman gently released his hold. But before Young Hunter could move, the big dog took three quick steps and placed itself between the young man and the water, which had, once more, grown as still and quiet as the surface of a small pond. The big dog stood in exactly the same way that he stood whenever he placed himself between the hearth fire and any small innocent child whose steps might lead too close to the flames.

Young Hunter smiled. But he did not protest. He did not try to go any closer to the lake. He stood, as Agwedjiman did, watching the water. He felt the warmth of the big dog as it leaned against him and he felt, as much as heard, the low guarding growl that still came from deep inside Agwedjiman's chest.

The round, calm face of the Night Traveler smiled down upon them. Beyond and all around her luminous halo, the Awatawesak, those far-off birds of fire, the dancing stars, added their fires to the brightness of their great chief. Patiently, in the tall grass of early summer, the wide-shouldered young man and the great dog stood. They were so still that they might have been figures carved of cedar. Only the occasional ripple of muscle across Agwedjiman's shoulder showed that they were not made of wood or stone.

One of the Awatawesak broke away from his relatives. The falling star streamed across the sky, fiery hair trailing behind it. Young Hunter saw, but did not turn his gaze away from the lake. It seemed now as if he, too, could sense something. But even with the deep-seeing powers that he was still struggling to control, whatever was there was not easy to discern.

Deep-seeing was like that. You could feel the thoughts of other beings, but those thoughts were not in words like those of the Only People, and the power of those thoughts was not always measured in human terms. Young Hunter remembered the day six winters before when he had first succeeded in doing as Bear Talker taught him. He had found a quiet place, close to the little stream that flowed into Kwanitewk, the Long River, above the great falls. There he had closed his eyes and readied himself. He had cleared away his own thoughts, like clearing away an old cobweb from the door of an abandoned wigwam, and then allowed himself to be filled in the way an empty cup is filled when it is thrust into a stream. Many things washed over him, but one impression was so strong, so hungry, so dangerous, that it had shaken him. It was a hunting hunger so powerful that it shook him deeply. He opened his eyes, looking around for that being that he knew must be one of the Ancient Ones, one of those terrible creatures that hunted the Only People.

It was two winters before Bear Talker would send him on that quest that would lead to his fight with the cannibal giants, and Young Hunter had yet to encounter any of those old ones whose very existence threatened the lives of all human beings. Yet that day by the little stream, Young Hunter first experienced the kind of fear one felt when stalked by such a creature. He saw and heard nothing around him. He stood and ran back to Bear Talker's lodge, uncertain if he would reach that place of safety or be caught, killed, and eaten. That was how strong the wordless thoughts of that terrible being had touched him. He had told his story to Bear Talker, who had remained strangely calm.

"Show me where you sat," Bear Talker said.

They had gone back to the place by the stream.

"Here," Young Hunter said, indicating a flat stone next to an overhanging willow. His heart was beating so loudly that he was certain Bear Talker could hear it.

Bear Talked knelt and then reached deep into the stream. He groped about and then lifted something up. It wiggled in his grasp. "Here is your creature," he said.

Young Hunter came close and looked. It was a very big beetle. Its snout was thrust deeply into a minnow that was as large as it was. The minnow's eyes were glazing over and it moved its tail weakly.

"It is drinking the life of this fish," Bear Talker said. "Of all the water creatures, this beetle, the Life-sucker, is the hungriest one."

Young Hunter knew that Bear Talker was right. At the edge of his mind he could again sense the fierce thoughts of that small hunter of the waters. It would kill and eat anything.

Bear Talker nodded. "You see, nephew? This is the one you sensed. Just because something is small, does not mean its hunger is small. If this one was as large as a beaver, we human beings would be its prey."

Young Hunter sensed something else. He tried to speak. "Uncle . . . ," he said.

Bear Talker paid no attention. "But because the Life-sucker is so little, we have nothing to fear from it. Hiiii-yagggh!"

And then Bear Talker had quickly shaken the Life-sucker beetle from his hand so that it landed back in the water with a splash. Just as Young Hunter had sensed it was about to do, the little fierce one had released its hold on the minnow and driven its sharp beak deeply into Bear Talker's palm.

What Young Hunter sensed now was not as sharp and quick as the Life-sucker beetle. It was slow and deep, barely there at the edge of his mind. Once again, Young Hunter felt that familiar uncertainty. Was he truly sensing this or only wishing himself to do so, imagining something that was not there? There was a thin line between those two worlds, the one of imagination and the other of deep-seeing. Sometimes people fooled themselves into believing they were deep-seers. What was it that Medicine Plant said to him? Yes, that was it. Those who deceive themselves do not allow themselves to have doubts. A small smile touched the edge of Young Hunter's mouth. So, he thought, because I have doubts I am truly a deep-seer?

The Night Traveler moved across the skyland as the two of them stood there. A finger's width, two fingers. A hand's width, two hands. Young Hunter and Agwedjiman remained as they were.

Perhaps, Young Hunter thought, Willow Woman is now wondering why I have not returned. He knew, though she pretended to continue to sleep as he had gently removed her leg from its usual place over his thighs, that she had wakened when he woke. He knew that she had watched him as he rose and slipped out of their lean-to. Her eyes had observed as he made his noiseless way down the slope toward the lake that had beckoned to him in some way, the big lake that glistened far below their camping place. He was certain, too, that it was Willow Woman who had sent Agwedjiman after him. Young Hunter had motioned for the three dogs to remain with his wife as he left.

Now the Night Traveler had moved the width of three hands. And Young Hunter heard a sound. It came across the water. It was like a sigh. It was a call so deep and lonely that he felt it in his chest even as his ears heard it. It echoed across the bay. As if in answer to it, Agwedjiman, who had been silent, again began to growl.

Young Hunter looked for the motion that he knew must be there. At first he saw nothing. Then it was there. Far out. A ripple moving. It came closer. A shape like the head of a small bear sticking up out of the water. Dark lines and shadows moving back from it as it crossed the bay, heading toward the same shore where the young man and the big dog stood. All around that swimming creature, ripples were trembling the surface of the lake, trembling it as a spider's web trembles when a fly lands upon it and is caught.

As the animal came closer, Young Hunter recognized it. It was a fish-catcher, one of the water people found here in Petonbowk and in the deeper saltier waters that began where the land ended at the edge of dawn. Although they were animals of the day, sometimes the fish-catchers would come out on bright nights. They would dive and play together as the Night Traveler watched with wide eyes. The fish-catchers were often as big as a human being. They were awkward on land, but in the water they were as graceful as a gull in flight. They were as playful as otters and Young Hunter had always liked them. His people did not hunt them.

At times a fish-catcher might come and rise out of the water to look at a human being with wide, beautiful eyes. "Come and play with me," those eyes seemed to say. Yet the Only People hesitated to follow them into the water. It was said that once a human being shared the life of a fish-catcher, even for the briefest period, that human being would never return to his or her own life again. That human being would join the fish-catchers, put on their skin and be one of them. Such a life with plenty to eat and no need to ever gather wood or make fires or repair wigwams would be so easy. Such a life of playing and constant companionship would be hard to resist.

Yet this fish-catcher was alone. And it was swimming slowly, so very slowly. Was it injured? Young Hunter began to sense its distress. It was even closer now. It was going straight toward the very place where Young Hunter had tasted the waters of Petonbowk, there where the bottom fell away suddenly from the shore into depth and darkness.

The heart of the fish-catcher was pounding. Young Hunter felt his own heart beat faster. Faster, he thought. Swim faster. There was no reason for this fear. The night and the waters were calm. All was quiet. Too quiet. Was it the quiet of something waiting? Agwedji-man's growl grew louder and he pressed back against Young Hunter's legs. The fish-catcher was now only a spear's throw away from the land. Young Hunter could see its eyes. Its eyes, luminous and large as the Night Traveler's face, saw him.

Suddenly the surface of the lake surged behind the fish-catcher. A ripple rose like a muscle beneath the glittering skin of Petonbowk. The fish-catcher made a single cry, almost like a dog's yelp. Then, as if struck from beneath by a great club, it was hurled up. Water cascaded around it, white water. Something rose up, like a great arm. It lifted high, swift as thought, and Young Hunter saw the white glitter from the great mouth that gaped open. It caught the fish-catcher in mid-air and then struck down. THWOOM!

The force of that blow was so great that water was hurled far up onto the shore. A sudden brief rain fell all around the young man and his dog. It fell on Young Hunter's face, onto his forehead and his eyes. Onto his lips. He tasted that water with his tongue. It was warmer and saltier than he expected. He lifted a hand to wipe it from his eyes. He saw it was dark on his fingers in the Night Traveler's light. Darker than water. Blood.

In the bushes and trees all around the bay small birds began to call in distress, startled out of sleep. A series of waves, caused by that sudden explosion of motion and violence, lapped onto the shore.

Young Hunter watched and did not move. The surface of Peton-bowk again became calm. The birds fretfully settled back into sleep. Young Hunter knew what his dreams would hold when he next slept. In his dreams he would see that wide and hungry mouth, those white sharp teeth, those cool eyes that held his for the briefest of heart beats before vanishing again back into the depths. He knew he would see those eyes again, and not just in his dreams.

2 ▣ WATCHES DARKNESS

As he crouched in the darkest shadows at the base of a giant pine, Watches Darkness amused himself by imagining what would happen to those inside the wigwam if he wished. He imagined balls of fire flying out of the darkness and striking all around the base of the wigwam. He imagined dry birch bark catching fire, the shapes incised into it as decorations blackening with heat and smoke, then curling into the red of flame and the white of ash. It was good to see this in the eye of his mind, but it was even better to imagine those within. To feel them waking as they felt the sudden heat surround them. To hear them coughing from the smoke, screaming in fear as flames fell all around them. To see them stumbling out, blinded, burned, helpless. And then to feel their even greater fear at what they saw approach them on four legs. It would come toward them slowly at first, lazy with power. Its dark fur would ripple with that power. Its eyes would be red from the flames and from the promise of blood. It would circle them, keeping them with their backs to the fire, unable to escape as it moved faster. It would rear up on its hind legs, spread its paws wide so that its long claws reached out like spear points. Yes, yes! Then, shaking the earth as it walked, it would walk toward them like a man as they stared up at it. It would be the last thing they would ever see.

Watches Darkness laughed. It was a laugh that made no noise. He closed his arms and then sat back down again in the deep shadows. Yes, it might be that way. But there were other ways it might be, too. He would save the spirit fire and the One Who Walks Like a Man for another time. He might come to the wigwam as a traveler. A traveler who looked familiar, like a friend or even a relative from one of the thirteen villages. They would not see his pale skin that was afraid of the Day Walker's light. They would not see his eyes that were the color of a dying flame. They would see someone they thought they knew. He would not mention a name, but they would think him familiar. They would invite him in.

"It is late, my relative," they would say. "It is the middle of night. You must travel no further. You must stay here with us."

Then they would give him food to eat and the guest place by the fire. He would pretend to eat their food, but he would not eat it. He would pretend to sleep, but he would not close his eyes. He would wait until they slept. He would listen until their breathing was deep and regular with sleep. Then there were many things that he could do, silent things. Yes! And those silent things would make the silence in the wigwam even deeper. There would be no sounds of breath when he was done with his work.

Watches Darkness giggled. This time he did make a sound. It was a small sound much like the call of the great horned owl just before it hunts. He was close to deciding. Other possibilities were still there at the edge of his mind. A great dead tree could fall on the wigwam, perhaps. It would thrust its branches in through the sides like spears, piercing the bodies of those within. It was good to think of them trapped in this way. Struggling to escape in the dark. And then, yes, then he could send the fire so that the wigwam would burn. And he could also call forth the One Who Walks Like a Man to roar and fill them with terror. And then he, Watches Darkness, could stand in the light of that fire so that they could see him. Yes! They would see his skin like birch bark, his hair like winter snow and his eyes that could not stand the brightness of daylight. And they would be afraid of his power. They would not laugh at him as the people of his own village had laughed when he was a child. They would not tease him as the children teased him then, before he found his power. Before he was given the means to gain revenge.

The old woman who had raised him had not loved him. His birth had killed her daughter. She was always angry with him, always impatient when he dropped something or made some mistake.

"Go and cut me a switch," she would say. "Make it as thick as my thumb."

He would do as she said. At first he would cut switches that were thin or he would weaken them so that they would break after she had struck him only a few times. But he quickly learned that did not work.

"Go cut another stick. This one must be stronger."

And then she would beat him again.

But she had kept the boy for reasons of her own. She fed him and gave him clothing and a place to sleep—even though he slept when others were awake and woke when others slept. She taught him what she knew, and she knew more than the others in the village realized.

His grandmother's own mind was not a straight mind. Some in the village said that it was the old woman herself who was to blame for the ugly strangeness of her grandson. She was the one who had taken her daughter far from the village, far toward the Summer Land. Three seasons later, when they had returned, the young woman was pregnant—even though it could clearly be seen that she was still too young to have a child. Others said that her husband, a man no one would ever see, was not a human person at all. He was one of those from the Summer Land who was able to shift between the worlds of the human people and the animal people.

That was why the old woman, whose name was Sharp Tongue, had taken her daughter far away from the places where her people walked. That was why she had sought such a husband for her only child. Sharp Tongue was jealous of the things others had. Not their possessions. Anyone could have possessions. She was jealous of this one's strength, or of that one's wisdom. She was jealous of the respect that other enjoyed, respect she did not enjoy herself, and so she would always say hard things about everyone. There was always a little truth in what she said, even though that truth was as distorted as the shadow of a tree when the light of the Day Traveler is about to vanish. People winced when Sharp Tongue spoke. They tried to avoid her and they pitied her daughter, who was as quiet and shy as her mother was loud and forceful.

"No one will ever marry that girl," the people said of Sharp Tongue's daughter. "No man will ever accept having that woman as his mother-in-law or the grandmother of his children!"

So Sharp Tongue took her daughter on that long journey south. It was her plan that her daughter would come back and give birth to a child filled with power. Then everyone would respect her. But it did not happen as Sharp Tongue planned.

Revenge. Watches Darkness leaned back into the shadow of the pine, remembering. He put the side of his hand into his mouth and bit it to keep himself from laughing too loudly. Whenever he thought of the revenge he had taken it was so sweet that he could not stop himself when he did begin to laugh. He would laugh louder and louder until his wild laughter began to sound like the howling of the wind. He had taken his revenge. No one still lived who had ever laughed at him, no one drew breath who had ever pushed or teased him, who had ever told him to go away because his face was like that of a maggot, who had ever seen his face blinded by the light. All of them were gone. But it had not been enough. At the furthest edge of his dreams he sometimes thought he heard their voices still laughing at him, mocking him. In his dreams, where his power should be its strongest, unseen hands still shoved him and as he walked, unseen feet would trip him. He would wake, sweat on his pale forehead. He would brush back his white stringy hair with one hand and know that his work was not yet done. It might never be done. But then he would smile. He would remember his grandmother as he had last seen her and he would smile.

Yes. Yes. He knew the feeling of real power. Real power was to be slowly enjoyed. Slowly. Watches Darkness took his hand out of his mouth. Blood oozed from his hand where his teeth had broken the flesh.

Watches Darkness smiled to himself. Not now, he thought. It would be too soon, too easy. There would not be enough fear and it would be over so quickly. He stood and looked at the wigwam with hooded eyes. And it would be foolish. It would call attention to him-self before he was ready. He knew that there were other deep-seeing ones not far away. Their presence had drawn him here. Three of them, though one was even younger than himself. Barely a man. To destroy them would give him the greatest pleasure, but if they knew, too soon, that he was here? That would not be good. He would wait a bit longer. For now he would only watch and . . . imagine the possi-bilities.

He looked down at his feet. It still lay there, a small bundle of feathers. His dart had killed it before it could give the warning call. It would not be wise to leave it here. Watches Darkness scooped up the dead owl and pulled free his dart and dropped it into his large medi-cine bag. Then he picked up the blowgun that he had used to fire that dart into the owl's chest.

No one will know I have been there, he thought before he disap-peared into the deeper shadows. But he was wrong.

Inside that wigwam, Rabbit Stick sat wide awake. He did not know why he had wakened, but he knew that there was reason to be awake. He was not afraid, but he held his throwing stick in one hand and his spear in the other as he waited by the open door. He knew that there was something to be seen there in the night. He knew that as clearly as he knew that it would be death to go out and look for it. Close be-side him, on the other side of the door, which had been left open to allow the cool night air to enter, Sweetgrass Woman crouched. She held her own spear in both hands. Her eyes were better than those of her husband. It had been that way even before the two of them had become elders. That was why one of her nicknames among the Only People was "She Who Sees Everything."

She saw the movement at the base of the huge pine. Something white as a snow rabbit, though this was not the season for animals to wear their coats of winter. Then it was gone. She felt it as much as she saw it. She looked over at her husband.

"Unh-hunh," he said.

Sweetgrass Woman pointed with her lips toward the big pine tree. "When first light comes," she whispered, "we will look there at the base of that tree."

"Put your back against mine, old woman," Rabbit Stick said. "You sleep first and then I will wake you up when I am ready to sleep."

"You are always ready to sleep," Sweetgrass Woman said to him, her voice soft. She poked him with her elbow. "You sleep first."

Rabbit Stick chuckled. He leaned back against her, feeling her warmth and her strength support him. Together, both of them awake as they guarded each other, they sat that way until dawn.

Bear Talker was troubled. His back and his neck hurt. It felt as if the small cords between his back and shoulder had been tied together, pulled taut and then pinned in place with spear points. There was a knot in his stomach that moved about and burned. It was as if he had swallowed a ball of snakes that were biting him from within. He started to get up from his stomach, but a fist struck him hard in the shoulder.

"Stay there," Medicine Plant said, "if you want me to help you." Wearing nothing but the tattoo of a snow owl, which spread its wide wings above her breasts, she was straddling her husband's back. Normally, Bear Talker would have found this of great interest. But this morning he was in too much pain.

"If you are going to help me, then help me," he groaned. Medicine Plant struck him again, this time hard on his shoulder.

"Quiet," she said, "I cannot think when you are complaining. I am trying to see where the pain is centered before I work it free."

"It is centered in your knuckles," Bear Talker said. "Just look at where the bruises are from your fists."

Medicine Plant leaned forward to breathe hard against his neck. Then she put her tongue into his ear. "Do I need to clean out your ears, my husband," she whispered in a husky voice. It made Bear Talker forget the pains in his neck and back and stomach for a few heartbeats as another part of his body began to make itself felt. Medicine Plant reached back and slapped him on his hip. "Stop that, too!" she said. There was laughter in her voice. Despite his pain Bear Talker found himself thinking once again of the great luck which had found him. It was true that Medicine Plant was merciless, even rather frightening in her ability to be ruthless when it came to curing someone of their pain. But she could be as gentle as she was firm, as passionate as she was strong. And that was how she would be with him when she was through with her ministering to his pain. Just as long, Bear Talker thought, as she doesn't kill or cripple me while she is doing it.

Medicine Plant pressed both of her thumbs deeply into the place where the back of Bear Talker's upper arm joined his shoulder.

"Unnnhhh!" Bear Talker moaned. "Just kill me quickly and be done with it."

Medicine Plant did not answer him this time. She had found the place where the pain ran like a long line through her husband's body. Deep through the muscles, following the strings of energy, which she could see clearly now, pulsing through his body. There, where the color was different, where she could feel the heat beneath her fingers. That was one place. She pressed hard, then softer, and massaged open the channel that was blocked. Although Bear Talker was round and looked to be a man of not much strength, the muscles beneath his skin were firm and very powerful. But a man with such strong muscles was more likely to have such pains as these when he used those muscles wrong and twisted himself about in his sleep as Bear Talker had done last night, growling as he fought an unseen enemy. She concentrated more of the healing energy into her palms and felt them grow warmer as the energy pulsed there.

Medicine Plant took a deep breath, then leaned forward and pressed with the heels of her hands across her husband's back as if she was smoothing the wrinkles from a piece of tanned deerskin.

"Unnh-hunnnh!" Bear Talker sighed. "Yes."

The pain was going. It was being washed away just as snow is washed away by the flow of a stream in the moon of thaw. He felt the stiffness leaving his back and his shoulders, even though the knot in his stomach remained. Aggh-ahh! Now that his back pain was gone his stomach hurt even worse.

Medicine Plant slid off his back. Grasping him by the shoulder and the hip, she flipped him onto his back as easily as if he had been a small baby. Despite his size and his weight, Bear Talker knew that she could just as easily have picked him up and thrown him out the door of their wigwam if she had wanted to do so. In fact, she had done that very thing to him two nights ago—in play. Medicine Plant was almost as dangerous when she was playful as she was when she was angry. Once again Bear Talker felt his heart—and something else, too—swell with pleasure at the thought of having the love of such a person.

Medicine Plant snorted. "You are worse than Raccoon with all his wives," she said. "This is not the time for that." She punched him in his stomach just hard enough to make Bear Talker open his mouth with a loud "OOOFFF!" Then she spread her fingers open and thrust down. Her fingers seemed to reach into his stomach, below the skin, right into his belly. He felt her fingers reaching for that knot of twisting, angry snakes. He closed his eyes and forced himself to lay back, willed himself to relax as Medicine Plant did her work. Her hand withdrew. He opened his eyes. His wife stood by the door of the lodge, her hand open as if setting something free. All of his pains, from back to stomach, were gone.

Medicine Plant turned back toward him. She reached down and picked up her deerskin dress, wrapping it about herself. Bear Talker looked regretful. Though her long hair was gray, his wife's body was not that of an old woman. Far from it.

Bear Talker sat up. As he did so, a sudden chill ran through him. And with that chill came the memory of his dream. He reached back and lifted the edges of his bearskin robe to wrap it about him. Then he looked at the robe, the robe made from the skin of an Ancient One that had hunted the people in the generation of his own grandparents. They had called that one Fear Bear. Once, Bear Talker had thought it was the last of the Great Ones, the last of those who saw human beings the way a fox sees a rabbit. But the things that had happened over the last four winters had proven that thought to be wrong. First there had been the Gray Giants. But Young Hunter— that young man that he and Medicine Plant were training to be a deep-seer—had accepted that challenge. He had gone forth, walking far toward the sunset. There, with the help of his three dogs and with the power of that sacred and still secret weapon called the Long Thrower, the Gray Giants had been destroyed.

Yet that, too, had not been the end of it. Only two winters ago the Walking Hill had come to their own villages by the Long River. Its two great teeth were like spears and it was so large that it could crush a wigwam under one foot. Once again, Young Hunter had been able to accept the challenge. Somehow, one of the Gray Giants had survived and it had proven to be their ally this time. Another of the ones from the old tales, a little one this time, the tiny man they knew as Mikumwesu, had been the one to make that giant enemy into their helper. Bear Talker shook his head. So many things were walking into their lives out of the old stories that he would not have been surprised to see the One Who Shaped Himself rise up again out of the earth outside their wigwam. It had been nine seasons since the Gray Giant and then Mikumwesu had vanished. Perhaps one or both of them would return. Bear Talker did not know. He placed his hand on his forehead and rubbed his temples with his fingers.

But there was one thing that Bear Talker did know. He knew it ever more clearly as he brought back into his awake mind the dream he had been given during the night. That dream that made him growl and try to strike out and overcome a new enemy. Or more than one enemy, more than one danger. For it seemed for one breath as if he was swimming, swimming beneath the water wrestling with something huge and cold and as slippery as an eel, and then the next breath he was on dry land and trying to hold on to—or hold back— something else, which was warm and powerful. He grasped the bear robe in his hand. Like this bear. Like this bear.

Bear Talker growled. It was like trying to untie a knotted piece of sinew. Just as soon as he thought he had worked it free, he would find under that knot yet another knot. He reached back behind him for his medicine bag, which was made from the whole skin of a wolf.

Medicine Plant knelt down on one knee and looked at him as if she was looking into him.

"In your dream," Medicine Plant said, "were you deep in Peton-bowk?"

"Unh-hunh," Bear Talker said, digging into his bag even though he was not sure what he was looking for. It comforted him to hold that bag. He had not felt her there beside him in his dream, but it did not surprise him that she was there. Though he knew his own medicine strength to be the equal of hers—after all, they had the same teacher—he also knew that her ways could be more subtle. While she always seemed to have known what was in his mind and his heart, he was constantly surprised by her. It had not been that way with the women he had married—and then unmarried—before the two of them came together. Some of his previous wives had been afraid of him. Others, like Little Mink, had only married him to try to steal power from him. Yet he had always know what was in their minds. That knowledge of his had frightened them to the point that the day came when they could control their fear no longer—usually a day when the bear was strong in him and he was growling and speaking to the ones who live far under the earth. Then they would run screaming from his lodge and never return. Bear Talker had been married many times, but he had never found it necessary to ask his wives to leave him when the time came for them to no longer be married.

But Medicine Plant was different. Bear Talker knew that they would remain together until the time came when one or both of them would climb to the top of the great White Mountain and step onto the road of stars. Their souls were connected to each other like two great trees whose strong branches and deep roots were intertwined. Although one was a cedar and the other a pine they swayed together in the wind, drank the same rain, and supported each other when struck by storm.

"But there was more to your dream," Medicine Plant said. "You fought one who did not know you were fighting him. You forced him to flee without knowing he was fleeing. He left before he harmed those who are our friends. You did well, my husband. His waking mind did not sense what you were doing. I watched as your spirit wrestled his. First he was a man, then a bear, though I could not see his face. It was another deep-seer."

"Who will soon come to hunt us," Bear Talker said.

Medicine Plant nodded. She opened her mouth to speak, but before she could say anything a small figure burst into the lodge.

"Come quick, come quick, come quick," the little boy said.

Bear Talker reached out to gently grasp him by his shoulders.

"Old Eyes Looking Backward Over Bright Sky," he said, calling their son by all three of his names, "what is it?"

"A man," Old Eyes Looking Backward Over Bright Sky said. "A bad man flying across the sky."

Willow Woman watched the first light of the new day begin to reach up into the sky. The little far-above ones, which had been so bright, were fading. Their chief, the Night Walker, had already gone to her home below the hills. Only one star was still bright in the sky. She looked behind her. There he was. Old Morning Star, the lazy one. Willow Woman smiled. Her mother, Near the Sky, had told her the story of Old Morning Star many times. It was one of her favorites, and Willow Woman knew that, when she and Young Hunter had children of their own, her mother would tell that same story to them.

It was long ago. Chibai, the cannibal ghost, was chasing two children through the night. The children came to the river filled with rapids. Crane was on the other side.

"Crane," said the little boy, "help us get across. A monster is chasing us and will eat us."

"Look at my legs," said Crane, "are my legs not long and beautiful?"

"Crane," said the little girl, "your legs are very long and beautiful."

"Good," said Crane, "if that is what you think, then I will help you." And then Crane reached one long leg across the river filled with rapids. The children used that leg as a bridge and crossed over. Then Crane pulled her leg back.

Soon the Chibai came to the river filled with rapids.

"You there," the Chibai hissed, "help me across. I need to catch two children and eat them."

"Look at my legs," said Crane, "are they not beautiful?"

"Scabby and covered with crap," hissed the Chibai.

"Oh," said Crane, "if that is what you think, I know what to do." Then Crane reached one leg across the river filled with rapids. The Chibai started to cross, but when it was in midstream Crane shook her leg. The Chibai fell into the rapids and was swept away.

The children kept running, because they knew the Chibai would not be killed by the water. Only the light of the new day could kill it.

They ran until they came to a cave. An old old man lived in that cave. That old man was Morning Star. He was slowly, slowly, slowly getting dressed for the time when night would end and he would have to leave the sky.

"Can you help us?" said the boy.

"The Chibai wants to eat us," said the girl.

"Ahhhhhh, Chilllllldrennnnn," Morning Star said in his slow voice. "Comme, comme, commmme in heeeere."

The children ran into the cave and hid in it while Morning Star continued to sit in front slowly, slowly, slowly getting dressed. Meanwhile, the Chibai fought its way out of the rapids. It ran back up the river and found the children's trail. Soon the Chibai reached the mouth of the cave. Morning Star still sat there.

"Old Man," hissed the Chibai, " have you seen two children?"

"Waaaaiiit," Morning Star said in his slow voice. "Waaiiit untilll I get my legging onnnnnn." Then he slowly, slowly, slowly wrapped his leggings around one leg.

"Old Man," Chibai hissed again, "I cannot wait, I am hungry. Where are those two children?"

"Waaaaiiit," Morning Star said again in his slow voice. "Waaiiit untilll I get my ooooother legging onnnnnn." Then he slowly, slowly, slowly wrapped his leggings around his other leg.

Now the Chibai was growing angry. "Old Man," it hissed, "I cannot wait. Where are they?"

"I will tellll yooou," Morning Star said in his slow voice. "But firrrrrrst I must put my mokasin onnnnnn." Then he slowly, slowly, slowly put on his mokasin and laced it and tied it. And as he did so, the sky began to show the first glow of dawn.

The Chibai jumped up and down. "Old Man, Old Man!" it hissed. "Where are the children?"

"Firrrssst," Morning Star said, "I must put my ooooother mokasin onnnnnn." Slowly, slowly, slowly he put on his other mokasin, laced it and tied it. Then he stood up. When he stood, he did not look like an old man any longer. His eyes were bright and he smiled.

"Now," said Morning Star, "I will tell you. The children are here and so is the light of the new day."

And as Morning Star spoke, the light of dawn struck the Chibai and killed it.

That is how it happened then.

And so it is to this day, Willow Woman thought as she remembered her mother's story. So it is that the light of day always helps our people. So it is that the elders always care for the little ones. Willow Woman placed her hand on her stomach. She could just begin to feel the heartbeat of the little one there. She felt proud of the way she and Young Hunter had planned. It was not the way of the Only People for a man and a woman to have children immediately after they were married.

"We are not like Matagwas and Matagwaskwa," Near The Sky said to her the night before their wedding. "Those Rabbit People have so many children that they do not even know which ones are their own. They are always confusing one child with another and forgetting their names. That is why the Rabbit People are so often the ones who get eaten.

"Matagwas comes home and says to his wife, 'Where are our children?'

"She scratches her nose with a hind leg, looks around and then answers him, 'Ah, they are here. See, there is that one and this one. And there is that other one and this other one. Ah, and there is also that one and that one and this one and that one. Perhaps there are more, I am not certain.'

"'That is good,' says Matagwas and then he goes to sleep.

"The fox and the wolf and the bobcat, the black cat and the long-tail, the hawks and the eagles and owls, they hear the rabbits talking and they laugh. All of them have only a few children at a time. All of them always keep a close eye on their children. And all of them hunt and eat the children of Matagwas and Matagwaskwa."

"Unnh-hunnh, Nigawes," Willow Girl said, "Yes, Mother." She said it without looking over to the place where her mother stood with a birch-bark basket in her hand that would be filled with roots and dried berries and other food the next day. Willow Girl would hand that basket to the grandparents of Young Hunter to indicate that she would always provide the kind of food that women were best at providing. The food that the men brought back as hunters and fishers was important, but the family would starve if it were not for that which the women gathered. Although Willow Girl was too busy braiding her hair in a certain way to look up, she heard her mother's words clearly. She understood them. When a young man and a young woman first marry, they are still children. And when they first have their own children, they are still not truly adults. They are children with children. So it was best to wait a few seasons at least before having that first child.

Willow Woman looked over toward Young Hunter, who sat beside her on the hilltop above Petonbowk, not looking back over his shoulder at the lake far below them. Like his wife, his eyes were on the coming day. Willow Woman reached over to take his hand. She placed it on her stomach. Young Hunter smiled.

"I feel our daughter's heart," he said.

Willow Woman squeezed his hand. His words thrilled her. He

was like his grandmother, Sweetgrass Woman. It was said that she could always tell whether the child to be born was a girl or a boy or if there were two little ones and not just one waiting to draw their first breath. So, their child was to be a girl! The happiness that washed over her was like the warm waters of the big lake in summer. But as she thought of that lake, a cold chill tingled down her spine. She saw again, in the clear eye of her memory, what she had seen when she followed her husband as he made his quiet way down to the lake.

Willow Woman did not know why she had felt compelled to follow him. Something had spoken to her in a voice without words, telling her first to send the big dog after him. Then, only a few heartbeats after Agwedjiman had slipped quietly down the slope after Young Hunter, she, too, had followed. Her feet were just as quiet as her husband's, finding their way between the stones and the bushes of the hillside on the well-worn path that many generations of their people had followed. This part of the shore of Petonbowk was well known to the Only People and well loved by them. There were dugout canoes overturned or waiting with stones in them to weight them down just under the water in the shallow places in the many little coves. There were racks built of poles to dry the fish that would be caught here. There were circles of stone where fires had been made again and again from the abundant driftwood that always washed up here. As far as the eye could see in either direction up and down this shore, the Only People had been coming for as long as memory could reach.

But last night, as she followed her husband, Willow Woman had felt afraid—not only for herself, but for him. She was not sure that Young Hunter was ever afraid. He was so brave, so reckless, so ready to risk his life for his family and his people. She gave thanks that the last few seasons had been such quiet ones. But now, on this deceptively calm night, she felt that time of peace was about to end and she did not know why.

Danowa and Pabesis, Young Hunter's two other dogs, were close by her. Danowa moved down the trail just slightly ahead of her while Pabesis followed a few paces behind her. They were alert, ready for anything that might be a danger to her. Only two winters ago, Pabesis had been little more than a huge and awkward puppy, but now he was even larger than Agwedjiman, a dog who loomed over most of the other dogs in their village the way a wolf looms over a fox. Big as he was, his feet were silent on the stones and his eyes— large and bright with the light of the Night Traveler—glowed with purpose. With these two to guard me, Willow Woman thought, no one is safer than I am this night. But is my husband safe?

She had stopped them, only the distance of a long spear throw up the slope from the place where Young Hunter stood by the edge of the water. She sat down and the two dogs curled themselves around her. She leaned back against Pabesis. She felt as warm as if she was still in their little lodge near the hilltop, wrapped in a warm bearskin robe. But she could not be comfortable. Something was going to happen. As Young Hunter waded into the star-sprinkled water, she lifted her hand to her mouth. She was about to call out to him, call him back. But then she relaxed as she saw Agwedjiman pull his broad-shouldered master back out of the lake and up from the water and then stand like a log across a trail, keeping Young Hunter from again going too close to that deceptively calm surface.

Young Hunter stood and watched, not sensing his wife doing the same on the slope above him. From the place where she sat, Willow Woman could see further than her husband. She saw the fish-catcher swimming toward the shore before he did and she saw something else. Because she was above him, she could see what Young Hunter did not see. There, behind the fish-catcher, just close enough to the surface that it could be seen as a huge shadow, something was moving. It moved lazily behind and below the fish-catcher. Back and forth. Playing with it.

Willow Woman had seen something like that before. When she was a small girl, she had climbed up to the Deer Drive Place. Looking down from the edge of one of the cliffs, she had seen a bobcat walking in circles in the meadow below her. It reached out a paw, pushing at something in the grass, and then lay back on its stomach to watch. Its small tail whisked back and forth. Then the grasses in front of it moved and parted. A small woodchuck crawled out. One of its hind legs was injured and it dragged as the woodchuck tried to run. The bobcat jumped, placing itself in the small animal's path. The woodchuck's hole, its one hope of safety, was right behind the bobcat. And the bobcat knew it. The woodchuck tried to raise itself up, but fell backward instead. The bobcat lay itself back down again beside the woodchuck's burrow and waited, tail still twitching.

As she watched, Willow Girl had known what would happen. Her father, Deer Tracker, had told of such things. Sometimes an animal that was a hunter would not kill its prey. It would only cripple it and then play with it. When Willow Girl had asked why, her father had placed his hand up to his chin and nodded his head a few times, thinking. "Ah," he finally said, "perhaps the fear makes the meat taste better."

That day, looking down from Deer Leap, Willow Girl had been angered by what she saw. She had shouted, but the wind carried the sound away and the bobcat had not heard her. Then she had looked around her and seen what she needed. Stones. She began to throw them, arcing them up high so that they would fall into the meadow. One stone, two. Three. And on her fourth throw she succeeded. The stone fell right behind the bobcat. It leaped high in the air, twisting its body around as it leaped. It landed on the other side of the hole that led into the woodchuck's burrow. And as the bobcat looked around for whatever had startled it, the woodchuck reached its hole and ducked down into it so quickly that Willow Girl had felt certain that, injured though it was, it would recover.

As Willow Woman watched that huge shadow move back and forth beneath the fish-catcher, she knew that no stone she might throw would make a difference. The fear that she felt for herself and Young Hunter was so strong now that it paralyzed her. Pabesis and Danowa were standing now on either side of her as she sat there. They were pressed against her, watching the lake below. She knew that their eyes were not as keen as hers, but their other senses were telling them that something ancient and powerful, dangerous and hungry was there below them. And it was so large. It was like a great tree, swollen at the center, and it swam beneath the surface as a snake swims. Its long tail was sweeping back and forth, back and forth. The fish-catcher was almost to the shore now and the dark shape beneath the water began to grow smaller, sinking further beneath the surface. Perhaps it was going to go away. Then, so quickly that it made her gasp aloud, a wide, open-mouthed head and a long neck struck up out of the water, raising up as high above the surface as the height of three men. It grabbed the fish-catcher in mid air and then slammed down. The waters churned white in the light of the Night Traveler and then grew calm. The huge creature was gone and Willow Woman was walking down the slope to the place where Young Hunter still stood without moving.

She placed her arm around his shoulders and he turned to her. There was no fear in his face, only concern.

"Did you see?" he said.

"I saw," she answered.

"Padoskoks," Young Hunter said. It was a word that he had never spoken before. It meant the snake-being bigger than big. Greater than great.

"Unh-hunh," Willow Woman said. Then, the three dogs around them, they had walked back to their wigwam and walked beyond it to the top of the hill where they would be able to first see the light of the new day.

Young Hunter removed his hand from Willow Woman's stomach. He stood up and faced the dawn. The morning star was gone now from the edge of the sky behind them and the light of the new day was bright. Willow Woman stood with him.

Young Hunter pointed his chin in the direction of their village. "We must go and warn all of the people. They must know of the danger in Petonbowk. It is no longer safe to go to the Waters Between."

Rabbit Stick was the first to come out of the wigwam. He still held his throwing stick in one hand and his spear in the other. Half in and half out of the door, he smelled the air. There was nothing out of the usual, only the smells of the new day coming to him on the small breeze. He listened. Only the sounds of the small birds singing the arrival of the Day Walker. Then, after smelling and listening, he looked. It was as he had been taught by his own father. Human beings are too ready to trust their eyes, unlike the other beings—the wolf people, the deer people and all the others. A wolf or a deer will scent the air first, then listen. Then and only then will they look, for the eyes are often the easiest of the senses to fool.

Sweetgrass Woman placed one hand on his shoulder. "It is good that our grandson was not here last night."

"Hunhh, that is certainly true," Rabbit Stick said. "If he had been here with us, he would have gone out into the darkness to see just what it was that was out there."

"As would you have done, my husband," Sweetgrass Woman said, "if I had not hooked my hand through your belt."

Rabbit Stick tried not to laugh. He coughed to cover his amusement, but it was no use. Sweetgrass Woman could see that her words were accurate.

"Foolish courage," she said, "is something that all of the men in your family have always had."

"That is why we have always married cautious women," Rabbit Stick said. He meant it as a compliment, but Sweetgrass Woman shoved him so hard that he almost fell.

"Hah! How could that be so? If I were cautious I never would have married a man who thinks with his . . . hssst!" Sweetgrass Woman stopped in mid-sentence and held up her hand. Rabbit Stick looked in the direction that she was looking. She had heard something. Then he heard it, too. The soft shifting of feet. Someone was there in the brush, silently watching them. There, just behind that blueberry bush that was green with new leaves.

It could not be Young Hunter, Sweetgrass Woman thought. He was surely a full day's journey away from them by now in the camp he and Willow Woman had made near Petonbowk. For some reason of his own, perhaps a reason he himself did not understand, their grandson had left with his wife and their dogs for the long moons camping place much earlier than anyone else in their village. It would be a handful of days before anyone else would join them there. And if that person watching was a friend, someone who meant no harm, he should have identified himself by now.

Rabbit Stick thought the same as his wife. But instead of trying to see who was hidden there, he turned his back and pretended to look in the other direction. "Did you hear something over there, my wife?" he said.

Sweetgrass Woman understood. She, too, turned that way and took two steps away from her husband.

As soon as his wife had cleared the space between them, Rabbit Stick pivoted on one leg and swung his arm sideways across his body, letting the throwing stick fly straight into that place in the brush where someone waited. His aim was true, for the stick struck solid flesh with a loud thwack!

"Waagh-ahhh!" someone shouted. "You have killed me!"

Rabbit Stick and Sweetgrass Woman looked at each other. Rabbit Stick lowered the spear that he had raised up to his shoulder, ready to throw. They knew that voice.

"Slow Bird," Sweetgrass Woman said.

"Bear Talker," Rabbit Stick called. "Why are you hiding there?"

Holding his hip with one hand and the throwing stick with the other, Bear Talker came limping out from behind the blueberry bush. He threw the stick down at Rabbit Stick's feet. He glared at Sweetgrass Woman.

"Not only do you try to kill me," he said to Rabbit Stick, "then you," he glared at Sweetgrass Woman, "insult me by calling me names!"

Sweetgrass Woman's lips twitched, but she kept herself from smiling. She and Bear Talker had been children together. A heavy-bodied child wanting desperately to impress the girl who was a faster runner than any of the boys, Bear Talker had fallen flat on his own face when he tried to beat Sweetgrass Girl in a race. Ever since then, Slow Bird had been her nickname for him. Though she respected and cared for the deep-seeing man almost as much as she respected and cared for her husband, Sweetgrass Woman would die before she admitted it out loud—or ever stopped teasing him.

"But you are not dead," she said, "clearly, my husband is losing his skill." Then she did smile, for she had managed to tease both of them with a single statement. However, even as she teased the deep-seeing man who was one of the best friends, Sweetgrass Woman knew that something was wrong. For some reason, Bear Talker's medicine was clumsy medicine, even though it was powerful. Whenever he stumbled or did something foolish, it was because his medicine caused it. Perhaps Bear Talker had just flown here through the air, the way certain deep-seeing people were able to do. They were a two-day journey from the lodge that he and his wife Medicine Plant shared with their little son, whom Bear Talker persisted in calling Bright Sky, even though Sweetgrass Woman had named him Looks Backward— her right as the midwife who helped the child into this world.

Sweetgrass Woman stepped closer to Bear Talker and pulled his hand away from his hip.

"It is broken," Bear Talker growled.

"Only a little bruise," she said.

"It *was* broken," Bear Talker said, pushing her hand away, "but I cured it with my medicine."

Sweetgrass Woman put her hand on her old friend's arm. She

could see that it was hard for him to stand, but that it was not because of the bruise on his hip. The tiredness that had come upon him so strongly that he was unable to stand and walk to their wigwam was still there in his face. But it was only when Rabbit Stick reached out to take Bear Talker's other arm that the deep-seeing man allowed his friends to assist him.

"I came here," Bear Talker said, his voice slowed by exhaustion, "a little too quickly. I had to see if you were safe. Great trouble was close to you last night, so close that . . ." Bear Talker grew silent, as if the words were too heavy for him to speak them. Rabbit Stick helped him sit, leaning back against the side of the wigwam. Sweetgrass Woman brought a cup. It was filled with pine needle tea that had been steeped in the clay pot they kept in the fire pit. Sweetgrass Woman took some maple sugar from a pouch, crushed it between her fingers, and sprinkled it into the cup before she placed it in Bear Talker's trembling hands. He drank it in one thirsty gulp.

"Ahhh," he said. "Oleohneh. Thank you."

Sweetgrass Woman knelt by him and spread open her hands, asking him to continue what he had been about to say. Bear Talker shook his head. He handed the cup back to her.

"What trouble?" Sweetgrass Woman said. But Bear Talker said nothing. Instead, his eyes closed as his head dropped back against the side of the wigwam. He began to snore.

"It is no use," Rabbit Stick said, "I have seen him this way before. He will sleep like that until the Day Walker is in the middle of the sky."

Rabbit Stick walked over and looked near the blueberry bush where Bear Talker had crouched. The earth was soft there and he could easily see the shuffling footprints Bear Talker made when he came stumbling out. Rabbit Stick followed them behind the bush. They ended there. A single set of footprints was pressed deeply into the earth, as if Bear Talker had jumped down there from high in a tree. But there was no tree close enough to jump down from and no sign of any prints leading to those first deep ones.

Rabbit Stick shook his head. It was as he had thought. But he did not come back to the place where Bear Talker slept and Sweetgrass Woman stood. Instead, he continued to walk carefully around the wigwam, stopping now and then to squat down and angle his head first in one direction and then the other. Sweetgrass Woman watched him, but said nothing. She had seen her husband do this many times before and she knew that no one was a better tracker.

Rabbit Stick walked in a careful circle, moving further and further out as he went. At last, when he reached the base of the cedar tree with a bent top, he stopped. He sat down and looked for a long time. Then he dug into the soft earth that he had seen near its base, earth that was too smooth, too clear of leaves or small sticks. It was a track that showed itself because there was no track there. He did not have to dig far before he found the small one buried there. Gently, he lifted it up and then held it, wings spread open, so that Sweetgrass Woman could see it before he buried it again, deeper this time than before.

"I am sorry, my friend," Rabbit Stick said as he brushed the earth back over the dead body of the cat-owl. He knew that it had been killed because it was their guardian, the one who watched for danger in the darkness and would have warned them of such danger if its life had not been taken. Bear Talker was right. Great trouble had been close to them last night. Rabbit Stick knew that it would return.

6 ▣ TWO DIRECTIONS

The Sky Walker was now the height of two hands above the horizon. Willow Woman sat with her back against one of the great pines on top of the high hill. Pabesis, who was remembering that somewhere in his heart he was still a puppy, brought her another stick. She placed it in the growing pile at her feet. The big dog shook his head, whimpered softly, and then ran off to find another stick.

Willow Woman smiled. She could tell what the young dog had been thinking. Perhaps that stick had been too long or too heavy. Ah, he would find a better one. Sooner or later he would find one that was the right size and Willow Woman would throw it for him. She placed her hands on the back of Danowa, who sat next to her, waiting patiently for Young Hunter to be done with whatever he was doing as he sat on top of the great boulder just up the slope from them. Danowa looked at Willow Woman, looked in the direction where Pabesis had just galloped down the slope, and then seemed to shake his head in disgust as if to say, "Will he never grow up?"

The dawn light was warm on Young Hunter's bare back as he sat without moving. His broad forearms rested on his knees as he sat, cross-legged. His breathing was slow and his eyes only half-open. He looked down onto Petonbowk and also looked into the wide Waters Between. What he saw confused him. He could sense that ancient powerful being that had killed the fish-catcher as easily as a bobcat kills a meadow mouse. It was there, deep beneath the surface, resting and waiting. But what was it waiting for? And was it alone? And why was it here now? And where did it come from?

Young Hunter sighed. There was so much he did not understand.

Most of all, he did not understand why these things were happening in his lifetime. He had hoped that there would be no more of the sorts of problems that he had faced to help his people. But now, just when all had become calm and peaceful, now only two seasons before he would become a father for the first time, it was beginning again. There in the Waters Between.

From his vantage point Young Hunter could see the quiet cove where his dugout canoe still floated near the shore, tied with a thin but strong rope made of reverse-wrapped strings of supple basswood bark. This was the day when he and Willow Woman and their three dogs had planned to cross Petonbowk in that same dugout. There, on the other side, they would have camped for a moon or more. It was time, he had thought, for the people to make a new village. Their first village on the other side of the Waters Between. Was that the reason this great water creature had appeared now? To keep his people on this side of Petonbowk? There were reasons for everything in the world. Everything was caused by something else. Everything was connected by thin strands like those of a spider's web. Sometimes Young Hunter could see those strands of power and connection, floating in the air, touched by the light. But he could not see those strands here.

A tingling feeling began along his spine. Young Hunter shivered. It was as if a handful of snow had fallen on his neck and slid down his back. He turned to face the direction of the Dawn Land. He could not see what it was, but there was something to be seen. Young Hunter's stomach tightened and he almost said it out loud. Nda! No!

But it was so. Just as there was danger from the direction of Petonbowk, so, too, there was also another danger to the people that was now there among them. There in the thirteen villages of the Dawn Land. A danger at least as great as that hidden in the deep waters behind him. But this danger that was among his people was at least partly human. It was twisted with power.

Young Hunter realized that he had been feeling this presence of evil since the night before. But he had pushed his consciousness of it to the back of his mind because the one beneath the waters, Padoskoks, was so powerful and so immediate. He reached one hand up to touch the flint knife that hung at his chest from the cord around his neck.

Then Young Hunter saw something. He saw it with his eyes and with the eyes behind his eyes. It was flying toward him from the dawn. One breath it looked to be a white owl, the next a woman. Each wingbeat that it took carried it over another range of hills. He could see it and he could see through it. He closed his eyes and he could see it more clearly. A great white owl with a face that was human. A face that he recognized. It was Medicine Plant. She was traveling to him on her spirit, leaving her body behind her.

"My teacher," Young Hunter whispered, "I see you."

He began to hear the deep-seeing woman's voice. It was as soft as the wingbeats of an owl and the message that he heard, a message that did not enter his ears, was like a feathered wind that circled him and circled into him, linking him to her thoughts. Then, as quickly as it had begun, that wordless message ended.

Young Hunter opened his eyes. The bright early light of the Sky Walker almost blinded him. He shaded his eyes with his hands and squinted. There was no sign of an owl or of any other bird in the sky. Young Hunter slid down from the big rock.

Pabesis came trotting up to him, dragging a stick that was almost a log. It was as big around as a man's wrist and four times the length of a man's arm. Young Hunter shook his head. Pabesis dropped the stick and looked up at him, all of the puppiness gone as he sensed the seriousness in his master. Willow Woman came up to Young Hunter and took his hands.

"You have seen something," she said.

Young Hunter squeezed her hands gently and then released them. He reached up to brush his long hair back from his face and then rubbed his eyes with his palms. He let out a great sigh.

"My wife," he said, "it is very bad. A strange deep-seer has come among our villages. One with a twisted mind. His wish is to kill all of those who have power. We must go home."

Willow Woman did not hesitate. She had already lifted up the small bundle that contained those few possessions she had brought with them. A bone awl, a small knife, thin cord, a fire-making kit, a comb, a bag of woven basswood fibers. She slung it over her back. Everything else in their double lean-to had been made there after they had set up their camp. What they left behind—clay pots, sleeping racks of woven sticks, baskets and trays made of bark, stone-circled firepit—would either go back into the earth or be there waiting for them when they came to stay there again.

"If we hurry," she said, "we can reach the wigwam of your grandparents well before evening." Then she turned and ran down the slope with long, graceful strides. Pabesis followed after her.

Young Hunter picked up his spear and tightened his belt. His wife was a fast runner and he knew he would have to go as quickly as he could to keep up. He looked at Danowa and Agwedjiman, who were sitting on their haunches, looking at him with what seemed to be amusement in their eyes.

"Go ahead and laugh," Young Hunter said to his two dogs. "But you know as well as I do that we men are always trying to catch up to the women."

Then, his dogs beside him, he hurried down the hill.

Medicine Plant opened her eyes. She looked at the place where the Day Walker stood in the sky. A hand further along his path. She nodded. It was always hard to tell how long she was gone from her body when she sent her spirit out on the owl's white wings. This time, though, she had felt herself drawn back into herself even more swiftly than usual, so swiftly that the flight had seemed a blur. It was as if she had not just been flying back. It was as if someone had been pulling her. Then she felt the tug on her hand.

"Nigawes," Old Eyes Looking Backward Over Bright Sky said, his voice insistent as he pulled once more on Medicine Plant's hand, "My mother."

Medicine Plant looked at her son. Three winters old and yet he had the power to draw her back. Was it because he was the child of two deep-seers and thus, though so young, already becoming a medicine person? She remembered the day he was born. A storm had swirled about the hilltop where their wigwam stood, but directly above the wigwam the sky was bright and clear. So it was that Bear Talker, who struggled through that storm to return to their lodge with help for his wife in her difficult labor, had said that their son should be named Bright Sky. Though Sweetgrass Woman had brought more babies into the world than anyone could count, it had been a struggle for her to midwife this little one into breath. He had turned his back and fought to remain with his mother. So it was that Sweetgrass Woman had called him Looking Backward. But it was when she first looked into her son's knowing face that Medicine Plant had known his true name. His eyes were the eyes of her own mother's father. The old and wise eyes of her grandfather. And though he would have to relearn human words to fully understand the memories that he had carried back into this world with him, Medicine Plant knew that there would be days to come when her son would be an elder to his elders. Old Eyes was his true name.

Old Eyes tugged her hand again. It was as if he was tugging at her heart. The warmth she felt, the love she knew for her own son, the one who had danced within her for nine moons, sharing her breath and her blood, was so overwhelming that she almost wept. Perhaps his power to draw her back to him was nothing more than the power every child has over a loving mother.

"Kinosis," Medicine Plant said, "My little boy, what is it?"

Old Eyes slid into her lap and then reached up to place his small hands against her cheeks, wanting to feel her words as she spoke them. "Why does the bad man who can fly want to hurt us?" he said.

Medicine Plant did not answer him quickly. Neither she nor Bear Talker had been able to explain how their son had sensed, as they sensed, the passage above them like an angry wind, of that one whose name they did not yet know. That one who was a deep-seer who had turned away from the power of healing to embrace the twisted power of destroying. Somehow Old Eyes had known, as clearly as did his parents, that the one whose name they did not yet know, wanted to wipe out all of those who were, like himself, deep-seers. But why did he wish this? It was a question that she was not sure she could answer, for it was a question that she was now asking herself.

"My little boy," she said. "It is not easy to say. It is hard to see into someone else's heart and know how they feel."

"I see into your heart, my mother. I know how you feel."

"Ahh." Medicine Plant paused. She remembered her mother's father on a day when she was as small as her own son. His name was White Fox. He had held her on that day, a day when she was sad and did not know why. He had placed his hands on her cheeks and turned her face toward him. Then, in a voice that was as deep and gentle as the throb of a drum beat, her grandfather White Fox had said, "My little girl, do not think you are alone. I can see into your heart. I know how you feel."

Medicine Plant looked down into the knowing eyes of her little boy. "And did you see into the heart of the bad man?" she asked.

"Unh-hunh," Old Eyes said.

Medicine Plant took a breath.

"What did you see?"

"Snakes," Old Eyes said, patting her cheeks softly with his palms. "Snakes with no eyes. Snakes biting each other and biting themselves."

8 ▣ RUNNING

Young Hunter and Willow Woman ran together. They ran as young people run, with an easy stride that carried them along the long winding trail that led inland. It led down the ridge where the stones were open to the sky and into the long valley where the beech and birch and maple trees that lined the trail glowed with the green leaves of early summer. They crossed that valley, heading toward the next ridge of hills, which gradually became the highest of the mountains.

Although they ran swiftly, they did not run headlong, the way children run, heedless of what is in front of them. They ran the way their dogs ran, loping at times, slowing to a trot at others. And though they trusted the stronger senses of the dogs to warn them of any possible threat, they still used their own eyes and ears and noses as they ran. The trail they followed was not a single track, but a trail made of many trails, joining and diverging. So, when Willow Woman saw the tracks of a mother bear and her two cubs in the soft earth near the little stream that ran next to the trail, they took a fork in the path leading away from those tracks. Nothing is fiercer than a mother bear when she thinks her cubs are threatened.

As they ran, the sweet air of the early morning filled their lungs. Though Willow Woman and Young Hunter knew there was uncertainty in front of them and danger behind, they smiled as they ran or even laughed out loud as they brushed against each other, first one leading and then the other.

At last, when the Day Walker was in the center of the sky, they came upon a meadow that had once been a beaver pond. It seemed to be filled with tiny embers, little bright red pieces of the sun scattered everywhere in the grass. Strawberries. Young Hunter stopped.

"My wife," he said, "shall we pick some berries?"

Willow Woman handed him one of the two baskets she had made of the birch bark that she had picked up as they passed through the white stand of trees on the slope behind them. Young Hunter shook his head. She was always surprising him this way. He had not seen her pick up those two pieces of birch bark and fold them in her hands as she ran, pinning them together with sharp twigs.

Apart from love and respect and friendship, there are few things in life as sweet as strawberries warmed by the sun. The two of them filled their baskets. The sweet red juice of the berries stained their fingers and their lips as they tasted one berry for every four they picked. While the humans picked berries, three dogs wandered through the field, bending their heads down to eat strawberries themselves. Pabesis rolled onto his back and squirmed among the berries so that their sweet scent was on his coat.

Young Hunter and Willow Woman sat leaning back to back, eating strawberries. Young Hunter's strawberry basket was in Willow Woman's lap. Willow Woman's basket was in his. Young Hunter remembered how he had often seen his grandparents sitting this way together. Did they ever sit like this in this same strawberry field, eating strawberries from each other's baskets? He knew this field had been here for a long time. The people cared for this field, burning it over each autumn so that the grasses would stay short and the trees not fill in the field. The burning would make the earth sweeter for the berries, which were shared by everyone—humans and birds and animals. Young Hunter looked toward the far edge of the field. A mother bear and her two cubs were there, eating berries themselves and paying no attention at all to the humans and the dogs that they had surely scented.

How easy it would be to be a bear, Young Hunter thought. To have none of these worries that we human people have. Then again, he thought, bears also must worry. Certainly a mother bear worries about her little ones. And when it is nearing the moons of short nights and the leaves are falling, every bear worries about getting enough to eat so that it will be able to survive the long sleep until spring. Then bears must also worry about finding a den that will shelter them properly for that long sleep when they must stay hidden and silent.

Young Hunter remembered how, four autumns ago, he had watched a bear running about, looking for such a den. He had followed the bear for three whole days, staying upwind so that he could not be scented and far enough away—for a bear's eyesight is weaker than a human's—so that he could not be seen. Each place the bear went to find a denning place, other bears were there ahead of him. In one place, that bear spent a whole morning deepening an earth cave under the roots of a wind-toppled cedar only to have a larger bear come and chase him away from the shelter he had made for himself. That poor bear was still seeking a sheltering place when Young Hunter finally decided that his grandparents would worry about him if he stayed away another night. Perhaps, Young Hunter thought, bears look at us and think how easy our lives are compared to theirs?

The distant mother bear rolled over onto her back and the two cubs leaped on top of her. The three of them wrestled together in the field of green grass and red strawberries. But not today, Young Hunter thought. Today those bears are surely happy to be who they are and they envy no one.

Willow Woman poked him. "My husband," she said, "you must wait a few more seasons before you wander off to live with the bears. Now we have somewhere to go."

She placed the empty berry basket on top of a blackened stump and began to run. Young Hunter leaned over to drop the basket he had been holding on top of the same stump. Left there in plain sight, anyone who needed to use those baskets could find them easily. By the time he had gotten to his feet and picked up his spear, Willow Woman was halfway across the field, the three dogs frolicking around her. He ran as fast as he could to catch up to them.

9 ▣ WAVES

In the waters of Petonbowk, the dugout canoe that Young Hunter had left behind rocked in the small waves, which had been stirred by the wind. The wind came across Petonbowk, carrying with it a change of weather. Although the Day Walker still shone his light down upon the land and the rippling water, rain came walking across behind the wind, warm drops patterning the surface of the clear lake. From beyond the mountains on the sunset shore, a rumble could be heard from the sky land as the Bedagiak, the Thunder Beings, began to gather. Soon they would play their ancient game, rolling balls of lightning from cloud to cloud across the heavens.

The thunder and clouds on one side, the clear sky and light of the day on the other, and the deep waters of Petonbowk in between. It was as if the old lake was showing both of its faces—those ancient faces of power and peace, of storm and calm.

The willow bushes at the edge of the stone-strewn beach shook and then parted as a wolverine thrust his head out to look at the water below. The wolverine sniffed the air. The scent that had drawn him, carried up from the lake by the moist wind, was stronger here. He padded down onto the beach. The stones and gravel crunched under his feet. He looked around on the shore as he walked, turned over pieces of driftwood, tasting the salty stones with his tongue. But what he smelled was not here.

The wolverine had survived for many winters by being a good scavenger. He would eat anything, whether it was freshly killed or rotten. He had learned to follow behind other animals when they hunted—bears, wolves, the long-tail cats that bury their prey after they kill it. Sometimes he would even challenge them for their prey and take it away from them. Few animals dared to stand up to a wolverine. Even though he was no larger than a small bear, he was fierce. But the human beings were the best ones to follow. When they left their camps, there was always some food left behind. The wolverine enjoyed finding a human camp. Not only would he eat their food, he would destroy whatever he could and then leave his strong scent, almost as strong as that of the skunk, everywhere. If there was too much food for him to eat, he would cover it with his scent, knowing that no one would touch it then. It was almost as good to spoil the food for others as it was to eat it himself.

The wolverine stood at the edge of the water, rocking back and forth slightly. He was not sure that he wanted to go in, though he was a good swimmer. The rain-rippled surface of the lake was not threatening, yet he felt uncertain. Then a small wind gust wafted over the dugout that floated just off the shore. The scent came to him strongly. He smelled the fish that Young Hunter had speared the night before as he stood in the dugout with a torch in one hand, its light attracting the fish, and a spear in the other hand. Young Hunter had placed those fish in that dugout and then forgotten them.

The wolverine growled. That smell was so good. He placed one paw in the water and then pulled it out again. He walked back and forth on the shore, shaking his head, snarling and talking to himself as wolverines do. Then he saw the rope tied to the back of the dugout. The wolverine had seen ropes before. Such ropes were used by the humans to hang bags full of food from the trees so that hungry ones like himself could not get that food. But if he pulled hard enough on such a rope, that food would come falling down.

The wolverine grasped the rope in his teeth and backed up. The dugout came toward him. He let go of the rope and ran down to the shore. But the dugout floated back away from him. He grabbed the rope again and pulled once more, walking back even further. The end of the dugout ground against the sand. The wolverine ran down to it and jumped inside. He did not notice that the dugout bobbed free of the beach as his weight in the stern rocked up the prow. He was too busy gnawing at the big pike that he held between both his paws, sitting with his back against the side of the bow and his hind legs stretched out before him. The swirling wind pushed the boat out to the length of the rope. The rain began to fall a bit harder as the clouds came closer. The wolverine continued to eat.

Then something bumped against the boat. The wolverine jerked his head up and looked around. There was nothing to be seen above water. A small wave spread around the boat, embracing it. The wolverine looked back toward the shore. He moaned as he saw the stretch of water between the end of the boat and the land. Something bumped against the boat again. The wolverine turned toward the deep water and looked. Two huge eyes looked back at him from beneath the surface. Those eyes came closer and closer and then lifted out of the water. They were in the head of an animal bigger than any animal the wolverine had ever seen before. The wolverine snarled in defiance. The eyes rose up and up, as that animal's head was lifted above the boat on a long snake neck. The wolverine stood on his hind legs and spread his paws wide. He bared his teeth and screamed up at the creature, which stared down with cold eyes. Then a great mouth opened wide, teeth flashed, and, as a spear of lightning crackled across the skyland, the head struck down.

The rain fell harder now. The waves on the surface of the lake grew higher in the strong wind. They washed over the broken dugout canoe, which floated upside down in the Waters Between.

As Young Hunter ran, it was easy to follow the tracks left by Willow Woman. It was clear that she was not running to get away from him as a deer might run when a hunter follows it. Her tracks went straight on the path and did not curve off as an animal's track would when it doubled back to see what was pursuing. A mokasin print here, a twig pressed into soft earth there. A clear trail to read.

A friend always leaves a track, that is how Rabbit Stick had explained it to him. "My grandson," Rabbit Stick said, as they followed the trail of an elk across the rocky slope of a hill high above Petonbowk, "an enemy also leaves a track, but an enemy's track may be a hidden one. Sometimes the only trail left by an enemy is the absence of tracks."

Then Rabbit Stick had shifted his spear thrower to his other hand and bent to lightly touch the place where the elk's hoof had scraped a bit of moss away from a red stone. "But this elk," Rabbit Stick had said, "this one is our friend. It has agreed to give its body to us so that we can feed ourselves and others in our village. So it has left these small signs. It knows that we will respect its body after we cut its breath. Down there in that pass between the hills, that is where we will find it waiting for us."

As he continued to run, Young Hunter thought of the things his grandfather had taught him and continued to teach him. Even when the old man was not with him, Young Hunter could hear his voice.

"Look at yourself, grandson," Rabbit Stick had said earlier that same day as they rested by the shore of Petonbowk in a place where the water was calm and clear.

Young Hunter had leaned over to look at his reflection in the water.

"Where are your eyes?"

Young Hunter lifted his hand and his reflection did the same. Some said that a person's reflection in the water was actually another person, one who lived in a world where water was air and winter was summer. Young Hunter doubted that. He had dived into the water many times trying to find some trace of that land of opposites. No matter how deep he went, all that he ever found on the bottom were stones and mud and water plants. One would have to dive in a different way, perhaps, to find that deeper world.

"Here," Young Hunter said. "Together at the front of my face."

"Where are the eyes of the deer?"

Young Hunter raised both hands and watched as his opposite person did the same, placing those hands near his ears.

"Here, apart and on each side of the head."

"And the elk?"

"The same."

"The moose, the caribou, the rabbit?"

"All on the sides of their heads."

"That is so they can see to both sides, even behind them. That way they can better see the animals that hunt them. But what about the wolf and the dog and the long-tail?"

Young Hunter and his watery twin moved their hands back to the front of their faces.

"Unh-hunh," Rabbit Stick said. "Like us, they are hunters. So their eyes are in front. So they were made, like us, to hunt and follow the trail. That is how Ktsi Nwaskw, our creator, made us. So we must be thankful for the way we are made and be good hunters. It is a great gift."

Young Hunter ran, hearing his grandfather's voice. The trail led along the same way he had gone with Rabbit Stick ten winters ago when they had hunted that elk, which gave itself to them in the small pass between the stony hills. Young Hunter kept his mouth closed, his eyes and ears open. He smelled the air as he ran.

"Ktsi Nwaskw, the Owner Creator," Rabbit Stick had continued, "meant it to be that we would keep our mouths closed most of the time. When a bird is always singing, it cannot hear the hawk. When a wolf is hunting, it only speaks when to wishes to frighten its prey so that it will run toward the place where other wolves are lying in wait. Remember the story of The Speaker?"

Young Hunter had nodded. It was one of his favorite tales. Back when the world was new, the dust of creation that clung to the hands of Ktsi Nwaskw, the Owner Creator, had fallen on the earth. That dust shaped itself together into the first person who looked like a human being. That was Odziodzo, the One Who Shaped Himself from Something. But the One Who Shaped Himself from Something could not perceive the world about him because there were no openings in his head. So Ktsi Nwaskw, the Great Mystery, made the lightning strike seven times. Those seven strikes of lightning made seven holes in the head of the One Who Shaped Himself. There were two ears, two eyes, two nostrils, but only one mouth. That was because that new being was supposed to talk only half as much as he listened or observed or smelled the world around him. Then, when that One Who Shaped Himself did begin to speak, he became known as Gluskonba, The Speaker. And the only times when The Speaker got into trouble, it was said, were those times when he talked too much and did not listen.

Young Hunter's dogs had run ahead of him. There was still no sign of Willow Woman. Young Hunter was still surprised at times at how fast his wife could run. He knew that he was faster than her, but when she got ahead of him, it was not easy to catch up. The Sky Walker had now moved the width of three more hands across the heavens. Soon it would be evening and they would reach the village. They had traveled very swiftly, so swiftly that they no longer needed to hurry.

Young Hunter thought he saw a small motion from behind a oak tree that leaned slightly over the trail ahead of him. But he did not slow down, he kept running, his feet thudding more heavily on the trail now. He was almost to that tree. He slowed down slightly, but kept his eyes on the trail. He could see the clear tracks of Willow Woman's feet leading past the tree. The place where they doubled back would be around the next bend.

Suddenly someone leaped onto Young Hunter's back from behind that tree. He dropped his spear and throwing stick and allowed himself to be rolled over onto his back. Willow Woman put her foot on his stomach.

"Hah," she said, "you are as blind as the One Who Shaped Himself was before the lightning struck and gave him eyes!"

Young Hunter looked to one side. All three of his dogs sat there, amused looks on their faces. "Betrayers," Young Hunter said, but the three dogs did not move. They had seen all of this happen before.

"Get up," Willow Woman said, pressing down on Young Hunter's stomach with her heel. "Just because you are blind it does not give you an excuse to be lazy."

"My wife," Young Hunter said, "I have broken something. I cannot get up."

"Hah," Willow Woman said, "It seems to me that you can get up quite well. *That* is not broken."

Young Hunter reached up to take Willow Woman's hand and pull her down, laughing, beside him.

Although the Day Walker shone its light down now from the middle of the sky, Bear Talker was still asleep. Eyes closed, head back against the side of Rabbit Stick's lodge, mouth wide open, his sleep was not peaceful. Not only did he snore and growl as he slept, but every now and then he would strike out with both arms, his fingers clawed like the paws of a bear.

A group of small children had gathered to watch Bear Talker as he slept. Rabbit Stick, who was keeping an eye on Bear Talker, waiting for him to wake, also watched those children. He remembered what it was like when he and Bear Talker were both children of the age of those who watched the deep-seeing man now with a mixture of awe and amusement. Rabbit Stick had already earned his name then, for even as a little boy he had been able to use a throwing stick with as much skill as most grown men. He was tall and lanky for his age, a slightly smaller version of the erect elder he became.

But Bear Talker back then was still known as Slow Bird. Slow Bird had not looked then as Bear Talker looked today. Even though he was a round, awkward child, there was always a starved, hurt look in his eyes. It was only to be expected in a boy whose father was Two Sticks, a man too lazy to even bring wood in to make a fire in their cold lodge. Since the death of his wife, the mother of Slow Bird, Two Sticks had become too lazy and uncaring to even bring food home most days.

Rabbit Stick often had Slow Bird come to his wigwam to eat. Rabbit Stick's parents did not mind, they always had extra food for any guest, even little Slow Bird who would eat with both hands and scrape the bottom of the cooking basket with the sides of his hands. When they ate deer or caribou, elk or moose, Slow Bird would go so far as to keep the bones from the meal, even though they had the marrow sucked out of them. He would put them in his pouch and save them to chew later. Rabbit Stick's parents would look at each other and nod as they watched Slow Bird stuffing himself. They knew his hunger was more than just a hunger for food. Food would never fill his emptiness.

Rabbit Stick looked back over his shoulder. He could see the other wigwams of their village slightly down the hill from the place where his own lodge sat. Sweetgrass Woman was down there now, sitting and talking with the circle of Women Who Know. The Women Who Know would talk things out about the doings of the night before, the death of the owl, the way Bear Talker arrived at dawn. Among those women, all of them grandmothers, a decision would be reached. Then their words would be brought to Young Hunter's uncle, Fire Keeper, who was sagamon of their village, the one chosen to lead. But no man can lead the people unless the women have first agreed upon the direction in which he will go.

When evening came, Bear Talker would be awake. He would talk then to all the people in the village around the big fire. Rabbit Stick could see the wood being brought in to the center of the village circle by the young people of the village. These little ones who were watching Bear Talker were among those who were supposed to be bringing in that wood. Each of them had a few sticks in their hands. Rabbit Stick cleared his throat and the children looked up at him. He looked down the hill toward the place where the big fire would be kindled. Like a flock of grouse who have been pecking at the ground and then are startled by a sudden sound, the children scattered. Those who had a few sticks ran toward the wood pile. Those who had completely forgotten their duties disappeared back in direction of the pine trees where many dry sticks could easily be gathered.

Was I ever that young? Rabbit Stick asked himself. He looked again at Bear Talker. And was he? Then Rabbit Stick began to laugh as he remembered the time, many winters ago, when he and the round boy then known as Slow Bird had decided to go look for The Speaker's Island.

Old Muskrat was the one who told them the story. Muskrat was a skinny old man who usually did not live in their village. He traveled widely, and wherever he went he was welcomed. He was a great storyteller. Only Stands-in-a-Hole was a better storyteller than Old Muskrat. Whenever Muskrat sat down by a winter fire, slipped the braided strap of his brightly decorated basswood basket off his shoulder, and began to shrug his shoulders, everyone else would grow silent, waiting for the story to come.

"The Speaker, he did many things," Old Muskrat said, spreading his thin arms wide, as if to embrace the whole world. "Then he had done enough. He had done all that he needed to do to help make the world a safer place for the human beings. He saw the people relying on him too much." Old Muskrat laughed. "Hunh, hunh! They were getting lazy. So he took his grandmother, Woodchuck, and his brother, Marten. He took them and got into his dugout canoe and they went far out into the big water. There they live to this day on an island hidden in the mist. But if someone has a great wish, they can go to that island. If they find it, The Speaker will give them their wish."

Rabbit Stick still remembered how Old Muskrat had paused then, his arms spread wide open. You could clearly see the tattoos on his chest and his arms. A turtle, a series of blue lines circling his sinewy biceps, a wolf on each shoulder. But even though Old Muskrat had stopped talking, no one, from the smallest children to the gray-haired elders, said anything. Slow Bird had stopped chewing on the bone that he had taken from the torn pouch that hung from his fraying belt. All of Slow Bird's clothing was always like that. With no mother or grandmother to care for him, he was also usually dirtier than the other children. Rabbit Stick was his only friend.

Then Muskrat let his arms fall. "Once, they say, three men decided to look for The Speaker's Island. Each one of them had a wish.

One wanted to be a great hunter. One wanted all the women to want him. Hunh, hunh! And the third one, he was a joker. He wanted to be able to make a noise that everyone would hear and then everyone would laugh when they heard it. Hunh, hunh, hunh!" Muskrat paused and looked around at the children who surrounded him. "How do you think he made that noise? You show me."

All of them had tried various ways to make that noise until Slow Bird had taken a deep breath and then let out a loud, deep belch. All of the children looked at him with admiration and even Old Muskrat nodded.

"Maybe it was like that," Old Muskrat said, "But louder and deeper. And that was that man's wish. So they started to travel. It was a long journey. They traveled for seven winters! At the end of the seventh winter they began to hear dogs barking. Those were The Speaker's dogs, the two dogs that often are with him. One dog is black, one dog is white. They are bigger than wolves. They walked toward the sound of those dogs barking. It took them two moons to reach that place where the dogs were barking. They were barking from an island far out in the big water. That water was frozen. So they walked across the ice. It took them two more moons to walk across to the island. The Speaker was there. They told him their wishes. He gave the first man a little flute made of willow. 'Play this flute,' the Speaker said. 'The animals like it. Then if you respect the animals when you hunt them and never waste anything, they will always give themselves to you.' He gave the second man a pouch. 'This pouch will make all the women want you when you open it. Wait until you are in your home before you open it.' He gave the third man a root. 'Eat this root and you will be able to make a noise that everyone will hear. It will make them laugh. Do not eat it until you are home.'

"Then the men left The Speaker's island. It only took them two steps to cross the ice. They took two more steps and they could no longer hear the dogs barking. It had taken them seven winters to reach that place. It took them only seven days to get back to the edge of their village. They parted then.

"The man who wanted to be a great hunter went to his lodge and played his flute there. He became the best hunter of all. The second man did not go to his home. He was in too big a hurry to see all the women who would want him. He opened his pouch there in the woods. Women began to come up out of the ground. Their faces were white as snow. They wanted him. They grabbed him, they threw him down on the ground. There were so many women that he could not breathe. So many women wanted him that it killed him there. Hunh! Then those women went back into the ground and were gone. The third man, he was impatient, too. He ate that root there in the woods. Then he began to make that noise. It was very powerful. He walked into the village and everyone laughed. Hunh, hunh! He was happy at first, but he could not stop making that noise. When he went to hunt, he made that noise and all the game ran away. He could not sleep because that noise kept him awake. Finally he went to a cliff to jump off and kill himself. But before he could jump, the Culloo, the great bird, flew down and grabbed him and flew off with him. That is what happened."

Rabbit Stick remembered how Slow Bird had looked over at him and nodded when the story was done. But he had not understood until the next morning came and someone scratched on the door of their wigwam before dawn.

"Rabbit Stick," a voice whispered.

Rabbit Stick went out. Slow Bird was there, standing in the snow.

"We should leave now," Slow Bird said. His voice was more serious than Rabbit Stick had ever heard it before. "It will be a long journey."

Rabbit Stick understood. He had a wish, too. He quietly packed a bag with food, being careful not to wake his parents and their guest. Slow Bird was waiting impatiently. Rabbit Stick looked at him and put more food into the bag. Then he pulled a wolfskin cape around his shoulders, and followed his friend.

The snow was deep on the trails, but Slow Bird took the lead. Breathing hard, he pushed on, his taller friend behind him. The other children sometimes said that the two of them together looked as The Speaker, who was tall and strong, must have looked when he walked with his uncle Turtle, who was short and very round. Wherever they had gone together before, Rabbit Stick had always taken the lead. But it was not that way this day.

"Slow Bird," Rabbit Stick said, "do you know which way to go?"

Slow Bird turned to look at him. His face was red with cold. "Do not call me that. I hate that name."

Rabbit Stick paused. He had never thought about his friend's name.

"What shall I call you?"

"Anything else."

"What does your father call you?" Rabbit Stick said. As soon as he asked he knew it was a mistake.

Slow Bird looked down at the snow. "He doesn't call me anything."

"My friend," Rabbit Stick said, "that is what I will call you. I will call you my friend."

"Good," Slow Bird said. He was smiling now.

"My friend, what way are we heading? And how long will it take us to get there? I do not want to walk for seven years."

Slow Bird looked up at the sky. "We are going the same direction that the Sky Walker is going. And I am certain it will not take us seven years. The men in that story were grown men. That is why it took them so long. We are much smaller. So it will not take us long at all." He turned and began walking again, growling as he fought his way through the heavy drifts of snow.

Shaking his head, Rabbit Stick followed his friend.

By the time the Sky Walker was in the middle of the sky, they were very tired. All of the food was gone, most of it eaten by Slow Bird. Another hill was ahead of them.

"Over that hill," Slow Bird said. "I am certain."

When they reached the hill top, they could see a big lake in the valley below. It was covered with ice. In the middle of the lake was a small island with trees growing on it. Smoke lifted from among the trees.

"Listen," Rabbit Stick said. They listened. They could hear it clearly.

"Dogs barking," Slow Bird shouted, "dogs barking!" He began to run down the hill, tripped and began to roll. He rolled almost to the edge of the lake, Rabbit Stick running as hard as he could to catch up to him.

"My friend," Rabbit Stick said, "are you hurt?"

"Nda," Slow Bird answered, standing without even brushing off the snow which clung to him. "Follow me."

They walked together across the thick ice toward the island, which was further away than it looked to be. When they were almost there, four dogs ran out to greet them. The dogs, which licked their faces and jumped up on them, were as large as wolves. One of the dogs was pure white.

"The black dog must be off somewhere else," Slow Bird said. "It is clear that The Speaker has more dogs now because that story happened long ago."

Rabbit Stick shook his head again. This was all happening faster than he had expected. They walked together up the path to the lodge built among the cedar trees. It was a double lean-to, covered with boughs.

"Kwai, kwai!" Rabbit Stick called, announcing their arrival to whoever was inside.

"Hunh!" A laugh came from within the wigwam. "Come inside."

The two boys ducked their heads and entered. There, sitting next to a fire, cooking a fat goose on a spit, sat none other than Old Muskrat. He stood up and the boys noticed how tall he was. The tattoo of Turtle on his chest seemed to come alive, moving and breathing in the flickering light of the fire.

"Are you The Speaker?" Slow Bird said.

"Hunh, hunh, hunh." Old Muskrat's laugh was louder and deeper than usual. "I am an old teller of stories. And you must be hungry after your journey. Sit and eat."

They sat and shared the goose with the old man. Rabbit Stick remembered how good it had tasted, like no goose meat he had eaten before or since. When they were done, Slow Bird moved closer to the old man. He looked up at him, right into Old Muskrat's eyes.

"Will I get my wish?" he said.

Old Muskrat did not laugh. He looked at Slow Bird and then at Rabbit Stick. "Are you certain about your wishes?" he said.

Neither of them hesitated. "We are certain," they said.

"Unh-hunh," said Old Muskrat. "Now it is time for you to return home. You took the long way to get here. Let me walk with you part-way and show you a better trail."

They went outside and crossed the ice at a place where the shore seemed much closer. They climbed another hill behind the old man and went through a valley. He stopped at a place where the trails divided.

"Go straight here," he said. "You will be home before night."

"We will not stop before we get home," Slow Bird said. He began to walk, not looking back. Rabbit Stick followed his friend, but not before looking back once. Though the trail behind them was long and clear, there was no sign of Old Muskrat to be seen.

Not even, Rabbit Stick remembered many winters later, a track in the snow. They had arrived home before the night. Slow Bird had gone straight to his lodge. The next day, when he woke, he had stood and then fallen. He had fallen and kept falling, falling through the earth down to a place where voices spoke to him. Those voices claimed him as a deep-seer. Two winter later his name, Bear Talker, had found him and he was Slow Bird no longer.

Rabbit Stick had gone to his own lodge and found his parents waiting for him as he had expected, food prepared and no questions asked. What he had not expected to find was that their guest was still there with them. Sitting in the same spot where he had been sleeping when Rabbit Stick had left that morning, Old Muskrat smiled across the fire at Rabbit Stick and then laughed.

Rabbit Stick looked at Bear Talker as he slept. "My friend," he said in a soft voice, "we both got our wishes that day. Did we not?"

Bear Talker's eyelids fluttered and then opened. He stretched his arms out and yawned. "I have been sleeping," he said.

"All day," Rabbit Stick answered. "You came a long way."

"I went even further while I was sleeping," Bear Talker said. He held out a hand and Rabbit Stick pulled him up to his feet.

"You hear the dogs?" Bear Talker said. "Young Hunter and Willow Woman have arrived. It is time to go to the council fire."

Then, limping a little from the bruise on his hip, Bear Talker headed down the hill and Rabbit Stick followed him.

12 ▣ WHITE DARKNESS

Watches Darkness narrowed his eyes against the light. It was not yet dark enough. But soon it would be. The one-eyed being that he so despised would finish his long, slow crossing of the sky land. He would sink again behind the hills and trees and the shadows would caress the face of Watches Darkness. But not quite yet.

Watches Darkness retreated back around the corner of one stone wall. There it was very dark, especially because of the other wall of evergreen boughs that he had woven thickly together to block out the rays of sun. That was one thing that the old woman had taught him, perhaps the only useful thing. Then Watches Darkness giggled. No, there was one other thing she had taught him, taught him too well. To cut a stick that was strong enough so that it would not break.

His grandmother, Sharp Tongue, had been a very strong old woman. He remembered how glad he had been about her strength. It made her last that much longer.

"Is this stick strong enough, grandmother?" Watches Darkness said, giggling. His voice echoed off the walls of the stone chamber.

No one had ever thought he would become a person of power, least of all the old woman. He saw in his mind the thin, cowering child that he had been then. He saw himself walking out of the village that night, no, limping because of the pain in his legs where the old woman had whipped him. He had traveled all the night, growing stronger the further away he went from the village. That was when he had first realized that his strength was greater when he was away from people. Human beings drained his strength from him.

He traveled and kept traveling. He slept during the days in hollow logs or caves or shelters he made of branches. He set snares at the end of each night and when he woke with the sweet touch of night, he checked his snares and ate what he caught. It tasted better, he discovered, without a fire. Especially if the animal was still warm with the fires of its own fading life.

Moon after moon he lived this way. Seasons passed and more than one winter as he traveled. He grew taller and stronger without noticing the changes in his own body. His dreams grew in strength, too. He noticed that. He listened to his dreams. The voices in his dreams called to him. Told him what to do and where to travel. One night, he took his stone knife and used it to strip a roll of birch bark from a tree. He folded the bark so that he could hold it with one hand. Then he took a stick with his other hand. He tapped out a heartbeat rhythm on the birch bark. Then that rhythm became slower. It was now the same sound as the beating of the drum he had heard from the lodge of the man who was the deep-seer in the village where he had been an unwanted guest in his grandmother's lodge. He played his birch-bark drum and began to chant. He did not know the meaning of those words, but he felt those words deep in his belly as he chanted them. The words called something out of the darkness. He watched as it came to him. It came in the shape of shadows and it had no face. It whispered a deeper darkness into his ears and into his heart. It gave him his name and it gave him the beginning of his power. Watches Darkness.

When Watches Darkness returned at last to the small village where he had been a small beaten child, seven winters had passed. He did not come alone. In the medicine pouch that hung around his neck he carried seven helpers. To the normal eye they would have seemed only pieces of bone and stone. But Watches Darkness saw their power. And in the eye of his mind he saw the faces of those who had died to give him those seven helpers. He saw the darkness of seven villages grow bright from his fire. He heard first the screams and shouts and then the silence. He tasted the salty warmth in his mouth as he ate the hearts of the deep-seeing people who had not been able to stand against him.

As he crept close to that village, watching the darkness, he saw something. It was in a pit dug into the earth in the center of the village, a pit surrounded by sticks driven into the ground. The something was white and it whimpered and growled as it moved about the pit, trying to escape. Watches Darkness looked down into the pit. The one within it stood on its hind legs and looked back at him. Eyes as red as flame met his own fiery eyes. The one in the pit grew silent. It sat on its haunches and waited.

Watches Darkness went first to the wigwam of Crooked Hand, the deep-seer. It was said that Crooked Hand could hold a spearhead in his hand and blow on it. Then that spearhead would fly through the air and pierce the chest of an enemy far away. It was said that Crooked Hand could watch things happening beyond the farthest hills. He could walk into deep water and sleep at the bottom of the lake. But Crooked Hand did not sense the one who watched him from the darkness. Holding one of his helpers in his palm, crooning a low song, Watches Darkness slid into the deep-seer's wigwam. He crouched down by the head of Crooked Hand. He placed the flat piece of stone on the man's forehead. Crooked Hand did not wake. Watches Darkness giggled. It was always so hard to decide what to do at that point. Should he wake his victim before or after the blood began to flow?

He pulled back the bearskin robe that covered the man's chest. He lifted the obsidian knife, which was sharper than any blade of flint could ever be, sharp enough to easily cut down through flesh and cartilage, separating bone from bone.

"Wake up," Watches Darkness said. Crooked Hand opened his eyes. Then Watches Darkness struck.

That night he had visited every wigwam, saving his grandmother's for the last. Unlike the others he killed, he had allowed her to talk. He had hoped that she would beg for her life, but she had refused him that pleasure. Still, she had not refused him her pain.

When he went at last to the pit in the center of the village, Sharp

Tongue's wigwam was burning along with all the others. The stakes around the pit were driven in deeply and stones had been wedged around them to hold them tighter. Watches Darkness wrapped his long arms around first one stake and then another, pulling them out with little effort. His winters in the forest had made him stronger than most men. He shoved two of the stakes down into the pit, making a ramp for the one trapped there to use. Its red eyes glittering in the fire light, the white-skinned bear came up out of the pit. It was skinny from a lack of food and only half-grown, but when it reared up to its hind legs it stood as tall as Watches Darkness. He looked at it. It went down to all fours.

"You are hungry," Watches Darkness said. "Eat. There is cooked food all around you."

The One Who Walks Like a Man made a low moaning sound. It went to a wigwam where the fires had burned down now to almost nothing—the wigwam that had belonged to Crooked Hand. It did not have to dig long before it found the cooked food that Watches Darkness had spoken about.

Four winters had passed since Watches Darkness had gone home for the first and final time. The One Who Walks Like a Man had stayed with him. It had eaten well as it grew to its full size, twice as large as its black-coated cousins. Together they had visited many villages before they turned their steps this way. And now they were here.

But Watches Darkness was not pleased. For the first time, he had sensed someone sensing him. Despite their so-called power, none of the other deep-seeing people had known of his presence before they took their final breaths. Here, though, it was different. Somehow, he had been seen. So he would have to be more careful. He would not try anything this night. He would wait one night. He would strike at another village than the one where he had watched. There was no doubt in his mind, however, that no one could defeat him. His bag now held thirteen helpers. Among them was the spearpoint that had once belonged to Crooked Hand.

13 ▣ COUNCIL

Young Hunter knew all of the people who were gathered in the council circle. His friends, his family, the people of his village. He knew them all and knew that he would do whatever he could to help and protect them. The only ones who were not there were Sparrow and River Woman. His closest friend and his wife had traveled toward the winter land, to see the village where River Woman was born. Although that village had been destroyed by the Walking Hill, people had come back to rebuild it. The pain that had once twisted River Woman's heart and her face, even more than the fading scar on her cheek, had been healed by her life with Sparrow. They were the kind of couple that were said to share one spirit. Young Hunter smiled as he thought of them.

Young Hunter sat by the shoulder of his uncle, Fire Keeper. It was an honor for Young Hunter to be seated there, beside the sagamon of the village. Across the fire he could see Raccoon, Fire Keeper's son. Raccoon was no longer the little child who would sit in his father's lap. Raccoon was now almost as tall as Young Hunter had been when the Only People sent him out to face the danger that came toward them from the direction of the sunset, the Gray Giants who sought to kill all that lived around them.

Raccoon still looked up to his father, but whenever he could, he followed Young Hunter around. Sometimes he followed him so closely that Young Hunter would turn and almost trip over him. But Young Hunter was patient. He remembered how he, himself, had been that same way once with his grandfather. So much so that for a time they had called him Rabbit Stick's shadow.

Bear Talker sat on the other side of Fire Keeper. It was clear that he, too, had something to say to the people. Young Hunter had been surprised to find Bear Talker waiting for him when he reached his grandparents' wigwam. Now that the son of Bear Talker and Medicine Plant was old enough to speak, Bear Talker seldom was far away from his family. "I have much to learn from my son," he had said. Yet here he was, back in their village.

Young Hunter began to feel uncomfortable. It was a familiar feeling to him. He had felt this way twice before. Once was the time when he had been sent to keep the danger of the Gray Giants away from the people. The second time was when the Ancient One they called the Walking Hill had come among their people in their fishing village along the Long River. Young Hunter wiped the sweat from his forehead. I am sitting too close to the fire, he thought. But he knew it was not the fire that was making him sweat.

"My nephew will speak," Fire Keeper said.

Young Hunter cleared his throat. It was easy for him to tell a story, but to speak like this with the weight of his words being measured by all of his elders was much harder. He reached one hand out to take the hand of Willow Woman, who sat on his other side. She squeezed his hand, reassuring him.

"It is not safe to go to Petonbowk," Young Hunter said. "There is a great creature there now. It is a bigger than big snake creature. Padoskoks. We saw it strike a fish-catcher and swallow it whole. The neck of this creature lifted up was as big as that pine tree there. It would surely do the same thing to a human being who went into the lake or even stood too close to the shore."

Young Hunter looked around the council circle. He could see that no one doubted his words.

"Where did this great water snake come from?" The question was asked by Fisher, a man who was respected for both his courage and his generosity. Fisher had been planning to help Fire Keeper finish a new dugout canoe big enough for both of them to use in Petonbowk. Young Hunter had seen that unfinished canoe turned upside down and waiting for its makers to return. It had been left there in the bay just a look up the lake from the place where Young Hunter had seen the creature. "Why did we never see it before?" Fisher said.

Bear Talker cleared his throat. It was like the growling of a bear. "Do you remember when the earth shook?" he said. He looked around the council circle. Everyone remembered. It had happened twice during the winter. It happened first during the moon of long nights. That first time had been the most powerful. The trees had swayed as if they were struck by a great wind, even though the air was calm. A great rumbling and cracking sound had rolled through the hills around them. The earth beneath their feet had twitched like the skin of a giant animal. Then it had been calm again. Though the people had been frightened by it, their fear did not last long. No one had been hurt. Such things happened. Some said it was caused by the passage of great beings under the ground. The second time had been two moons later, during the moose hunting moon. It had not been as strong as the first time, yet several men who were out on snowshoes following a moose had been thrown to the ground. When they got up again, they had stopped tracking that moose and gone straight back to the village. As before, no one was hurt.

"What does the shaking of the earth have to do with the great water snake that Young Hunter saw?" Fisher asked.

Bear Talker growled again and Fisher became silent. Bear Talker had not yet finished what he was going to say. "I see things you cannot see," Bear Talker said, his voice so deep that Young Hunter felt it like the reverberation of a drum beat.

Bear Talker took a stick and drew a long shape on the earth with two legs toward the winter land. Young Hunter recognized it, as did everyone else. It was the shape of the Waters Between.

"Which way does Petonbowk flow? Where is the river that drains it? You, who want to talk so much, you show me!"

Fisher reached out and drew a line leading out from one of the legs of the lake. "Here," he said, his voice tentative. "Toward the Always Winter Land."

"Nda!" Bear Talker roared. He took his stick and scratched out the impression of Fisher's finger. "When the earth shook, the land changed. Petonbowk is no longer connected to the river that flows there. It no longer is connected to that river that flows out to the great salt water. I have seen this."

Bear Talker looked around the circle. No one questioned him or asked how he had seen this. They knew it to be true because he said it. He paused, as if waiting for someone to interrupt him again. But everyone, especially Fisher, remained silent.

"This bigger than big snake, Padoskoks. Yes, that is the right name for it. I see what has happened. When the earth shook the first time, it drove that great creature down into the Waters Between. Then when the land changed, it could not get back to the great salt waters. Once it hunted in the great salt waters. Now, when it hunts, it can only hunt here. Maybe there is food enough for it in Petonbowk. Maybe not. So we must warn all the people of the danger that is there."

Bear Talker became silent. Young Hunter waited, certain that there must be more. Bear Talker looked over at him and nodded.

"I can go to the other villages, those villages that will soon be going to their summer camps by the Waters Between. I can warn the people," Young Hunter said. He looked over at Bear Talker. The deep-seeing man nodded again. He looked pleased. Young Hunter sighed inwardly. Perhaps there was nothing more.

Fire Keeper looked around the circle. "You have all heard the words of Young Hunter and Bear Talker. Who else wishes to speak about this?"

Everyone else wished to speak about it. Each person had an opinion. Those who did not, simply repeated all that they could remember that had been spoken by the people who spoke before them. By the time everyone had finished speaking it was very late. They had talked all through the night. Soon it would be dawn. But the decision had been made. Everyone had agreed. Young Hunter would visit all of the villages and warn the people of the danger in the Waters Between.

As the people walked away from the council fire toward their wigwams, Young Hunter stood and stretched. His legs were tight from running through one whole day and then sitting through almost an entire night. Bear Talker stood, too. He came over to Young Hunter. Young Hunter noticed that he was limping. As Bear Talker came closer, Young Hunter began to feel as if he was watching from a distance. He was looking down, seeing a broad-shouldered young man with a scar on his ankle being approached by an older man who was as round and burly as a bear.

"There is more," the bear-like man said. "We must go into my spirit lodge."

Then Young Hunter found himself back in his body again, looking at Bear Talker. It was beginning again. And all that he could do was agree.

Throughout the land, the people of the Thirteen Villages were beginning again to follow the rhythms of the long days and short nights that the Moon of Strawberries brought them. In some of the villages, men and women were rolling the birch bark off their lodges into long bundles, leaving behind the frameworks like skeletons stripped of flesh. They would unroll that birch bark over the summer lodges they had left behind two seasons ago. Children were making smaller bundles of their favorite possessions to take them along when their families moved to the places where they would fish or gather berries. Dogs barked around them or played as if they were puppies again, carrying sticks in their mouths and chasing each other. There was a happy rhythm to the things done by both big and small alike. It was a good time for those who loved the light.

At the edge of one such village, deep within a stony and tangled thicket where even the village dogs did not venture, a great leaning rock formed a natural shelter against the hill. It was not a good place to camp. It faced the north, and the cold within it was so deep that ice remained there even in the warmest of moons. Everyone avoided that place. They called it the Hill Where No One Walks and the Stone Lodge. Stories were told of how the Frost Spirit himself made that his dwelling place during the Moon of Long Nights. In the darkest corner of that stone lodge, two who did not love the light waited for the end of the day. One was a tall angular man, whose muscles looked like knots tied to his long bones. The other might be called a bear, though it looked like no bear that had ever walked the land of the Only People before. Not only was it more than twice as large as the largest black bear, its head was surprisingly small for its huge body. Its jaws, though, could gape wide enough to cut a deer— or a human being—in half with one bite. The man and the bear were not only alike in their dislike of the day. Both of them were pale-skinned and white-haired. And when the light struck their eyes, those two sets of eyes both glowed red. As the long day wore on, the two waited. They slept and did not sleep. And when the Sky Walker reached his resting place at the edge of the sky and dusk began to set-tle over the land, they left the Stone Lodge. It was now their time.

At the sunrise edge of Otter Creek Village there was a single wig-wam. It was set on a sandy rise above the now empty settlement of stripped wigwams and deserted lean-tos. It looked down on the vil-lage the way a grandparent looks down on grandchildren who need an elder's protection. That wigwam was shaped like a cone and on its sides were designs of water animals. Beaver, otter, mink, and muskrat were there. A small fire burned in front of that wigwam. It was a fire that always burned there when the one who owned that wigwam was inside. Even though no one in the Otter Creek Village ever saw him go out to gather wood for that fire, it burned steadily in every season, even in the hardest of rains. Others might leave Otter Creek Village in this long day season to go and set up camp nears the fields of berries or the fishing places, but not Gray Otter.

The deep-seeing people of the other villages might take long jour-neys to dwell for a season or two in other villages or go to stay in dis-tant places that ordinary human beings could never go, but that was not Gray Otter's way. He had been born many winters ago in a wig-wam on the site of that one where he now lived. When anyone asked, Gray Otter would simply nod and look toward the Hill Where No One Walks. "I am waiting for something," he would say. And that was how it was. He would remain in that wigwam, watching over the village where the bones of his parents and grandparents were buried beneath him, under that always-burning flame.

Now it was not that Gray Otter never moved from that lodge

where he could be found faithfully sitting every night. He had another lodge in the village where his wife and his daughters lived. His days were often spent with them. He would stroll through the village during the days, nodding to people, exchanging a greeting with then or just listening to their stories. He was not a storyteller himself, but he loved to hear stories—especially those the children would tell him. Or he would appear among the people when they were walking far from the village. He would be there among them, listening as he always listened, and then he would not be there.

A party of men might be hunting moose in the season of snow-crust. They would stop to make a fire and rest and then notice that Gray Otter was sitting with them around that fire.

"The moose you are hunting can be found on the other side of that hill there among the alders," he might say. The hunters would look that way, look toward the place where, indeed, later that day they would find that moose. Then, when they turned back, Gray Otter would be gone.

Sometimes people, especially children, would come to Gray Otter's Lodge to sit with him. They would try to sit all through the night as he did. Gray Otter was one of those who was a no-sleep person. As far as anyone knew, he never slept, and it was said that he drove his parents to despair when he was a baby who could cry all through the night without resting. Perhaps that was why, now that he was an old man, Gray Otter spoke so little. He had used up most of his talking by never sleeping.

Others came to his lodge and sat waiting to see him do something wonderful. But it was not Gray Otter's way to do anything wonderful that people could see. He did not make fire fall from the sky or flowers blossom in the Frost Moon—as did some deep-seers. He did not call the animals to come and talk with him. Instead, he went about quietly. He would give the people medicine when they were sick, give them advice when they asked, sometimes even tell them where to find things that were lost or gently and indirectly advise them against things they were planning to do that were not wisely planned. People usually listened to such advice—if not the first time, then after they had fallen and broken a leg following a certain trail that Gray Otter would not have walked had he been planning to go walking or after they had tipped over their dugout in the deep cold waters of the big lake on a day when fishing had not seemed, to Gray Otter, to be a good idea.

That night, as Gray Otter sat waiting in his wigwam, he was contented—even though he knew his contentment would soon end. Early that day he had said, in his offhand way, how good an idea it might be for everyone to pack their things and make their way to the summer village. How, for one reason or another, it might not be comfortable here when darkness came. How, in fact, if he wished to see another sunrise and he was one of the people in this village, he would leave well before twilight. Everyone grew very quiet as he strolled about saying those words. Even the dogs stopped barking. Then the people began to pack more swiftly. Some of them came and embraced Gray Otter before they left—especially the children. Every child in the village hugged him and more than one had tears in their eyes. But no one hesitated to follow his advice. Well before twilight, all of them were gone. The last of them were his wife and his daughters. His wife looked hard at him, but said nothing.

The last light from the Sky Walker faded from the edge of the sky. The full face of the Night Traveler had not yet risen above the trees. Gray Otter knew that it was time. He sat in front of his fire so that its light was at his back. When one looks into darkness across a fire, one cannot see the shapes that darkness holds.

"I see you," Gray Otter said. His voice was calm and quiet. He was prepared. Yet the answer that came to him out of the darkness shocked him. It was not just the words that were spoken, spoken from just in front of him, closer to him than he had expected. It was the absolute coldness of that voice, the sort of voice that flint might have if that hard, sharp stone could speak. Ice and stone. It was the voice of one whose mind was more twisted than Gray Otter had imagined.

"I will eat your heart," Watches Darkness said.

"Have you eaten many hearts?" Gray Otter's voice was still calm.

He made his heart beat more slowly as he breathed out and breathed in.

"Not enough of them," answered the cold voice of Watches Darkness. This time the voice came from the side, even though Gray Otter had neither seen nor felt the twisted mind one move.

"Heart Eater? Is that your name?"

"You will know my name soon enough." This time the ice voice came from Gray Otter's other side. But he had expected that. Just as he expected what happened next.

A ball of flame kindled in mid-air and came shooting at him out of the night. Only Gray Otter's arm moved. He caught the ball of fire in his hand and dropped it into the fire that burned behind him.

"Fire Thrower? Is that your name?" Gray Otter chuckled. He was not amused, but he was certain that laughter would displease the one who sought to take his life. An angry enemy might be more careless in his attacks. A second and then a third ball of flame came hurtling at him. Gray Otter caught them both, one in each hand. He clapped his hands together and the flames vanished.

"A good trick for a bad child," he said. "Is that your name? Little Bad One?"

As he spoke, Gray Otter tensed himself. He could feel the anger of the one who would, indeed, eat his heart if he won this contest. It made his enemy easier to see. He was standing still, a tall man with hair as silver as an old man's. But this was not an old man who stood so silently in front of him, allowing himself to be seen. Gray Otter ducked low. A huge paw swung over his head. It was the paw of the other one he had felt creeping toward him from behind his wigwam. Through the corner of his eye he saw, in the light of his fire, the gaping jaws and the great teeth, the red tongue and even redder eyes of the monster that had sought to rip his head from his shoulders. Gray Otter rolled to one side, stood and then dove head first into his wigwam and swung the door flap closed behind him.

Watches Darkness took two steps forward and began to reach for that door flap. The One Who Walks Like a Man stood towering over him, waiting. Watches Darkness stopped. It was not wise to enter the closed wigwam of a deep-seer, even if it was only a small old man. Watches Darkness stepped back.

"I will not just eat your heart," he said. "I will also dig up the bones that you guard. I have seen them in your thoughts. Yes! You try to protect them. They strengthen your power. They are the bones of your parents. I will scatter some of them. Some I will keep. Maybe I will use one of your father's leg bones to make a pipe stem. Maybe I will use one of your mother's arm bones to make an awl. Yes, yes! I will make drinking cups from their skulls." Watches Darkness laughed, a high long laugh that turned into a howl. "But first I will eat your heart. I will eat it cooked!"

Watches Darkness reached into his pouch and took something out. He worked it with his hands and then threw it at the base of Gray Otter's bark covered wigwam. Flames burst forth and the wigwam began to burn, the flames encircling it. The door to the wigwam did not open, though Watches Darkness heard a frantic, scraping sound from within, a sound that grew fainter and then could no longer be heard as the fire's own voice grew louder. Watches Darkness smiled. Even easier than he had expected.

One Who Walks Like a Man went back to all fours. He lifted first one front foot and then the other, weaving his head back and forth. He looked over at Watches Darkness, who made an impatient sign of dismissal. The great white bear turned and shambled back into the shadows.

Watches Darkness stood there, rubbing his hands together and waiting. The incised shapes of beaver and otter, mink and muskrat and fish-catcher blackened and twisted and then vanished into smoke and flame. The bark wigwam collapsed in on itself quickly. The fire ate its own heart and fell into glowing embers. Watches Darkness stepped into the ashes and burned sticks of the wigwam, which stuck up like charred bones. But they were not charred bones.

He began kicking the sticks aside, searching for the body. It was not there. All that he found was a hole dug deep into the earth. It had been hidden by the remnants of a mat woven from reeds. The hole was not fresh. It was worn smooth by time and frequent use—like the entrance hole to an otter's den dug deep into a stream bank. Watches Darkness howled. This time there was no mad pleasure in his voice.

Gray Otter was gone, and he had taken the bones of his parents with him.

15 ▣ THE SMALL VOICE

As Young Hunter walked away from the council circle with Bear Talker, Willow Woman watched. The whisper-small voice within her that sometimes spoke was speaking now. It had always been so when that man whose life she would share as long as she drew breath was walking toward danger. It had first begun when they were children.

She remembered the day when Young Hunter was only seven winters only and he had taken the trail that led to the whirlpool below the big fishing falls. That whirlpool had frightened him as he stared at it the day before with a group of other children, Willow Girl among them. Even back then, Willow Girl had known what he was certain to do. She had seen the way he was. She had seen how, when a bigger boy tried to bully him, Young Hunter would lower his head and charge straight at that bigger boy. So she had followed behind him at a little distance as he made his way down the rocky trail that led to Great Falls. He had paused for only a few heartbeats before leaping into that swirling water. Willow Girl's own heart had felt at if it was about to burst out of her chest like a frightened woodcock fluttering up from the brush. Then she had seen a small movement on the other bank closest to the place where Young Hunter was being carried around and around by that dangerous current. It was Rabbit Stick. Young Hunter's grandfather was there, watching. Rabbit Stick had a long pole in his hand, ready to use it to fish out his brave but foolish grandson.

Young Hunter had found his own way out of that whirlpool. He had stopped struggling, allowed the current to move him downstream, and then swam free. But it would not be the last time that he would lower his head and leap into danger. And each time, as a girl who was one of his most loyal playmates and then as the woman who married him, that small whispering voice had spoken to Willow Woman. It had been so when he had gone out to hunt the deer without any weapons and had been struck on the ankle by the poisonous fangs of one of the close to the earth people. The voice had whispered to her, not once but many times when Young Hunter had been sent toward the sunset by the deep-seers to do battle with the Ancient Ones, the gray cannibal giants. It had woken her from her sleep ten seasons past just before the great Walking Hill attacked their fishing camp village by the Long River. And now, just two nights before, it had whispered to her, telling her to follow her husband when he rose and walked from their lean-to lodge to stand by the seemingly quiet waters of Petonbowk. There, together, they had both seen the head of the huge snake lift up and strike down with such terrible power.

That voice within her was quiet now, yet she knew that it would speak again as certainly as she knew the strong, swimming motions of the little one she carried within her or the feeling of the earth beneath her feet as she walked.

Willow Woman's feet had carried her now away from the center of the village where the council fire was almost burned to ash. The sky was gray with clouds. The new leaves of the aspen trees that grew around this village fluttered over her head. As the leaves fluttered with the gusts of wind, they made the trees shine and flicker. It was a sure sign that a storm was coming. The fluttering of the leaves hid the dark-winged shape of the one who peered down at Willow Woman from above as she walked.

The dark-winged shape dropped closer. Still she did not see. Deep in her thoughts, she continued along the trail. Closer still. Then, spreading its wide wings, it dove toward her head. Its claws spread wide as it reached for her.

"Hello, my friend. Hello, my friend. Hello, my friend."

The loud rasping voice of the big crow struck her ear at exactly the same moment as Talk Talk's feet lightly grasped her shoulder.

Willow Woman turned her head to look at the crow she had rescued from a long-tail when it was only a little one. Beak open, Talk Talk made a chuckling sound. He could tell that he had startled her.

"Talk Talk," Willow Woman said, "you are a bad crow."

"Wli gahgah, wli gahgah," Talk Talk said, spreading wings as wide as a fire-tail hawk's. "Good crow, good crow." He cocked his head and then leaned forward.

Willow Woman sighed. She lifted her hand up and stroked his head with one finger. Talk Talk made a small happy crooning sound.

"My friend," Willow Woman said, "I am worried."

Talk Talk lifted his head up and began to nibble her ear. "Wli nidoba, wli nidoba," he squawked. "Good friend, good friend."

Willow Woman laughed. Talk Talk knew how to make her smile. She continued walking, circling back toward their village. She was certain now where she had to go.

16 ▣ SPIRIT LODGE

Bear Talker's spirit lodge was not located in the place where his wigwam once stood on the sunrise side of their village. Only the wooden framework of that wigwam remained. Though the poles were still strong enough to support the weight of the birch-bark covering, which had been unrolled from its sides and hidden away, Bear Talker no longer lived there. He now stayed with his wife and their son on the high place far above the village of the Salmon People.

As Bear Talker and Young Hunter walked, neither of them spoke—at least in the words of human beings. Bear Talker was already growling and rumbling in that bear talk language that the Only People heard him use when he spoke to the ones that live beneath the earth. No one among them but Bear Talker understood that language. Young Hunter said nothing at all. In part it was because he knew that his silence was appropriate. When a person does not know what to say, that person does best by saying nothing at all. Young Hunter also remained silent because of his surprise. It was well known that no one, even another deep-seer, ever entered another person's spirit lodge. Yet Bear Talker had indicated that they should go there together. So Young Hunter walked in silence with Bear Talker while that other part of himself, that distant observer who could step out of Young Hunter's body, watched them as they went through the village.

Everyone who saw them stepped aside. Not only did they respect the two men, they knew that standing in front of Bear Talker when he looked this way was not at all safe. He would brush anyone who blocked his path aside as easily and as violently as a mother bear would swat away anyone foolish enough to approach her cubs. Bear Talker was always strong, but when he spoke with the voice of the bear, he was even stronger.

There was a story told about Bear Talker's strength when he took on the bear's power. A man who was a very good hunter had teased Bear Talker one clear winter night as a group of men sat together around the fire. That man was named Three Jaws. He had been given that name because he talked so much that everyone said he must have an extra jaw. Three Jaws had first complimented Bear Talker on his ability to find game for the people. Then he had said the wrong thing.

"You are a great finder of game for the people, but only hunters such as myself can bring that game in to them."

"Unh-hunh," Bear Talker had replied.

That was all that he had said. He went into his lodge and took down his drum which hung by a loop of sinew that could be slung over Bear Talker's shoulder. He came back to the fire and began to play it, singing a song that no one had ever heard before. A wind began to blow in the forest. They could hear that wind walking closer. When he stopped, everyone could hear feet breaking the snow crust. Some could see dark shapes moving among the trees.

Then, still singing and playing his drum, Bear Talker stood and walked out of the circle of light. They all heard the drum in the darkness, circling around the village. Then the drum stopped. Bear Talker came walking back to the fire, dragging a live full-grown moose with him. He held it by its back hooves. Bear Talker pulled it as easily as another man might pull a rabbit. Each time he stepped, the moose stepped with him. Everyone watched, their mouths wide open.

When he reached the fire, Bear Talker stopped and looked at Three Jaws. Three Jaws looked down at the ground. Then Bear Talker let go of the moose's hooves. Everyone watched as it walked back into the darkness.

There was a long period of silence. Then Three Jaws spoke in a nervous voice, still not lifting his eyes up from the ground.

"I was wrong," he said. "You not only find the game, you can also bring it in even better than I can."

They were now nearing the winterland edge of the village again. They were not walking straight to their destination as ordinary people walk. Instead, they were circling the village, each circle taking them further away from its center. Instead of following the ordinary path, they were taking a medicine trail. It was a trail that everyone could see, but few would ever try to follow.

Even Willow Woman, who was never afraid of anything, had made it a point to look away from them when they passed her as she walked back into the village. Out of the corner of his eyes, Young Hunter had watched her. Talk Talk was on her shoulder and she was walking in that determined fashion that Young Hunter knew all too well. He wondered what decision she had made now and where she was going. Then he brought his thoughts back to what he was doing. As always, it was easy to lose track of what he was doing when he thought of her. But to follow a deep-seer, one must focus one's thoughts.

Bear Talker was not moving fast. He was walking as a bear walks on its hind legs, shambling along. His shoulders were rolled forward and his head was down. To many people, Bear Talker was a fearful sight when he was like this. He had placed the two long teeth of a black bear into his mouth. Tied together with a piece of sinew, those teeth stuck out over his lower lip as if they were his own. Only Young Hunter, who had a similar set of bear teeth in his own pouch, knew that they did not really grow out of the deep-seer's mouth when he took on the power of the bear.

They walked around the small hill on the winterland side of the village. A group of children, who had been playing the stick game on the trail, shrieked at the sight of Bear Talker and then dove off the trail like frightened partridge chicks. Young Hunter could hear them as they thrashed through the brush for a few steps and then were silent as each of them found a hiding place from which to watch, wide-eyed, the passage of two men of power. Is that me? Young Hunter thought. Am I a person of power? How can that be so when I still see myself as a little one? Then Young Hunter almost laughed

One child, a little taller than the others, had not run. Instead, he stepped back to one side up onto a mossy stone that leaned against a beech tree. From his vantage point, Raccoon watched them, with eyes that were not afraid. Seeing his nephew standing there in that way was like seeing himself at that same age—curious and stubborn enough to not allow his fear to tell his legs what to do. Young Hunter found himself remembering the day he had followed the fox up that stony and steep trail that led to Medicine Plant's lodge. Even though she had walked knee deep in stone toward him, he had not allowed his own legs to carry him away in fear. He had held his ground.

Raccoon had that same kind of determination. Young Hunter knew that his brave nephew was ready to follow them. Young Hunter lifted his hand and made a small motion off to the side. Raccoon nodded, even though his eyes showed his disappointment. He would do as his uncle asked and not trail behind.

At last, as their circle went wider, they reached a small, overgrown trail that no one had taken for several seasons. Even the deer had not traveled this way. Bear Talker turned and went down the small trail. As Bear Talker kept up his constant growling speech, pushing through the overhanging branches as a bear does, even biting at some of them that brushed his face, Young Hunter lowered his head and stayed close behind. No one was with them. Even Young Hunter's dogs were not there. They had listened and obeyed when Young Hunter told them to stay and guard the wigwam of his grandparents.

Suddenly, Bear Talker vanished. It happened so quickly that Young Hunter was surprised. He blinked his eyes twice and then saw what he had not seen before. There, in front of him and just a single step to the side, was a pile of what seemed to be nothing but brush in a small round clearing circled by many tall birch trees. Thickly covered with branches that were green with new leaves, it was round and wide as a wigwam, but no higher than his hips. Rather than being made of cut saplings thrust into the ground, this little brush lodge, so short that it might belong to Mikumwesu, had been fashioned of living saplings, which grew in a circle within the circle of birches. The saplings had been bent and bent and woven together so tightly that he doubted he would be able to see through them.

Young Hunter began to bend down to look closer. But before he could do so, two arms were thrust out of the bottom of the brush pile. Two hands grabbed his ankles and pulled his legs out from under him. The next thing Young Hunter knew, he had been yanked through the doorway that he had not seen, out of the light and down into the depths of the earth.

17 ▣ GEESE

The geese circled the bay twice. Their wings took them over the great stone that sat in the deep water. The leader of the geese turned her head from side to side as she flew, barking back to those who followed. Ka-hankh. Ka-hankh. Ka-hankh.

They would not land where the water was deepest, so dark that they could not see to the bottom. They had done so the day before this and now their flock was only half the size it had been before. The great-mouthed snake had swallowed them up, striking first from below and then back and forth on the surface of the water, killing and stunning many as the birds tried frantically to take flight, wings beating, feet running across the surface. Even when they were in the air they were not safe. The great snake's head snaked on its long neck high up from the water, to snatch three more of the flock in mid-flight.

Lower they went, but not too low. The sharp eyes of the old goose watched the water. She could see what seemed to be a shadow under the surface. A long shadow, wider in the center. It was following beneath, moving toward the place where their flight might take them.

The leader of the geese lifted the edge of one of her wings slightly and turned toward the shore. There a river emptied into the bay. That was the way to go. Inland. She called a single time. Ka-ronkh.

Her eyes taking in the long flow of the river toward the range of mountains, the leader of the geese flapped her wings. The others followed in formation, currents of air linking them together like sinew thread. The wedge of geese rose higher and higher, still going toward the direction of the dawn. Now they were level with the tops of the highest peaks and then they were above them. Wide wings spread, wing tips fingering the wind, they sailed over the mountains and valleys. Away from the wide salty waters between mountains.

As they cut through the clouds, the leader spoke to the others. Ka-ronkh, ka-lonkh. Ka-ronkh, ka-lonkh. Calling, calling as they answered from either side. They could feel her wingbeats, hear her voice. Even when the whiteness of cloud was all around them, they did not break their formation. They continued on, following her, trusting her memory and her feel of the land no longer seen below. The water of the clouds glistened on their feathers as they flew. Moisture streamed off their wings and fell down as rain.

At last she knew she had gone far enough. She locked her wings, barked two quick times. Kankh, kankh. She cocked her head to look down and began a wide descending circle. As her head broke through the clouds she saw what she had already seen in the inside eye of her remembering. The long river stretched beneath her. There, where it was wide, was the place. The marsh there was full of food. They were far from the reach of the great hungry mouth of the big snake. She turned back and made four quick barks. Ka-lunkh. Ka-lunkh. Ka-lunkh. Ka-lunkh.

They would land there. There where the water was not deep. There the river was full of the sweet taste of plants and small creatures in the soft mud. Down they came. Their wings fanned open to catch the air. Their webbed feet reached out for the touch of the warm currents of the shallows. And as they approached, hidden eyes watched them from below.

The water opened like a hand as the leader of the geese folded her wings back, slid forward on the surface and bobbed down. She looked around. All of the others had landed about her. Though her flock was much smaller than it had been the day before, there were still many of them. Her mate swam over to her. They touched each other's beaks, nibbled at the small feathers of each other's necks. They had been together for seven winters. Like all of the others of their kind, they were mated for life and true to each other. Together they raised their young. Side by side they slept through the nights.

Even in the darkness, the two of them were ready to defend their eggs or their nestlings against any that came to attack them. Their wings were strong. When a full grown goose struck with its wing it was like a blow from a war club.

But here there were no enemies to be seen. The geese began to paddle about slowly, ducking their heads down to seek food. They dug in the mud and around the base of the water plants with their mouths, seining out water and earth through the grooves in their beaks, leaving only the small creatures good to eat. As they did so, two geese whose necks seemed stiffer than the others drifted toward them.

The two stiff-necked geese approached the leader of the flock and her mate. They paused and then passed them by. None of the other geese paid them any heed. They were too busy feeding. It had been a full day since any of them had eaten.

The stiff-necked geese drifted on into the heart of the flock. There were younger geese there, full-grown and fat, but not yet mated. A group of four such geese were feeding together. One of the stiff-necked geese came close to them. It paused. Two of the four geese dove under the water in a strange way and were gone. All that was left was a slight ripple on the water. The stiff-necked goose continued on its way. It moved away from the others toward a tangle of big logs and brush that had been washed down and lodged by the bank when the long river was high with the floods that always come in the Moon of Frogs.

The other stiff-necked goose circled toward the upriver edge of the flock. As it passed through, two more fat geese dove in that strange way—not head first, but all at once. Then that stiff-necked goose headed in the same direction as the other. Like the other, it swung around the tangle of logs and brush and was lost from sight.

When he was, at last, deep within the shelter of the logs and brush that screened him and his brother from the sight of the geese, Red Hawk stood up. The brush that the two of them had added to the driftwood and logs still screened them from sight. He reached up one hand to remove the cap from his head, which was made of the

feathered skin on an entire goose. Smoked over the fire, stuffed with
cattail down and then sewn together, the neck and head held stiffly
up by a stick, it was a perfect disguise. He placed it carefully in his
large carrying bag made of woven basswood fibers. Then he used a
piece of braised basswood twine to tie together the legs of the two
dead geese so that he could sling them around his neck. Across from
him, Blue Hawk did the same.

Aside from the hawk tattoos on their arms, the two young men
were identical. But Blue Hawk's tattoo was of a hawk perching. Red
Hawk's tattoo showed that same red-tail hawk in soaring flight. Blue
Hawk held up the two geese that he had pulled beneath the surface
and strangled before they could struggle. With a smile, Red Hawk
held up his two geese in the same way.

"We have caught . . ." Red Hawk said.

"Enough for today," Blue Hawk finished.

"Let us leave them . . ." Red Hawk continued.

"To eat in peace," Blue Hawk said.

It would not be respectful to frighten those geese now that four of
them had agreed to give their lives. The two tall young men quietly
moved out of the river, using the willows by the bank to screen them
from the sight of the feeding flock of geese until they were around
the bend in the river. They moved with the quick strength and grace
that had earned them the respect of all of those who knew them.

Aside from Young Hunter, no one could beat them in wrestling.
No one could run faster than Red Hawk, unless it was Blue Hawk.
No one could throw a spear further and with more accuracy than
Blue Hawk, unless it was Red Hawk. Yet there was no real rivalry and
no argument between the twin brothers. Even before they had drawn
breath, they had shared everything—whether it was hunting or eating, joy or danger, the two of them were together.

Only two summers before, they had almost died together when
the Walking Hill trapped them under the ledge of stone some distance downstream from the spot where they had just caught their
geese. Only Young Hunter's quick thinking had saved their lives. He
was their best friend, in the oldest and strongest sense of friendship.

The three of them had mixed their blood together, and even though Young Hunter was becoming a powerful deep-seer, they did not fear him. And they still tried, without success, to beat him at wrestling.

As they walked along the trail that led to their village, their feet made little noise. It was doubtful that anyone heard them coming. But there were still people waiting—several of them. Red Hawk was the first to notice as they were about to come down the hill. He looked over at Blue Hawk. Blue Hawk looked as unhappy as he felt. It meant that Blue Hawk had also seen those who were waiting for them along the trail.

It was a group of the young women who were about the same age as the twins. All of those young women were unmarried and all of them admired the two young men. Because of that admiration, they teased Red Hawk and Blue Hawk without mercy. It made it very hard for the brothers, who had decided when they were small children that neither of them would choose a wife and marry before the other one did. And neither of them would marry a woman unless that woman truly touched his heart and spirit. Thus far, two such women had not yet come along.

Although they were still far away, Red Hawk could see that one of the waiting young women—her name was Laughs a Lot—was holding something in her hand, something that appeared to have been removed from between the legs of a bull moose. He groaned. The teasing would really be bad this time. He looked over at Blue Hawk.

"Shall we . . ." Red Hawk said.

"Run for our lives?" Blue Hawk answered.

As one, the two young men left the trail and began to run. The young women tried to follow them, but were slowed by the tangle of maple and birch and beech saplings. Red Hawk and Blue Hawk could hear a few of the words that the young women were shouting after them.

"Is this why you will not marry any of our women?" Laughs a Lot called in a loud voice. "Should we give you one of these so that you can act as a man should act?"

It made the twins run that much faster. But they were slowed by the fat geese that they still carried slung around their necks. They were determined not to drop them. If Laughs a Lot or one of the others saw them do so, they would pick up the geese and then claim that they had been given as a token of love.

The young women had spread out now. There was only one way that the two young men could flee. They took the rocky trail that led up and up, high above the Salmon People Village. As the brothers climbed, the muscles of their legs beginning to burn from their effort, the voices of the young women grew fainter and then could no longer be heard.

At the top of the slope, Red Hawk turned to look back. Blue Hawk turned with him, placing his hand on his brother's shoulder.

"I think," Blue Hawk said.

"We are safe now," Red Hawk continued.

"I think," said a familiar voice behind them, "that you have brought me some fine geese to eat."

The twins both cringed. But they tried to smile as they turned to look up into the powerful face of Medicine Plant, who stood on the slope above them with her hands outstretched.

"I have been waiting for you," she said.

As she wove the moist strands of basswood together, Sweetgrass Woman hummed a song. Willow Woman handed her another long, fibrous strand. Twice as long as the height of a tall man, it had been shaped down to the width of a finger and such thinness that the light shone through it. Yet that strip of basswood was supple enough to tie into knots and strong enough to support a grown person's weight without breaking.

Sweetgrass Woman held the length of basswood bark up and looked at it, remembering. When she was a child and helping her own mother prepare basswood bark, Sweetgrass Woman would sometimes do just that. She would tie a long piece of the inner bark of the basswood tree to two low limbs and then sit on that thin strip to swing back and forth.

Willow Woman was using a flat piece of stone to smooth the bark and break away the rough pieces that still clung to it as she sat back on one of the fallen tree's branches. She held the end of the basswood strand pressed tight between one foot and a flat stone that stuck up above the swampy earth. Pulling the long strip tight across her knee with one hand, she ran the stone down the length of bark.

"Old Man," Sweetgrass Woman said, "stop being so lazy. Our daughter needs more bark to prepare."

Rabbit Stick, who stood knee-deep in the mud a few spear lengths away from them, working on the trunk of the wind-thrown basswood tree, did not reply to his wife with words. Instead he made a grunting sort of whimper. It sounded exactly like a porcupine. Whenever Rabbit Stick stripped bark from a tree, whether it was basswood for basket and rope making or the good-tasting inner bark of the pine tree for food, he always thought of himself as a porcupine. Of all the animal people, porcupine was the best at stripping bark from a tree—even better than beaver. Rabbit Stick had watched porcupines at work and learned from them. So he spoke their language when he was stripping bark. It helped him do it better and it also was his way of giving them thanks for what they had taught him.

"Hunh," Sweetgrass Woman said. "You see what it is like for me, my daughter? I am not married to a human being." She pointed with her chin at Rabbit Stick.

Rabbit Stick tried to keep a straight face, but smiled in spite of himself. Though he would never admit it out loud, he enjoyed being teased by his wife. It had been that way since they were small children together in the village. No girl ever picked on a boy more than Sweetgrass Woman picked on Rabbit Stick. When they were little she was always tripping him, poking him, throwing mud balls at him. He worked his bare feet in the warm swampy earth that was all around them. Mud just like this. When they got a bit older, she was always complaining about him to her own parents, who smiled knowingly at each other when she told them how much it bothered her that Rabbit Stick always seemed to be looking at her.

"Enhhh, enhhhh-ugggh," Rabbit Stick whimpered, trying to keep the laughter out of his porcupine voice.

"Hanh!" Sweetgrass Woman said. "Say that to a porcupine women and see what she says back to you."

Rabbit Stick could stand it no longer. He put down his flint knife and let go of the strip of bark he had been peeling from the fallen tree.

"I just did," he said. Then he began to laugh, holding his hands up as he did so, for he knew what was coming. The ball of mud that Sweetgrass Woman scooped up and threw at him in one quick motion struck him in the stomach.

"Ooonnghh," Rabbit Stick groaned, as the mudball knocked the air out of him. But he was still laughing.

Sweetgrass Woman smiled and Willow Woman smiled back at

her. It was a very good day. The air smelled moist and sweet. The many small birds that fluttered in the trees above them were as brightly colored as the small flowers that grew here. The little stream that trickled out of the hillside from a spring formed a pool just below them. The sound of that sweet-tasting flowing water was a good sound. Many of the agwalegedjisuk, the little ones who change into something else, swam in that shallow pool. Some of them were already growing legs from their small dark bodies as their tails shrank. At night, the voices of their parents could be heard singing all around them from the trees. Perhaps the song they sang told the story of Big Mouth, the lazy one.

Sweetgrass Woman always remembered that story when she saw a pool filled with the agwalegedjisuk. Big Mouth was a man who lived long ago. He was very lazy, so lazy that he would not hunt or gather food like the other people. He expected everyone to take care of him. Every day he grew more lazy. It reached the point where he would not even crawl out of his own wigwam. People had to bring food to him, and his wigwam was so smelly and dirty that everyone moved their wigwams further away from his. One day, he woke up at his usual time, when the Day Walker was in the middle of the skyland. Everything was very quiet. He crawled outside and looked around. Everyone in the village was gone. Everyone had packed their things and moved. Big Mouth was the only one remaining.

The people had told him that they were all moving to the fishing place, but he had not listened. They had told him they would leave at dawn, but he had been too lazy to get up that early. So they left him, thinking he would follow after them. But they were wrong. Big Mouth was too lazy to do that. He stayed where he was. But as the days passed he grew hungrier and thirstier. He was too lazy to go look for food. He was even too lazy to walk to the spring to get water. At last he became so hungry and thirsty he could stand it no longer. He could see a little pool of water not far away. It was dark and dirty looking and filled with the little ones who change into something else. Big Mouth did not care. He put his face down in the water and began to drink. He drank and drank. He stayed there drinking.

Meanwhile, the people who had left him behind became worried. Days had passed and Big Mouth had not followed them. Two men were sent back to see what had happened. When they came to the village they looked into Big Mouth's wigwam. It was as smelly and dirty as ever, but he was not there. Then one of the men saw something down in the swamp below them. They went down there and saw Big Mouth, his head still down in the water. They thought he had drowned, but when they came close he lifted his head up and looked at them,. His head was no longer that of a human being. It was like the head of a frog, but it was lumpy and ugly looking.

"I am going to stay here," Big Mouth said. "I am no longer going to be a human being. Go back and tell the people that this happened to me because I was too lazy."

Then Big Mouth crawled into the water and began to change even more. As they watched, he changed into a toad.

Sweetgrass Woman looked over at Rabbit Stick. He was busy peeling more bark from the basswood tree. Willow Woman had a pile of strips ready for Sweetgrass Woman to braid and was working on more. No one here was being lazy. But all around them everything was changing, changing in such a good way. All around them everything was greeting the spring. It was calm and peaceful. Yet Sweetgrass Woman knew that such calm often was followed by a great wind—like the one that had broken the trunk of the big basswood tree and hurled it down the slope to land here in the swamp.

But the old tree's sacrifice would not be in vain. They had already thanked it for the gifts it was going to give them. Rabbit Stick had walked around the tree, talking to it, treating it with the same respect one would give to a moose or some other game animal that had fallen to the spear.

"We thank you, Grandfather. You have fallen here because you knew that we needed you. We will make good use of you. Our hands will join with your hands and together we will make something. For a long time you stood here. For many winters you gave shelter to your children under your arms. Now you have chosen to rest. So we come to take your coat. We will borrow it to make things. When we use those things we will always think of you. So we come to use your body. Your body will give us warmth and when we feel that warmth we will always think of you. We thank you, Grandfather. We give you thanks. We give you great thanks."

Sweetgrass Woman turned back to helping Willow Woman with her work on the rope. She began again to hum her braiding song, singing that song into the rope. Anything that was sung into being was always stronger and better. Something had told her son's wife that there would be need for such a rope in the days to come. Sweetgrass Woman felt it, too. This rope would have to be a long and strong one.

Young Hunter pushed himself from his stomach and wiped what felt like a moist leaf from his face. He slowly slid back into a sitting position. He could see nothing inside the midnight dark of the spirit lodge, but sight was only one of his senses. He closed his eyes and reached out with his other senses. His hands felt the moist, cool earth behind him and he could smell that he was at least partially underground. The cool air on his skin, cooler than the air outside had been, also told him that. So that was why the lodge had seemed so small and his fall—when Bear Talker had yanked him down—had seemed so surprisingly far. The lodge was dug down into the earth and the webwork of bent, growing trees was only a roof above them. The living earth itself made up the walls, held firm by the interlaced roots of the trees. From the smells of their roots and the quick look he'd had at the little trees before he was pulled down, at least three kinds of trees made up the lodge.

"Sweetdrink tree, Thunder's tree, snowshoe tree," Bear Talker said, answering Young Hunter's unspoken question. "Those are the three that make up the roof of this lodge. Maple, birch, and ash. But I did not make this lodge. It was made for me by the trees. They bent themselves together and joined their arms. They wove their fingers so tight that no light shines within." Bear Talker growled, a deep growl that reverberated off the earth walls. "And I did not dig out this lodge. It was done for me by the ones who live under the earth. The mole and the squirrels and the mice, the woodchuck and the fox, they are the ones who dug out this lodge. That is why you can hear their voices in here."

Bear Talker stopped speaking, but the silence that followed did not last for long. The whistle of a woodchuck pierced the air, then the barking of a fox. The small thin chattering voices of the mole and the squirrel and the mice quickly followed. In the vision place behind his eyes Young Hunter saw them all. They danced around Bear Talker's head and then dove down into the earth by his feet and were gone. Again it was silent in the lodge.

Young Hunter said nothing. He knew that he had not been brought to this place for him to talk.

"Here in this lodge, we can hear things from far away." Bear Talker growled. "Listen!"

Young Hunter listened. He heard the distant sound of a paddle in the water. It came closer and closer as the person inside brought the boat toward them. Young Hunter saw it clearly through his closed eyes. It was a strange boat, unlike any boat he had ever seen before. It was not made of a single log. It was almost as white as snow or the wings of certain great birds. Its white was the white of the smooth stone which was found along the mountain sides. That canoe made of snow or bird wings or stone was closer now. It moved lightly in the water that rippled and trembled. It floated high in the water, graceful as a whistling swan. Young Hunter saw that it was made of birch bark, many pieces of birch bark stitched together. A frame was inside that boat, like the skeleton of an animal over which the birch bark was stretched tight as a skin. The paddles held by the one who manuevered that boat were also thin and graceful as was this strange, lovely canoe. The one paddling that canoe seemed familiar, as did the waters on which he paddled. It was the bay near the Guardian's Rock. And the one who paddled the boat was himself. As soon as Young Hunter saw that, he opened his eyes. And he saw only darkness.

"Dark, use your ears to see," Bear Talker growled.

Young Hunter closed his eyes again, but the birch canoe was gone. There was nothing and then he began to hear the sound of feet drumming on the earth. Running feet. He saw those feet running. The feet of a human being, the feet of more than one human. The feet of a dog, the feet of more than one dog. Only their feet, running and running. They were not running from something, they were running somewhere. As he watched by listening, he felt himself running with those feet. They ran from one village to another, carrying a message to every village of the people of the Dawn Land.

As Young Hunter ran in that place behind his eyes, he heard his own heart beating. His heart was beating as loudly as a drum. Louder and louder. Then he realized that it was a drum he was hearing. It was a drum that rumbled and rattled from the string that was tied across the drum head. The sound filled the spirit lodge and Young Hunter could no longer see anything. The running had stopped and the drumming filled all of his senses. It was like the roaring of an animal he could not name and the sound of thunder at one and the same time. Then it became the actual sound of thunder and the rattle of rain coming down all around. He could not feel that rain on his skin, but he saw it with his ears. Suddenly there was a flash of lightning. In the lightning flash he saw it. The shape that stayed etched in his mind was as clear as one of the drawings carved into the stone of the ancient rocks below the fishing falls. It was the shape of a thin, angry man shaking his outstretched arms. Behind it, almost part of it, towering above it, the shape of a great snake was lifting its head up from the deepest waters of Petonbowk.

The rainstorm and the thunder were gone now. Young Hunter could hear something else now, the sound of something rubbing wood, something being twirled between two rough palms. Then he heard a blowing sound. He opened his eyes, knowing that he was supposed to open them. His open eyes saw what he thought they would see. A light appeared in midair. A flame. Bear Talker was wreathed in smoke as he held the tinder bundle—which appeared to have once been a mouse nest—up and blew into it one more time so that the fire lifted high. The fireboard was still held between his bare feet and the hand spindle that had sparked the coal lay across his toes. Bear Talker leaned forward and placed the flaming tinder beneath the little pile of dry bark and twigs arranged within the hearth in the center of the spirit lodge. Long shadows began to flicker around them.

"I will tell you about the one you saw," Bear Talker said. He no longer growled now but spoke in his normal voice, the voice of a teacher speaking to his best student. "I do not know his name, but we have felt him watching us out of the darkness. He has come a long way to get here. His mind is so twisted that he sees nothing but darkness. " Bear Talker paused and then laughed. "Unh-hunh," Bear Talker said to himself. Then he became silent.

Young Hunter waited. He knew that it was not yet time for him to speak.

At last, Bear Talker continued. "Perhaps that twisted one who watches darkness has drawn the great snake here through his power. If so, I do not think he knows it himself. He is hungry for only one thing."

Bear Talker stopped. He sat looking into the fire. Young Hunter waited. He asked nothing, not even with that breathless voice which was inside his thoughts. The fire burned down and Bear Talker added more sticks. Again, Young Hunter remained silent. Those sticks, too, burned down. Twice more the fire ate itself and Bear Talker built it back up. At last, Young Hunter spoke.

"What is he hungry for, Uncle?"

"He is hungry for the spirits of all who are deep-seers. He wants to eat our hearts."

Within his lodge of stone, Watches Darkness was filled with a hunger that was as dark as the anger twisting inside him. He felt as if his head was filled with black stone. He had not thought that the old man would be so strong. He had not thought that the old man would be ready for him. Though he had moved within the shadows, someone had seen him. Someone had warned or was warning the other deep-seers about him.

It had not been that way in his own land beyond the mountains. There those who had great power were jealous of each other. They would not speak to each other. They would not warn or help each other. When they spoke to each other it was like two bobcats snarling from either side of a fallen log, each one daring the other to cross to their side. In his own land, when deep-seers met only one walked away. Here it seemed to be different. Here, as in all the other places he had traveled, each one had his or her own village, yet here they seemed to communicate with each other. There were even two who lived together as husband and wife and had a child. It was strange.

Watches Darkness smiled. But there will still be weaknesses in them. I will seek out those weaknesses. It is certain that there will be pride in the hearts of some of them. Such pride could be like the little hole in the covering of a wigwam that one could stab a spear through to kill the person within. Watches Darkness smiled even more broadly. Yes, yes, he thought as he remembered.

He had done just that in the Village of Black Stones far toward the summer land. There it was much warmer than here in the Dawn

Land. So the people were lazy and did not repair the bark covering of their lodges. There were many holes in their wigwams. He had defeated the deep-seer of that village almost too easily. That old woman did not even wake up after he sang his medicine song outside her door. His song made her sleep, just as it made everyone else in her village sleep until they woke to their own dying. The old woman had reminded him of his own grandmother, but even so he had killed her relatively quickly. There were so many other people in that village and he had wished to save his strength for the long night ahead of him. The spear that he found in her lodge, one with a finely made head of black stone, was better than his own spear. That spearhead shone in the firelight so brightly that it seemed to be made of black water. It was sharp enough to slice through clothing and skin with only a little pressure. So he took it. But, to keep things in balance, Watches Darkness left his spear in the old woman's chest.

"Yes, yes. I have traded fairly with you, Grandmother," he said, giggling.

A spear thrust into the side of the neck was best. Deep enough to cut the hollow tubes that carry the blood so that the one stabbed could not speak. But not so deep that it would kill immediately. This new black stone spear was so sharp that it took a few tries before he got it just right. The ones stabbed properly in that way would wake and sit up, choking on their own blood that flowed out like dark water gushing from a spring. They would be unable to speak. Their limbs would grow so weak they could not raise their arms up or support themselves and they would fall back. But their eyes would still be open. Then he would lean close so that they would see his face, a face as pale and cold as the white stone of a distant mountain. He would put his face very close to theirs and hold their heads in his hands to be certain that he was the last thing they saw.

He did not know how many he had killed in the Village of Black Stones. He kept count of only those whose hearts he ate and he only ate the hearts of those with power. But of those who had lived in that Village of Black Stones, none still were living when he left. Men and women, children and old ones. In that way, Watches Darkness was different from the other deep-seers who sought only to take each other's lives or the lives of their enemies. The enemies of Watches Darkness were all those who laughed at him and mocked him, all human beings. There had been so many in the Village of Black Stones that the One Who Walks Like a Man had been forced to leave much good meat behind, even though he ate only the tenderest parts of each person's flesh.

Watches Darkness shook his head. It would not be that easy here. He had met only one of the thirteen deep-seers who walked the Dawn Land and that first one had been clever enough to escape him. Of course that first one would not escape him forever. He would find that old otter man again and defeat him. But for now he would try others. Others who had weaknesses. Others who were too proud . . . like that one he had watched earlier this night. The one who lived with the snakes. He had sensed much pride in that one who lived only two valleys away.

Watches Darkness kindled the fire. He let it burn until it was down to coals. Then he took the moist rotten log from beside him. He had chosen that log carefully, knowing what was within it. He placed it on top of the coals.

"Little Spirit Creatures," he chanted. "Come out and help me."

There was a small movement at the hollow end of the log which stuck out beyond the fire. Four little ones came crawling out. Two of them were spotted and two had red stripes down their backs. Their smooth moist skins glistened like the black stone of his spearhead. They crawled toward Watches Darkness and then stopped and looked up at him. One of the little spirit creatures reared up on its back legs and tail and pawed at the air. Its dark eyes reflected the light. Its mouth was open as if it was talking, but no sound could be heard.

Watches Darkness leaned forward, listening, listening.

"Yes, yes," Watches Darkness said. "That is good. I will accept your sacrifice."

He leaned over and picked up the little spirit creature carefully so that its tail would not break off. Part of the power of these little ones was to sacrifice part of their bodies. Those broken-off parts would wriggle and twist with life—so that the creature itself could crawl away to safety and grow back a tail or a leg. But Watches Darkness did not want to lose any of the power the little spirit creature held within itself. He dropped the little one into the container he had made of green bark and filled with water before placing it on the coals. The water was boiling in that container. There was a hissing sound as the little creature struck the water. It twisted once and then grew stiff. Its mouth still open, it rolled belly-up in the bubbling water. White foam began to appear all over its body. It was a powerful poison.

Watches Darkness nodded. "And so that you will not be lonely, I will accept your brother and your sisters as well."

He picked up the remaining three little ones and dropped them into the water as well, watching the white foam thicken around them. He added a handful of carefully chosen leaves and roots and the liquid grew clear again. No scent rose from it. It seemed to both eye and nose to be only water. Powerful poison. Strong poison. Yes, yes.

21 ▣ FEEDS FOXES

The view around them was as wide as any spot in the land. They could see the hills rolling to all sides like the limbs of great resting animals, furred with the green of countless trees. Ponds sparkled, the many eyes of the living land looking up at the light of the Sky Walker, which shone brightly above them. The rivers and streams wove the land together, connecting it, giving it life as the flow of blood does through a living body. In the valley to one side of the high place where they stood, flocks of small birds, dancing in the warm air of the new season, wheeled and darted above the trees. Just below the level of their hilltop, above the valley on the other side, two red-tailed hawks were circling, calling back and forth to each other. All of it was beautiful to see and hear.

But Red Hawk and Blue Hawk found it hard to appreciate that beauty. It was hard for them to think of anything with Medicine Plant there before them. It was not that they disliked the deep-seeing woman. They had known her since they were small children and she had never been unkind to them. However, ever since they were small children, they had been told stories about her power and warned not to come too close to her lodge on the high stone slope. Those who came too close, it was said, might be struck by the lightning that shoots out from Medicine Plant's eyes when she is disturbed. Or they might be attacked by the animals that were always somewhere nearby, guarding her solitude.

* * *

Everyone knew the story of the man, many winters ago, who decided that Medicine Plant—then still a young woman—should be his wife. That man had another name then. No one could remember it now. He asked his mother to go and tell Medicine Plant about his intentions. The man's mother, who was wiser than he, refused.

"Would you not prefer me to go and tell someone less dangerous that you want to marry her?" she said. "Perhaps someone like a female bear or a thunder being woman?"

The man did not listen to his mother. Although he had only seen Medicine Plant from far away, he was certain that she was the one for him and equally certain that she would accept him. After all, he was tall and good-looking. He was a good hunter and he was generous. So he made a courting flute and practiced a song that he was sure could win the heart of any woman.

Then he waited until a night when the face of the Night Traveler was full and bright in the sky. He loaded a pack with venison and started up the trail to Medicine Plant's lodge high on the stony slopes. He was gone a long time, so long that some people thought Medicine Plant might actually have accepted him, though wiser people said it was more likely that she had just thrown him off a cliff.

When the man finally did return, late the next morning, he did not look like a man who had just found a wife. His clothing was torn and tattered and he was bruised and scratched all over. His pack of venison and his courting flute were gone. At first he would not speak of what happened to him, but gradually the story came out.

He was not yet within sight of Medicine Plant's lodge when he first heard the growling. It came from the bushes in front of him. Then it came from the bushes behind him. Then it came from all around him. He stopped walking. The growling came closer. A small animal poked its head out of the brush right by his feet and snarled up at him. In the bright moonlight the man could see clearly that it was a fox. The man backed up slowly and the fox came out, still snarling. Another fox came out of the bushes behind him. Foxes came out from all around him. He was surrounded. All of the foxes were growling and yipping. They did not look happy.

The man did the only thing he could think to do. He threw a piece of venison to the foxes. They ate it and then started growling again. He threw another piece. That piece, too, was quickly devoured. Piece by piece, he fed them all of the venison. But when it was gone, the foxes began to come closer. He threw down his pack. They tore that apart and came closer. The only thing he had left was the courting flute. He threw that down, too. When one of the foxes went to grab it, he leaped over that fox's head and started to run down the trail, away from Medicine Plant's lodge. But each way he ran, the foxes got in front of him. They nipped at him, tearing his clothing. They drove him all around the mountain, all through the night. Finally, when the dawn came, the foxes vanished.

From that day on, the man had a new name. Feeds Foxes. At first, he was not pleased with that name. But it was what everyone called him and he finally accepted it. He accepted it just as he accepted that Medicine Plant did not want him for a husband. Those foxes had made her message to him more than clear.

Eventually, Feeds Foxes found that story as funny as everyone else in the village of the Salmon People did. Perhaps what made it easier for him to accept that name was what happened when his attentions turned to another young woman. She lived in the village of the Spearstone People and she was not a deep-seer. When he asked his mother to go and speak for him, his mother was happy to do so. She came back and told him that the mother of that young woman was not opposed to the idea of his courting her daughter. Feeds Foxes was happy. The next night would be a night when the face of the Night Traveler would be full. He would play his song for her. Then he remembered that he had thrown his flute to the fox that night when he tried to reach the lodge of Medicine Plant. His heart sank. Just then, he heard a sound outside their wigwam. It sounded like a fox barking. Feeds Foxes went outside. There on the ground in front of his wigwam, surrounded by fox tracks, was his courting flute.

His wife-to-be, Two Fawns, had not been able to resist the courting song he played. The children of Two Fawns and Feeds Foxes were now almost as old as Red Hawk and Blue Hawk. Those children themselves told the story of how their father got his name. And that story was only one of the many tales told that showed why it was important to be cautious about coming too close to Medicine Plant's lodge.

It was true that Young Hunter, the best friend of Red Hawk and Blue Hawk, had become the student of their village's powerful deep-seeing woman. It was true that Red Hawk and Blue Hawk had been allowed to come close to her, even sit next to her wigwam, during the last few seasons. But they were still wary of Medicine Plant. And when a medicine person says that they have a job for you to do, you can be certain that it is not something simple like gathering firewood.

But Medicine Plant was not telling them what that job was. She was too busy preparing the geese to cook. Covered with moist clay, only their feet sticking out, she finished burying them in the coals of the fire. Her son, whose eyes were as deep and full of knowing as the eyes of any elder, sat with his back against the wigwam. He was watching his mother as if he had seen this done many many times before. As he watched, little Old Eyes played with a piece of sinew string webbed between his fingers, bringing it together and pulling it apart to make different shapes.

"We will eat together when they are done," Medicine Plant said at last, looking up at Red Hawk and Blue Hawk. "Now sit down."

The two young men sat.

"You will need to eat well," Medicine Plant continued. "You have a long journey ahead of you."

Red Hawk looked at Blue Hawk. Blue Hawk looked at Red Hawk. Neither of them said anything. There was nothing to say.

Agwedjiman lifted his head and sniffed the air. He looked back along the trail. Danowa whined softly.

Young Hunter sighed. "I know, my friends. I know. We have not lost him."

Young Hunter turned around and cupped his hands around his mouth. "We know you are following," he called. "We will wait for you to catch up to us."

He sat down in the middle of the trail, one hand on the back of Agwedjiman, the other on the back of Danowa. Pabesis had remained behind with Willow Woman and his grandparents. For this part of his long journey from village to village, Young Hunter had expected to travel with his two dogs as his only companions. But it was not to be.

Soon a tall boy appeared trotting along the trail after them. He carried a spear in one hand and a throwing stick in the other. Although he had lived only eleven winters, he already looked much like his father, Fire Keeper. And the look on his face was so determined that Young Hunter found it hard not to laugh.

"Hello, my uncle," Raccoon said.

"Nephew," Young Hunter said, "you are far away from home. Are you hunting?"

"I am hunting, Uncle," Raccoon said, petting Danowa's head as he avoided Young Hunter's eyes.

"Ah," Young Hunter said. "And you just happened to choose this trail to follow, this trail that leads to the Village of Many Pines?"

"That seems to be so, Uncle," Raccoon said.

"Tell me, my nephew, did you hear me speaking with your father about my own plan to travel this trail? Did you hear me telling him how I was going to carry the message to their deep-seeing person, to the one called Carries Snakes?"

Raccoon paused. He made small circular shapes in the well-trodden earth of the trail with the tip of his spear, then wiped them away with his throwing stick. Finally he spoke. "I may have heard you speaking about that plan, Uncle."

"Was it your idea to travel with me, nephew?"

Raccoon looked up for the first time. "Uncle," he said, "I can carry things for you. I can bring wood for your fire. I can cook, too. I am a good cook!"

"Should I call you Skunk, then?"

Raccoon smiled. "Nda, Uncle. Call me Raccoon. We both know there will be no snow in this moon." Then both of them laughed as they thought of the old story.

In that story Skunk had never done anything great. He wanted to do great deeds. He lived in the village of the One Who Made Himself from Something. By then, the One Who Made Himself from Something was also known as The Talker. That is because he was the first one made on this earth to speak words and tell stories. The Talker was always going out and doing great deeds to help the people. Then he would tell stories about the things he had done. Skunk wanted to do the same. He wanted to be like The Talker, who was always going on adventures.

One day, a group of people came to the village of The Talker.

"You must help us," said those people, who were shivering with cold. "The Snow Bird has come to our country. He stands on top of the mountains with his wings open wide and the snow keeps falling. There is so much snow that we cannot hunt or even gather wood. Soon we will all freeze or starve."

"I will help you," The Talker said. "I will go and talk to the Snow Bird."

Skunk had been listening. This was his chance to be part of an adventure. He begged to go along with The Talker. At first The Talker refused.

"You are very small," The Talker said. "It might be hard for you."

But Skunk begged to come along. What finally made The Talker decide to let Skunk go with him was Skunk's final argument.

"I am a great cook," Skunk said. It was a good argument. In those days, Skunk's coat was pure white and he smelled very sweet. He was known by everyone to be a very fine cook. And everyone also knew how much The Talker loved good food.

"You may come with me," The Talker said.

But it turned out to be harder than Skunk thought. It took many days to reach the mountain where the Snow Bird stood. Each day Skunk cooked big meals for The Talker and The Talker was pleased. However, as they got closer to that place, it began to snow. The Talker was a giant and found it easy to walk through the deep drifts. But little Skunk had to jump from one of The Talker's footprints to the next and his thick white fur became covered with ice and snow. He was not happy.

When they reached the mountaintop, Skunk was so cold that he could barely crawl. The Talker walked up to the Snow Bird and spoke to him.

"Uncle," said The Talker. "There is too much snow for the people. If you do not close your wings, I will have to bind them."

The Snow Bird looked at The Talker. He knew that The Talker was the one who had tied the wings of Snow Bird's brother, the Wind Eagle.

"I will do as you ask," said the Snow Bird. He closed his wings and the snow stopped falling. It began to grow warm.

By the time they got back to the bottom of the mountain, the snow had all melted away. Skunk was warm again and he was feeling happy.

"When we get to the village of those people who were freezing," Skunk said to himself, "they will praise me for helping them."

As they walked along, Skunk saw another big bird on a mountain-top. Light seemed to be coming from that bird.

"What is that bird?" said Skunk.

"That is the Day Eagle," said The Talker. "When his wings are open, it is day. When they are closed, it is night."

Soon they reached the village. The people were happy to see The Talker. They praised him and brought him food. But everyone ignored little Skunk. Skunk became very angry.

"It is not right," Skunk said. "I froze myself to help these people and they do not even see me. I will do something great. Then they will remember me!"

That night, when the Day Eagle closed his wings, Skunk sneaked back to that mountaintop where the bird of light slept. He tied the Day Eagle's wings. Then he sneaked back to the village and pretended to sleep. The next day, there was no light.

"We cannot see," the people called to The Talker, "help us."

The Talker found his way through the dark to the Day Eagle's mountaintop. He found the great bird's wings were tied. Those knots were so strong that he was only able to free one wing. Ever since then, it has been hard for the Day Eagle to hold up that one wing as long as he used to hold up two wings. So it is that the days grow shorter for part of the year as he grows tired.

"Who did this to you, Uncle?" said The Talker.

"The white one who travels with you," said the Day Eagle.

The Talker found Skunk's tracks. He followed them to the place where Skunk was still pretending to sleep.

"Why did you do this?" said The Talker.

"I wanted to do something great, so that everyone will notice me," said Skunk. "I am not sorry for what I did."

"The thing you did was not great," said The Talker. "But I will make sure that everyone notices you from now on."

Then The Talker knocked the ashes out of his pipe and covered Skunk with those ashes, making him black and bad smelling. With his fingers, The Talker drew two white lines down Skunk's back and across his tail.

"These white stripes will remind people of what you looked like before you did this bad thing. Now everyone will notice you and they will stay away from you."

And so it is to this day.

Young Hunter stood up and placed his hand on Raccoon's shoulder. He felt how strong his nephew's muscles were. It was no wonder that Raccoon was one of the best of all the boys in throwing a spear or wrestling. Raccoon looked up at him, waiting.

"You may accompany me," Young Hunter said. "But you must do as I say."

"I will do so, Uncle. Truly I will do so." Raccoon jumped to his feet. "Tell me what I must do and I will do it. I will!"

Young Hunter laughed. "First," he said, "do not talk so loudly." He patted his nephew's back. "Now walk with me." He looked into the boy's face and nodded. "And if you have any questions to ask, ask them now."

"Any questions, Uncle?"

"Any questions, nephew."

"Then I will ask them," Raccoon said, taking a deep breath. A very deep breath.

23 ▣ CARRIES SNAKES

The huge boulder was shaped like a great snake, a snake of darkly patterned stone coiled into a ball with its head hidden. The man who sat on top of that boulder sat exactly where the head of the snake would have been.

As he sat, unmoving, there was motion all around him. A long black snake, draped about his neck, lazily swung its head back and forth. Its tongue flickered in and out, tasting the air. Every now and then it would raise its head up and gently nudge its mouth against the man's cheek. But the man did not move. On the flat surfaces of the big stone were many other snakes. As they moved about, coiling and uncoiling, shifting their bodies as they crawled, it seemed as if the huge stone snake itself was alive and pulsing with breath.

It was a strange thing to see. It was not just that so many of the snake people were together in one place. It was common for a warm spot such as this to attract many of the close-to-the-ground people during the moons of long day. What was strange was that these snakes were of all of the different kinds living in the Dawn Land. They would not have been seen together anywhere else, for some of those snakes were hunters and eaters of other snakes. Here, though, they did not bother each other. Each kind of snake seemed to have its own place on the wide, rippling top of the great rock. The tangle of striped snakes of all sizes was separate from the small grass-skinned yellow wanderers. Several bright-patterned spotted snakes, those quick hunters, lay sunning themselves an arm's length away from two of those who carry the rattle with them to warn their enemies.

The man who sat there, his black, unblinking eyes narrowed

against the light, was almost as strange as that congregation gathered about him. There was no hair on his deeply tanned head, which had been rubbed with bear grease and shone in the bright light of midday. Blue patterns like the scales of a snake had been tattooed on his forehead and his cheeks. A soft smoke-tanned deerskin, patterned with swirling designs, was draped around his midsection. Aside from the small pouch that hung around his neck and the belt around his waist, the man had no other clothing. Blue tattoos of snakes crawled over the exposed parts of his body—his back and chest, his arms and legs. His long arms, which were wrinkled with age, were still heavy with muscle. Although he seemed small where he sat on top of the huge boulder, he was larger than any of the other men in his village. This, too, was strange. When he was a young man, he had been the smallest. A large woven bag lay empty on the rock next to him. A rattle made of folded bark hung from his belt.

The man's head—and the heads of all of the snakes—faced in the direction of the South Land. There a trail ran down the ridge past two huge trees, a pine and a hemlock, which had twisted themselves together so tightly that they seemed one tree. That trail led toward the village that was beyond the other side of the river and two more ranges of hills. The one who was coming to him would come up that trail.

The black snake lifted its head up again and nuzzled the man's face the way a dog would. It touched the man's nose with its delicate tongue. This time the man smiled. He lifted one hand to stroke the snake's back.

"Sssss," the man said, speaking as a snake does, "Ssskoks. Be calm. We will protect each other asssss we alwaysssss do. Sssssss."

He picked the bag up and opened it. The black snake slid off his neck with a motion as smooth as water being poured from a bucket. It flowed into the bag and coiled itself in the bottom. The man placed the bag into his lap and slung the handle over his shoulder. But he did not stand up or move from the place where he sat. The Day Walker moved across the sky as the man sat there, still watching the trail.

As the man sat there, he thought of what he felt. He felt his death coming toward him. He saw it with a self-confidence and certainty that some might have felt was pride. But it was not pride, only a knowledge that he knew was larger than himself. Step by step, his death was stalking him. He did not regret it. Perhaps he could delay it. But it was coming to him sooner or later. The sooner way would be the quicker one.

Better that it should reach him while his old limbs were still supple and his mind was strong with the deep wisdom that had given him strength for so many winters. He had outlived all those in the Village of Many Pines who had been born before him and a good many of those who had been born many winters after. He saw the possibility of avoiding the quick death that hunted him. The slow death would be harder. He would lose his strength, not just the strength of his body, but the strength of his dreams. No one would care for his children, the beautiful close-to-the-ground ones who had taught him so many things.

He cast his mind back to see himself as he had been when it started. As had so often been the case, he was sick. He was sick so often that the name he was called by was Little Cougher. It was the end of the moons of snow and somehow he had lived through another winter, even though his arms were as thin as sticks and his chest rattled when he breathed. Although the nights were warm and the days bright with the life of the new season, his own life seemed to be very small. He held no more than a handful of breath. His parents still looked at him and shook their heads sadly, thinking that the time was near when he would cough no more. Then they would wrap his cold body in bark and place him high in the branches of a tree.

That night, though, a voice as soft as the wind had whispered to him and continued to whisper. Its sibilant voice had called him out of the wigwam that he shared with his parents and his three brothers. He had walked down to the edge of the Lake of Many Springs. He had walked into the cold water, not feeling its cold. Then, even though the water was deep and he had always feared deep water, even though the distance was far and his limbs were weak, he had begun to swim. He swam at first as a dog swims, head up, paddling the water beneath him. The light of the Night Traveler was shimmering on the surface of the calm water. Something came toward him through the water. A head thrust up, a long body sinuously moving behind it. It was so beautiful in that glittering light that he felt no fear. He felt only delight.

As it came very close he saw what it was. It was a black snake, as long as the height of a tall man. It swam in a circle around him and then brushed against his face. It swam away and he swam after it. He no longer paddled as a dog does. He moved in a way he had never moved before and he felt strength coming into him from the water's flow. There was a rocky island in the center of the Lake of Many Springs. The people of his village seldom went there. There was no reason to go there and the people also felt that the island did not wish them to go there. As he swam, he saw that island before him, its head lifted up from the water like a giant relative of the black snake that swam beside him. He felt it speaking to him. It was calling him home.

The whispering breeze stirred the leaves of the birch trees that grew all over the stony island. The island itself seemed to shift and move, as did the leaves of the trees. From the water, he saw clearly what caused that motion. There were snakes everywhere and though it was night, they were not sleeping. He stepped carefully from the water onto that island. He was not afraid.

He did not return to the Village Among the Pines until the moon when leaves fall. He was thin and sickly no longer. He no longer coughed when he tried to breathe deeply. His chest had grown broad. His skinny arms and legs were sinuous with muscle, his eyes no longer filmed with pain. He had grown a hand's width taller and he walked with the assurance of one who sees beyond the things that an ordinary person sees. He wore a pouch around his neck and carried a bag slung over his shoulder. The head of the black snake stuck out of that bag, its eyes seeking the eyes of anyone who looked in their direction. The eyes of the snake were dark and glinted like wet stone. It made people turn their heads away to look elsewhere.

Some people had been afraid. But his mother had not. She recognized her son and she saw who he had become. He was no longer Little Cougher. She walked up to him—on the side away from his bag—and placed her hands on his shoulder.

"This one is now Carries Snakes," she said. "He will help us." Her voice was proud.

So Carries Snakes had been given his name.

Unlike other men, Carries Snakes had continued to grow. He did not grow swiftly, as a young tree grows, but slowly with the seasons—as does a snake. Even as an old man, instead of growing stooped and small he had continued to grow taller. He was now two hands taller than anyone in their village had ever been before. The people had begun to notice it many winters ago, but it had not troubled them. By then they were grateful for the help he had been giving them. He knew medicines for their sicknesses. He saw where things were that had been lost. He told them where to go to find the game animals. When their spirits became lost, he would seek their confused spirits out and return them. So the people did not mind that Carries Snakes seemed to have the power to keep growing.

Although it had surprised Carries Snakes himself, he had accepted that growth. It was another of the gifts that the island of snakes had given him. But like all gifts, even the gift of breath, he would have to give it back to the earth. Soon now. His spirit would move on. And he did not regret it.

He turned his head and looked in the direction of the sunset. But there was one thing he did regret. He would not live long enough to see the great one there in the Waters Between. Seven sleeps ago he had felt its presence in his dreams. He had tried to lift from his body and go there to see its beauty, a beauty as great as the power of the whirlwind or the quaking of the earth, or the rumble of water over the great falls. But he had been unable to do so. Perhaps it was because of the one coming for his life, the one he sensed growing closer, preparing to strike in the night. Perhaps it was only that the great one did not wish for him to bother it. Padoskoks.

The black snake lifted itself out of the bag and rested the top of its body against the chest of Carries Snakes. Its heart was over his heart. It touched his chin with its nose. Carries Snakes stroked the head of the black snake.

"Sssss," he whispered, "Ssskoks, ktsssi nidoba. My old friend, you will live to sssee the great sssnake. I promisssse you thisss. Sssss."

The two young men walked slowly and carefully on the trail that led through the cedar swamp. They had been running since dawn of the day before but they were not tired, even though the Sky Walker was already moving again down the sky toward his lodge. Alone, each of them could run for two days and two nights without rest. Together, for the brothers always drew strength from each other, it was said that they could run forever. They had eaten as they ran, taking from their pouches handfuls of the dried meat and maple sugar and berries, which were ground together to make a good food for one who must travel swiftly and without rest.

They had crossed one wide river valley and three smaller streams since they had left the high rocky slope where Medicine Plant gave them their instructions. Each time they had crossed a stream they had paused to give thanks to that flowing giver of life before they drank sweet water and then continued on their way. They had passed out of the hunting grounds of their own Salmon People and through the hunting grounds of two more villages, following the trails on which anyone who was a friend could travel without challenge.

As they ran, Red Hawk and Blue Hawk ran with the land and not against it. So it was that their strides grew longer and they ran as water runs, flowing with the earth. They had stopped only once, when they reached the place they had been told to go first. Otter Creek Village. What they saw there at first had filled them with despair. But what they heard before they arrived had prepared them. They heard nothing.

Though their running feet were soft on the earth, the two brothers knew that each step they made was like a drumbeat to the ears of the four-legged ones who chose to live with the people. Whenever a man came running toward a village, the dog people would alway be the first to know and they would announce his arrival long before he came into sight. And in the long day moons, even when the human people of a village pack and travel to the berry picking spots or the fishing camps, some dogs always choose to remain behind. But no dogs barked as they came close and closer to Otter Creek Village.

Red Hawk looked over at Blue Hawk as he ran and Blue Hawk looked back. They did not have to speak. They were both thinking the same thing. Where are the dogs? What has happened here?

Red Hawk fitted a short spear into his atlatl and cocked his arm back, ready to throw. Blue Hawk held his own, longer spear across his body as they slipped off the trail and circled into the village. What they saw first was the lodge of the man who never moves. His name was Gray Otter. He was the deep-seeing man of the village and had been so for as many winters as the two brothers had drawn breath.

The lodge of Gray Otter was burned and the ashes were cold. The charred sticks of his lodge had been scattered and broken and there were footprints in the sandy earth and the ashes. The two brothers read the footprints and looked at each other. They did not like what they saw. Each of them felt the hair rising on the back of their necks.

Blue Hawk used the tip of his long spear to move aside some of the charred and trampled sticks of the lodge. There, in the center, was a hole that was almost big enough for a man to go down. For some reason, he found himself smiling when he saw that hole. He did not understand why. He looked at his brother. Red Hawk was smiling, too.

Red Hawk motioned with his chin toward the village below. The two brothers left the mystery of the deep-seeing man's lodge behind. What they found in the village surprised them, as well. The wigwams had all been broken. It was as if something like an angry wind had gone through the village. But they knew it was more solid than a wind, for they found more footprints and places where the poles of wigwams had been bitten in half by very large teeth. Yet, despite all the destruction, there was no sign of blood, no feeling of death. The village had been destroyed after it was deserted.

The trail of the ones who had done this led out of the village toward the direction of the winter land. Red Hawk and Blue Hawk had no intentions of following that trail. When a big man walks with a giant bear, it is best to let those two walk alone.

Blue Hawk looked at Red Hawk. He saw his brother was thinking as he thought.

"If this many people . . ." Red Hawk said.

"Have left the village . . ." Blue Hawk continued.

"We should be able to find *their* trail," they said as one.

It had not been an easy trail to find. The people of Otter Creek Village had been careful. But Red Hawk saw the place where a child's foot had scuffed the moss from a stone on the slope to the sunset side of the village. From then on, the way was easy to track. They began to run as they followed that cold trail, a trail left at least four nights gone. It led eventually to the cedar swamp and went inside. More slowly then, they had followed.

When one travels through a cedar swamp, it is wise to move with care. When a deer is wounded and would escape its enemies, it often goes into the swamps, knowing where it is safe to go and where a wrong step will plunge a pursuer into deep cold water. When they were children, the brothers had never been told directly by their parents not to go into the cedar swamps. But they had been told about the monsters that were to be found in such places. Those monsters were especially fond of eating curious children.

The worst one of all was the Toad Woman. She was a creature who could take the shape of an old woman. If she saw a child, she would call out in a sweet voice, like that of a grandmother.

"Little One, come and help me. I need you. I have hurt my foot. Come close and help me. I have maple sugar in my pouch and I will give it all to you. Come here, Little One. I need you. Come here."

If you were foolish enough to come close enough to her, you would see that her face was lumpy with warts and you would notice how bad she smelled. But by then it would be too late. Her long fingers with sharp claws on them would have grabbed you, pulling you down into the depths of the swamp. There she would drown you. And when your dead flesh was rotten and soft, she would suck the meat from your bones. And you would never be seen again.

Now that they were grown, Blue Hawk and Red Hawk realized that Toad Woman was just one of those stories grown-ups told to make children think twice before doing foolish things. It was best not to interfere with the wishes of children, but to allow them to learn by doing and by making their own mistakes. Cautionary stories helped prevent them from making mistakes that would be too dangerous.

Such stories did not always work. After hearing that story many times from his grandparents, who had adopted him after his own parents were killed, their friend Young Hunter had decided that it was his job to rid the world of such a terrible monster. Even though he was less than six winters old, he had taken up his little spear and gone down into the swamps to hunt for Toad Woman. But he had never found her. His conclusion had been that he had frightened her away. After all, he had heard something thrashing around in the swamp like a wounded deer as he sought out his enemy. It was many winters later when Young Hunter understood why his grandfather, Rabbit Stick, had been sound asleep from exhaustion when he came home that evening and why his grandfather's mokasins had been caked with drying mud.

Still, even though they no longer believed in Toad Woman, both Red Hawk and Blue Hawk thought that in such a place as this they would not be surprised if they did really see her. They moved even more slowly now, walking as a weasel does, turning their eyes and their ears in every direction. As they followed the trail, the brothers noticed how dark it was within the swamp. The trees grew closely together and they could not see far in any direction. There was more water around them now and the trail underfoot was moist, the ground sometimes moving and trembling as they stepped. Little streams, which seemed to be flowing in all directions and in no direction, were everywhere. The smells of the swamp rose up as they walked. They knew that it was in a place such as this that spirit lights would be seen glowing in the darkness.

Red Hawk and Blue Hawk were beginning to worry now. Soon they would be wading knee-deep if this trail continued down. Soon there would be no trail at all. They had been to Otter Creek Village before, ten winters ago when they were children traveling with their parents to see their cousins. Since only ten winters had passed, it had been easy for them to remember the way. But they had never been in this swamp before. In the old days, when the people were hunted by the great beings, the Ancient Ones, each village had secret places where they could seek refuge, hiding places like this deep swamp. But only the people of the village knew those places.

Soon it would be dark. And darkness would come even sooner and more quickly in a place such as this. It was too wet here for them to make a fire and they found themselves worrying about what might walk in the darkness in such a place as this. They had gone in so far on this trail that even turning back would not bring them to dry and higher ground before the night came. It would not be easy to back-track. This would be a night when the Night Traveler's face might not be easy to see through the clouds, which were beginning to fill what they could see of the early evening sky.

Something moved ahead of them and to one side of the trail. The two young men jumped back. A brown head stuck up from the swamp. It lifted up higher and its long brown supple body could now be seen. It was a large male otter. It slid out of the water and stood on its hind legs in the middle of the trail, right in front of them. It shook the water from its head, lifted up its front paws and stared, first at Red Hawk and then at Blue Hawk.

As those deep-set brown eyes looked up at them, the two brothers felt certain that the otter was going to speak human words. Instead, it chattered in a way that sounded like laughter. Then it dropped back to all fours and turned. It ran up the trail swiftly, humping along almost as a caterpillar travels. When it came to two age-black-ened hemlock stumps, the otter looked back at them and chattered again. It disappeared from sight between the hemlock stumps.

Red Hawk looked at Blue Hawk. Blue Hawk looked back at his brother. Shrugging their shoulders, the two men turned off the trail to follow the otter.

The otter's tracks were clear in the dark wet soil. They led through a thickly grown screen of small black spruce to the place where another trail began. There the otter tracks disappeared. But the tracks of people, some of those tracks made that same day, were there.

As they followed that second hidden trail, the ground around them began to change. In places it was drier as islands of earth rose out of the cedars. On those islands giant pines grew, and now they heard the evening songs of the birds who live among the tall trees. There would be dry places to make a fire here and sleep. The two brothers felt their hearts begin to rise as they left the swamp further and further behind.

The trail led around one of those giant pines. Red Hawk and Blue Hawk suddenly stopped. A man was there on the trail, lying on his stomach. He was a small, compact man of middle age. His hands, which were under his chin, rested on a woven bag and he was facing them. His deep-set brown eyes looked into theirs.

"Hello, my friends," Gray Otter said, rising to his feet. "I have been waiting for you."

25 ▣ FERN LEAVES

Young Hunter rubbed his palms across his forehead. Raccoon was still waiting. He sat there, leaning against Danowa, who had closed his eyes and stretched himself out in a shady place under the ferns that grew thickly all along the uphill edges of the trail. Agwedjiman, ever watchful, had disappeared up the path. Young Hunter knew that the big dog had gone to scout ahead of them.

Raccoon's eyes were bright with eagerness. He had asked even more questions than Young Hunter had expected. Usually his nephew was one of the quietest of the boys of his age. He had been so slow to talk as a baby that his parents had worried about him. Perhaps he was one of those who had not been given speech. But his eyes and, as it turned out, his ears had been open when his mouth was not. Raccoon was a listener. It was as if he was born understanding the teaching that the Owner Creator had made a part of every human being's head. We were made with two eyes and two ears, but only one mouth. So, if we live as the Owner Creator meant, we will talk only half as much as we listen to others. We will look twice at the world around us before we speak once.

Like his namesake, Raccoon was always watching and listening. He was filled with curiosity and aware of everything around him. But all of the listening and observing that Raccoon had been doing over the past few days had built up so many questions in him that they had burst forth like water from a broken beaver dam.

It was hard to remember all of Raccoon's questions. Young Hunter's nephew had sat there, holding a twig in his hands and making a mark in the sandy soil at the edge of an ant hill each time he asked a question. There were far too many such marks.

Who is the one bringing danger to our people? Why does that person want to hurt us? What makes a person want to hurt other people? Why does he wish to destroy our deep-seeing people? How can he hurt our deep-seers? Don't they have the power to defend themselves? Why don't all our deep-seers band together and fight this enemy? What was it that you saw in the Waters Between? What can we do about it? Can we catch it as one catches a big fish? If I swim there, would it eat me? Why are you traveling to the Village of Tall Pines? What will you say to that person who is called Carries Snakes? Is it true that he can turn himself into a snake? What can I do to help you?

Young Hunter rubbed his forehead again. Was this how his grandfather, Rabbit Stick, had felt when he asked similar endless strings of questions of the old man during his own childhood? So many questions. And for every one of them Young Hunter knew what he could answer, with great truth. I do not know. I do not know. I do not know. I do not know.

Once, Young Hunter had thought that his grandfather and grandmother knew all things. Then, when he was older, he had imagined that Bear Talker held within him the knowledge of everything. If he became a deep-seer himself, like Bear Talker, he would be able to answer all of his own questions. Now he was beginning to realize that no one can ever answer all their own questions. Sometimes you simply have to follow a trail, using what you know as you travel. You prepare yourself before you set out on your journey, but what will happen along the way cannot completely be forseen. Only the possibilities. It was like hearing a story told for the first time. You might have a sense of how it will end, but you could not be sure until it was over. And even a familiar story could take its own twists and turns.

Young Hunter looked at the lines his nephew had drawn in the sand. A single ant was trying to find its way between them, confused at the ranges of hills that had suddenly appeared in the midst of what had been a well-marked trail.

"Nephew," Young Hunter said.

"Uncle," said Raccoon.

Young Hunter went back to studying the ant. It went first one way and then another. At last it turned and hurried back to the top of the mountain of sand that was its wigwam. It disappeared inside. What a story it would have to tell all of its relatives. Young Hunter smiled.

"You know the story about Alebis, the ant?"

"How does the story go, Uncle?"

"You know what Alebis is like. He has a big, big head and a very small neck. And Alebis likes to go on journeys."

Once, long ago, Alebis had been gone a long time. When he came back all of his relatives were surprised to see him. They thought he had been killed, perhaps stepped on by one of the great giants or eaten by one of the many terrible monsters that love to eat the ant people.

"Hanh," Alebis said, "I am fine. I have a great story to tell you all. It is the finest story ever. You will all love this story. You will be glad when I tell it to you."

All the ants were very excited. This would be a special story. They gathered everyone together in a big circle around Alebis. Alebis waited until they were all there. Then he looked slowly around the circle and took a deep breath.

"Hanh," Alebis said. "Good. You are all here. But first I have to have something to eat."

Everyone ran to get food for Alebis. They were eager to hear that story. He ate very slowly while all the other ants waited. He ate a great deal of food. At last he was done eating.

"Hanh," Alebis said, "That was good food. I am full. But now I am tired. I need to rest. Let me sleep a little while. Then I will tell you my story. It is worth waiting to hear that story, and I will tell it better when I have rested."

Then Alebis went to sleep. The other ants waited patiently while he slept. He slept for a long time. At last he woke up and stretched.

"Hanh!" Alebis said. "It is good that you waited. And I will now tell you that story. It is a story you will never forget. You will want to tell it to all the coming generations of our people. But first I need something to drink. I am feeling thirsty. My story is a very long story and so I need something to drink before I start. I cannot tell my story when my throat is dry."

All the ants ran to get something for Alebis to drink. They were so excited. This would be the best story ever told. When they brought Alebis his drink, he drank it very slowly. Then he cleared his throat.

"Hanh," Alebis said. "Now I am completely ready. I will tell this story. You will love this story. Everyone listen closely."

The ants all leaned forward, ready to hear that wonderful story.

"Hanh," said Alebis. "Now hear my story. Oh, wait. First I must sneeze."

Then Alebis sneezed. He sneezed so hard that he sneezed his big head off his little thin neck. So no one ever heard his story.

Raccoon laughed. "That is a good story, Uncle."

Young Hunter nodded. "Maybe it is the story that we are in right now, Nephew. I am not sure that I can answer your questions. I only know that I have been sent out to follow this trail. It is as my grandfather told me. When we are on a journey, we have to go along step by step. We have to follow the trails the best we can."

Young Hunter reached out his hand and touched a group of fern leaves by the side of the trail. Some of them were still tightly coiled while others were open. The delicately fringed open leaves swayed as he brushed against them.

"These fern leaves hold a message. See how they are coiled up. We cannot see what is inside them until they open. But they must open on their own. We cannot force them open or make them grow the way we want them to grow. If we do, they grow in a twisted way or they turn brown and die. We have to wait."

He looked at Raccoon. Raccoon nodded.

"Why do people want to hurt others? I cannot answer that question. It is hidden inside them. But I think that sometimes people become twisted in their minds from anger or fear or pain. Otherwise they would not want to hurt their own people. A wolf does not hunt other wolves. It hunts the deer people and the rabbit people. It does not hate or fear the deer people or the rabbit people. It is not angry at them. It hunts them because they are its life. In its own way, the wolf cares for the deer people and the rabbit people. It does not want to destroy them. If it destroys them all, it will destroy itself. But when a human being hunts other human beings, that is a twisted thing. Hunting your own people is like hunting yourself. Although you may destroy them, in the end you destroy yourself as well."

Young Hunter indicated one of the curled fern leaves. Then, with one finger he drew a straight line in the sand that ended in a curl like that of the uncoiled fern.

"You know this pattern, don't you, Nephew?"

Raccoon reached out his own finger and copied the shape his uncle had made in the soil. Then he nodded.

"I know it. It is one of the patterns that we cut into the bark of our lodges."

"It has many meanings. It means that what is hidden will reveal itself if we are patient. It also stands for the trail that an animal takes when it is being pursued. It will circle back so that it can see the trail behind it. That way it can see what is pursuing it."

Young Hunter stood up and brushed the sand from his hands. Raccoon jumped to his feet followed by Danowa, who yawned and shook himself so hard that his ears made a noise like wings flapping. Then Danowa stretched, arching his back and thrusting out his feet. It was a long, satisfying stretch. As he stretched, the dog's big front feet wiped out the marks that Raccoon and Young Hunter had made in the sandy earth. All of the lines and circles marking questions and trails disappeared back into the soil.

Young Hunter whistled softly as he looked up the trail. Then he turned and looked back. Agwedjiman stepped quietly out of the ferns down the trail behind them. His mouth was open and he seemed to be grinning. The big dog had made a circle.

"Uncle," Raccoon said, "I understand. We will follow this trail, but we will keep looking back."

A storm was coming across the lake. Walks-in-a-Hole could feel it coming as clearly as he could see its path being marked in the sky land above him. He had also seen it the night before when he slept. The motions of the clouds and his dreams both spoke to him with equal clarity. It would be a strong storm.

Walks-in-a-Hole tapped his long staff against the red rocks, which stood in powerful shapes here at the edge of the Waters Between. In some places, like here next to him, the great blood-colored stones leaned together in ways that made them look like wigwams for giants. One story his uncle had told him, back when he was a child, explained why those rocks were red. That story told him whose blood it was on those rocks. It was a story told for his family and his family alone. It was not a story known to the other villages of the Only People or even to the other families within their village. It belonged to his family. He would not even think too much about that story or tell it in his head. The red rocks would hear him thinking of that story.

His uncle had explained it clearly to him about the rocks. Rocks are always listening. Perhaps it is because they cannot move away as people do. Because stones have no hands, they cannot cover their ears. Because they have no eyes to close, they cannot sleep. Even the trees sleep, dropping their leaves in their slumber during the season of long nights. But stones remain the same. So they are always awake. Walks-in-a-Hole felt how wide awake these stones were. The stones would not like it if he was to tell that story of how they became red. That story of how those certain monsters shed their blood here and who it was who did it to them.

The great stone on which he was standing moved slightly. Perhaps it was only because it was balanced just so and he had just shifted his weight as he stood on top of it. Or perhaps not. Walks-in-a-Hole tried hard to change his thinking. Trying to not think of a story sometimes made one think of it that much more. His uncle, who had been the greatest of storytellers, had told him that. Walks-in-a-Hole smiled as he thought of his uncle. His uncle had taught him many things.

Like his uncle, Walks-in-a-Hole was a very short person. And, like Stands-in-a-Hole, his name did not just mean that he lacked height. Like his uncle, Walks-in-a-Hole was a deep-seer. He was one of whose who, when he walked with power, could make his feet sink into the stones so that it seemed as if he was walking in a trench where there was nothing but solid rock. His uncle had taught him that. His uncle had taught him how to scream as only a deep-seer can scream, a scream as loud as the fierce storm winds and as terrifying as the nighttime cry of the long-tail cat. Done with great strength, it was said that such a scream could frighten someone to death.

From Stands-in-a-Hole, he had also learned to see more deeply into his dreams than did most people. It was well known to all human beings that dreams held power and knowledge. But those who were trained as Walks-in-a-Hole had been trained were able to walk through their dreams, look around the other side of the mountains that remained distant visions for ordinary dreamers.

So it was in the way he sensed this storm. He did not just sense that a storm was coming. He felt it. He saw already how the waves would come across the lake, like great herds of animals running through tall grass. They would leap up on the shore, hurling white plumes of foam, lifting branches and logs to drop them on the rocks. Sometimes, Walks-in-a-Hole would swim far out into the lake when such a storm was about to begin. He would close his eyes and laugh as the storm lifted and tossed him. It was great fun to see where the storm would finally wash him ashore.

Like his uncle, Walks-in-a-Hole was a very round man, even rounder than his friend Bear Talker, who was the deep-seer for the village that was a three-day walk from his own. People said that his roundness was the reason why Walks-in-the-Hole would never drown. He would simply bob on the surface of the water like a piece of wood that has been rounded by the waves and floats back and forth from one shore to the next.

But today, Walks-in-a-Hole thought, I will not swim out. I will fish!

Walks-in-a-Hole was a great fisher. He liked to fish in a special way, not with the spear, but with bait and hook he had made by binding together three sharp bones with sinew. He only fished for very big fish, ones big enough to swallow that bait. He had a song that would bring the biggest fish to him and he knew the trails that they followed through the water. He knew that most people who fished as he did and had no luck were simply fishing in the wrong place at the wrong time. Just as the deer and caribou and moose and elk people have their own trails and pass along them with great regularity, so it is true of the underwater people, especially the biggest ones. A big sturgeon, for example, will always swim a certain trail.

Walks-in-a-Hole had been watching one sturgeon in particular. He had need for that great fish and so had made up a song to call it to him. He would share its meat with all the people of his village and he would use the other parts of the fish in special ways. A small flock of crows passed overhead. Walks-in-a-Hole had always had a special love for crows.

"Gah-gah," Walks-in-a-Hole called up to them. "Do not go far away. I will have good food to share with you soon."

He had no doubt that the great sturgeon would give itself to him. He had watched for a long time from the red stones higher up on the cliff. He had seen it moving lazily along, sucking its food from the bottom and coming close to the water's edge where the lake was deep and clear. From high above, it had looked like a small fish, but Walks-in-a-Hole knew it was very big. It was big around like a tree. It would weigh four times as much as he weighed. Walks-in-a-Hole was certain that he would catch that great fish. His dream of the night before had told him that he would hook the largest of the underwater people that day.

Because of that dream, he had braided together not just one line, but three. They were strong enough to tie down a moose. Just to make certain, he had wrapped the end of that long line around a gnarled cedar tree that grew close to the end of the Waters Between. Then he had come down to wait, watching the sky for the right moment. If it went well, he would hook the great fish just before the storm struck. Now the waves had begun. They whitened the top of the water and Walks-in-a-Hole could no longer see beyond the surface. But he knew that far below, the lake was still clear and calm. The lake's power was such that even the greatest storm barely touched its deep places.

Walks-in-a-Hole sensed that the time was right. He leaned his long staff against the tall red rocks. Picking up the baited hook in one hand and the loops of line in the other, he walked further out on the rocks until he stood at the very edge of the water. He swung the baited hook at the end of the line back and forth, gathering momentum until he could swing it around his head. With each circle it made, he sang his song.

> Biggest one who swims
> Come to me now
> Biggest one who swims
> Come take what I give you

At the end of the seventh circle, he let go of the line. It whistled through the air. The baited hook, which was the size and weight of a fat muskrat, landed with a splash among the waves and sank quickly out of sight, pulling the line after it.

"So, do you travel a great deal?"

Red Hawk and Blue Hawk looked at each other over the head of the small, energetic man who walked between the two of them as they continued along the trail that led up out of the cedar swamp.

"We travel . . ." Red Hawk said.

"No more than most people do," Blue Hawk continued.

"Ahhh." Gray Otter stopped turned and looked up at the two tall young men. "Gray Otter has never traveled before," he said. "This one, Gray Otter, has never traveled."

Gray Otter turned and continued on. Though his legs were short, there was a familiar bounce in his gait and it was not easy to keep up with him.

Blue Hawk looked at Red Hawk. Red Hawk looked back and nodded. The small deep-seeing man moved just as an otter might move if it walked on two legs.

Gray Otter stopped and turned around again so swiftly that Red Hawk and Blue Hawk bumped into each other.

"I mean," he said, "I have not traveled this way. Walking this way. It is enjoyable this way, you know? Do you enjoy traveling?"

"We enjoy traveling," Red Hawk and Blue Hawk said together.

"Hmmm. Is that your name? Talks Together? One name for two brothers? No. I know your names."

Gray Otter reached up both hands to place them on the tattoos on their shoulders.

"You are Red Tail and Blue Tail. No, I am teasing you. Red Hawk and Blue Hawk. Two brothers who talk together, just as do two others I have met. But we are not talking about talking together. We are talking about traveling, are we not? The three of us enjoy traveling. But I have never traveled before, not before I was pushed. The way Raccoon pushed the Big Stone. You know that story?"

Both Red Hawk and Blue Hawk smiled. Gray Otter was a very amusing man, even though he talked like an otter chattering, talking so fast and so much that it hardly gave them a chance to say either yes or no. But this time it seemed that he was waiting for an answer.

"Yes," Blue Hawk said.

"We know that story well," said Red Hawk.

Raccoon had been out traveling around as he always does. Things were too quiet. So Raccoon went looking for trouble. Trouble was interesting. And if there was no trouble to be found, Raccoon would make some.

As Raccoon walked along he saw someone standing on a high hill.

"Who is that?" Raccoon said. "I will go and see."

When Raccoon reached the hilltop he found the one he had seen was a great stone, balanced on its end.

"Grandfather," Raccoon said. "Hello. How are you?"

The big stone said nothing.

"Unh-hunh," Raccoon said. "So you are well. That is good. Do you like this place here on top of this hill?"

Again, the big stone said nothing.

"Unh-hunh," Raccoon said. "I like this place, too. But there are other places that are also good to see. Have you ever seen any other places?"

As before, the big stone was silent.

"Unh-hunh," Raccoon said. "You have not seen other places because you have never traveled. Myself, Raccoon, I love to travel. Would you like to travel, Grandfather?"

Just as Raccoon expected, the big stone did not reply.

"Unh-hunh," Raccoon said, "I am glad that you would like to travel. So I will help you."

Then Raccoon began to push against the big stone. He pushed and pushed until it began to move. Raccoon took a deep breath and pushed hard one final time. The big stone fell over and began to roll down the hill with a big rumbling noise.

Bada-rum, bada-rum, bada-rum.

"Grandfather," Raccoon shouted, "you are traveling!"

Bada-rum, bada-rum, bada-rum, went the big stone. It went faster and faster as it rolled.

"You are a fast traveler," Raccoon shouted, "but I am faster."

Then Raccoon went running after the big stone. In those days Raccoon had long legs and was even faster than the deer. He caught up with the big stone easily and began to run back and forth in front of it.

"Look, Grandfather, " Raccoon shouted, "I am faster than you."

Then Raccoon caught one of his feet on a root and tripped. He fell right in front of the big rock, which ran over him and squashed him flat. When Raccoon managed to get back up again, his legs were short and he was very close to the ground. And ever since then, whenever Raccoon hears a sound like a rolling stone, he will run up a tree as fast as he can.

Gray Otter smiled. "I can see you know that story. Me, I am like that big rock. Once I have started to roll it is hard for me to stop. I have discovered, you see, that I like to travel. And here is the place to which I have traveled."

They stood now on top of the little hill. All around them, the cedar swamp stretched. But below, on a piece of land elevated above the swamp and circled by great trees, was a fine clearing. In that clearing were the wigwams of Gray Otter's people. A dozen of them seemed to be completed and people were working on a dozen more. A small packs of dogs were wrestling and fighting over the scraps they were being given from the carcass of an elk, which was being dressed out as it hung from the overhanging limb of a maple tree.

"How did . . ." Red Hawk said.

"You find this place?" Blue Hawk asked.

Gray Otter smiled again. "Yes, you are right," he said. "I am the one who found this place. It is a good place. There is a good spring over there. The land is dry and everything was here that was needed for the people to make their homes. How did I find it? I found it by traveling. But not in the way we just traveled." Gray Otter waved a hand above his head. "I traveled here in my dreams. I saw this place. I saw, too, that long ago, people came here to hide from the Ancient Ones. Unless you know the trails through the swamp, you will not find this place. You two did well to come as far as you came before I guided you. So we are here now. Here we will be safe for a while. No one will find us unless we want them to find us. Unless someone comes with a message. What is the message that my cousin, Medicine Plant, has asked you to give to me?"

Blue Hawk spoke first. "There is . . ."

". . . great danger," Red Hawk said.

"A deep-seer with a twisted mind . . ."

". . . is hunting all the others who have such power."

Gray Otter nodded. "Unh-hunh. And there is a great naked bear with him. I made their acquaintance four nights ago. You have been to our village, the one we left behind. You have seen that they were there, have you not? Because I am the man who stands out, they came to my lodge for food. But since I was the food, I, Gray Otter, did not invite them to eat."

Gray Otter chuckled as an otter chuckles. "I had seen them coming. So I told my people to leave. But I stayed. I wanted to meet that one who only comes out at night. I know that one's name, now. He was so sure of his power that he was careless. He is dangerous. Because I got away from him, he is angry. He will not be so careless again."

Gray Otter paused and looked up again at the two brothers. "There is more that you have to say, is there not?"

Blue Hawk continued their message. "There is also a great one . . ."

". . . within the water of Petonbowk."

"It is no longer safe . . ."

". . . to go to the Waters Between."

"Unh-hunh," Gray Otter said. "That I did not see. It is good that you have warned us of this. Some of the young men planned to go to the Waters Between tomorrow to fish and bring back fish. But now they will not go there." Gray Otter nodded. "But I want to see that one. I will have to look there. But I will not travel there," he slapped one of his feet, "this way. And my people will not suffer if we must all stay here for a while. We have enough food for two moons, plenty of water, and work to do. Maybe you would like to stay with us and help?"

Gray Otter whistled. It was a short piercing whistle that could be heard from very far. Red Hawk and Blue Hawk had heard otters whistle in just that way.

In answer to that whistle, one of the people who was working on finishing a wigwam stood up gracefully from behind a wigwam where she had been busy tying a bundle of reeds onto the bottom. The young woman wore a necklace of stones that sparkled like the light of the morning sky. Hidden by the wigwam, she had not been visible before, even from their vantage point on the hill. She looked up from the meadow below them, shading her eyes with one graceful hand. Catching sight of them, she smiled, a smile that was as bright as the light reflecting from the stones around her neck. Waving once, she bent back to her work, disappearing out of sight behind the wigwam. Blue Hawk looked at Red Hawk. He liked that tall young woman's grace and the way she had smiled.

Gray Otter whistled once more, a longer whistle this time. Once again that same young woman stood up, but this time from behind a second wigwam, some distance from the first. Just as before, she looked up at them, smiled, waved, and bent back out of sight. Red Hawk looked at Blue Hawk. Even from the hilltop Red Hawk had seen something in her eyes that he liked. But how had she managed to get so quickly from one wigwam to the next? And why did the necklace of bright stones around her neck seem darker in color?

Gray Otter looked up at the two young men and laughed. He whistled yet again, a whistle combining the short and long whistles he had done before. This time both of the young women stood up. Apart from the different color of their necklaces, they were as similar to each other as Red Hawk and Blue Hawk were.

"Two young women," Gray Otter said, "who talk with one voice. You will want to know their names. I call them Talks Together. But their real names are Light at the Edge of the Morning Sky and Light at the Edge of the Evening Sky. They are the daughters of Gray Otter."

"Sisssikwa, sssisssikwa."

Hearing its name, the same name by which the Only People call a rattle, the big flat-headed snake raised its head and looked up at the man who sat on the big stone. It was the one that the Only People call the bravest of the close-to-the-ground people, for it always tries to warn its enemies before it strikes at them. This brave one was so large, its body as big around at its thickest as the arm of a powerful man, that its strike would be a deadly one to a human being.

The tall, long-limbed man, whose face was patterned with shapes like those marked on the back of the rattlesnake, lifted one hand. It held the bark rattle that had been hanging at his belt. He shook the bark rattle twice and it made a sound much like that of the snake's own rattles. Then he gestured toward the tumble of rocks to the side of the trail. The rattlesnake uncoiled and crawled swiftly into the piled stones. The softly purring rattles on its tail were the last to disappear from sight.

The man hung the rattle back in its former place, slipping the toggle at the end of the wrapped cord of plant fibers under his belt. Then he held out a flat palm and slapped the rock four times. The snakes that had been sunning themselves all around him, striped snakes, tiny red-necklace-wearers, green snakes and beautifully spotted ones began seeking shelter with the first slap. By the fourth, all of them were gone. Only the big black snake remained. Most of its body was inside the bag that hung over the man's shoulder. Only an arm's length of black neck and its head were still visible. That head was lifted up next to the head of Carries Snakes. Its alert, intelligent eyes, along with his, watched the trail. Both the man and the snake knew that their visitors would soon arrive.

As they walked up the stony trail, Raccoon began asking questions again. Young Hunter was not surprised. The surprising thing had been how long his nephew had been able to maintain his silence. When the boy spoke, however, he spoke as he had been taught to speak. He used that low voice that hunters use when they are on the trail. It was a voice that could not be heard from far away.

"Uncle," Raccoon said, "was it not in a place such as this that the brave one struck you?" His eyes searched the rocks around them, a worried look on his face.

They were climbing the steepest part of the trail now and Raccoon's face was at a level with Young Hunter's ankle. The twisting brown scar, which almost resembled the shape of a snake, was clearly visible to the boy. That, and the stones around them, just the sort of stones where the close-to-the-earth people like to sun themselves, had made Raccoon's question a logical one to ask.

A ledge covered thickly with moss opened to one side of the trail. The sun shone down brightly there and from that spot one could see the distant gleam of one of the arms of the Waters Between. Young Hunter snapped his fingers. The two dogs, whose eyes had been on the trail upslope, turned toward them. Young Hunter gestured toward the ledge. Agwedjiman and Danowa leaped up onto the ledge, sniffing around it carefully. They looked back at Young Hunter, who nodded.

"Our friends here," Young Hunter said, "will smell any of the close-to-the-earth people long before we see them. And the close-to-the-earth people will hide when they hear a dog. Yes, this is something like the trail on which I was struck. But I was alone then. I was hunting in the old way, as a Pure Hunter."

Raccoon nodded. He understood that way. At a certain age, when a young man wanted to give a gift to his people, to prove

his devotion to them as a hunter, he would hunt that way. In only
a few winters, Raccoon planned to do that himself. He would
leave behind his weapons and his dog. He would seek the trail of
a certain deer, one that would be the right one to follow. Then he
would trail it night and day, never letting it rest. At last, when it
was no longer able to run from him, he would come close to it.
He would thank it for giving its life to the people and he would
use his hands to hold shut its mouth and nose, cutting off its
breath. He would carry that deer back to the village—as Young
Hunter had done, even though he limped from the bite he had received on his ankle. The mud of a medicine spring had drawn out
much of the poison, but he had still walked awkwardly for several
days after that. Then, Raccoon promised himself, when he had
taken a deer as a Pure Hunter does, he would give it all to the
people. He would neither use nor eat any part of it himself. Like
his uncle, he would show his respect for the Deer People and his
life for his human relatives.

Young Hunter looked around. "Maybe," he said, "this is one of
the high places where the foolish people came after The Talker
changed them when they did not listen to him. Perhaps the waters of
Beaver's flood did not reach this high."

Raccoon leaned back on the moss and watched the eagle that circle above them. They were very high now, far above the valley where
they had found the Village of Many Pines. The people there had
greeted them as friends and relatives. They had listened carefully to
Young Hunter as he told them about the great being, the bigger than
big snake that he had seen in the Waters Between.

"We hear your words, my relative," the people said to him. "We will
not go to the Waters Between. We will go to the smaller lakes to fish."

The Many Pines People had given them food and laughed with
them.

But Young Hunter said nothing to them about the other danger
that threatened them. He knew that those words should be spoken
first to the one who was a friend of the close-to-the-earth people. Finally, Young Hunter had asked about their deep-seeing man.

The people's faces had become serious then. They had looked toward the highest peak.

"Up there," they said. "That is where he is waiting for you. He told us to send you to him as soon as you asked about him."

The Day Walker had moved the width of four hands across the sky since they had begun their climb. Raccoon was glad that they were resting now. Even though he was not tired, the backs of his legs had begun to feel tight. They had climbed a long way. If this peak was only a little higher, it might even be the one on which the Wind Eagle stands. Perhaps it was high enough to be one of the mountain tops that was not covered by water when Beaver made the great flood.

It happened long ago. Some said it was just after the mountains of ice suddenly pulled back from the northern part of their land. Some said it was even before that. Back then, Tamakwa the Beaver was very large. He was a giant. And he decided to build a big dam. He began cutting the biggest trees to make that dam. The Talker saw what he was doing. If Beaver's dam was so large, it would flood the whole world. The Talker became worried about the human beings. If the world became flooded, they would drown. So he went to the people.

The people were glad to see The Talker.

"The Talker has come to visit us," they shouted. "Let us all get together and have a dance to celebrate his visit."

"I have come to warn you of danger," The Talker said. But the people paid no attention. They were too excited.

"Get your rattles," they shouted. "Get ready to dance. We will have fun."

"Hear me," said The Talker. "Beaver is cutting down great trees. he is making a huge dam."

"Unh-hunh," the people said. "We hear you!"

They began to shake their rattles and sing a song, dancing around and around The Talker as they sang.

"Beaver is making a dam,
Beaver is making a huge dam.
Beaver is making a dam,
Beaver is making a huge dam."

The Talker could not believe it. They were acting in such a foolish way.

"Listen," he said, "you can hear the water rising now."

Hearing his words, the foolish people made up a new song. They played their rattles and danced as they sang it.

"Hear the water rising,
We can hear the water rising.
Hear the water rising,
We can hear the water rising."

The Talker was surprised. Did they not understand what was about to happen?

"Do you not understand me?" he said. "The whole world will be flooded soon."

The people stopped dancing and looked at The Talker.

"Unh-hunh," they said. "We understand."

Then they began to sing a new song.

"The world will be flooded.
The whole world will be flooded soon.
The world will be flooded.
The whole world will be flooded soon."

Now The Talker was beginning to lose patience with these silly people who thought of nothing but singing and dancing.

"Listen," he said, "when the world is flooded, you all are going to drown."

"Ah," the people said. Then they shook their rattles again and they began to sing and dance to yet another song.

"We all are going to drown,
We all are going to drown.
When the world is flooded,
We all are going to drown."

The Talker saw that it was no use. These silly people would never listen to him. He changed them into rattlesnakes.

"Now crawl up to the highest place you can find. Maybe you will be safe there."

And that is what happened. The whole world was flooded, but the rattlesnakes survived by crawling to the highest rocks. As the water rose, The Talker climbed onto the trunk of a big dead tree. When the water had risen as high as it was going to rise, he sat there on that tree along with muskrat and otter.

"Dive down and bring up some mud," he said. "I am going to make a new earth."

Then with the mud that the water animals brought up he made a new earth on the back of the big turtle.

"My nephew, are you awake?"

Raccoon opened his eyes. He blinked at the light from the Day Walker, who had moved yet another hand's width across the sky land. The eagle that had been circling overhead was gone. Young Hunter stood over him. Raccoon looked down at the expanse of land below them, the hills and valleys, the thin lines of streams, the distant gleam of the big lake. It seemed as if he could see the great sea that had once covered all of this land.

Young Hunter placed his hand on his nephew's shoulder and looked out with him over the land. He smiled as he did so, remembering how he had become lost in stories himself when he was his nephew's age.

But now, Young Hunter thought, I am no longer just hearing stories and imagining what it was like. I am walking into those stories myself. And, unlike the old tales, I do not know how these stories in which I find myself are going to end. He sighed.

Raccoon jumped to his feet. "I am ready, Uncle. Let's go!"

29 ▣ THUNDER

The shapes of the clouds were changing. As the wind from the sunset direction grew stronger, those clouds took on long and sinuous shapes. They twisted and swirled as they swam across the sky land. At first, Walks-in-a-Hole thought that they looked like fish, but they grew longer and longer until they were too long to be fish, even the snake-fish, the eels. It was unusual. The shapes of the clouds often told him what to expect. He was sure that he could see some sort of a message in the clouds that were being swept ahead of the coming storm. But this message was either too hard for the deep-seeing man to interpret or a much stranger message than he had expected.

Walks-in-a-Hole shook his head. Perhaps he was looking so hard that he was not really seeing. Wishing to see something can sometimes make you think you have actually seen it. It is like the man who stands with his fishing spear held high so long that he thinks he sees a fish coming up to the light of his torch. But when he strikes, he hits only shadows.

Walks-in-a-Hole held his long line tight with one hand and plucked at it with the other, making a sound almost like drumming. Tummmb-tummb, tummmb-tummb, tummmb-tummb, tummmb-tummb. He began to sing his song again.

Biggest one who swims
Come to me now
Biggest one who swims
Come take what I give you

Now the clouds were beginning to join together, darkening and thickening as they rose. He could feel the thunder beings within the cloud. He considered them his friends. The Bedagiak helped The Talker cleanse the earth of many of the dangerous beings who lived long ago. Even now, when they ride through the sky on the backs of the clouds, floating on them as water birds float on the waves, they watch the land below them. Sometimes they give a great shout of thunder and then strike a tree with one of their spears of fire. That is because something was hiding in that tree, something with a twisted heart. There, at the base of such a tree, one might find a stone buried, all that remains of a Bedagi's great fire-spear of lightning.

Walks-in-a-Hole kept such a stone in the pouch that always hung at his waist. He had heard the roar of the thunder one night, four summers ago. It was so close that it shook him from his sleep. Many people would have stayed inside, knowing that the Bedagiak were so close, but Walks-in-a-Hole was not like many people. He ran outside into the driving rain. The lightning was still striking and the Bedagiak giving their great shouts, but they were moving away, riding the clouds over the next ridge and into the valleys beyond the Red Stone Village of his people. Even in the heavy rain, he could see the tree that had been struck by lightning.

It was a huge, hollow pine and it had been split in half. One half of the tree had fallen to the side. The other half, which still stood, was burning at the top like a great torch. Walks-in-a-Hole went straight to that tree, pushing aside the shattered branches that blocked his path. The smells of pine needles and resin, of fire and flint, of moist earth and windy rain filled the air.

The rain continued to pour down. He pushed his wet hair out of his eyes. Sparks were falling from the burning tree, showered out by the wind that roared through the broken treetop. Walks-in-a-Hole paid no attention to the fire or the rain. He placed his hand on the scarred bark of the tree, following the black line that had been drawn by the lightning as it cut down and drove into the sandy soil. Where it touched the earth he dug. A hand's width below the surface he found the white stone. It was still warm to the touch when he picked it up. It glittered like fire made solid. He knew that it was a gift to him from a Bedagi, a thunder being. He would always carry it with him to show that he was a friend of the Bedagiak, a friend of the thunderers.

The rain was beginning to walk across the lake. He could see how misty it appeared to be on the the far side of the Waters Between. Walks-in-a-Hole turned his gaze up the lake, its surface shimmering with waves. He could not see them, but the islands of the Thunder Brothers were there. On those seven islands, islands where human people never went, were the lodges of the Bedagiak. Distant thunder sounded from the direction of the islands. The Thunder Brothers were awake and getting ready to ride on the clouds.

Walks-in-a-Hole turned his attention back to his fishing. The great sturgeon should be swimming its trail now. Soon it would see his bait, smell it, touch it with its mouth. Soon it would swallow it. He sang his song for what he was certain would be the final and decisive time.

Biggest one who swims
Come to me now
Biggest one who swims
Come take what I give you

Something tugged at his line. Unh-hunh! Walks-in-a-Hole felt the familiar excitement. It was as if not only the line had been tugged, but some part of himself deep inside had also been touched by that first nudge to his bait. But he felt certain that the bone hook had not been swallowed. It was not time for him to pull. He must coax it along. He sang his song once more, changing it slightly.

Biggest one who swims
You have now come to me
Biggest one who swims
Pull hard on my line

The line jerked so hard that it pulled him forward.

"I have you!" Walks-in-a-Hole cried.

As he shouted those words, the rain began to fall. The line moved back and forth, more swiftly than Walk-in-a-Hole had expected. The great sturgeon was strong, but it was not one to move so quickly. Walks-in-a-Hole walked with the line, trying to hold back the one on the end, the one who had swallowed his bait. But he could not do so. The line pulled so hard that he had to let loose of it or be pulled into the water.

The strong line, strong enough to tie a moose, was pulled in as far as it would go. The end of the line, which was tied to the largest root at the base of the cedar tree on the hill behind him, held tight, but the line was so taut that it made a singing sound. The small tree trembled and small stones began to roll away from its base. The big crow that had been sitting on a broken limb high in the tree took flight and began to circle overhead.

"This sturgeon," Walks-in-a-Hole said to himself, "is a larger fish than I thought it would be!"

He placed his hand on the line as he walked to the edge of the lake and looked down into the waves, trying to see into its depths, which were clouded by the waves and the rain. A wave washed up by his foot, bringing a big log to rest just below him. Walks-in-a-Hole wiped the rain out of his eyes and blinked. It was not really a log. The wave rolled it and Walks-in-a-Hole saw one large dying eye look up at him. It was the head and the top part of the great sturgeon. That it had been bitten in half so cleanly showed how large the mouth that did it must have been, how sharp the teeth. In a last dying reflex, the sturgeon's head opened its mouth, gasping for the life that had been torn away from it.

"Biggest one who swims," Walks-in-a-Hole whispered. Then he realized that his song had not called the sturgeon. Big as it had been, it was clearly not the biggest one that now swam in the Waters Between.

A part of Walks-in-a-Hole was amused. A part of him was laughing at himself. His song had done its job well. Too well, it seemed.

And now whatever was on the end of his line was about to come to him! But the part of Walks-in-a-Hole that was not amused was already thinking about how to escape what was surely about to happen.

The line grew tauter still and the cedar tree shook. But the strong line still did not break. The roots of the tree pulled free from the earth and stones and the whole tree came flying through the air. Walks-in-a-Hole threw himself down into his belly. The end of one of the roots whipped across his back, cutting the flesh. Then the tree splashed into the water. Walks-in-a-Hole felt the blood flowing across his back, but the wound was not deep. He was able to stand.

The wind was blowing hard. The rain came hissing down like water poured from a pot, striking and cooling the stones that had been warmed by the sun only a few heartbeats before. Walks-in-a-Hole could see the cedar tree floating out in the deep water offshore. It was spinning around in the waves, around and around, then back and forth. He knew that he should run. But he had not yet decided in which direction to go. He wanted to see the one who had come to his song. A part of himself would not leave until he had seen the one who was, without a doubt, the biggest one who swims.

The thunder rumbled again. It was coming down the lake, coming closer. Walks-in-a-Hole placed his hand into his pouch. He felt the smooth thunderstone. It calmed him.

"Bedagiak," he said, "protect your foolhardy friend, Walks-in-a Hole."

He walked along the edge of the lake. He looked out through the rain at the cedar tree, which floated calmly now, bobbed only by the waves. It was no further away than a long spear cast. Had the line finally broken? Suddenly the cedar tree straightened up in the water as if it was trying to root itself in the surface of the deep lake. Then, just as swiftly it sank out of sight. It was gone.

Walks-in-a-Hole breathed in and out. Once, twice, three times, four times. The tree shot up out of the water like a thrown spear and landed on the beach just below him. An arm's length of broken line was still tied to the thickest root.

Walks-in-a-Hole stared at the cedar tree. There were big gashes along its length and the bark was torn away. Toothmarks. He slid his hand out of his pouch, the thunder stone still held tightly between his thumb and his fingers.

"Bedagiak," he whispered, "I ask it again. Protect your foolish friend, Walks-in-a-Hole."

It was the sound of the thunder from behind him, still far away but closer than before, that made him turn around. A dark shape was rising up out of the deep lake. A long neck like that of a goose, but a goose bigger than any bird that ever swam. Walks-in-a-Hole began to walk backward, up the rocky slope, away from the Waters Between. He held the thunder stone up in front of him and his eyes were on that long-necked shape, which continued to rise up and grow larger as it swam closer.

When he reached the top of the slope where the cedar tree had stood, Walks-in-a-Hole stopped. Large as that great being was, long as that neck might be, he was sure that it could not reach him from the water. Like most who are deep-seers, Walks-in-a-Hole was one who respected power. But he was also one who liked to walk close to power. That was why he would swim out into the lake during storms. That was why he spoke to the thunder beings. This being, this biggest one who swam, was a being of great power. He wanted to see it more clearly.

The head at the end of that long neck swung back and forth. It was looking for him. Then it stopped. Even though the rain was thick between them and he stood without moving, somehow it had seen him. It surged forward—out of the water! It had legs, strong legs. Walks-in-a-Hole turned to run. Out of the corner of one eye he saw something flying not far overhead, its head cocked to watch. It was a big crow.

"My friend," Walks-in-a-Hole said, as he began to run as fast as he could. "I wish I had your wings." Some deep-seers who were said to be able to fly, to leap great distances through the air over the hills. But he was not one of them.

As Walks-in-a-Hole ran, he could hear huge feet thumping the earth, closer and closer behind him. He headed toward the piled red stones, which might give him shelter. They were not far now, perhaps he might make it. The wigwam of great red stones was only a few steps away. But he could also feel hot breath on his back.

Holding the thunder stone above his head, Walks-in-a-Hole called out to the sky.

"Begadiak, help me!"

The world around him exploded into light and then he saw and heard nothing.

30 ▣ TWINS

Red Hawk took a handful of berries from the bark plate. He looked over at Blue Hawk. Blue Hawk looked as worried as he felt. There should have been no reason for them to be worried. They had done as Medicine Plant said they should do. They had found Gray Otter and his people. They had warned them about the danger to be found in the Waters Between. Gray Otter and his people had listened carefully to their words. Everyone had agreed that no one would go to Petonbowk. It had been a long and sometimes difficult journey to find Gray Otter's people, but they had done so. Now they were being fed and well treated. They were in a comfortable, safe village surrounded by people who seemed to like and respect them. Yet they were worried.

Red Hawk put the strawberries into his mouth. They were so ripe and sweet that there was almost no need to chew them. Yet he almost choked on them when he thought of the hands that had picked those berries. He looked again at his brother. Blue Hawk's expression was the same as his. Just as his brother did, Blue Hawk felt like a rabbit caught in a snare.

It was always this way, Red Hawk thought, when one did the bidding of deep-seers like Bear Talker and Medicine Plant. They would tell you one thing, but they would always be thinking about another. Go there and do that, Bear Talker and Medicine Plant would say. But they would be smiling inside at the thought of what else the unsuspecting one they sent out would encounter.

Just as it had turned out to be this time. Red Hawk now understood that their job had not just been to take a message. The two brothers had been sent here by Medicine Plant for another purpose as well. Red Hawk now saw that purpose as clearly as he saw the two hands that thrust the bark plate at him again. That purpose described itself in a silent voice that he could hear inside his head as well as the deceptively gentle one that now spoke to him.

"Take more berries," said Light at the Edge of the Morning Sky.

Red Hawk took the berries, but he did not look up into the young woman's smiling face.

How could they have allowed themselves to be trapped this way? Even the Walking Hill, that monster large enough to crush villages beneath its feet, had not been able to catch them. But now, it seemed, now they were ensnared. He and his brother had been caught by these two young women. These two young women, just like Red Hawk and Blue Hawk, were twins. Red Hawk shook his head as he remembered again what everyone in their Salmon People Village always said. Only when Red Hawk and Blue Hawk found two young women who were exactly the same would they marry.

But Red Hawk knew that he was not ready to be married. He *and* his brother were not ready. It did not matter how attractive these two young women were. It did not matter that Evening Sky was tall and as graceful as a young deer. It did not matter that her face was rather pleasant to see or that her hands, when they happened to brush against his shoulder, felt warm and soft. It did not matter that her voice was as musical as the song of a thrush. He felt confused when he was around her! He had only known her for the length of a single day, yet she acted as if she had known him all of her life.

Red Hawk had already discovered, as Gray Otter had been very careful to explain to both the young men at the moment when they first saw his daughters, that the twin sisters had no interest in any of the young men in their village—or in the villages closest to them.

"The problem, "Gray Otter said, "is not just that my two daughters are taller and stronger than most of the young men. They are great wrestlers and both of them are as good at hunting as any of the young men of their age. Even when they were little girls, they were always fighting with the boys—and beating them! They have continued to do so as young women. As a result, though I cannot really understand why, some of the young men are afraid of them. This seems foolish to me, for they have seldom broken the bones of any of the young men they have beaten."

Gray Otter smiled broadly. "They are like my wife, Big Pine Woman. When I was a child, she always protected me from the larger children who tried to pick on me before I heard the voices that called me into being a deep-seer. She used to carry me around on her shoulders. When she chose to marry me, she explained that she was only doing so out of pity."

Gray Otter chuckled and then poked the two brothers who stood on each side of him with his elbows. "Pity had nothing to do with it, of course! We, who are otters, have our ways, you know." He chuckled again.

"What is the problem?" Blue Hawk said.

Red Hawk stared at his brother. It was not what he had expected him to say. This never happened. Blue Hawk looked back at him and shrugged his shoulders. He did not understand why he had spoken those words either.

Gray Otter smiled even more broadly. He reached out his hands and grasped each of them by the elbow. He began to walk down the hill with them, down toward the two young women who were standing next to each other now and looking up the hill with pleased looks on their faces. Those pleased looks, Red Hawk thought, were like those might see on the faces of two wolves who see a pair of fat geese waddling into their den!

"The problem," Gray Otter said, "is that both of them are so much alike, that they would surely choose the same man to marry." Gray Otter chuckled, "Or the same men."

Unfortunately, Evening Sky had taken a liking to Red Hawk from that first moment she saw him, looking him over much too carefully from top to bottom. Worse yet, Morning Sky, her sister, seemed to have taken a similar liking to Blue Hawk. Somehow, as soon as they had seen the brothers, each of the sisters had decided which one was to be theirs and theirs alone.

It is lucky, Red Hawk thought, that Evening Sky is the one who likes me. It was quite clear to me that my brother liked her sister better when he first saw her. I see now that my brother will need help. I will have to protect him from this young woman who seeks to come between us.

Red Hawk looked again at his brother. Light at the Edge of the Morning Sky was sitting very close to him. In fact, one of her hands was on Blue Hawk's wrist as she leaned over to whisper something in his ear. Blue Hawk began to cough. Light at the Edge of the Evening Sky leaned across Red Hawk to poke her sister in the arm. As she did so, her breasts pressed hard against Red Hawk's chest. He suddenly found it hard to breathe. His heart began to pound so loudly that he was certain everyone could hear.

"Sister," Evening Sky said, "what are you saying to our visitor there? Are you trying to kill him?"

"Sister," Morning Star answered, "what are *you* doing to our visitor there? Are you trying to crush him?"

Then the two young women burst into giggles.

Blue Hawk grabbed Red Hawk's arm and pulled it. Red Hawk understood. He disentangled himself from Evening Sky's arms, which had just happened to rest themselves around his neck as she talked to her sister. Blue Hawk slid out from under Morning Sky's legs, which, purely by accident, had come to rest over his own legs. The two young men stood. Everyone who had been sitting around the fire stopped talking and looked up at them.

"We must," Red Hawk said.

"Go over there," Blue Hawk said, indicating the ravine at the edge of the woods where the people went to relieve themselves.

Evening Sky looked up at Red Hawk. "Do you know the way?" she said in an innocent voice.

"Shall my sister and I accompany you?" Morning Sky said.

"Agggghhhh," Red Hawk said. Words had deserted him. He felt

as if he could not move his feet. Blue Hawk pushed him and then pulled his arm.

"Nda!" Blue Hawk said, his voice a bit louder than necessary.

"Nda!" Red Hawk managed to say. "No!"

The two brothers stumbled off into the darkness. Behind them they could hear the two sisters start to giggle. Red Hawk and Blue Hawk did not look back. It was important to keep their dignity. They squared their shoulders. Together, as one, the two brothers took another step and together, as one, they tripped over a stick and fell to the ground. All of the others around the fire behind them joined in the laughter.

The dark bird soared high up from the village. It spread wings almost as wide as those of an eagle as it flew higher and higher until it could glide on the warm river of air that rose up from the marshy land below. Cocking its head, it looked in the direction where the wide lake glittered in the distance, marking one edge of the dawn land. It held itself in mid-air, thinking. It considered for a moment the idea of flying over the Waters Between, looking down to see what it could see. The last time it had flown over the big lake, two days ago, it had seen something new in its waters. It would be interesting to see it again. Then it lifted one wingtip to bank itself in the opposite direction. It would fly to to Petonbowk later, not now. Now, it was looking for wolves.

A flock of geese was crossing the sky. The bird flapped his dark, shining wings to rise above them. The bright face of the Day Walker was behind him and they had not yet seen him. He waited until they were passing below. Then he dove down at them, straight at the leader of the flock. Wings flapping, almost falling out of the sky, the female goose tried to dodge her attacker. The formation broke, like the calm surface of a lake broken by a stone.

"Ka-honghhhh," the female goose called, urging the flock back together. "Ka-honnghh, ka-honnghh." Then she dodged again, as her black-winged tormentor returned.

"Gah-gah," the big crow squawked, as he dove again at the geese. He would not hurt them, but it was such fun to disturb them this way. "Wli gah-gah."

Back and forth across the sky, he played his game—though it was not a game for the irritated geese. He swooped at them and then flew above them. He placed himself below them, rolling upside down to watch as they turned their angry heads in his direction, scolding and threatening him. He plucked at their tail feathers with his beak and then added himself to their formation, placing himself in the midst of the flock. All the time that he did this, he avoided their beaks as they snapped at him and complained. He had little to worry about from the threats of the geese. Even an eagle could not challenge him in the sky.

Finally, after having changed the direction of the flock a dozen times, Talk Talk grew tired of it. Below him now was the area where his favorite pack of wolves hunted. It was mid-day and he was hungry. He set his wings and dropped from among the irate geese, who barked abuse at him as he spiraled away.

A flock of the small crows, those who looked like him but lacked his size and strength, called warnings to each other. They took flight and disappeared among the trees over the next ridge. Talk Talk continued on his way, following the downstream curve of a stream. His sharp eyes took in everything that happened below. He watched small animals take shelter as his shadow passed over, heard the warning cries of a jay. Then he saw what he had hoped to see. He circled twice over a stand of beech trees, watching intently. He was certain of what he saw. It was good. Then he flapped his wings and continued down the stream.

At last he came to the place where rocks were jumbled together into a series of small caves. Talk Talk circled lower. There he saw the one he was seeking. A big black-coated wolf lay there near the widest part of the stream, watching the rippling water.

Talk Talk dropped with a flutter of wings behind him. The wolf looked at Talk Talk, growled softly, and went back to watching the water. A big trout was coming to the surface to snatch at flies. The black wolf liked to watch that trout. Perhaps one day it would figure out some way to catch that trout. But it did not feel like going into the stream.

Talk Talk hopped close.

"Gah-gah, wli gah-gah," Talk Talk said. The black wolf paid no attention.

Talk Talk hopped closer. "Gah-gah!" he said. Then he grabbed the tip of the wolf's tail in his black beak and pulled.

With a snarl, the wolf whirled round to snap at the big crow. Somehow, even though Talk Talk hopped back only a little ways, the wolf's jaws missed him. The wolf looked at Talk Talk and then wagged his tail. He thrust his front legs out and put his head close to the ground. But Talk Talk had not come to play.

"Nolka," Talk Talk said, ruffling the feathers around his neck. It was the word that the human people used for deer. Perhaps the wolf did not understand human speech, but it looked with new interest at the big crow. It sat down on its haunches and whined, looking eagerly into Talk Talk's dark eyes.

Talk Talk flapped his wings and flew up to the top of a small birch, which bent under his weight. He jumped up and down on the small tree, making at swing up and down. "Nolka," Talk Talk squawked again. "Nolka."

The black wolf whimpered twice. Six more wolves came trotting out from among the rocks. One of them came up and licked the face of the black wolf. The seven wolves played together, leaping over each other, biting at each other's feet. It was a game that clearly had rules. None of the other wolves did anything that would truly challenge the black-coated wolf, who was their sagamon. One of the younger wolves bit a little too hard at the black-coated one's front foot. With a loud growl and a sudden leap, the black-coated wolf knocked the younger one off its feet. The younger wolf whimpered and stayed on its back, exposing its throat to its chief, who backed off and sat on his haunches. Their play resumed.

Finally, the black-coated wolf yelped once. The other wolves stopped playing. They sat on their haunches. Then, following the gaze of their leader, they all looked up at Talk Talk. The wolves waited.

Talk Talk preened his feathers. He had seen the small herd of deer not far down the stream. Among them was a small buck that still limped, even worse than it had limped the day before when he had first noticed it just as evening was coming and he was flying back to the lodge of his greatest friend. Although he could easily care for himself, he had no wish to stay away long from her wigwam. He felt warmth within him as he thought of the touch of her fingers as she stroked his head. It would be good to be back sitting on the shoulder of Willow Woman. But that would be later. Now it was time to get food. Food would be good now.

Now, Talk Talk would lead the wolf pack to that deer. As he had done before, he would be their guide. When they had killed it and eaten their fill, he would get his share of the meat. The fresh meat of the deer would be good to eat.

"Gah-gah," he called. Then he took flight, heading downstream. Fanning out below him, the wolves followed.

"My second mother," Willow Woman said as she finished off the end of the long braided rope, "I would ask you a question."

"My daughter," Sweetgrass Woman said, "ask it."

She looked over at Willow Woman. It was so good to have a daughter again. Her own daughter, Young Bear Woman—who was the mother of Young Hunter—had been killed by the same falling tree that had taken the life of Young Hunter's father. So it was that their grandson had come into their lodge, to be raised as their son. Sweetgrass Woman and Rabbit Stick had other children, but Young Bear Woman had been her only daughter. There were things that a woman could say only to her daughter. Small secrets that she could share with her. There were ways that only a mother and daughter can laugh together. When Young Bear Woman died, it was as if all of those things had died with her. Now, though, those things had returned with the laughing voice and the quick intelligence of her new daughter, the wife of her grandson Young Hunter.

There had always been happiness in Sweetgrass Woman's heart, but with the arrival of Willow Woman in their lodge, that happiness had turned into song.

"How was it that you and my second father met?"

Sweetgrass Woman pushed back her gray braids from her face and sat back against the side of the wigwam. She could hear Rabbit Stick. His breathing was soft, but he was there on the other side of the bark wall. He was trying to listen to them. But, as always, her hearing was far superior to his.

Sweetgrass Woman held up two fingers—like the ears of a rabbit.

Then she made a motion with her hand as if she held a stick and was about to throw it. She pointed over her shoulder with her chin and saw from the smile that came over Willow Woman's face that she had understood her signs. Rabbit Stick was listening to them from inside the wigwam.

"Which of my husbands do you mean?" Sweetgrass Woman said. "You know I have had many of them."

A scraping sound, as if someone had slipped and caught themselves, came from within the wigwam. Neither woman paid it any attention.

"My second mother," Willow Woman said in an innocent voice, "How many husbands have you had?"

"Many," said Sweetgrass Woman. "Too many to count. All of them were great hunters, powerful men. It is sad that the one I live with now is so weak and pitiful. Other men, who have great power, wear necklaces made of bear claws. This last husband of mine, on his necklace he carries his own dried-up toe."

Sweetgrass Woman made a sniffing noise. "At least I think it is his toe. It might be something else."

The sound of someone hitting their shin against a bowl and a muffled shout came from within the lodge. The skin flap which hung over the door was flung open and Rabbit Stick came out.

"If you are going to talk so loudly," he said, "I will go elsewhere to sleep."

With as much dignity as he could muster, Rabbit Stick limped off. Remembering the importance of respecting her husband's grandfather, Willow Woman did not smile until he was well out of sight.

"We never met," Sweetgrass Woman said, still looking in the direction that her husband had gone.

"I do not understand," Willow Woman said.

"Rabbit Stick and I never met. How can two people meet when they have always been together?" Sweetgrass Woman picked up a stick and drew a circle on the ground. "Rabbit Stick and I have always shared one life. Which part of it is his? Which part is mine? It is all connected, like this circle." She smiled. "When we were little children, we played together. I knew from the first time I saw him that we were supposed to be together. That is why I beat any of the other girls who tried to get too close to him. Men are so foolish."

Willow Woman nodded. It had been the same way with Young Hunter. Before they were married she had to keep a close eye on the other young women. Sometimes she had to do more than just watch. She remembered sitting on the back of one young woman in particular, a slender girl named Elk Daughter, who had gotten into the habit of stumbling over things she could not see and falling against Young Hunter. As Willow Girl sat on Elk Daughter's back, she had pressed her rival's face into the mud.

"This mud will help clear your vision," she had said to Elk Daughter. "Now you will not stumble so often."

Sure enough, her medicine had worked. From then on, Elk Daughter had been very careful to walk, quite sure-footedly, some distance away from Young Hunter.

"Of course," Sweetgrass Woman continued, "Rabbit Stick suspected that I liked him. That is why I always teased him so much when I was a child. You would not believe how much I teased him."

Willow Woman said nothing. Considering how much her second mother teased Rabbit Stick now, it was be hard to imagine her doing it more when the two of them were children. She must have made Rabbit Stick's life miserable.

"I remember how we would sit around the fire listening to the one who was the deep-seer then tell stories. His name was Stands-in-a-Hole and he was the greatest storyteller I ever heard. I would sit as far away from Rabbit Stick as possible, but he was still always looking at me. Sometimes I would hit him with a stick when he looked at me. That only made him look more often—and duck more often, too. It was very hard for him to listen to Stands-in-the Hole's words."

Sweetgrass Woman laughed and Willow Woman laughed with

her. The two women sat together smiling. Then Willow Woman spoke.

"I have heard a name like that," she said.

"What name?"

"Stands-in-a-Hole."

"You may have heard me speak his name when I have told the stories he taught to me. Stands-in-a-Hole was the grandfather of my uncle," Sweetgrass Woman said. "He climbed the great white mountain and stepped onto the star trail many winters before you were born."

Willow Woman rubbed her hands together. "The name I heard was another name. It was spoken by someone else to me. It was spoken to me while I was sleeping. The one who spoke it is one you know very well. She is your friend."

Willow Woman was careful not to say the name of the person whose voice had come to her in her sleep. It was not proper to speak the name of a dream speaker until that name had been guessed by another.

"It was Medicine Plant who spoke this name?" Sweetgrass Woman said. Her tone was not happy.

"It was her voice."

"Ahhh-ahhhh," Sweetgrass Woman said. She shook her head. It was always this way with Medicine Plant. Medicine Plant wove people together the way they had just woven their rope. One strand always led to another. "And so we are making this rope for the one whose name it is."

"So we are, my second mother."

"What was the name spoken?"

"It was Walks-in-a-Hole."

"Unh-hunh. I know him. He is a nephew of Stands-in-a-Hole. He is a deep-seer himself."

Willow Woman said nothing more. She did not ask where Walks-in-a-Hole lived or how far it was from their own village.

Three days walk, Sweetgrass Woman thought. Three days to the Village of Red Stone. If that was where they were going to go.

* * *

Sweetgrass Woman held up a length of the rope they had made. It was thicker and longer than any rope she had ever seen before. It was so heavy that she knew they would need help carrying it. Where they would carry it, she was now certain. She knew now what it was for. She suspected that her second daughter, Willow Woman, knew also.

"We have made a strong rope, my second mother," Willow Woman said. "Your song has given it even more power."

"It is a strong rope," Sweetgrass Woman agreed.

But, she thought, will it be strong enough?

33 ▣ SEEING

From the point where the four had stopped, the trail made a wide swing out away from the edge of the hill, then dove down, disappearing into a rocky pass. Three of those who stood on that trail could not see further along it. Yet Young Hunter could. He saw with that other sight, the sight that lifted a part of himself up out of his body and then looked down as a hawk looks down on the land below it.

With that sight which went beyond his eyes, he saw the broad-shouldered young man and the tall boy there. The man squatted back on his heels without moving, one hand on the ground, the other held against his chest. The boy sat cross-legged at the man's feet, holding a spear cradled in his arms. The two others, the four-legged ones who stood watchfully on guard, looked up at the sky. Perhaps most people could not see a spirit in flight, but dogs, it seemed, were different. There was concern in the eyes of Danowa and Agwedjiman as they looked up at Young Hunter, seeing him where he was and was not, seeing beyond the body that would wait for his return.

With his spirit sight, Young Hunter gazed beyond the dip and bend in the trail. His vision moved him the distance of two looks—for human eyes—beyond the place where the four waited. He saw a great coiled stone. Like small circles of warmth, he sensed the many beings gathered around, within, and beneath that stone. A human person sat on top of that stone. He was a man of great size, with many beautiful designs tattooed onto his body, his long arms and his face. He was looking down into a large pouch that hung from his shoulder.

Then that person lifted his head up to look toward the place of Young Hunter's sight. The man's eyes were dark, but there was no cold in their darkness. He smiled and Young Hunter felt the warmth of that smile. Then the dark-eyed man spoke in the same way that Young Hunter saw him. Seeing without eyes. Speaking without breath. Young Hunter listened. He did not hear words, yet he understood. The man on top of the stone raised his hands up, as if offering something to him. Young Hunter reached out one hand, closing his spirit eyes as he did so.

When he opened his eyes, he found himself looking down not from the height of the sky, but from the normal height of his own body. Raccoon was looking up at him. He did not appear concerned. Young Hunter had never spoken to his nephew about the things a deep-seer could do, about the things that he had learned to do himself. But from the way Raccoon smiled up at him, Young Hunter knew that someone had been telling his nephew things. Was it Bear Talker or Sweetgrass Woman? Was it Rabbit Stick or Fire Keeper? Or, more likely, was it all of them? Raccoon had a way of asking a question and then asking it again until he received an answer that satisfied him.

"Hello, Uncle," Raccoon said. "Did you travel well?"

Some people felt uncomfortable around a man or woman who was able to—do things. Everyone had some power, that was well known among the Only People. But when someone had the power to do things that others could not do, that person was respected or even feared. Some had such great fear of that ability to do things that they would even make it a point to avoid a deep-seer—unless they had a great need for that person's help. Raccoon, though, did not seem to have any such fear. After all, Young Hunter was his favorite uncle.

If I were to turn into a bear in front of him, Young Hunter thought, my nephew would probably ask me if it made me itch to have so much hair on my body.

"Nephew," Young Hunter said, "you ask many questions."

"Do I, Uncle?" Raccoon said. "What do you have in your hand?"

Young Hunter felt something move inside the closed hand that he held against his chest. Something was nudging against his fingers. Had he picked something up from the ground when he squatted down and then let his spirit take its seeing flight? He opened his hand and looked.

No longer than two fingers, a little red-bellied snake uncoiled itself and lifted up its head from Young Hunter's palm. Its gentle eyes, which were dark and warm, looked straight into his.

"Uncle?"

"Unmh-hunh," Young Hunter said, nodding to his nephew. "Take him."

Raccoon reached up. The little snake glided from Young Hunter's palm into the outstretched hands of the boy. The little red-bellies were the favorite close-to-the-ground ones of children. They were shy, hiding inside rotting logs and under stones. There they hunted the small many-legged ones. But they would never bite a human person, even a child. The children of the Only People loved to find the little red-bellies to play with them for a while before returning them to their homes. Raccoon stroked its back with one finger as the little snake lay calmly in his hand.

Young Hunter pointed with his chin toward a poplar tree that had fallen many seasons ago. Raccoon walked over to it, knelt, and placed his open hands on the ground. The red-belly slid out of his hand, looked back once, and then crawled into a hole at the base of the uprooted tree.

"Good hunting, small one," Raccoon said.

He looked back up at Young Hunter, who nodded. Young Hunter was pleased to see how much respect his nephew showed for the small one. He was not going to grow up to be one of those who walks through the world with heavy feet. He had already learned that one must always be careful. To harm anything without reason—even something as little as one of the close-to-the-earth ones or a small plant growing at the edge of a trail—was a foolish thing to do. It was as foolish as dirtying the water of a spring. One never knew when one might need to drink that water in the future. Even the smallest beings might one day be the ones you would have to turn to for help. But if you had treated them badly in the past, they would hide from you in your time of need. Although his nephew was one who asked many questions, he was also one who listened to the answers. He could be trusted.

"Wait here," Young Hunter said to Raccoon. "If all goes well, I'll be back before the Day Walker has traveled the width of four hands across the sky."

Raccoon said nothing. He looked up at Young Hunter with serious eyes and nodded his head.

"Our two friends will wait here with you," Young Hunter said, touching the heads of Agwedjiman and Danowa. He put his hands under the lower jaws of each of the dogs in turn and lifted their heads up so that they would look straight into his eyes. That way neither of the dogs would be able to pretend they had not heard him and just happened to follow him. They had done so before. But this time it was important that they should hear his request clearly and stay behind.

"Do you hear me, my friends?" Young Hunter said to the dogs. "You will stay with Raccoon till I return."

Danowa sat down and wagged his tail, eager to please his master. Agwedjiman looked decidedly displeased. The big dog's intelligent eyes asked the question that Young Hunter was already asking himself. Are you sure that you are doing the correct thing?

"Everything will be good," Young Hunter said in a soft voice to Agwedjiman. "You will see. But you must remain here. The one I am going to visit has many small friends who do not like dogs. I must go to him alone."

The hunger twisted in his belly like a stick sharpened at both ends. It had been two sleeps since he had eaten. There should have been food for him, but there had been none.

Wait, he had been told. Wait. You will eat well.

He had not eaten well. He rolled to his side and moaned. The one who lay not far from him in the deep hole under the roots of a rotted pine did not wake. He moaned again. The thin man, whose eyes were as flame red as his own, did not move.

The great bear pulled himself to his feet. He leaned toward the man, sniffing him, smelling his flesh. This was the one who gave him food. Sometimes much food. But the memory of that food was thin and his hunger was growing. All he had eaten recently was the carcass of a deer that had been killed—he could tell by its strong smell—by a wolverine and then abandoned. That had been three sleeps ago. And he was hungry. He sniffed at the man. His smell was not a good smell, but the man was made of that same kind of meat that the giant bear had grown used to eating. The man was bony, thin, but there was meat on his bones. Good meat.

He growled and lifted a front foot as if to strike or paw at the man. Then he pulled back. The man gave him food, but the man had also given him pain. More than once. Sharp pain that struck deep into his eyes, throbbed inside his head. It was a pain like the light from a sky filled not with just one but with many day fires. It was a pain given to him when he did not do as the man wished. He would not risk that pain again. He was not yet that hungry.

The roof of the cave dug out under the big tree roots was low near the entrance. Walks Like a Man crawled on his belly until he was almost at its mouth. The trail that led past their hiding place was only a short distance away on the other side of a deep ravine. Even with his day-weak eyes, he could see it. He could see motion on that trail. It was food. Two-legged food. The food stopped. It was close enough for him to smell it. But the ravine and the brighter light were twin barriers between that food and his hunger. His hunger hurt him, but he could do nothing about it. Not now. But later, later he would eat. That night. It had been promised to him that he would eat that night. With the darkness he would be given his food.

Young Hunter stopped walking. The small hairs on the back of his neck prickled. He was being watched. He knelt as if to tighten the strap of his mokasin. Without moving his head, he looked to either side. There. On the other side of the ravine, the broken trunk of an ancient pine tree rose up. Its gnarled roots arched over a dark opening that led back into the earth under the tree. Something was watching him. He could feel its hunger. That was not unusual. There was hunger everywhere in the world.

It was one of the things that Rabbit Stick had taught him when he was only six winters old. Young Hunter had been watching a black striped butterfly as it sat in the center of the trail. The butterfly was busy with something that was hidden under its wide wings. Suddenly there was a flutter of wider wings and the butterfly was gone. A brown bird with a dark cap had darted down and grabbed it up. Holding the butterfly in its beak, the bird landed on a branch over Young Hunter's head. Thwap! Thwap! It began to strike the butterfly against a twig. One by one, the bright wings were snipped from its body and floated down past Young Hunter's upturned face. Then the bird lifted its head as it gulped down what was left.

A hand was placed on Young Hunter's shoulder.

"Everything must eat, grandson. It is the way things are. If you are quiet and open yourself to it, you can feel that hunger. It is in the birds as their eyes seek out insects. It is in the wolf as it watches the passing of a herd of caribou."

Rabbit Stick put his hand on Young Hunter's stomach. "It is in you, too, grandson. Everything around us is always feeling hungry or eating or feeling glad that it ate. And everything gets eaten. Many beings, from the very tiny ones that fly down to bite us, to the very big ones, look at us as food, too. That is the way it is. If you are feeling hunger or eating or trying to not be eaten, you are alive. And often, what is eaten gets turned into something beautiful. Look at what that butterfly was eating."

Young Hunter looked more closely at the trail. He began to laugh. There where the butterfly had been was a fresh pile of little round pellets. Rabbit scat.

Hunger was the way of the world. Young Hunter felt that hunger from within the cave. But he felt a wrongness about that hunger. Something within that cave was not good.

Bedagiak, Young Hunter thought, Thunder People. Look at that place. There is something in there to strike with your spears of sky fire.

But there was no answering rumble from the sky. Perhaps the Thunder People were asleep on this bright day. Perhaps they did not recognize his voice. He knew that others were better able to speak to the Thunderers than he was.

He knew, too, that whatever it was that watched him from within that cave was something that he should not disturb. Even as he sensed it watching him, he sensed its hesitation.

Young Hunter stood and continued up the trail. Nothing followed him, but he walked a little faster now. He must reach the man whose wordless voice was calling more strongly to him now. And when he had done whatever had to be done, he would return even more quickly. He would find another trail back down this hill to reach the place where Raccoon and the dogs waited for him. He would not pass that cave and the hunger within it again.

35 ▣ A SMALL GAME

The Sky Walker was less than a finger's width above the trees. Red Hawk and Blue Hawk sat together, their backs against the cedar they had slept beneath the night before. The light from the Sky Walker's face was warm on their own faces. It was a time of day that the two brothers had always loved and looked forward to in the past. But this morning was different. This morning they would have to face Evening Sky and Morning Sky yet again.

"You do not need to sleep under a tree," Evening Sky had said to them the night before.

"There is room in our wigwam," Morning Sky had added, looking into Blue Hawk's eyes.

"The days are warm now, that is true," Evening Sky said, placing her hand on Red Hawk's shoulder.

"But it can be very cold at night," Morning Star said, reaching for Blue Hawk's hand . . . and missing it as Blue Hawk and his brother backed away from the central fire of the village as fast as they could.

Once again, laughter had followed their retreat. But they had made their own fire between the roots of the tall cedar and then slept fitfully in the little hollow between those roots.

Red Hawk leaned back against his brother.

"Did you hear . . . ?" he said.

"Someone whispering near us last night?"

"Then it was not . . ." Red Hawk said.

". . . a dream," Blue Hawk continued.

Blue Hawk reached out and picked up the deerskin blankets that he and his brother had kicked off as they sat up with the morning light. He looked them over and then tossed one of them to his brother. The soft deerskin smelled of the wood smoke that had been used to tan them. It was a good smell, but Red Hawk took the blanket between his thumb and forefinger and held it out in front of himself as if it was a skunk. These deerskins were not theirs. Somehow, these deerskins had appeared in the night. Someone had placed them over the brothers. In the corner of the skin that he held a small mark had been burned in. It looked much like a star in the evening sky. He dropped the skin.

"Brother," Red Hawk said.

"Brother," Blue Hawk said.

"It is time that we returned home," both brothers said together.

The cedar tree that had given them shelter was downhill from the new village that was still being built by the Otter Creek on the big island in the center of the great cedar swamp. The tree was also on the far side of the wide clearing from the trail which led up over the hill and down into the swamp again. Whether they liked it or not, they would have to pass through the village on their way out. And there really was no choice. Their host, Gray Otter, was a deep-seer. One did not leave the village of a deep-seer without being courteous.

The two brothers tightened their belts and pulled on their mokasins. Red Hawk threw their traveling bag over his shoulder. Aside from their flint knives, Red Hawk's atlatl, and Blue Hawk's spear, they had nothing else with them, but they were well enough equipped to travel for many days.

Red Hawk picked up the deerskin with Evening Sky's mark on it. Blue Hawk picked up the other deerskin, carefully folded it once, and placed it over his shoulder as one would wear such a deerskin blanket when one was traveling. Red Hawk looked at him. Blue Hawk quickly pulled the deerskin off his shoulder and slung it over his arm.

Red Hawk shook his head. It was clear that they must leave this place fast. His brother was becoming forgetful. How could he have forgotten that to wear a blanket in that way meant that he accepted it as a gift? And that accepting a gift from a young woman in that way also meant accepting that young woman? Or had he forgotten? Red Hawk looked hard at Blue Hawk, who began to busy himself with checking the flint point on his spear.

Slowly, Red Hawk led them uphill toward the place where the Otter Creek people were gathered. He absent-mindedly stroked the deerskin over his arm. It was well tanned, indeed. Only one who was careful and skillful could make a skin this soft and supple. He found himself imagining Evening Sky's hands as they scraped and worked the deerskin.

As they came closer to the people assembled in the center of the village, Red Hawk began to feel more ill at ease. There seemed to be some purpose in this gathering. Usually, early in the morning, everyone would be about their own tasks. But it seemed as if everyone was waiting for something. Or someone. They were only a few paces away now and everyone had stopped talking. All of the faces, Gray Otter's face, the faces of his two tall daughters, the faces of young and old alike—including the faces of several unfriendly looking men of their own age—were turned now toward the two brothers as they approached.

They are waiting, Red Hawk realized, for us!

"Wli?" Gray Otter said. "It is good?" It was a simple greeting, but it held many meanings. Had their sleep been peaceful and their dreams good? Did they feel well in body and spirit on this new day? Were their hearts good toward Gray Otter and his people?

"Wli ogun," Red Hawk and Blue Hawk replied. "Everything is good."

Then the two brothers looked at each other. Until they had spoken those words, they had not realized how true they were. Things, indeed, were good. They felt well and strong and, for some reason, excited and happy. It was very confusing.

Red Hawk remembered the deerskin he was carrying over his arm. He placed it carefully in front of Gray Otter and then gently nudged Blue Hawk in the ribs with his elbow. Blue Hawk placed the other skin blanket on top of the first.

Evening Sky, who sat on one side of her short father, looked over the top of his head at her sister. For some reason, the return of their gifts did not seem to displease them. Instead, the two sisters nodded to each other and then turned back to smile up at the brothers. Each of them reached out to reclaim their deerskin blankets, placing them in their laps. Evening Star began to stroke her hand over the blanket that was now draped over her well-muscled thighs. For a moment, it seemed to Red Hawk as if he could feel her hands. He shook his head and looked at Gray Otter.

"We must thank you. . ." Red Hawk began and then paused. But Blue Hawk said nothing. Red Hawk looked at his brother. Blue Hawk was staring at Morning Star, who was rubbing her blanket against her cheek. Red Hawk elbowed Blue Hawk so hard that he almost fell over.

"We must thank you . . ."Red Hawk said again.

". . . for treating us well," Blue Hawk said.

"But now we must leave," the two brothers said as one.

Gray Otter smiled up at them. "I see that this is true," he said. "We are grateful to you for warning us about the danger in Petonbowk. But before you leave, we wish to honor you."

Red Hawk and Blue Hawk looked at each other. They knew there was no way they could refuse whatever honor Gray Otter wished to give them. Perhaps it would only be a small present.

"We have heard," Gray Otter said, "that you two are great runners and that you enjoy playing ball. So we are going to have a ball game, just a little one. It will be played hard, so that it will be a good gift to you. Our Owner Creator likes to see our people play together in this way. So this game will also be a good prayer."

Gray Otter looked over toward the summer land edge of the big clearing. Everyone looked with him, except for the small, rather hostile-looking group of young men who kept staring at Red Hawk and Blue Hawk. Two poles had been set up there at some distance from each other. Red Hawk and Blue Hawk recognized them as the opposing goals for a ball game.

It was a game that the brothers knew well and had played many times. To score a point, one had to strike the balls against the pole on their opponents' side. The balls were two tightly wrapped bundles of rawhide connected together by a skin covering that narrowed into a band the width of a finger between the two balls. Each player carried two sticks to throw the balls, which would wrap themselves around a stick thrust up to catch them. The rules of the ball game were simple. Only the two sticks, which had to remain in your hands throughout the game, could be used to catch and throw the balls as the players ran up and down the field. The side that scored an agreed-upon number of points first was the winner. Aside from that, there were no rules. The sticks, as well as one's arms and legs and whole body, could be used to block and strike the opposing players. Fingers, and sometimes arms or legs, were often broken in a good ball game. If someone became very badly hurt, they were allowed to quit.

Red Hawk and Blue Hawk looked at each other and smiled. They liked the idea of playing a ball game. Then the same thought crossed both of their minds. Who were they to play against? Ball games were usually played between the men and boys, but there were times—big games—when everyone in the village might play. And even in a small game, sometimes the women played against the men. In some villages, a game would be played once a year between the men and the women. The side that lost would be required to bring in the firewood for the rest of that year. In those games, the women—who were much better at cooperating with each other and played more fiercely than the men—were often the winners. What if they were supposed to play against Evening Sky and Morning Sky?

Red Hawk and Blue Hawk looked at the two sisters. But the sisters did not look back at them, Instead they looked in the same direction their father was looking.

"Over here," Gray Otter said, "are the young men who wish to play that small game with you."

The four unfriendly-looking young men who had been staring at the two brothers stood up. Although none of them were as tall as the two brothers, all of them were well muscled and rugged looking. One of them was as broad as a bear and his thick hair fell across half of his face. The second, the tallest of the four, had a scar that ran from his shoulder down to the middle of his chest. It was the kind of scar that might be made by the claws of a long-tail. The third young man had very large hands and had clearly played ball often, from the bends in three of his fingers where they had been broken and then healed. The fourth young man, who already held his ball sticks in his hands, was more slender than the others and seemed to be having a harder time looking angry. A smile flickered at the edge of his mouth as he looked at them. His eyes were as quick as a bird's.

That fourth one, Red Hawk thought. He looked at Blue Hawk, who nodded back to him. The fourth one was the one who was going to be the hardest to play against. It did not matter that it would be four against two. It was possible for two who played with one mind to beat many times their number.

"Is it good?" Gray Otter said. "This game? Would you like to play?"

"It is good," Red Hawk and Blue Hawk said.

"The first side to score four goals will be the winner."

The voice that spoke to him was both quiet and powerful. It was a voice as sibilant as the wind's whisper through the trees at the first approach of a storm. Soft, barely noticed at first, but building in strength until even the great trees must bend before it or break.

"Thissss way," the voice whispered. "Come thisssss way."

As he walked, hearing the deep strength of that voice that could be heard by no ears but his own, Young Hunter began to understand more clearly something that Bear Talker had explained to him about becoming a deep-seer. Like the seed of a plant falling into soft earth, the words Bear Talker had placed within him were growing stronger now and he could see the shape of the tree that lifted up from that little seed.

Two springs ago, as they sat beside the river, watching the ice of the season of long nights wash away, Young Hunter had asked his teacher about those voices that now were always with him.

Bear Talker took a stick and poked at a piece of ice that was lodged against the bank. It floated free, spun once in the current, and then went rocking down the river. He watched until it was out of sight before he spoke.

"They call to you from inside. The voices that speak inside your head are always there with you, like the sound of your heartbeat. You may hear them coming up from deep in your chest or flying back and forth between your ears like the wings of birds. Sometimes you cannot hear them, sometimes they become very loud. They may ar-

THE WATERS BETWEEN 183

gue with you one time and guide you another. It can be confusing, it
is true. And who are those voices? They may be your own voices, the
voices of the person inside you and the ones who come to help you.
Or they may be the voices of others. Some of those others are friends.
Some do not care if you live or die. Some may be your enemies."

Bear Talker snorted and struck his wide chest with the palm of his
hand. "That is when you find out how strong your own heart is.
When your enemies seek to take your life, you must wrestle with
them. You cannot ignore them when they have come close enough
and are strong enough to speak inside your head."

Bear Talker paused, waiting for the question that he knew Young
Hunter would ask.

"What if you do not listen to any of the voices? What if you decide to turn away from them and not become a deep-seer?" Young
Hunter said.

"If you do not listen to them, your mind will become lost—like a
child who has wandered into a swamp. When you are one who hears
those voices, you must listen to them. Your body may remain, but
your spirit will leave you. It will be like the ice in this river, washed
away bit by bit until it has vanished into the flow."

Bear Talker growled and shook his head like a bear. "Then you
will be like the one of the men caught by the daughters of Great
White Hare."

Young Hunter understood. The story about the daughters of
Great White Hare was a very old story. Great White Hare lived far to
the north, there where the giant mountains of ice rose in the Always
Winter Land. Great White Hare had many daughters.

In the old days, when a man went to that cold north land to hunt
and trap, he might see one of those daughters. After seeing her, he
would be able to think of nothing else. She would smile at him and
beckon to him. He would drop his spear and follow her back to her
lodge made of ice and snow. He would go inside with her, unable to
see anything but her. She would tell him to sit down by her cold fire
and then ask him to remove his hunter's hood from his head.

"You hair is tangled," she would say. "I will comb it for you."

Then with a comb made of bone, she would comb his hair. And, as she combed his hair, she would also comb out his brains. When she was done, he would no longer be a man. He would be a white-coated hare and he would wander across the snowy land for the rest of his life. Prey to the fox and the wolf and the owl, he would be forgetful of the fact that he had ever been a man.

"That," Bear Talker said, "is how a man who tries to turn away from the voices inside his head and his heart will become—as brainless as a white hare."

Young Hunter left the trail and began to make his way among the many large stones of the hillside. He was careful where he stepped. The stones underfoot were loose and it would be easy to slip and fall. It was not an easy path to follow, but he could tell that at least one other person came this way more than once. There were small markings on the rocks. Scored into the flat faces of the stones were shapes of circles and stars, half moons, and wavery lines like the sinuous bodies of rivers and streams. Looking at those shapes, it seemed to him that they were visible echoes of the whispers, which he heard more clearly now.

"Thissss way. Come up thisss way."

He climbed higher and higher until, at last, he came to the top of the ridge and stopped at the base of a great, smooth boulder. Young Hunter leaned back against the great boulder, which had been warmed by the touch of the Day Walker's light, and looked back. The wide land stretched out below him. He saw the flow of rivers and the glitter of ponds and lakes, the green rolling hills covered with green blankets of trees. He could see all the way to the Waters Between. It was all very good to see.

As he saw that land that would always be a part of him, the life and breath of the Only People, feeling its beauty in his heart, something vanished. He listened. The voice which had been speaking to him suddenly became silent. One heartbeat it was there, calling him, and the next it was gone, leaving an emptiness behind.

But Young Hunter knew that he was not alone. He could smell something. It was not a bad smell, but it was a strange one. It was a human smell and also the smell of one of the close-to-the-ground people. Like all of the Only People, Young Hunter knew the scents of the world around them. Their noses were not as good as the dog people, but human beings were meant to learn from the world around them by using all of their senses.

The different close-to-the-ground people each had their own smells. The little striped ones had a musky scent, which was not pleasant to the nose. That was to discourage the larger beings that sought to eat them. There was a sweet scent to the little yellow wanderers, the green snakes. Young Hunter had learned to recognize that scent when he had lost his first set of teeth. His grandmother, Sweetgrass Woman, had taken him in search of one of the little yellow wanderers. They sat together in a meadow and she had sung a song for the little ones. Before long, a small green head had lifted up from the grass not far from them. Sweetgrass Woman picked the little green snake up carefully.

"Little friend," she said, "my grandson wants to have strong teeth, teeth strong enough to crack a hickory nut. You can give him that strength."

Then she had handed the snake to Young Hunter, who did as his grandmother had told him he must do. He held the small snake stretched between his hands and gently bit along its body from its head back to its tail. When each of his new teeth had touched the body of the snake, he was done.

"Thank you for my strong teeth," he said to the green snake. Then he placed it, unhurt, back on the ground. It slid away into the tall grass. And, like all of the other children who asked the little green one for its help, Young Hunter had always had strong teeth since that day.

This scent, though, was not that of a striped one or a yellow wanderer. Nor was it the scent of a rattlesnake, one of those brave ones who warn their enemies before striking. A rattlesnake's scent was pungent, almost like the smell of green butternuts when someone treads on them, breaking their husks. This scent was different, much more subtle. It was the scent of the strong-muscled snake that wrestles with its prey, the black snake.

Young Hunter knew where that scent of man and black snake came from. He stepped back far enough so that he could see more of that huge stone, which was shaped, he now saw, like one of the close-to-the-earth people. From the top of that stone snake, the eyes of the long-bodied man who sat there looked down into his.

37 ▣ DOUBLE BALL

Red Hawk and Blue Hawk faced each other. They knew that everyone in the village was watching them, especially the four men who were to play against them. The sticks with which they would soon play the game lay on the ground beside them. Those sticks had obligingly been provided by Evening Sky and Morning Sky.

"We hope that our men will not hurt you too much," Evening Sky said as she handed her pair of sticks not to Red Hawk, but to Blue Hawk.

"No one has ever beaten Black Marten and his friends," Morning Sky said, smiling as she handed a second pair of sticks to Red Hawk.

"You will not beat them," Morning Sky and Evening Sky said as one.

Then the sisters had linked arms and walked away, whispering to each other as they went.

Red Hawk looked down at the sticks that lay on the ground. The two that had been given to him had designs burned into the handle. Those designs stood for the evening sky, just as the designs on the sticks Evening Sky had handed Blue Hawk stood for the morning sky. The sisters had switched their ball sticks. Red Hawk shook his head. They are playing with us. Or perhaps, he thought, they are deliberately doing things backward for another reason. Perhaps, when they told us we would not beat their young men they meant just the opposite?

Red Hawk shook his head a second time. Thoughts like this were too confusing, like thinking what it would be like if water was dry and fire wet. Young Hunter was able to think of such things. He loved to talk of such things. But such thinking and talking made Red Hawk's head ache. He shook his shoulders, bent his knees slightly, and held his arms out toward his brother.

"One," he said.

"One," Blue Hawk repeated.

The two brothers grabbed each other's wrists, then, still holding tight, they spun around so that they were back to back. Red Hawk leaned forward and flipped Blue Hawk over his back. Blue Hawk landed on his feet with a shout, once again facing his brother.

"Two," Blue Hawk said.

"Two," Red Hawk repeated.

This time Blue Hawk was the one who flipped his brother and shouted when his feet touched the ground. They continued doing this, faster and faster, until they had reached the count of ten. By that time, almost everyone in the village was shouting with them. But the four men who were their opponents stood together in a group, their arms crossed. They were not impressed.

Red Hawk dove forward toward the ball sticks, ducking his head as he did so. He rolled and came back to his feet, holding one stick in each hand. In perfect unison with his brother, Blue Hawk had done the same.

Red Hawk threw one of his sticks at his brother. Blue Hawk struck it in midair and it went spinning back toward Red Hawk, who caught it at the same moment that he threw his second stick. Back and forth between the two brothers the sticks flew, never touching the ground. By now the bodies of both young men were gleaming with sweat.

Red Hawk stopped and held both of his sticks tightly together in front of himself at the level of his knees.

"Unh-hunh," he said.

Blue Hawk ran toward him and placed one foot on the two sticks at the same moment that Red Hawk lifted. Blue Hawk went sailing high over his brother's head, flipped in the air, and landed on his feet. It was a trick that their friend Sparrow had taught them. Blue Hawk turned around, grasped his own sticks and held them the same way.

But when he flipped, Red Hawk went backward and landed on his feet facing his brother.

Everyone in the village shouted—with the exception of the four young men, who were having a much harder time now looking unimpressed. The one with the scars on his chest, whose name was Three Scars, nodded his head. Many Fingers, the one with the large hands, linked those two big hands together and then cracked his knuckles. The young man who was as broad as a bear uncrossed his arms and pushed the hair away from his eyes. His name was Bear Paws and he had never seen anything like that before. He leaned forward, shaking his head. His mouth was wide open. Black Marten, the slender young man with the quick eyes, quickly nudged his friend. Bear Paws recovered. He closed his mouth and crossed his arms again.

Black Marten stepped forward and looked up at Red Hawk and Blue Hawk. His eyes sparkled. "Are you ready?" he said.

Red Hawk and Blue Hawk said nothing. As one, they turned their heads toward the ball field.

"Kiiiiiyiii!" Black Marten let out a great shout. He held his ball sticks over his head and ran toward the field, followed by his three friends, who did the same. It was impressive, though the impression was spoiled just a bit when Bear Paws tried to roll forward and come up on his feet as Red Hawk and Blue Hawk had done. He landed on his back with a loud thump and his friends had to pull him to his feet.

Blue Hawk and Red Hawk went to the center of the field and stood, not together but with Red Hawk a dozen arm lengths behind his brother and to the side.

Gray Otter came forward, the double ball in his hand. He threw it high up in the air, backing away quickly so that he would not be caught in the play of the game.

Instead of trying for the ball, Red Hawk stepped back. It was a wise thing to do. The body of Bear Paws flew through the space that had been occupied by Red Hawk. The broad young man was moving so fast that he lost his footing when he did not make contact as he had expected. He rolled like a ball into Three Scars, knocking him off his feet.

Red Hawk leaped high and caught the ball on his stick. Before his feet touched the ground he flipped it back over his head toward Blue Hawk. Black Marten shouted at Many Fingers, already guessing their plan. But Many Fingers did not listen, he charged toward Blue Hawk.

Red Hawk lowered his head and ran as fast as he could in the opposite direction, toward his opponents' goal. Black Marten tried to keep pace with him, but Red Hawk was too fast. Soon he was many strides ahead of the smaller man. He looked back over his shoulder as he ran. Just as he expected, he saw Blue Hawk throw the double ball before Many Fingers could reach him. No one could throw a double ball further than Blue Hawk. It sailed half of the length of the field to Red Hawk, who caught it just in front of the goal, swinging his stick down to strike the ball against the upright pole. Thunk! Red Hawk and Blue Hawk had scored the first goal.

As Gray Otter collected the double ball to bring it back to the center of the field, Blue Hawk limped up to Red Hawk. There was a large bruise on Blue Hawk's thigh.

"They play . . ." Blue Hawk said.

". . . very hard," Red Hawk answered.

They nodded at each other and got ready for the second play of the ball, this time with Blue Hawk taking the position in front.

But the play did not go as it had before. Black Marten had been whispering to the other three. Instead of attacking at the start, the four young men dropped back, allowing Blue Hawk to catch the ball. As the two brothers started forward, Black Marten and Many Fingers ran for Red Hawk while Bear Paws and Three Scars attacked Blue Hawk. The strategy might not have worked, had not Blue Hawk stumbled on a root. He threw the ball as he fell and Red Hawk caught it. But before Blue Hawk could rise, a very heavy weight came down on him as Bear Paws thumped down onto his back, pinning him to the ground. By the time he got up, he looked down the field to see his brother, Red Hawk, doing the same. Many Fingers had knocked him to the ground just as he caught the ball and Black Marten had stolen it. Black Marten and Three Scars were standing by the goal post, tossing the double ball back and forth between them. As soon as they were on their feet, Black Marten took the ball, smiled downfield at them and tapped it gently against the post. The score was now tied.

"They play . . ." Red Hawk said.

". . . even harder than we thought they would," Blue Hawk answered.

Then they both smiled. This was going to be a better game than they had expected.

By the time the game was over, Red Hawk and Blue Hawk had won by a single goal. All six of the young men were bruised and Bear Paws was carefully feeling one of his front teeth, which had been struck hard by Blue Hawk's elbow. But there was no anger in any of their faces. It was good to score goals, but it was better to play. The game itself was a sacred thing, a prayer and a giving of thanks. That they had played so well and so long made their prayer that much stronger.

Black Marten thumped each of the brothers on their chests with his fist. "You play well," he said. His eyes were sparkling like those of the small quick animal that gave him his name.

"It was a good game." Many Fingers said. He was busy pulling one of his fingers, which now stood out at a very odd angle, back into place.

Three Scars nodded. "I am glad that we took pity on you."

"My tooth is loose," Bears Paws said, his hand still in his mouth.

Everyone burst into laughter.

People were all around them now, congratulating each of the players on how well they had done. Gray Otter stood before the two brothers.

"Now we must do something very important," he said in a serious voice.

Everyone stopped talking to look at the deep-seeing man.

"Now," he said, "we must eat!"

The fact that they were tired and bruised made the food that was waiting for them taste even better. All six of the young men sat together, sharing food and joking with each other. The game had made them feel like brothers.

The Day Walker was in the middle of the sky. It was close now to the longest of the days and there was still much time ahead for Red Hawk and Blue Hawk to travel before it was dark. They should be able to travel through the cedar swamp and back onto the trail toward their own village of the Salmon People. The two brothers said their words of thanks and made ready to leave, but Gray Otter stopped them.

"My young friends," he said, "you will need guides to help you through the swamp. You might go off the trail and be lost. The way out is more confusing than the way in. And you must go quickly so that you will not be caught there when it is dark. To travel quickly, you must be helped by those who know the way. "

"Will you . . ." Red Hawk said.

". . . travel with us again?" Blue Hawk added.

"Nda," Gray Otter said. "There are things that I must do here now. But you do not have to worry. I have arranged for guides to help you."

"Un-hunh," Red Hawk said.

"That is good," said Blue Hawk.

The two brothers looked over toward Black Marten and the other ball players, certain that they were the ones who would guide them. But there was a strange smile on Black Marten's face. He pointed with his chin behind them. Red Hawk felt something like a fist clutching inside his stomach. He knew that his brother felt the same. They both knew, all too well, who was standing behind them.

"My daughters," Gray Otter said, turning the brothers around so that they faced Evening Light and Morning Light. The two sisters looked at Red Hawk and Blue Hawk through narrowed eyes.

"They are good guides," Gray Otter continued. "They will show you the right ways to walk. They will accompany you all the way."

As Young Hunter watched, the man on top of the stone, whose eyes were locked onto his, leaned toward him the way a snake does when it brings its head back down. Then he slid forward, head first, in an easy, almost boneless way. In that same head-first way, moving as the close-to-the-ground ones move, he came down the slanted side of the stone. He used his hands as he came, yet he kept them so close to his body that it seemed as if he had actually become a snake. The tattoos across his face and forehead made his resemblance to a big snake even greater. Arms still close to his side, he rose to his feet—and kept rising until he stood at his full height, two heads taller than Young Hunter. Swaying back and forth gently, his eyes unblinking, the man looked down at him.

It is the way, Young Hunter thought, that a snake controls the mind of one that it plans to eat. He had seen it more than once, watched without interfering.

He had been very small when he saw it the first time. He sat on a log just above a small branch of Little Otter Creek. As he watched the flow of the water, it seemed as if that water became more alive, pulling itself together into a long muscled body on top of the surface. It was a water inhabitant, a quick-tempered snake whose home is the water. Such snakes were not poisonous, but they were so easily angered that they would chase a child—and even an adult—who disturbed them. Young Hunter did not move. He was small then, but he had already learned that the best way not to be seen is to stay still.

The water snake swam past him, its head and neck lifted out of the water. It was a big one, its body as long as Young Hunter was tall, but it did not see him. Its eyes were on something else, on a mouse that sat on the bank of the stream, pulling seeds from a branch that hung over the water. As the snake drew closer to the mouse, it lifted its head higher, swaying it back and forth, back and forth. The mouse saw it and stopped eating, but it did not run. It was fascinated by the movement of the snake. It seemed unable to tear itself away. Back and forth, back and forth, the water snake came. Closer and closer, swaying, swaying and then—it struck! The mouse struggled, but it was quickly wrapped in the snake's coils. The snake worked its jaws around to the head of the mouse, gaped wide, and began to swallow it. Soon all that was left to be seen of the mouse was a bulge in the snake's belly.

Young Hunter held up a hand. "I am not a mouse," he said.

The tall man understood. He stopped swaying back and forth and a wide grin spread across his face. "Yesss," Carries Snakes said, "you are not a moussse."

Young Hunter looked up at the man. He could see now that Carries Snakes, even though he stood strong and tall, was a man of great age. The lines around his eyes, the wrinkles about his neck, the grey of his hair all were marks of many, many winters. He saw, too, now that Carries Snakes was smiling, the warmth in the deep-seeing man's eyes, the warmth in his heart.

"Grandfather," Young Hunter said, showing his trust and respect for the old man by his use of that word, "you have called me to you."

"Grandssson, I have called you to me."

Carries Snakes made a small flowing gesture with one hand. It was a gesture Young Hunter had never seen before, yet somehow he understood it. It meant come with me and it meant more than that.

Carries Snakes turned and began to walk. Young Hunter followed him. As they walked, Young Hunter found it hard to look at the land around them. It seemed as if all he could do was keep his eyes on

Carries Snakes, for if he turned away for even a heartbeat, the tall old man would be gone. They walked between some of the tall stones and, it seemed, through others. They walked upon the earth and they walked beneath it. They walked only a few paces and they walked for a long long time. When Carries Snakes stopped at last, Young Hunter did not know where they were.

"We are here, grandssson," Carries Snakes said, answering the question Young Hunter had not asked. He sat down, cross-legged, and Young Hunter sat in front of him. There was a bag slung over the old man's shoulder. It had not been there before and Young Hunter had not seen Carries Snakes pick it up as they walked. Yet it was there. As Young Hunter looked at it, the bag moved.

Carries Snakes took the bag off his shoulder and placed it on the stone floor in front of him. They were in a bowl of stone. It circled around them and there was no way into that stone bowl. All that could be seen was the red stone around them and the cloudless blue of the sky above.

"Now," Carries Snakes said, "before we sssspeak, we musssst see if my friend acceptsss you."

The bag moved as something large rippled the woven bark from within. Then a head poked its way out. Two bright eyes looked around as that dark head moved back and forth. A pink tongue poked out of its mouth and flickered rapidly up and down. Slowly, that head was drawn back, almost of sight into the bag. Only one bright eye could be seen now, looking shyly up at Young Hunter. Young Hunter smiled. It made him think of the way a child comes into a lodge when there are visitors, looking first around one side of the door and then the other.

"Kwai, kwai, nidoba mehkazewigit skoks," Young Hunter whispered. "Hello, friend black snake."

The black snake slid its head fully out a second time and looked up at Young Hunter. The tongue flickered out, up and down so fast that it almost could not be seen. It was like the beating of a hummingbird's wings. Then, as if a decision had been made and there was no longer any reason for hesitation, the black snake came flowing out of the basswood bag. It went straight toward Young Hunter, lifting itself higher as it came until its head was at the same level as his eyes. It leaned forward and its tongue flickered against his cheek. Young Hunter did not move, but his smile grew broader. So much like a child, he thought.

The black snake leaned against him. Its skin was warm from the sun, smooth feeling. It wrapped itself around his neck and lifted its head to look over at Carries Snakes.

Carries Snakes nodded. "There is no quesstion. Black Friend is your friend, too."

Then Carries Snakes began to speak. He spoke with words and without them. And all the time he spoke, the black snake hung around Young Hunter's neck, its head up as if it, too, was listening and ready to add its own words to those of the tall old man.

Young Hunter listened hard. He knew that the things he heard were important, especially those things that he did not yet understand. But he would remember them and one day, perhaps, their meaning would come to him. A child who has not yet seen snow can be told about the time of long nights, but that telling will mean little until one has lived through more than one winter. As Carries Snakes spoke, Young Hunter understood one thing very clearly. Carries Snakes was giving him a great gift. The old man was passing on to him a long lifetime of wisdom. Young Hunter hoped he would be worthy of it.

"Grandsson," Carries Snakes said. "You will do your bessst."

Young Hunter looked at the old man. He looked strong and well, yet there was something in his eyes. Where had he seen it before? Then he remembered. It had been in the eyes of old Muskrat, the day that old man took him out into his dugout and showed Young Hunter how to make a muskrat call. No one had seen old Muskrat again after that day. He had poled his boat out into the water and not returned. Even his boat had never been found. Some said the old man had been so old that he simply walked into the sky land, body and all. Others thought he might have turned into one of those cedar trees that were to be found at certain places along the river, bent over like an elder waiting to tell a story.

"Nda," Carries Snakes said, "you cannot help me thisss night. The one who huntssss usss, I mussst face him alone." He paused and looked for a long time at Young Hunter. The black snake still lay draped around Young Hunter's neck and over his shoulder.

"You will sssssee me again," Carries Snakes said.

Carries Snakes stood and began to walk, leaving the basswood bag on the ground. Young Hunter picked it up and followed him. The old man's legs were long and it was hard for Young Hunter to keep up. He tried to run, but it was as if he was in a dream in which running is not possible. The old man was getting further and further ahead of him. He was now at the top of the hill.

"Carries Snakes," Young Hunter called. It was the first time he had spoken the deep-seer's name.

Carries Snakes looked back over his shoulder. "Young Hunter," he said, "Grandsssson, it issss your turn to carry him now." Then he took one more step and was gone.

Young Hunter stopped walking. It was no use to follow a deep-seeing person when they did not wish to be followed. He looked around. Somehow, he did not know how, he had come back to the place where he first met Carries Snakes. The trail was under his feet, the great coiled stone in front of him. It was as it had been before. He looked up. Even though they had walked for what seemed a great distance and talked for what seemed a long long time, the Day Walker was in almost the same place in the sky where it had been when Young Hunter first reached this spot.

The trail was the same. The great stone was the same. But other things were not the same. Carries Snakes was gone and Black Friend now hung about Young Hunter's shoulders and neck.

The snake lifted itself up so that its head was in front of Young Hunter, its eyes looking into his. Young Hunter slung the bag over his shoulder.

"Black Friend," Young Hunter said, "you will travel with me for a while?"

The black snake dropped its head and nosed open the bag. It slid its long glistening body in and coiled itself together so that it rested next to Young Hunter's heart.

Young Hunter nodded and shifted the bag slightly on his shoulder. It would not be hard to carry. He started back down the hill.

39 ▣ PILED STONES

His grandmother would not stop talking.

"You are a fool and a coward," she said. It did not matter than her bones were broken. It did not matter that her eyes could no longer see. Her voice, which had at first been weakened by pain, kept growing stronger.

"Skuksis walaguk wudji! You are a little worm who crawls into a hole in the ground. Fool. Clumsy, ugly, worthless little fool. You are nothing."

He covered his ears, but he could still hear her voice. It gave him greater pain than any of the beatings she had given him when he was a child. He tried to speak, to tell her to once again be silent, but his own voice was gone. He tried to lift the heavy stick to strike her, but the stick was gone and he had nothing to hold a stick with. He had no arms. He tried to look at himself, but he no longer had any eyes. He had become a worm and he was wriggling on the ground.

Although he could no longer see her, he sensed his grandmother there above him. Somehow she had escaped from beneath the stones he had piled on her body. Somehow her wounds had healed. All that he had done had been for nothing. He, himself, was nothing. She stood above him, her foot lifted. She was going to crush him with her foot. He crawled as fast as he could, trying to find a hole in which to hide. But he could feel her looming over him, closer and closer.

"Fool. Little fool. Worthless little worm."

He could not even scream.

Watches Darkness opened his eyes. His grandmother was gone,

though he felt her spirit still hovering around him. It was often like this when he slept. She would wait until he was deep in slumber and then she would walk into his dreams, her tongue even sharper than it had been when she drew breath. There seemed to be no way he could rid himself of her. Perhaps, though, when his power was great enough he would be able to do it. When he had stolen the lives of the deep-seers of this land and eaten their hearts his strength might be great enough to drive his grandmother's spiteful spirit away from him once and for all.

She was gone now. Sharp Tongue was gone. Now that he was awake, she could not remain. But there was something else here. That feeling of some great presence just above him. Something warm and moist fell on his face. Watches Darkness slowly reached up his hand in the darkness. His hand touched the open mouth of the huge bear. He felt its breath on his face and he sensed the depth of its hunger. Its hunger was so great that it had almost overpowered the bear's fear of him as it stood, drooling over his body.

Watches Darkness spoke a word. He spoke it without using his breath, using it like a spear. The One Who Walks Like a Man felt that word deep inside its head. It burned like fire. The great bear stepped back, moaning from the pain.

Now that its bulk was no longer over him, Watches Darkness stood. He could see his dangerous ally in the darkness, cowering back into the corner, rubbing its shoulders against the earth walls as it tried to move even further away from the pain. It feared him, but it was still hungry. It would not wait.

Watches Darkness walked outside. The despised light of the face in the sky was gone now. The wind of night was in his face. It was his time. He listened. He could hear the feet moving softly on the trail that led just below the cave under the roots of the great fallen tree. Watches Darkness took the black stone knife from his bag and then crouched to wait. The feet came closer and closer until they were just below him. Watches Darkness leapt like a panther. One of his arms circled the neck of the one who had come too close as his legs wrapped about the warm body. There was only time for one brief despairing cry before the sharp edge of the knife was drawn across the throat that spurted out blood and life.

The others ran. Watches Darkness paid them no heed. This one would be enough. He placed the knife back into his pouch and picked the dead one up. It was a large female. Much meat on it. He carried the warm body back up to the cave, bent down and dragged it in. He threw it at the feet of the One Who Walks Like a Man. The great bear growled as its long teeth tore into the flesh of the deer that Watches Darkness had slain.

"Eat," Watches Darkness whispered. "Remember that I am the one who feeds you. Follow me tonight and I will give you more food."

Carries Snakes sat on the great stone, an elkskin blanket around his wide shoulders. He touched his chest with his hands, feeling the place where the bag had always hung. It was strange to be without Black Friend. But it was right that he had done as he did. Seeing as he did, seeing what walked toward him, he had seen that he must face it alone. He had walked for a long time in this body. He had done good things. When the time came for him to leave this body behind, he would do it by himself. It did not matter if that time was this night or some other night. No one would be with him to show him the start of the Sky Trail. His spirit would have to take those steps up the great mountain alone.

Carries Snakes picked up the round stone. It had been the easiest one to carry up to the top of the great rock. It was just the shape of a person's head.

"Are you me?" Carries Snake whispered to the skull-shaped stone.

The one who was coming was awake now. Carries Snakes felt his presence growing closer. The one coming was like a dark flame. As he burned, the darkness around him grew. Carries Snakes smiled. The one coming was arrogant in his power.

Perhaps, Carries Snakes thought, this old man will surprise him.

It was a dark night, but it was not a night as full of darkness as it would be when clouds came between the earth and the sky land. The campfires of the little far-above ones could be seen. There were more of them than could be counted. The great sky road led through their camps toward the land where the hunting was always good and the berries always ripe.

Carries Snakes thought of the taste of berries. Would it be strange to always have all the berries ripe at the same time? As he thought it, he seemed to taste those berries. He shook his head. It was said that those just about to die could already taste the berries of the sky land. Better to think of something else now. The one who was coming was close. He thought that he was walking silently, but Carries Snakes could feel his feet as they walked, the small vibration of that one's feet came through the big stone.

And that one was not alone. Carries Snakes could smell the other one. Its hunger and its fear were part of its scent, which was like that of a bear and yet stronger than any bear he had smelled before. An Ancient One. One of those who hunted the human beings in the time of his ancestors. Once there had been many such beings. But the Owner Creator had seen how the people suffered. So he sent The Talker to change those great animals, to make them smaller and less dangerous. But a few did not come to The Talker when he called them together. A few of the Ancient Ones survived. This, it seemed, was one of them. A stick snapped in the brush two spearcasts down his hill behind him. It was not yet close enough to charge at him. Two cowards, not one.

Carries Snakes balanced the round stone carefully on top of the pile of rocks and leaned back to look. It was good. In the darkness, the pile of stones looked like a large seated man. Only one thing was needed to complete the effect. Carries Snakes draped his elkskin blanket around the piled stones. Now it would not just look more like him, it would also smell like him. Then, quieting his mind until it was as still as the piled stones, Carries Snakes slid from the top of the great boulder.

* * *

Watches Darkness could see him clearly now. He tried to touch his adversary's mind, but he could not. Perhaps the old man was even stronger than he thought. Or perhaps not. Look at how he sat there like a fool, waiting to be destroyed. Like a fool. A fool. A worthless little fool. For a moment, Watches Darkness heard again the words spoken to him inside his dream by Sharp Tongue. It made him angry and his anger made him impatient. He would not play with this old fool after all. He would do it quickly. He would use the bear to do it.

He saw that the great bear was on the other side of the large round boulder with the flat top. It could be on the man who sat so stupidly up there with one leap. All he had to do now was distract the old fool.

Watches Darkness stood up from his hiding place in the shadows. His red eyes shone in the starlight.

"Old one," he shouted up to the figure who remained unmoving on top of the boulder. "I am here to kill you."

His shout had been the signal to the One Who Walks Like a Man. Before his words were finished the huge, pale beast was there, on top of the boulder, looming over the seated figure and then striking down with teeth and claws.

The great bear bellowed. It was not a roar of victory, but one of surprise and pain. It came sliding off the top of the boulder, the stones that it had struck rolling with it and over it. One of them, as round as a human skull, bounced and came to a stop next to the feet of Watches Darkness.

Anger darkened his eyes. He strode over to the place where the huge bear was tearing apart something. An elkskin blanket. He spoke a single word and the One Who Walks Like a Man lifted its head to look at him. Blood was dripping from its mouth. It was its own blood—from the teeth that had been broken when it bit the stones piled to look like a man.

"Stay here," Watches Darkness growled.

He turned and began to walk up the hill, past the great stone. The old man was not far from here. He could sense him now. Watches Darkness spread his arms wide, leaned his head back and howled.

"Maaaaaaguuuaaaa!"

It was a howl that split the night. It was heard by those who were far away.

"You are a coward!" Watches Darkness screamed. "Face me!"

"Faccccce me," said a soft voice beside him.

Watches Darkness slowly turned his head. Carries Snakes stood there, only an arm's length away.

His head lifted toward the sky, one hand cupped behind an ear, Bear Talker stood listening. He listened as a deep-seer listens, as he had been taught to listen so many winters ago by his first teacher, Oldest Talker. She was the one who had taken in the hungry boy he had been then, the first to see that his deepest hunger was in his spirit, not his body. He had been so full of talk in those first days with her that nothing said to him remained in his head.

"Listen," she said to him then. "But do not listen with words and talk. Words and talk are like a wind. They blow everything out of your head. Listen with the silence."

Then she had giggled. It had confused him, that way she had of laughing after saying the most serious things. It had taken him a long time to realize that taking yourself too seriously was as bad as talking too much. Everything in the world around you knows that it important sometimes to play. The animals, the birds, even the winds play—whirling together in pleasure as they dance across the land and the waters. Being too serious prevented a human person from really being a part of everything. Too much seriousness was also a barrier to real listening.

It was a warm night, the kind of night when people usually sit outside their lodges, enjoying the touch of the wind that is scented with flowers and pollen. The Night Traveler had not yet shown her face, which would be this night, as it had been the night before, still partly shadowed by her long hair that hung across one cheek. But the little far-above ones had lit their many fires and the sky glittered with their countless lights. With only the star people for company, Bear Talker stood. Listening and waiting.

Despite the warmth of the night, the people of the village were not outside their lodges. They sat inside. They, too, were waiting, though they did not know what they were waiting for. Uncertainty hung in the air like smoke blown over the hill from a fire that has not yet been seen. Something was happening throughout the Dawn Land. The shaking of the earth that had happened two moons ago had been the start of it. People hesitated to go out in the night after the usually solid ground beneath their feet had trembled like the surface of a mossy bog. When Nanamkiapoda, the earthquake maker, traveled beneath the earth, no one knew which way he would go.

Young Hunter's story of the great being in the Waters Between made the people even more uncertain. Had they known about the killing of the village guardian, the cat-owl that sat among the cedar trees watching for strangers throughout the night, their worries would have been greater still. But Rabbit Stick had told no one of finding its small body buried in the soft earth beneath its favorite perch. The sudden arrival of Bear Talker and the equally sudden departure of Young Hunter—off to do battle with other deep-seers, some people whispered—had been noted by everyone, however.

Usually this was a time of travel between villages, of small parties of people going out to the fishing places or to gather plants and berries. It was not that way now. Great things, terrible things, perhaps, had happened and more were soon to happen. Although the deep-seeing people felt it more clearly than others, everyone sensed it. And at a time when great changes were happening, it was best to be as safe as one could be, to remain with one's family, to be in one's lodge during the time of darkness. Darkness was not the enemy of the Only People, but an enemy could hide more easily in the dark.

Bear Talker felt a presence close behind him. It had come upon him so silently that he felt startled. An open mouth with long teeth pressed against the side of his leg. Bear Talker's heart filled his throat. He took a stumbling step as he turned around, almost falling as he did so. Then he shook his head, breathing easily again. He should have known.

Mouth open, Pabesis smiled up at him as only a dog can smile. He had grown so much over the last two winters that his shoulders now came to Bear Talker's waist. He was even larger than Agwedjiman, who stood two fingers taller than any of the other village dogs. Pabesis was now almost as large as one of the great wolves that lived in the time of the great-grandparents. Bear Talker looked into the eyes of Pabesis. It was the first time that the big young dog had played such a trick on him, sneaking up behind him and then gently biting him to make him jump.

But, although Pabesis had never played it before, it was a familiar game to Bear Talker. Pabesis was named for another dog who had been faithful—to the death—to Young Hunter. That dog had been named Pabetciman. From the time he was a puppy, he had been the one of Young Hunter's three dogs who was the fondest of Bear Talker. It was Pabetciman who had played that game with him, creeping up quietly behind and then nipping Bear Talker when he was unawares. Bear Talker had always roared and shouted and chased him, but Pabetciman had taken that as part of the game, running in circles and staying just far enough away to not be caught. When the roaring and shouting and running was done—and no one was around to see them—Pabetciman would trot up to Bear Talker, place his front paws on the deep-seeing man's shoulders and gently kiss his face with his tongue.

Pabetciman had met his death in a place which was a journey of many days toward the sunset. His body was broken in a battle against a creature that hunted human beings. Pabetciman had closed his eyes for a final time as he accepted the arrival of the Sleep Maker. Even though it happened far away, Bear Talker had known the moment when his four-legged friend had died. He had felt a small emptiness within himself, an emptiness that had remained until now.

Bear Talker looked into the eyes of the big young dog. It was that way sometimes. When a spirit is born again in a new body, that spirit may not remember everything from its previous life. Not at first. But then, as the moons and the seasons pass, things come back. Memories held by the wind return again.

"I have missed you, my friend," Bear Talker said.

"Uncle," whispered a voice from behind him.

For a second time Bear Talker almost fell as he spun around. Twice in one night! First because he had been listening so hard to hear something—he was not certain what—but something, something from far away. Now this time because he had been lost in that place between memory and vision where the circle completes itself. Again, just as before, he was not surprised to see the one who stood there. Of course! The big young dog had not been alone. Part of Pabesis's teasing game with Bear Talker had been to distract him so that he would not hear her approach.

There was laughter in her eyes as she looked at him, but she kept her voice respectful. Bear Talker was thankful for that. He saw, too, that the laughter in her eyes covered the worry that was in her heart.

"Uncle," Willow Woman said, "do you hear anything in the wind?"

"Your husband is safe tonight," Bear Talker growled, answering the question that she was really asking. "He will return two dawns from now."

Bear Talker lifted his head again and held up one hand. Willow Woman understood. He was still listening. She knelt down beside Pabesis, her arm over the big young dog's neck. They waited silently as Bear Talker stood there. The new leaves of the maple trees moved with the night wind, but Bear Talker stood as unmoving as a figure shaped from stone. The branches of the pines whispered above them. Except for the wind and the trees, it was quiet around them. The many small ones who sing in the darkness were as silent as the two humans and the four-legged one. The silence grew in strength. Finally even the wind died down and the trees settled into quiet. Everything lay in silence. Silence and listening. The fires of the star people circled overhead in the great dance that filled the sky.

Then it came, a call from so far away that Willow Woman was not sure that she heard it with her ears. It floated across the sky as if it came down from the road that leads up into the stars. Silence. And then that call was repeated. It was closer now, though distant still. It seemed to come from the hills beyond the hills. Willow Woman recognized it this time. It was the call of the Nighteyes, the owl who brings a certain message. She looked up at Bear Talker, who had not moved. He was still listening. The owl's call came a third time, this time from the hills beyond the valley. The Night Traveler had risen now above the hills and, though shadows fell around him, her light was bright on Bear Talker's face. Still, the deep-seeing man had not moved, but the look on his face seemed changed somehow. Then the fourth call came. It came from the top of the tallest pine tree at the edge of the village clearing.

"Kokokhassss, kokokhasss, kokokhasss, kokokhasss," the Nighteyes called. I am sorry, it said, again and again and again.

Willow Woman looked at Bear Talker's face. She saw what was there. Bear Talker's eyes were filled with tears.

"My old friend," Bear Talker said, "travel well on the sky road."

41 ▣ POISON

The pain inside his head was worse. It had not gone as he had planned. He pressed his head hard against the cold stone of the cave where they had finally found shelter against the painful light. They had not tried to go back to the burrow under the unrooted pine. The night had not been long enough for them. They had come, limping and stumbling, down the hill until they reached the stream. Its waters had cooled them, but they had to continue on. They went downstream further and further as the sky grew lighter.

Then they had found this cave. But it had not been empty. The long-tail cat crouched within it had spat and snarled at them, trapped inside when they entered. But the fire thrown from his hands had blinded it and, though its hind claws raked bloody lines into the side of the One Who Walks Like a Man, one bite and a shake of the great bear's head had ended it. Although the bear's mouth still ached where its small front incisor teeth had been broken by the stones, it began to eat. In the far corner of the cave, it was still gnawing at what was left of the long-tail.

Watches Darkness held his hands up in front of his face. There were no wounds on them, not even small puncture marks on his fingers. He looked at his legs and his chest. They, too, were free of wounds. Yet he felt the poison burning within him, heating his blood. His hands shook as he opened his pouch, taking out the medicine that he needed. A drip of water came from the wall of the cave. He filled his cup, which was made from the top of a skull, and mixed the medicine in with the water. He drank it in one gulp. Then he crouched down, feeling the cramps begin in his belly as the medicine started its work. He closed his eyes and in the space behind his eyes he saw the face of the old man. The old man was smiling at him. Laughing at him. Watches Darkness leaned his head forward against the cool wet stone, seeing it all again as it had happened on the hilltop. He had not expected the old man to be so strong.

"Faccce me," Carries Snakes said.

Watches Darkness turned his body slowly. The man who stood before him was old, but he was taller than Watches Darkness. Watches Darkness had seen him before, seen him in the way a deep-seeing person can see another from far away. This was not the same. Watches Darkness could feel the power in the old man, see it in the eyes that looked at him without fear. Those eyes looked at him with—anger swept over Watches Darkness—amusement. The old man was laughing at him.

"I will eat your heart," Watches Darkness said. His voice was like a cold wind. Others had heard that voice and recoiled from it, but it had no effect on Carries Snakes.

"Your friend broke hissssss teeth trying to eat me," Carries Snakes said, looking over at the place where the One Who Walks Like a Man sat. "What will you break?"

Watches Darkness put his hand in his pouch as he stared at the old man. Carries Snakes had not moved from the place where he stood. Watches Darkness thought of pulling out the black knife, plunging it into the old man's throat. But as the old man's deep eyes held his, Watches Darkness knew that would not work. The old man was at least as strong as he was physically. Then he noticed it. Something was missing. The bag that the old man always carried. The one in which he carried the black snake that was his helper. Where was it?

Carries Snakes read the question in the eyes of Watches Darkness. "Where issss my friend?" he said. "I know what you planned for him. You will not hold him up in front of my facccce and bite hissss head off. He issss gone." Carries Snakes pointed down the trail with his lips. "Another carriesssss him."

The anger that filled Watches Darkness blinded him for a heart-beat. It was as if his vision was filled with sparks from a fire that burned behind his eyes. Then his vision cleared and he realized that anger would not help him. He quieted his heartbeat, spoke in as calm a voice as he could.

"You are afraid of me. You cannot beat me fairly," Watches Darkness said.

Carries Snakes smiled. "Nda. I am not afraid. What isss your challenge?"

Now Watches Darkness smiled. The old man had fallen into his trap. "A simple test," Watches Darkness said, "to see which is stronger. Nbizon. We will give each other medicine. I will see if it is true that no poison can harm you. I am Watches Darkness and I will defeat you."

Carries Snakes turned his back on Watches Darkness. "I accept your challenge," he said. "Follow me and we will sit together as we try each other's medicine."

He walked back down the trail toward the great rock where the piled stone figure had been, ignoring the great bear that still sat warily beneath it. The One Who Walks Like a Man shuffled back away from him as Carries Snakes came closer. Carries Snakes took four steps in footholds that Watches Darkness could not see and was on top of the rock. Watches Darkness followed more slowly. The stone was smooth and it was not easy to climb on top of it, but he managed to do so without slipping.

The two deep-seers sat facing each other.

"You challenged me," said Carries Snakes, "sssssso, you may tesssst me firsssst."

Watches Darkness reached into his bag with both hands. With one hand, he pulled out the bark container. In it was the moist bundle wrapped in green leaves. The white poison made from the bodies of the little Spirit Creatures was soaked into that bundle. One hand still concealed in his bag, he opened the bark container and lifted out the moist bundle. A pungent smell filled the air. He held it toward Carries Snakes, as if giving it to him. Carries Snakes reached out a hand to take the bundle, but as he leaned forward to do so, Watches Darkness dropped the bundle and grabbed the old man's wrist. As he pulled Carries Snakes toward him, Watches Darkness whipped the black-bladed knife from his bag and struck as hard as he could.

The back of a hand whipped across the face of Watches Darkness. It broke his grip, stunning him and hurling him backward. He struggled to keep from falling off the the great stone. There were cracks in the top of the stone and he dug his fingers into them. He found himself on his belly at the very edge. He looked up.

Carries Snakes was still sitting in the same place. The face of the Night Traveler had lifted from the trees and it shone down on him. Slowly, the old man reached over and grasped the handle of the black knife that had been driven deeply into his side. He pulled it out.

"Who isssss the coward?" Carries Snakes hissed. He smashed the knife down on the stone in front of him. It splintered into shards that spun away in the moonlight. One of the shards struck the cheek of Watches Darkness. He felt the warmth as blood began to run down his face.

Carries Snakes held up the poison bundle that he had grabbed from the hand of Watches Darkness. He smelled it. "I know thissss," he said. He placed it in his mouth and swallowed it. "Now," Carries Snakes hissed, "I give you my mediccccine. You do not have to take it. It will come to you."

Carries Snakes held out his palm and slapped the surface of the great stone slowly. One, two, three, four times. The stone vibrated to his touch and Watches Darkness heard a hissing sound that seemed to come from within the rock. Then, close to his cheek, he heard the sound of a rattle. It was answered by other rattles on all sides of him as he lay there on his belly, trying not to fall. Then, from all sides, the snakes struck. They struck his hands and fingers, his arms and legs.

Watches Darkness screamed and let go of his hold. He went rolling off the great stone and landed hard on the ground. The pain of strong poison pulsed through him. He howled like a wounded wolf and began to run. The One Who Walks Like a Man ran behind him.

Sitting on the top of the great stone, his limbs weakening as his life's blood left him, Carries Snakes heard them crashing down the hillside. He stopped singing his snake song and put down the rattle that he had slipped from his belt. The poison that Watches Darkness had given to him was strong. It would have killed him if he had truly swallowed it. Carries Snakes opened his other hand. The bundle that he had pretended to put into his mouth was still there. He put it down on the stone in front of him. As he pressed one hand against the deep wound to slow the flow of blood, he pulled dry sticks together with the other. There was still enough strength left for him to make a fire and burn the poison bundle. Its bad medicine would be wiped away by the cleansing touch of flame.

Despite the pain, Carries Snakes smiled. The mind of that deep-seeing person was so twisted that it had been easy to turn it against him. To make him feel the strike of snakes that were not there. To think he felt their poison, when the only poison was in his own heart. It was the poison in his spirit that had defeated him, but it was only the defeat of one night. That twisted spirit person, that one whose strange eyes saw only darkness, would strike again. Only death would stop him from striking again out of that darkness.

42 ▣ THE TOP OF THE MOUNTAIN

He stood, waiting for the dawn. His hands held out, his chin lifted up, he felt the warmth of the new day entering him and giving him the strength he would need for this long day. Raccoon stood beside his uncle, copying his every motion. Together, along with the birds, they gave thanks. They sang the welcoming song to the giver of all life as the Day Traveler showed his generous face.

Agwedjiman and Danowa sat on their haunches to either side of their human friends. Like Young Hunter, Agwedjiman had his head lifted toward the first light. Danowa kept looking over nervously at the large bag that rested at Young Hunter's feet. His nose told him what was inside. If his master carried it, he would accept it as necessary, but he would not trust it.

Now the Day Traveler was fully arisen. Young Hunter turned to Raccoon. He looked up the trail and then back at his nephew. Raccoon nodded. Young Hunter picked up the bag and slung it over his shoulder. He lifted his hand. Agwedjiman trotted up the trail ahead of them while Danowa hung behind. The two dogs would make certain that no danger came upon them without warning. His spear in one hand and his throwing stick in the other, Young Hunter started up the hill with Raccoon two steps behind him.

As they climbed, there was no sign of uncertainty on Young Hunter's face, but his thoughts were a different story. He did not remember sleeping during the night. And if he had slept, it was a sleep in which he dreamed that he was still listening and waiting. If he had slept, that sleep ended with the terrible cry that echoed through the night. He saw, in the eye of his mind, the things that might have happened on the hill above them. He could sense that the danger that had been there was no longer there—though it was not gone from the Dawn Land. The one with the twisted mind had not been finally defeated, only driven back for a time. He could sense, too, that the old man who had fought that battle alone was alive, though hurt. The smoke that rose from the fire on the hill high above them was a sign that he still lived. Not knowing what it was that he had to do when he got there, Young Hunter knew that he had to go to that fire.

As they walked, he watched himself walking. His spirit wanted to pull free and fly ahead, but Young Hunter held back from that flight. Part of it was because of his feeling of uncertainty about what he would find. Carries Snakes was a strange man, but he was an elder with a good heart. Though they had only met the day before, things of great power had passed between them and the old man felt like a grandfather, not a stranger. Young Hunter was afraid for him. He would climb the hill step by step. It would give him time to think about what he could do.

But when they reached the great coiled boulder, no certainty had come to him. Young Hunter took a deep breath to calm the beating of his heart. Then he began to look. He saw with his eyes and felt with his inner sight the things that had happened here. The tracks of the great bear led to the great stone. There was the place where it gathered itself and jumped up, its claws pressed deep into the earth and stones thrown back from its leap. He saw the marks scratched onto the side of the boulder by its claws.

Something round lay on the ground. He knelt to look closely at the broken stone the size of a man's head. It was scored by tooth marks and patterned with blood. Something as white as snow glittered among the dark stones. Young Hunter picked it up. It was a broken tooth, its hollow center still bloody. It was the tooth of a bear, one of the smaller teeth between the two great fangs. Yet even broken in half it was more than twice the size of any such tooth he had seen before. That tooth, the tracks, the way it reached the top of the tall boulder in a single leap, told him how huge the great bear must be.

Still moving slowly, his hands touching the ground, he found the tracks of the man next. Their size and depth in the soft earth told him that this man—the deep-seeing one whose mind was twisted—must be almost as large as Carries Snakes. He saw how the tracks also led to the great boulder, found where the man had fallen from it hard onto the ground at its base. The running tracks of that man joined those of the bear and led down the other side of the hill away from them, down that hill in the direction of the Waters Between. From the scattered stones and broken branches, their flight had been a headlong one.

Young Hunter motioned to Raccoon to wait. Smoke was still rising from the top of the stone. Stepping carefully so that he would not surprise any of the close-to-the-ground ones, the snakes who were the friends of the old deep-seer, Young Hunter climbed to the top of the boulder. It was empty of life. Though the warm touch of the sun was spread across its flat top, not even a single snake was there. Only the fire still burned, the smoke that rose from it a strange color.

But though no one was there, there were signs. Blood, too much blood, had been spilled in the place where Carries Snakes always sat. The bloody imprint of a hand was there on the surface of the boulder where Carries Snakes had placed it to push himself back up to his feet. The dark red splotches of dried blood led off the back of the boulder to the trail that climbed further up toward the very top of the mountain.

Young Hunter looked up the trail. A large birch tree leaned over it. There was another bloody handprint on the white skin of the tree. The old man had gone that way. Young Hunter walked back to the edge of the boulder and looked down.

"Nephew, I must ask you again to wait for me. Danowa will stay with you."

Raccoon nodded. He would do as his uncle asked him. He walked back to another birch tree, sat down beside it, and leaned his back against it, his spear across his lap. He would watch and be ready.

Agwedjiman stayed close by Young Hunter's side as they climbed the trail together. The trail wound in and out among the trees, dipping and then climbing again. It was not an easy climb. Aside from the frequent patches of blood, there was no sign yet of Carries Snakes. Young Hunter wondered how a man who was so badly wounded could continue on this way. Now the trees were growing smaller as they climbed higher. The wind that blew over the highest mountains of the Dawn Land was so strong that only those who were humble could remain up there for long.

They reached a small crest and Young Hunter could see the top of the mountain ahead of them now. A fire had washed across the peak long ago and the stones were bare of trees and bushes. A figure, made small by distance, was slowly, slowly climbing up that final slope. It was Carries Snakes.

Young Hunter shifted the weight of the bag to his other shoulder. He placed his hand on Agwedjiman's shoulder. The big dog understood. He sat down to wait. Young Hunter would continue on this final part of the trail without him.

By the time Young Hunter reached the place where he had seen Carries Snakes, the old man was out of sight. The trail led up so straight that it seemed as if there was no trail at all. But the old man had gone that way. Using his hands as much as he used his feet, Young Hunter climbed up to the very top of the mountain. As he pulled himself up over the edge of the final ledge, he saw Carries Snakes at last. On top of that mountain was a boulder that was a smaller twin of the one on the hill now far below. Four bloody hand prints were marked on that boulder, showing the way Carries Snakes had climbed to its top. The tall old man sat on that boulder in his familiar cross-legged pose, although his body was slumped forward. One hand was pressed to the wound, which no longer bled. His eyes were closed and his chin rested on his chest. It seemed as if his spirit had already left his body.

Young Hunter climbed to the top of the boulder. He sat down in front of the old man, a hand's distance away from him. It did not seem that Carries Snakes was breathing. A whirlwind came across the mountain top, stirring the dust to turn itself red and sparkling in the sunlight. The wind came and swirled about them, spinning and spinning, coiling the air around them, brushing the face of the old man. It seemed as if the whirlwind embraced him and then vanished within him. Carries Snakes opened his eyes and, with what seemed to be as great an effort as it would take to lift the boulder on which they sat, raised his head.

"Grandsssson," he whispered through dry lips. "You are here."

Young Hunter's eyes filled with tears. To be called grandson at that moment was almost more than he could bear. He swallowed hard and found his voice.

"Unh-hunh, Grandfather."

The bag that hung across his chest rippled. The head of the long black snake came out. Its eyes were on the old man's face. The snake leaned out further until its head was almost against the lips of Carries Snakes. The long, delicate tongue flickered out, caressing the deep-seeing man's cheeks.

"Ktssssi nidoba," Carries Snakes whispered. "My great friend."

The black snake drew itself further out of the bag. It slid over one of the tall old man's shoulders and then around the other until it was looped around his neck. Then Black Friend continued on, back around the neck of Young Hunter. Now the two men were linked together by the long body of the close-to-the-ground one, a living circle joining their lives.

"Grandsssson," Carries Snakes whispered.

Young Hunter leaned closer. He understood that the old man had only a handful of words remaining before his breath went back into the wind forever.

"Twisssted one. Hissss name Watchessss Darknesss."

Young Hunter nodded. To know the name of one who sought to harm you would give you strength.

Carries Snakes moved his eyes. Young Hunter looked toward the direction they indicated. He saw the glitter of the Waters Between.

"There, grandfather?" Young Hunter said. "I must fight the one whose mind is twisted there?"

"Yesssss." The voice in which Carries Snakes spoke was as small as the little breeze that barely trembles the leaves. His eyes began to close, but he forced them to open. He looked at Black Friend, whose head was close to his, and then away from the Waters Between toward a smaller lake beyond the next range of hills in the direction of the dawn. An island, which seemed no larger than a pebble from so far away, could be seen in the center of that lake.

"Menahanskoksssss," Carries Snakes whispered. "Hisssss home."

Young Hunter nodded. He knew now the home place of Black Friend, the companion of Carries Snakes.

Carries Snakes looked up and smiled. "Sssspemkik. Sssssskyyy laaand," he whispered. This time, his eyes did not close. They remained open toward the great road that goes into the stars.

His whispered words trailed away as the small whirlwind circled them again, danced toward the edge of the mountain, and then was gone.

Black Friend uncoiled from around their necks and drew back into the bag that hung over Young Hunter's shoulders.

"Wlipamkaani. Travel well, grandfather," Young Hunter whispered.

He floated over the hills, feeling the currents of air beneath him, rippling the feathers in his long dark wings. Another of his kind called to him from a stand of aspen trees below, the leaves of the trees shimmering like ripples in the water. He did not answer. The Day Traveler was beginning to tire and was taking his final steps toward his resting place beyond the farthest mountains. Talk Talk had a destination to reach and his beak was full of fresh deer meat that he had stripped from the kill made by the wolves.

He passed over the bare peak of a mountain. There, on top of a great boulder, was a pile of stones that had not been there the day before. He circled once around that pile of stones shaped like a seated man. There was nothing there that held breath. Talk Talk set his wings to glide downslope toward the lower hills that ran between the mountains and the wide blue of the Waters Between.

Willow Woman and Pabesis had been standing for some time, watching the trail that led down into the village. The looks on their faces were so much the same—like children who have been told that they will soon go berry picking—that Rabbit Stick found it hard not to laugh.

"Granddaughter," he said, "if both of you feel them coming, then they will surely soon be here. Go on and meet them."

Willow Woman and the big young dog both turned to look at Rabbit Stick, who was busy at work, sharpening pieces of bone and tying them together with sinew. Again, the looks on their faces were so much alike that it amused Rabbit Stick deeply. This time he could not keep from laughing.

"Go," he said.

Willow Woman and Pabesis had begun to run even before he spoke that word. The shadows were growing long on the trail, but their eyes were keen and they knew the way. Willow Woman carried her spear with her, its point forward, held on the side away from the dog who ran with her. Like many of the other women of her age, she was a good hunter. She knew how to use her weapon and how to care for it. She had made this spear herself, smoothing its shaft so that its balance was good in her hands, flaking the flint spearpoint and keeping it sharp.

They crossed the path that led to the spring and went around the hillside, their swift feet striking the earth softly. They made little noise as they ran together. It would still be several moons before the little one within her would be so large that Willow Woman could no longer run. As it was now, she felt as if her daughter yet unborn gave her more strength and she ran with a full heart, thinking of Young Hunter's face.

It was almost completely dark now, that time between day and night when shadow and light have blended together, when some begin to sleep and others begin to wake. The light of the Night Traveler would shine over the mountains soon, thinning the darkness. In only a few nights, that light from the Sky Grandmother's face would be at its brightest. But now, in that time between worlds, it only became darker with each stride they took along a trail becoming less familiar.

They ran further and further along the trail that led toward the sunset. The red light was gone now from the sky. It was taking longer than Willow Woman had thought it would take to meet her husband. She slowed to a jog. Had she really felt his presence coming toward them? A shadow of uncertainty tugged at her mind. Perhaps she should turn back? She hesitated and then shrugged. They would go a bit further. Before long they would come to a high place and be able to see for a long look down the trail. She could call from that spot and wait for a response. If there was no reply, then she would turn back to the village.

Willow Woman and Pabesis splashed together across the shallow place in the wide creek. Then, as they climbed the hill on the other side of the stream, they heard a sound.

Pabesis and Willow Woman both stopped. The sound had not been loud. It had been as subtle as the scrape of a claw against a stone. But they had heard it in the same way. It was a sound that meant danger. It was the sound of something or someone hunting. As clearly as the deer knows that the wolf is after it, Willow Woman understood. The voice inside spoke clearly to her. She was the prey.

But when the deer scents the wolf, the deer runs in panic—not knowing that another wolf lies in wait on the trail ahead. Willow Woman would not run. She would remain calm. She placed one hand on the big young dog's back. She could feel the rumbling growl deep in his throat. He was ready to protect them. If there was only one who sought to hunt them, perhaps that one would not attack. But if there were two who hunted them, that would be different. They needed to leave the open trail.

Willow Woman looked around her. Even in the deepening darkness, she recognized the part of the trail they were on. She and Young Hunter had played together in this same area when they were children. They still came here often to swim in the stream. Just over that next hill was a great hollow tree. Perhaps she should take shelter in there. But the great hollow tree was dead and dry. When a hunter chased its prey into the hollow of a fallen log or a dead tree, there was an easy way to drive it out. She saw in the eye of her mind the fire that could circle that tree, the smoke that would fill it, choking whoever took shelter within it, forcing them out. That place would not do. There was a cave among the rocks back down the trail. But that cave was shallow and its mouth wide, too wide to easily defend. She could seek shelter up among the branches of one of the great pines. But it would leave Pabesis behind her on the ground. She knew that the big young dog would not desert her, but would wait to face whatever followed their scent to that tree.

It had taken her no more than a handful of heartbeats to consider each of those possibilities. None of them would work. Whatever hunted them, she was certain that it would be able to follow their trail. But if the ones who hunted them could find no scent, it might be different. She placed her hand on the nape of the big young dog's neck, took a handful of skin and fur and pulled him back with her. His legs were stiff, braced and ready to attack. But she would not let him charge forward into the darkness.

"Follow me," she whispered into his ear. She turned and ran back to the stream, Pabesis by her side. When she was halfway across, she turned and waded from the sand into the deeper water. It was soon up above her waist and Pabesis swam beside her as she pushed upstream, ducking her head under the overhanging branches. They rounded a corner and came to the place where the stream cut down between the stones, forming a small gorge. The air was filled with a soft roar. A series of waterfalls came rushing down there. It was so dark now that she could not see them, but she could hear them. She knew this place so well. The water at the bottom of the creek was cold, but the water on the surface was still warm from the light of the Day Walker.

Now she found herself swimming, the big young dog's head close to hers. The waterfall that she sought was the second one. Her hands found the stone step of the waterfall and she pulled herself up like an otter in one quick, lithe motion, throwing her spear ahead of her through the waterfall that was striking her face. She turned, reached back, and grabbed Pabesis by the shoulders. His hind feet scrabbled at the slippery stones, and then he was up and vanished through the falls. Willow Woman followed.

The hiding place behind the falls was not large, the roof only high enough for a person to crouch or lie down. But it was dry inside and deep enough for two people to stretch out as it widened back from its mouth, which was just wide enough for a person who was not large to squeeze through and enter the cave. There was plenty of room for Willow Woman and Pabesis.

Young Hunter could no longer fit into that cave. His shoulders had become too broad. Willow Woman had teased him about it when they swam there before.

"I have decided to become an Otter Woman," she had shouted to him above the roar of the falls as he tried to reach inside the cave to pull her out. "This is a fine place in here. I am sorry that you cannot live in here with me. You must find another wife."

Willow Woman faced the mouth of the cave. She leaned against the big young dog. His warm wet fur felt comforting to her. It was growing lighter outside as the Night Traveler lifted into the sky. She could see the gleam of the rushing stream falling down like a shimmering doorflap made not of deerskin but of living water. If anything came close, climbed up onto the step of the waterfall, she would see its shadow through the water. Her spear held tightly in her hand, Willow Woman waited.

"More trails than one . . ." Evening Sky said.

"End in the same place," said Morning Sky.

Red Hawk and Blue Hawk said nothing. It was now the third dawn since the four had been traveling together. Although they had tried to protest, Evening Sky and Morning Sky had not turned back once they had guided the two brothers through the cedar swamp—on a trail they had not followed going into its depths. Instead, they had made it clear that their next destination was the same as that of Red Hawk and Blue Hawk. Since the brothers had themselves been uncertain of where they were to go next, it had been doubly confusing.

"Our father has seen," Evening Sky said in her calm voice, a voice that made Red Hawk think of the breeze that crosses calm water just as the first stars can be seen. It was strange how a woman who was so annoying could make him think of such pleasant things.

"The place of red rocks," Morning Sky said. For some reason, her voice made Blue Hawk think of the way it felt when the first light of a new day came through the open door of a lodge. It was very confusing to him.

Although it had grown dark as they walked, the night had felt warm and safe to them and the brothers found themselves trusting the judgment of the two tall sisters. It was not uncommon for the oldest children of deep-seers to have those gifts of far vision themselves. Evening Sky and Morning Sky moved with the kind of confidence held only by people who trusted their own strength and saw their way with clarity. It was enjoyable to be with them, even if they did a bit too much teasing. They told funny stories as they walked about things that had happened in their village. More than once, the brothers had to pause because they were laughing so hard.

If these two young women were only men, Red Hawk found himself thinking, we would be great friends. He looked at Evening Sky. But is it just as well that she is not a man, he thought, before quickly looking away as her eyes began to turn toward his. Just as well.

The Red Stone Village was further along the lake, where the stream flowed in. They had been following the stream for some time now on an old, well-worn trail. Evening Sky was leading them, as she had been since the first onset of darkness. It had been her intention that they reach the village before the dark, but they had stopped so many times. It had been easy to stop, there were so many good excuses to pause—not just to laugh over funny things that the sisters had said—and there had been many of those. There had also been the marshy place where they stopped to pull cat-tails and eat the delicate, crunchy lower stalks. In another spot there were coiled ferns that were sweet to the taste. For some reason, all four of the young people were very hungry as they traveled together.

The trail by the stream led straight to the Waters Between. It would soon be in sight. Evening Sky paused and held up a hand.

"Why do we . . ." Red Hawk said.

"Stop now?" Blue Hawk continued.

They were not that far now from the village and the trail along the edge of the moonlit lake was the most direct one. The night was calm and quiet, the only sound the soft flow of the stream, which had grown very wide and deep here as it drew close to the lake.

Evening Sky leaned close so that Red Hawk could see her and placed the back of her hand against her lips. Next to him, Morning Sky was doing the same with Blue Hawk. They must be silent.

Red Hawk lifted his head, closed his eyes, and breathed in deeply. There was a faint scent on the air that he had never smelled before. It was down the trail from them around the bend where the stream made a wide curve and then entered the Waters Between. Evening Sky's hands pulled down on his shoulders. He opened his eyes as he crouched down beside her. She held her own hands out and felt the trail in front of them. Red Hawk understood. It was strange how smooth and deep the trail was here. She pointed ahead of them with her lips and shook her head. Then, moving with little sound and as slowly as a stalking heron, she left the trail. One behind the other, Red Hawk, Morning Sky, and Blue Hawk followed. The ground began to rise and they went on all fours, carefully pressing their hands and feet down as they went so that no leaves rustled, no sticks snapped.

The Night Traveler had shown her face now, a face still partially obscured. There was more light for them to see, but even had there been no light at all, they would have been able to find their way as they moved with deliberate care. Now they were out of the small shrubs and bushes that lined the river bank and among the taller trees. The earth beneath them was soft and springy now with pine needles. On a hilltop just above them was a great pine tree. It was the tallest of all the trees here, so large around that six men with their arms outstretched could not have joined hands around it.

Evening Sky did not stop when she reached the tree. She began to climb. As before, Red Hawk, Morning Sky, and Blue Hawk followed. The first thick stubs of broken branches were just above their heads and they were able to leap up and grab those stubs to pull themselves into the tree. From then on it was easy. There were so many branches worn smooth from the touch of hands and feet that it was clear many people had climbed this tree before them. It was another trail. As they climbed higher they could see the land around them in the moonlight. Although the green of the living boughs began to cut off their vision as they climbed higher, there were spaces where the great winds had broken off the end of branches and they could see more and more of the Waters Between through them as they went higher.

At last they reached a high place where they could see both the trail they had been following and the wide lake beyond it. The wide branches, which were as big around as a man's waist, were twined together here in a way that made a sort of nest. The four of them could sit comfortably there, as high above the land as eagles.

It was a good place to be, Red Hawk thought. And as he thought that, he wondered why his heart had been pounding so hard at that faint scent that he could no longer smell and why he felt so certain now that had they rounded that bend in the trail, something terrible would have happened. He had felt as if the air had grown thick and hard to breathe. It was like the feeling in his chest the day when he and his brother had waited by the Long River, knowing that the monster the people called the Walking Hill was close by, watching them from the forest, ready to crush them beneath its huge feet.

"Look down," Evening Sky said.

"At the trail we would have followed," said Morning Sky.

The four of them looked. The trail was easy to see, for it followed the wide stream almost to the edge of the Waters Between. Either side of the trail was clear of trees and there were no large stones to obscure their view of it. The great red rocks that gave this part of the shore its name did not begin to appear until further up the lake. When the melting of the snow and the rains of early spring filled that river, it came roaring down into the Waters Between, rising high and washing away everything close to its banks. It look peaceful. Yet Red Hawk knew that there was something wrong. But what could it be?

They sat for a long time, watching. Nothing moved upon the trail or along it. That, in itself, was strange. It was a trail that had shown the tracks of many deer cut into the soft earth only a bit further up the stream. Deer always followed the same trails. They did so with such regularity that you could hide and wait, knowing you would see the same deer pass back and forth along that trail several times before the end of the day. But no deer, no animals of any kind, walked along this part of the trail where the river deepened and emptied into the lake.

What would stop them? Red Hawk thought. There was nothing that he could see. It would be easy enough for a deer to leap over that long, smooth log which had clearly been washed across the trail by the flood waters. Red Hawk looked again at that log. It was completely free of any branches, so smooth that it glistened where the light from the Night Traveler's face touched it. It lay partly in the water and partly across the trail, widening as it came to the place where it disappeared in the deep flow.

He touched his brother's shoulder.

"Do you see . . ." he said.

"That strange log?" Red Hawk answered.

"I see . . ." Evening Sky said.

". . . that it is moving," said Morning Sky.

It was so, the log was sliding into the deep water of the river. As it slid in, just before it disappeared, the end of that log swung from side to side like the tail of a giant snake.

"We will spend the night here."

Red Hawk looked at Blue Hawk. Evening Star looked at Morning Star. Then they all laughed, for all four of them had spoken those words at the same time.

The thoughts that filled his head troubled him. They were as insistent as the continued beating of his heart as he ran, the two dogs keeping pace with him. As they came closer to the village, his head filled with so many images that it seemed as if it would burst. So he ran faster.

Raccoon had stayed behind. The first day of travel from the Village of Many Pines had not been hard and the boy had kept up easily with his uncle. But on the first night after the death of Carries Snakes, after Young Hunter had built the cairn of stones around the still-seated body of the tall old deep-seer, the dreams had begun. After that long night of dreams, Young Hunter knew that he would have to travel as quickly as he could.

"My nephew," he said, "we have almost come to the fishing camps on The Lake Shaped like a Spearhead. I would like you to stay there. Your other cousins will be there. My dreams have told me that I must hurry."

"I hear you, Uncle. I will do as you say," Raccoon said. He would have liked to continue on with him, but he knew that he would not be able to keep up. There were others who could run faster than Young Hunter for short distances, but no one else could run as fast for as long. In a few winters, when his own legs were longer, Raccoon would be a great runner. But those winters had not yet passed.

"Nephew," Young Hunter said, seeing the disappointment in the boy's face and, once again, seeing the boy that he had been a handful of winters gone, "you have been a good traveling companion. You have not been like Skunk."

Young Hunter did not approach the village from the usual way. Instead, he circled. Those images in his mind had troubled him in ways that he could not understand. And because he could not understand them, he understood that—as urgent that it was that he reach his home quickly—he must also be careful.

He had been running, almost without stop, for all of the day before and most of the past night. He had stopped to drink water, to eat food, to relieve himself. Each time he stopped, one or the other of the two dogs had gone ahead, scouting further down the trail. More than once Danowa or Agwedjiman had come back, barked, and then led them off in another direction, down a different fork in a trail, over a hill rather than through a valley. Running, always running, with the tireless loping stride of a wolf.

Young Hunter no longer noticed the weight of the bag over his shoulder. Sometimes, when they stopped, Black Friend would slip his head out of the bag and look about, then draw back in. Once, when Young Hunter knelt by a stream, the long black snake slid from the bag into the water. It seemed to become a part of the water, a long dark ripple. It swam around a bend in the stream and was gone for only the space of a dozen breaths. When it returned, the hind legs of a frog were disappearing into its mouth. It finished swallowing and then flowed up Young Hunter's outstretched arms and back into the basswood bag.

The Day Walker was disappearing beyond the hills and Young Hunter was now within sight of the village. He stopped beside the tall cedar tree where he and Bear Talker often sat. He crouched down to listen, the two dogs close beside him. As he opened the circle of the wind, he heard more and more. First he heard those things close, the sounds of the night singers, the little many-legged ones in the trees and grasses. Then he began to hear the sounds of the village. The crack of the wood in the few fires that burned— only for cooking, for the night was as warm as the breath of a child. Most of the people of his village were here. Those who had not gone to the fishing camps on the smaller lakes were close to their lodges at the end of this long day. Some were already asleep. He hear the murmur of voices, the sound of a few children still playing. Things were as they should be when he listened with his ears.

He began to listen with the ears inside. Again, he widened the circle around him as he listened. He could sense the beating of many hearts, the rhythm of thoughts. He heard in that inside ear the things one hears when one is around many people. He heard contentment and uncertainty, like twin waves washing across the spirit. He heard happiness in the heart and anger, small angers that twisted inside but could still be washed away as easily as mud washes away from your hands when you thrust them into a clear flowing stream. There was nothing deeply wrong here, only the lives of people living as human beings were told to live by The Talker. Never perfect, often failing, but always growing, always part of something larger than themselves, their varied heartbeats meshing together to make the one great, healthy heartbeat that was the Only People.

Young Hunter opened his hearing further, listening beyond the village. He looked in the direction of the trail he would normally have taken to return from the direction of the Waters Between. Someone was on that trail, moving away from the village. That worried Young Hunter. Traveling in the dark was usually not a dangerous thing to do this close to their village. But this was not a normal night. Who was it who was moving away from the safety of the people along that trail?

But as Young Hunter tried to listen more closely, to sense who it was, he heard something else. It struck his inner hearing in the same way that the bad smell of rotten flesh might fill a hunter's nose. Young Hunter shook his head and growled. It was not far away, but it was beyond the other side of the village, moving next to the trail that he would normally have followed. It was a presence connected to the dream that had stayed with him as he ran. That dream was not a dream sent by a friend. It was a dream filled with hunger and self-hatred, with pain and with loathing for the light. The death of all those who walked would not be enough to satisfy the hunger of the one who sent that dream to him.

Young Hunter had learned from Medicine Plant how to deal with unfriendly dreams, how to close his mind against them. Yet he did not do so with this dream, for it showed him how that one saw. By holding it he was able to keep a connection with the one who had sent it. By holding that dream in all its twisting anger and pain, he could tell where its sender was going. That, of course, was part of the reason the dream had been sent to him. That dream had been meant as a trap to bring him running headlong into danger.

In that dream he saw through the eyes of the one who sees darkness and turns from the light. He saw, and when he first saw this it shocked him deeply, an elderly man walking back toward his lodge. Before he went in, that old man turned and his face could be seen. It was Rabbit Stick. He looked around once. Young Hunter knew his grandfather's face well. While another might have seen no concern there, Young Hunter knew from the look in the old man's eyes that Rabbit Stick sensed he was being scrutinized by an unseen watcher. Then Rabbit Stick vanished into their lodge and the memory vision of the deep-seer's twisted mind showed him others. His grandmother, Sweetgrass Woman, going to get water just after dusk. His wife, Willow Woman, coming out to look up and smile at the little far-above ones gathered around their countless campfires in the warm night sky.

What troubled Young Hunter was not just that the dream sent to him, sent as bait, showed him clearly how close the twisted mind deep-seer had come to those he love most. What also troubled him was that he felt how that dark-minded one saw the Only People. He saw them as a starving bobcat sees fat rabbits.

As Young Hunter ran, he had tried to keep his mind clear of his own thoughts. That way the dark-minded one might not sense him as he grew close. Though the dream was there, beneath the surface like something dead floating just under the current of a clear stream, it was not his dream. It belonged to the one with the twisted mind. As Young Hunter ran, he ran with the thoughts of all that lived and moved around him. He ran with the wind in the grass, with the swaying boughs of the pines, with the wings of the small birds flickering through the air, with the feet of his two dogs who were close by him with every stride, he ran with the flow of the waters in the streams. He ran with the earth, running, running from the center of his heart.

Now, as he looked down on the village, he saw Bear Talker's lodge before him. Placing his hand against the tree, Young Hunter called to him with a whistle that he knew his teacher would recognize.

Before the third note of that whistle was done, Bear Talker stepped out from behind the cedar tree. The two dogs wagged their tails and pressed their noses against his outstretched hands.

"You did well," Bear Talker said, his voice a soft growl. "The one who hunts us is close."

"Little one," the voice said, "I am hungry. Come to me."

Pabesis growled and tried to push past her. He, too, heard that voice, even though it had not been carried by the air but seemed to come from a place which was behind them, around them, and within them all at once.

Willow Woman pushed hard against him with both hands. And, though he was bigger and heavier than her, Pabesis sat back down and did not thrust himself out the mouth of the cave and through the shimmering blanket of water just beyond it. He whined once. Willow Woman placed her hand on his head and leaned close to his ear.

"Be quiet," she whispered. "Quiet."

Pabesis sat back on his haunches, his head brushing the top of the low roof of the cave. A low, almost noiseless growl continued from deep in his throat, but he did not whine again.

"Little one, little one. I am hungry."

The voice that was not a voice had been calling them. It had called again and again. Each time it called, it seemed to be closer. And even though Willow Woman knew that answering that voice would be a foolish thing to do, it had been hard to remain silent and to stay hidden. That voice was not the voice of a friend. It mocked her even as it called to her. It was a voice chilled by hunger.

"Little one, I am hungry. Come to me. Come to me."

That voice was like the fright-call of the great horned owl, the best of the night hunters. Great horned owl's voice was a voice that seemed to come from the land of the chibaiak, the ghosts. When great horned owl was hunting, he would sit silent on a branch and wait. Then he would cry out his hunting song. That song was so powerful, so frightening in its certainty of death, that the small animals horned owl hunted would be unable to remain still. They would try to run away from that voice, leave their places of concealment. Horned owl would hear them, spread his wide wings, and swoop down in a flight as swift and noiseless as the strike that would take the small one that horned owl's hunting song had called out to be killed.

I will not run like a foolish mouse into the dark, Willow Woman said to herself. I am safe in this cave beneath the waterfall.

"Little one," the owl voice called, "you are a mouse. Come out to me."

Willow Woman felt her blood run cold within her and a chill went down her body as if a pine branch had dropped an armful of snow on her. The one who owned that voice had heard her thought. And that voice was closer, so much closer.

Willow Woman looked at the blanket of water. She did not move her body, but she placed her thoughts in that water, letting them flow into it. Water flowing, water flowing. The sound of the waterfall, a breathless endless song.

"Little mouse, I am hungry. Come to me."

Even if the one who hunted her found the waterfall, he would still have to find this cave. Water flowing, water flowing. The waterfall a long breathless song.

"Little mouse, little mouse. I am hungry, I am hungry. Come to me. Come to me. Come to me."

And this cave at the base of the longest waterfall is not easy to find.

Willow Woman shook her head. That owl voice was calling to her thoughts, calling her out of the flow of water, finding her place of hiding by seeing through her eyes. But it would not call her out. She braced herself against the wall of the cave, one knee on the stone floor, her spear held in two hands. The growl from the throat of Pabesis became deeper and louder, echoing off the sides of the small cave.

"Nda," Willow Woman said between her teeth. "You come to me!"

Bear Talker dropped a stick into the fire. Sparks rose up and flew high above their heads, seeming to join the campfires of the little far-above ones. He looked up toward the road of stars. "I did not think," he said, "that his feet would walk the sky road before mine, the one who has gone before us."

Young Hunter nodded. He had said nothing about the death of Carries Snakes, but Bear Talker knew. He knew even before he saw that Young Hunter carried the bag that held the long-bodied friend of the tall old deep-seer. Like Bear Talker, he would not speak the name of Carries Snakes aloud. He was on his long walk along the trail that crosses the sky land. To speak his name might cause him to look back and lose his way. Only after the moon of falling leaves had passed would they be able to talk of him by name. Until then, he was the one who had gone before. Perhaps that part of his spirit that could join again with breath would return to their village this time and they would see him once more in the eyes of a newborn child. Or perhaps so many winters would pass that only their children's children would be given the gift of that wisdom the old deep-seer's spirit would bring to another life.

"Is my wife still with my grandparents? Or has she gone to stay in the wigwam of her mother and father?" Young Hunter asked.

Although it was often the custom that a young man would live with the family of his wife and help hunt for them, Willow Woman's father Deer Tracker was still once of the best hunters in their village. It had been decided, without the need of any discussion, that the young couple would make their home with the Young Hunter's grandparents. But sometimes, when Young Hunter was away, Willow Woman would take her deerskin blanket back to the lodge of her first family and spend the night with them, staying awake late into the night talking softly with her mother about all those small, important things that mothers and daughters need to share.

"She is with your grandparents," Bear Talker said. "She and your grandmother," Bear Talker shook his head and growled as he always did when mentioning Sweetgrass Woman, "have been making something. Something that you will need."

Bear Talker walked with Young Hunter and his dogs down along the small winding trail that widened as it came into the heart of the little village. Rabbit Stick was standing in front of the two, joined together wigwams that made up their home. He looked surprised when he saw them.

"Grandson," he started to say, about to ask why he had come from the side of the village away from the trail which led toward the Waters Between.

The look that passed between the three men made further words unneeded. Young Hunter understood who he had seen on that night trail, moving away from the safety of the village. Bear Talker knew where the one who hunted them was waiting. Rabbit Stick looked toward the trail that Willow Woman had taken, thinking that she would meet her husband on his way home. He knew that he could not have stopped her, but his throat felt as if it held a great stone. He coughed once, trying to dislodge that stone, then he spoke in a choked voice.

"Just at dusk. Pabesis was with her."

Young Hunter felt as if he was about to fall down. The world was spinning around him. He made the small movement one makes when he is about to run. Bear Talker grabbed his arm with a grip so strong that it surprised the younger man. He shook Young Hunter so hard that the dizziness went away.

"Nda," Bear Talker growled. "We follow the night trail together."

Rabbit Stick reached down and picked something up. Young

Hunter wiped his eyes and his vision became clearer as his grandfather shoved something at each of them.

"We will use these," Rabbit Stick said. "Fishing torches."

Young Hunter thrust the end of his torch into the fire that burned in front of their wigwam. The dry birch bark that had been wrapped tightly in the fork at the end of the torch burned brightly. Such torches were made to burn for a long time. When one fished with a spear at night, the light from a torch held out over the water would draw the fish to the surface where the sharp double points of the spear could reach them.

Young Hunter held the blazing torch above his head and to the side. Now they would see into the darkness. They would also see each other and stay together as they ran. The one who hunted them knew they were coming. But Young Hunter remembered the name that Carries Snakes had given him.

"The one who has gone before us gave me the name of the one who hunts us," Young Hunter said, "His name is Watches Darkness."

"Good," Bear Talker growled. "One who sees only darkness is afraid of the light."

With Young Hunter in the lead, the three men and the two dogs set out on the night trail.

He stood at the edge of the water. Leaning on his spear, he looked into the water. Even though it was night, he could see that it was deep. He had no liking for deep water. But the one he hunted was there, there in the throbbing heart of the water. He looked again at the waterfall, which shimmered the light from the Night Traveler's face. The water itself seemed filled with pale fire. He took a deep breath, drawing the air of the night into his mouth as if it was dark smoke. Then he breathed out slowly, sending his words with his breath. Making them powerful with his breath.

"Where are you? I know you are there. Little mouse, where are you? I hear you answering me. You are there! Yes, yes! Come to me now. Come to me. Yes, yes."

There was no answer. No words spoken in return. The one he called would not be drawn out to him. Stronger than he had expected. These were stubborn people.

It was not easy to see through the water, to hear through the walls of falling water as they crashed down without stopping. But the one he hunted was there and could run no further. Even if she would not come to him, she was trapped.

The One Who Walks Like a Man rocked back and forth, his front feet already in the water. He moaned and growled. He was hungry and he still felt the pain of his broken teeth. The great pale bear would surely kill anything it caught, its hunger and its pain mingling to make it even more deadly.

Watches Darkness nodded. He had thought to take her alive, to keep her alive for a while to play with her, play as a long-tail plays with a rabbit before crushing its spine with one bite. He had thought to use her as bait, to draw out the young deep-seer into a trap. The young are strong and brave but they are also foolish. It would not have been hard to do.

But he did not like deep water. It would be wet and cold. He had been wet and cold too often as a small child when his grandmother threw him out of their wigwam and made him sleep without shelter. He would not go into deep water to get her. Yes, yes. He would let his hungry companion do as he wanted to do.

He lifted the spear and prodded the side of the great bear. The One Who Walks Like a Man reared up on his hind legs, turned his head and glared at Watches Darkness. The bear's red eyes glittered with anger and hunger as it towered over him, but Watches Darkness did not step back.

"Go," Watches Darkness said, thrusting his spear toward the heart of the waterfall. "Go and pull it out. Food. Eat it."

The huge bear roared, its voice shaking the night air. Then with a speed that it seemed no animal of its size should possess, it whirled and splashed into the stream, thrusting itself against the current toward the waterfall.

Even above the deep shouting voice of the waterfall, Willow Woman heard the roar. It came, she knew without any doubt, from the throat of one of those Ancient Ones whose prey was human beings. Pabesis worked his front feet up and down, the hair on his ruff standing up, his mouth open and his long teeth bared. His growl was almost as loud and deep as the rumble of the falls.

He knows, Willow Girl thought, feeling the big dog beside her in the half darkness as it readied itself. He knows.

No other words shaped themselves in her mind. There was no room for other words. There was only room for a wordless song, one that she had heard Young Hunter sing to ready himself for danger. Young Hunter told her that it had been given to him by a hawk, who sang that song to him one dawn as he sat on a high ridge watching the trail that wound toward the Waters Between. As the hawk lifted up on the wind from the valley far below and hung in front of his face, Young Hunter had greeted the hawk as a brother. Its head cocked, its hunter eyes locked on his, that heavy-winged hawk had whistled four times and sung the song. The hawk sang that song as a gift from one hunter to another.

"It is your song, too," Young Hunter told her. "It was given to our family."

But until now, she had never sung it. Until now, she had not known that she remembered it.

> Keweh-yoh, hey-yo
> Keweh-yoh, hey-yo
> Keweh-yoh, hey-yo
> Keweh-yoh, hey-yo

That song filled her throat and then she was singing it, singing it in a high trilling voice. She felt the song's strength enter her hands and her arms as she held the spear. She felt the hawk's danger song steady her legs as she crouched on one knee staring at the white roaring wall of water washing down just outside the cave mouth two arm lengths in front of them.

Suddenly, that wall of water grew dark as a great shape loomed between it and the light from the Night Traveler's gentle face. Even more suddenly, a head burst through that darkened wall, the spray gushing into the cave as water cascaded off the wide flat skull of the giant bear. Turning its head, it looked into the cave, seeing them there. But the pale head of the bear was too large to fit into the cave. Its mouth open, it roared louder than the waterfall. Its voice reverberated inside the small cave and it seemed to Willow Woman as if her ears would burst. Its breath washed over her with the heat of a great fire. That heavy breath smelled of rotting flesh and death. Yet she did not fall back with fear. Instead, with a clarity of vision that seemed to come from inside her heart, she saw.

Willow Woman saw that its eyes were as red as two glowing campfires. She saw the shape of its long stabbing teeth, each of them as long as her hand. She saw that the smaller teeth between them were broken. She saw deep into the great bear's mouth, a mouth that was open, yet not open wide. She saw that it could not thrust its whole head into the cave, only the front part, for its skull was too massive. She saw its tongue was red as blood. She saw that its hair was the color of snow. She saw that only its nose was dark in color. She saw all those things at once, saw them with the speed of a hummingbird's wings. But, most of all, she saw where to strike. And, as she saw it, she struck. Holding the spear firmly in both hands, leaning into it with her back and shoulders, she stabbed.

The great bear's roar became a deafening bellow, and the spear twisted in her hands. Her feet were braced, but she was thrown to the side of the cave as she held onto that spear. She refused to let go. She would not lose her only weapon, and she pulled back with all her strength, pulling it free. Then, as suddenly as the mouth of the cave had been filled with rage and violence, it was silent. The waterfall flowed as before, luminous and unbroken.

The shaft of the spear had struck her high in the ribs when the huge bear twisted against the spearpoint thrust into its eyesocket. Her side was beginning to ache. Willow Woman removed one hand from her spear and placed it on her stomach. She felt a soft kick from within. Her little one was not harmed. She would not allow her to be harmed. She pulled back the spear and looked at the point. It had been fastened strongly with sinew wrapped many times. It had not pulled free. The sharp stone glistened with a wetness that was not water.

Willow Woman heard a whine at her side. She had forgotten Pabesis, though she remembered now the dark blur of movement and the flash of his fangs beside her as he attacked at the same moment she struck. She turned to look at him. He sat on his haunches. There was a wound in his shoulder, but the blood flowed slowly from it. He lifted up his head toward Willow Woman and whined again, seeking her approval, as he offered her the bloody piece of white-furred skin that his own powerful jaws had torn from the cheek of the great bear.

Willow Woman stroked his head.

"Good dog," she said, "good dog."

Once again, no other words would come into her mind. She knew it was not yet over. She pulled the big young dog away from the cave mouth. He faced the cave mouth and began to make his low, warning growl once more. Willow Woman wiped her palms against the back of her deerskin dress and then gripped her spear tight. She braced herself again, leaning back as far as she could away from the opening where the attack would surely come. She did not know when she had begun to sing it again, but the danger song was coming once more from deep in her throat.

Keweh-yoh, hey-yo
Keweh-yoh, hey-yo
Keweh-yoh, hey-yo
Keweh-yoh, hey-yo

Sweetgrass Woman was ready to run as she ducked through the door of the wigwam. Although almost all of the others in their village had been asleep when the sound cut the air like a spear of lightning splitting the trunk of a huge tree in the village, she had already been long awake.

She had only pretended to sleep when Rabbit Stick had gone outside to watch the trail for the return of their grandson. He had not wanted to wake her with his own restlessness, his eagerness to see their grandson's bright face. He will have a long wait, she thought, a smile on her face. After Willow Woman meets him on the trail, they will not hurry. She understood how it was when a young husband and wife have been separated, even for the space of a few sleeps. She thought of the two of them walking slowly up the trail together with their arms around each other—just as she and Rabbit Stick had walked when they were young. It would not have surprised her if they had not arrived at their wigwam until just before the light of dawn.

She had been surprised, though, when she heard Rabbit Stick's voice and someone else's reply. It was Bear Talker. She knew his voice all too well. Their voices had been soft, spoken so that they would not wake her, but she had already been awake. Although her hearing was keener than most, she could not hear the words, but she heard the tone of their voices. Why was the deep-seeing man at their lodge? Through the open lodge door she saw the flare of torches. Sweetgrass Woman thought of sitting up, of going out to see what was happening. Then she heard feet going quickly away, down the trail. More feet than just the feet of two men. It was strange.

She sat up on one elbow and looked out into the partial darkness beyond the small fire Rabbit Stick had kindled to one side of the door of their lodge. It was a bright night, for the face of the Night Traveler was in the middle of the sky land. On such a night, there should have been little to fear, but a feeling of uncertainty came over her. The night was warm and quiet as a baby's sleep, but something was wrong.

The small voice of the one who lives inside each person began to whisper to her. The one who lives inside has a small voice, but that voice always speaks the truth. The words of that small voice are always simple, always clear. Some do not listen to that voice. Some only listen when they want to listen. Some pretend that there is no one inside them, no voice to heed. But it is always there, waiting to speak, waiting to guide, waiting to be heard. Sweetgrass Woman listened. The whisper slowly began to shape itself into words. Do not sleep, the voice inside said, Do not sleep. Watch and listen. Watch and listen.

Sweetgrass Woman drew herself up into a crouch. She reached her hands out to feel the shafts of the spears that were kept leaning just inside the door of the wigwam. Her fingertips counted them. Only two of them were there. Two were missing. One of them had gone with Young Hunter when he left several dawns before. The other one must have been taken by Rabbit Stick as he left. Crouching by the door, Sweetgrass Woman watched and listened as her small voice had told her to do. Not knowing what it was that she watched and listened for in the silence that surrounded her, she held her breath.

Because she was watching and listening, the roar that came echoing over the hills like a deep-throated rumble of thunder did not startle her as it did the rest of the people in the village. As others in the village sat up wide-eyed or shouted in fright as they were shaken from their sleep, Sweetgrass Woman was already ducking through the door of her wigwam, two spears in her hands. That roar had come from down the trail, somewhere near the stream crossing.

That cry, her heart told her, came from some terrible creature, one of the Ancient Ones that hunted the people. It came from the direction where those she loved most in the world would be. Whatever fear might have been lodged in her heart by such a roar was chased away by her own fierce desire to protect her grandchildren and her husband. Her anger boiled like water in a cooking pot that any being would seek to harm them. She thrust herself through the door of the lodge like a spear aimed at an enemy's heart.

"Sister." The voice that came out of the night was as calm as the surface of a windless lake and just as deep. It stopped Sweetgrass Woman in mid-stride.

Sweetgrass Woman turned. Medicine Plant stood there, holding her little boy in one arm. The old eyes of Looking Backward met those of the woman who had helped bring him into the world. He reached out his arms to her.

Sweetgrass Woman leaned her spears against the side of the lodge and took the small boy into her own arms. He brushed her gray hair back from her eyes and then gently patted her cheek with his hand.

He is calming me, Sweetgrass Woman thought, as if I were the one who was the little child frightened in the dark. And, as she thought it, she felt calm fill her heart like cool water poured into a wooden bowl.

"Sister," Medicine Plant said, "you must stay here. The people have been frightened. Walk among them and ease their fears. Do not let anyone leave the village. Our boy will stay with you."

Medicine Plant began to turn to go down the trail. Sweetgrass Woman held out her hand.

"Protect them," she said.

Medicine Plant nodded. "With my life," she said. Then she turned and began to walk. Her steps seemed slow, yet they took her along the trail more swiftly than the long strides of a running man as she vanished into the night.

"Nda! Nda! Nda!" Watches Darkness struck the butt of his spear against the earth with each of his words. "No! No! No!"

It was not supposed to go this way. No! The one hiding in her little cave under the waterfall was not supposed to fight back. A little mouse was not supposed to have a weapon. Watches Darkness stared across the stream, shaking his head at what he saw. The One Who Walks Like a Man was standing in the midst of the waterfall, roaring and shaking its head. The light was gone from one of the great bear's eyes and it was striking at the water with its paws.

Watches Darkness looked again at the water. The water seemed to look back at him. It asked him to come into it. Come now. Come now. Step in, wade in. Come now. Come now. He leaned forward and then drew back. No! He would not listen to the water. If he ever went into deep water, he would never come out again. He knew this to be so. The water wanted him, but it could not have him. He would not let the water swallow him. He stepped back from the bank of the stream. No! No! He would not do it. He would tell the One Who Walks Like a Man how to do it. The great bear would listen to him.

Hear me, Watches Darkness said, speaking without breath. Hear me now!

The great, pale bear turned toward him, its mouth open. The light from the sky was so bright that Watches Darkness could see the blood that came from the deep gash within one eyesocket and the wound on the cheek of the bear.

A small inside voice spoke to Watches Darkness, a voice that he made even smaller so that it would not touch the edge of the bear's confused thoughts.

That one, the small inside voice said, will be of little use to you now.

Watches Darkness knew that voice was right. Even if his wounds healed, the One Who Walks Like a Man would not trust Watches Darkness after this. Too much pain had come to the great bear as a result of doing his bidding. First its broken teeth, then its eye. Now the bear would be resentful, dangerous, untrustworthy. Hungry. Watches Darkness remembered waking inside the cave of piled stones with the heavy breath of the One Who Walks Like a Man on his face as the huge bear stood over him, mouth open, drooling, its empty belly rumbling. The One Who Walks Like a Man had not been fed well for far too long. It was hungry. Too hungry.

I will have to . . . Watches Darkness did not finish his thought, knowing that the great bear would hear it. Instead he quieted that small voice, closed his eyes, and concentrated. He shut off all other awareness, all hearing, all vision, all other thoughts but one command that the great bear must hear and obey.

Hear me, he said again, his breathless voice as loud and insistent as a hysterical scream. Reach in with your paw and claw her out. Do it. Do it now!

Although they ran swiftly, they made little sound as they followed the trail. The flames of their torches left brief streams of light behind them as they went. A part of Young Hunter that was detached from the body that ran so urgently saw those swirling and leaping shapes of light. They were like the spirit lights that dance around the villages, the ghost lights that can be seen in the marshy places. His grandfather had shown him how those lights were not always spirits. Sometimes that glow came from rotting logs or from those plants that had no green in them and thrust their pale, thin roots into decaying things. But sometimes, sometimes, those lights lifted up from the earth, circled and danced or lifted so high in the air that they joined the spirit trail. Such lights were the signs of a traveling spirit, a deep-seer or another being who could leave the flesh and become one with the light.

Young Hunter urged that detached part of himself to go ahead, to see where Willow Woman was, but it would not obey him. Instead, stubbornly, it watched.

My second self, Young Hunter thought, why are you holding back? But even as he asked himself that question he could not give himself back an answer. Unless the answer was that caution was needed. Even in the midst of their urgency, there was still need for caution.

The trail divided, but there was no question which way to go. The two dogs swung to the side that led to the stream, following Willow Woman's familiar scent. They splashed across the stream, reached the top of the rise, and then stopped, turning back. Their eyes gleamed in the torchlight as they looked back down at Young Hunter, Rabbit Stick, and Bear Talker.

The three men understood. Willow Woman had discovered that something was hunting her. She had turned and headed back at an angle, off the trail, back toward the running stream where the water would be her friend. It was a good way to try to evade a being that is using its nose to follow you. Water cannot hold a scent.

Young Hunter took a few quick strides toward the spot where he was certain she would have entered the stream. He had learned as a child that a good tracker does not always follow every footprint. A good tracker also understands the one being tracked. A good tracker can sense where those prints are leading and go to that place. He held his torch low to the soft earth and gravel at the stream's edge. There were the marks of her mokasin tracks, so familiar that he knew the shape of each stitch on the soles. The tracks led into the stream.

He held up a hand toward Bear Talker and Rabbit Stick, their heads shadowed and outlined by the torches that they held above them. But before Young Hunter could speak, the terrible roar that filled the air took away all memory or thought of speech.

Bear Talker's hand jerked and he let go of his torch. Rabbit Stick caught it before it touched the ground. He held it out toward Bear Talker, but the deep-seeing man's eyes were turned away from it. He was staring upstream, his shoulders slouched, his head forward, toward the source of the great sound that had shaken them like nearby thunder. It was the same direction in which the mokasin tracks of Willow Woman had pointed.

"Fear Bear," Bear Talker growled. He lifted his head and sniffed the air like a dog. His growl deepened. "Not alone. The one who watches darkness is there."

Bear Talker bent low and began to run along the stream bank. In the soft light cast by the moon it seemed as if the deep-seeing man had become a bear himself. It seemed as if he went not on two legs, but on four legs like a bear. He moved more swiftly than Young Hunter had ever seen him move before. Agwedjiman and Danowa ran with him. Their torches in their hands, he and Rabbit Stick followed close behind. The sound had come from the direction of the waterfall, echoing from between the stone walls that rose up around the place where the stream was deepest. It was not far.

When it came, it did not come quickly. The wall of water slowly darkened and then it pushed through. It looked like a pale-skinned animal, crawling in. It was thickly furred and the size of a wolverine. It came crawling in slowly, a finger's width at a time, not walking but acting as if it was being pushed from behind.

Then Willow Woman saw it for what it was. It was not an animal. It was part of an animal. It was the huge paw of a bear, reaching in, feeling for her. The claws were twice the length of her fingers. Further in the giant paw was thrust, closer and closer, blindly reaching. She pushed herself back and to the side, but she could see that the cave was not deep enough. She lifted the spear up, ready to thrust, choosing the spot where she could pierce the thick skin, drive down between bone. But she had forgotten Pabesis.

The big young dog snarled once and then dove, mouth open wide to bite deeply on the back of that paw. The paw leaped up and swung toward him, but Pabesis had jumped to the side and bitten again, shaking his head as he did to drive his teeth in deeper, to tear flesh and skin.

Willow Woman stabbed down, aiming at the place where the paw joined the huge forearm, at the wrist place. There were tendons there that could be cut, weakening or crippling the giant animal. The tip of her spear blade ground into bone and then bounced off as the bear's paw came twisting toward her, striking against her arm and spinning her so that her head hit the cave wall. The lights of the night sky seemed to burst into the cave, spinning about her face and behind her eyes. The roar of the waterfall seemed to fill her ears from within. She did not drop the spear, but she could not strike again. Her arms would not do as she told them. She leaned against the wall, feeling how cold and smooth it was against her side. The bear's paw came clawing down.

It did not strike her. A solid strong body knocked her aside as Pabesis hurled himself forward. His growls filled the cave and he slashed at the bear's paw with his long teeth. Then, seeing an opening, his teeth sank deeply in the kind of grip that even death cannot break. The bear roared with pain and began to pull its paw back out of the cave, dragging the dog with it. The big young dog's toenails scraped against the stone of the cave floor, as it fought, still growling.

"Obey me," Willow Woman said to her arms, trying to force them to move. "Wake up!"

Her arms did not heed her command. They hung at her side like limp skins stuffed with wet earth. Willow Woman blinked her eyes. The lights that circled and filled her sight began to dim. She blinked again and her normal vision began to return. She looked down at her hands. Her hands opened as she told them to. The spear fell to the floor of the cave. Willow Woman reached her hands out, reached out as quickly as she could, even though it seemed the air was made of sand and she had to dig her way through it.

Her fingertips brushed the end of the dog's tail as he vanished through the wall of water. She was too late. Pabesis was gone.

51 ▣ THE FALLS

Someone was coming. His mind and his eyes had been focused entirely upon the bear thrashing about in the middle of the falls like a huge fly caught in a shimmering web woven out of water. He had not felt the others—there were several of them—coming until they were close. He had been expecting the young one, the one whose bravery would make him foolish, but more than one was coming. He had never fought more than one. And it was taking far too long to pull the woman out of her hiding place.

Watches Darkness felt the uncertainty creeping into his thoughts the way that the cold creeps into a wigwam in the moon of long nights. He could not do this alone. He looked across the deep water.

Leave that one there, he thought. Come back to me.

The One Who Walks Like a Man stayed as he was, reaching his paw into the cave, the water streaming over his broad head. He did not turn toward Watches Darkness. He would no longer obey him. The great bear's thoughts were directed toward one goal. To catch and kill the puny two-legged ones. First the one in the cave. Tear it with his teeth and jaws, eat the flesh and crush the bones between his teeth. Then, when the tall one was unaware, he would do the same to the one who tormented him. He would do the same to Watches Darkness.

Watches Darkness turned away from the waterfall. He began to walk quickly downstream. The ones who were coming up the stream bank were on the opposite side. A plan formed itself in his mind. He would call them before they turned the bend and saw the waterfall. He had listened carefully when he watched from his hiding place near the village. He had learned the voice of the one who was trapped in the cave. He would use her voice, lure with her voice.

Come and help me, that is what he would scream with her voice. The great bear has me in its jaws and is dragging me away. Come and save me.

They would hear it and they would hurry to rescue her. They would not doubt that it was her screaming for help. They would cross the stream and follow him into the night. Watches Darkness was certain. He was good at this, at taking the voices of others.

Watches Darkness smiled, showing his thin yellow teeth. Only two winters before he had done just that. He had used the voice of a deep-seer's own granddaughter to draw the old man away from his village and into a narrow gorge. Then he had dropped a heavy stone on him. Yes, yes! He would do the same now. He would lead them away from this place, lead them into darkness. He would confuse and separate them from each other. Then, one by one, he would take them. He shook with excitement at the thought. Yes! Yes!

"Wabiskoksis!" The scornful voice that spoke to him stopped him in his tracks. Who called him a white worm?

"You are a worm," the voice said again. It was the voice of an old woman, a voice made thin and sharp with anger. Then the one who spoke stepped from behind the birch tree that stood four arm lengths away from him. Her white hair shone in the light from the Night Traveler, though her face could not be seen. It could not be his grandmother, yet her voice held the same familiar contempt. She lifted her hands. Was she holding two sticks to beat him?

"Coward," she said. "Run away." Then she hurled one of the sticks at him.

As it came at him, Watches Darkness saw that it was not a stick. It was a spear. He twisted his body and the spear grazed his shoulder, tearing the flesh but not piercing into muscle and bone. He continued turning, stumbled, caught himself and began to run. It was not his grandmother, he saw that now. She was too tall, too strong to be the old woman's ghost. But her words had frozen his blood and he could hear her behind him now, calling his name and chanting a song. The song called on him to stop and face her. It was a deep-seer's song. Watches Darkness knew that if he stopped, the terrible old woman might destroy him. Summoning all of his strength, he leaped into the darkness.

Medicine Plant stopped. She bent and picked up the spear. There was blood on its flint point, but she knew that it had not struck deeply. The one with the twisted spirit had escaped, but she had driven him away before he could harm those she loved. However, this night of danger was not yet over. She turned back toward the canyon of the waterfall and what she heard there now. Men shouting, dogs barking, a great angry animal roaring.

Young Hunter knew that he would never forget what he saw that night. The canyon of the waterfall was a beautiful place, a place where he had played so many times as a child that he thought of it in the way he thought of the wigwam of his grandparents. It was a place of safety and peace. The glittering falls made bright by the Night Traveler's light, the smooth canyon walls, the deep water still warm on its surface from the long day—all of these were beautiful and familiar things. Yet in the midst of it was the twisting of powerful anger and the flow of blood. In the midst of it, like a huge log that has been swept into the stream by a flood and then lodged itself against the flow, was a giant bear as pale as a ghost. It stood in the middle of the waterfall, its hind legs on the ledge that was there just an arm's length under the surface. It was coughing as an angry bear coughs, clawing at the falls, reaching into the cave hidden by the swift-flowing falling water. Its back turned toward them, water cascading around its ears, it did not sense them as they stood there on the bank, a spear's cast away.

Young Hunter knew what the bear was trying to drag out of that cave. Willow Woman was in there. He started to enter the water. Bear Talker stopped him. The deep-seeing man shouldered him aside and waded in hip-deep. He was breathing in and out, growling, gathering his breath.

Rabbit Stick put his hand on Young Hunter's shoulder. "Wait," he said. "Wait."

It seemed as if they had stood there forever. Yet a part of Young Hunter knew that no more than the space of a few heartbeats had passed. Suddenly the great bear roared. It leaned back, swinging its paw out of the cave inside the waterfall like a man throwing a rabbit stick. Something large flew from that paw, its legs twisting, and went tumbling end over end. For the space of a single breath Young Hunter thought what he saw was Willow Woman. But as the one who was hurled through the air struck the water with a great splash, Young Hunter saw that it was a dog. A big dog. Pabesis.

The pale giant bear held its wounded paw up to its mouth and licked it. Its eye, glowing like a flame, saw the shape of the dog floating limply in the water, being carried downstream by the current from the waterfall. That was the one who had hurt it. The One Who Walks Like a Man dropped to all fours, ready to slip into the water after it. Its mouth open, it was ready to tear the one who had hurt it apart, to crush its body.

Bear Talker shouted. It was the kind of shout that could be made only by one who has listened to all those things that speak with power. The cry of the long-tail cat in the night and the howl of the wolf were in that shout. The cold breath of the bear wind from the winterland and the moist strength of the moose wind that comes from the direction of the dawn and the water that has no end was in that shout. The rumble of the earth when it speaks from its heart and moves the mountains was in that shout. Such a shout, the scream of a deep-seer, was said to be able to shake the leaves from the trees and split the rocks. Such a shout could kill.

Inside the cave behind the waterfall, Willow Woman put her hands over her ears as the deep-seer's shout reverberated through the rock walls. Rabbit Stick fell to his knees, his head ringing. The two dogs fell to their sides. On the other side of the stream, Medicine Plant drew a deep breath and leaned on the spear that she had thrust deep into the earth. She knew how much strength such a shout took, how much it drew from the one who made it.

Young Hunter stumbled forward, shaken and drawn by that shout, until he was standing next to Bear Talker in the water. He could not see the great bear. It seemed to have vanished. He grabbed Bear Talker under his arms just as he began to fall forward into the water. The deep-seeing man was limp, his body heavy in Young Hunter's arms as he dragged him back toward the shore. Rabbit Stick was beside him now, helping him. And someone else was there. Medicine Plant.

"We will take him," she said. "Save your friend." She pointed with her lips toward the limp body of the dog floating further down the stream as she helped Rabbit Stick lean Bear Talker against the base of a balsam fir.

Young Hunter looked at Bear Talker. The light of the fishing torches that Rabbit Stick had thrust into the ground around the base of the balsam shone on his face. His face was calm. Almost too calm, as calm as the face of one whose breath has left him. Young Hunter stood up and ran quickly down the stream. The dog's body had floated down to the area where it became shallow. Young Hunter waded in and embraced the big young dog's limp body, lifting him up from the water and carrying him as if he was still a puppy, despite his great weight. Danowa and Agwedjiman were waiting for them as they reached the shore. As Young Hunter placed him on the moss, the two dogs leaped back and forth over the body of their companion, nudging at him with their paws as Young Hunter knelt beside him. Pabesis kicked his feet, coughed, and then whimpered. His eyes opened, clear, and filled with life again. He lifted his head to lick Young Hunter's face.

Young Hunter stood and ran back to the place where Bear Talker lay. Medicine Plant was bending over him, saying something. Was she bidding him farewell? Were his feet already on the sky road? Then Young Hunter heard her words.

"So," she said, "you have not decided to leave us. Have you not troubled me enough?" Then she poked Bear Talker in the chest with her fingers.

Bear Talker growled. It was a weak growl, but it made Young Hunter's heart leap inside his chest. Then he felt his head spin again. So much was happening at once. Where had the great pale bear gone? Most important of all, where was Willow Woman? Was she hurt?

"The great one is still alive. But it will not harm you," Bear Talker whispered. "Go, look for your wife."

Young Hunter turned and dove into the water like an otter. With a few quick, long strokes he reached the ledge at the base of the falls. He pulled himself up onto it. He paused and then ducked his head through the wall of water and into the mouth of the cave. Something hard touched his cheek. He put up his hand and felt the flint point at the end of the spear that had been held out toward him

"My wife," he said. "I am here."

"My husband," Willow Woman answered, "you are very late."

Then she dropped the spear and wrapped her arms around him.

Young Hunter sat just outside the door of their wigwam. Within, the three women who were most important in his life were talking in soft voices. Had he tried to overhear what they were saying, he felt certain that a good part of their discussion would have been about him. So he did not try to listen to their voices. He let them be part of the web of songs that surrounded him this new day. The wind that was stirred by the warmth of the dawn light, the small black-capped singers who fluttered down to land close by, the little many-legged ones, the morning voices of the people of their village all wove together into a song that said thank you for the great gift of life.

Young Hunter listened and then began to sing softly, blending the wind and the small birds, the people's words and the breathless voices of the many-legged ones into a healing song. He opened his hands and held them toward the Day Traveler's face. He felt his hands grow warmer as he sang. Then, still singing, he placed his hands on the wounded shoulder of Pabesis, who lay curled up next to him. Pabesis turned his head to lick Young Hunter's hand. The big young dog would be lame for a while, perhaps until the moon of blueberries, but he would be well and strong once more.

The small son of Bear Talker and Medicine Plant was playing in front of them. His face quite serious, Looking Backward—as Sweetgrass Woman always called him—was making a small wigwam of bent sticks and pieces of bark. It looked suspiciously like the little lodge that Bear Talker used when he spoke to the ones who live deep beneath the earth. Young Hunter had grown used to such things from the boy. He was one of those born with ancient eyes. At times

Young Hunter felt as if he was in the presence of an elder when he was supposedly watching over this little one. But there were also times when Looking Backward would beg to be lifted up or tickled or wrestle with him just as any other little boy of his age would do. Looking Backward loved to play with Young Hunter. Still, he called Young Hunter by the name of Cousin rather than Uncle, as Raccoon did. And some days Looking Backward would look at himself, at his small arms and hands, at his short legs and little feet, as if impatient that he was not yet at least as large as Young Hunter. On those days, he seemed more than ready to go traveling in search of adventure.

There are many things, little one with many names, Young Hunter thought, that you and I will do together in the seasons to come.

As Willow Woman and Medicine Plant and Sweetgrass Woman continued to talk, Young Hunter thought back on the night that had just passed. Despite all the many winters that he had known Bear Talker—all of the winters of Young Hunter's life—despite the fact that the deep-seeing man had been his teacher for many seasons, Bear Talker was still capable of surprising him. When he saw the giant bear, heard its roar like the storm wind, felt its anger so powerful that it touched them like the heat from a forest fire, Young Hunter had been certain that either it must die or they would be killed by it. He had gripped his spear tightly and readied himself for a great battle.

But Bear Talker had seen it in another way. Powerful as it was, dangerous as it was, wounded and twisted by anger as it was, that bear was still the deep-seeing man's relative. Bear Talker's powerful shout, a sound so great that it seemed no human throat should have been capable of making it, had stunned the great bear. It had struck the huge beast, not with killing force, but the way a mother bear's paw strikes a cub who has placed itself in peril.

When they came together from behind the waterfall, Young Hunter and Willow Woman had been amazed at what they saw. There, on the opposite bank of the stream, the light from the night sky shone down on Bear Talker standing close to the great pale bear.

The bear sat as a man sits, its back against the trunk of two birch trees that grew close together at the edge of the stream. Its back feet were stuck out in front of it. It looked, Young Hunter realized, like his grandfather looked when he sat leaning against their wigwam. The bear was moaning softly, moaning as a small animal does when it is hurt. It held its wounded paw out toward the deep-seeing man, whose head barely reached the big animal's chest as it sat there.

Bear Talker was singing a crooning song. That same song, Young Hunter thought, is the one that mother bears sing to their little ones. Bear Talker cupped water in his hands and washed the hurts of his relative. He cleansed the blood from its injured eye and placed mud from the streambank on the wound on its cheek. And all the time he continued his healing song. Healing more than just the wounds on its body.

"I will stay with my relative," Bear Talker had growled to Young Hunter.

And Bear Talker had done so, not returning to the village until the dawn. He explained to Young Hunter how he had made a shelter of evergreen boughs near the waterfall and the great bear slept there now, safe from the heat of the sun. He had given it medicine made from plants that he gathered, plants that were strong medicine for both humans and bears. He would go back again with food that night. There had been no evil in the spirit of the great bear. Only hunger and anger, fear and pain. The deep-seeing one with the twisted mind had used it as another man might use a spear. Without that one who saw darkness guiding it, the great bear would not trouble human people. When the great bear was well again, Bear Talker would send it away. He would send it walking long toward the winter land and away from the places where human people often walked. He would caution it to hide from human people and it would listen to him. He would send it songs to keep its mind strong, even though he would be far away. He and the great bear were relatives and they would never forget each other. It would be that way.

Young Hunter heard all this and understood. He had seen before how one gesture of kindness, one moment of true caring, could be stronger than many seasons of anger. Hunger and pain, anger and fear twisted one's mind like a leaf caught in a whirlwind. But kindness given freely from the heart could straighten those thoughts and restore the balance that had been lost in that endless twisting fall. He remembered the human face of the man who had been his enemy, the one once called Weasel Tail. Young Hunter had saved his life and washed his face clean in a distant river. He had given that man a new name, Holds-the-Stone. And Holds-the-Stone had grasped that name with all of his heart. He had given his life staying true to that new name and that new faith in his own spirit.

Young Hunter shook his head. It would not be that way with the one who had hunted them. That one, the one named Watches Darkness, was so strong that his pain and anger had deafened the ears and blinded the eyes of the good spirit that lives in every person. Whatever good spirit remained within him was trapped in ice—like the heart of a cannibal giant. Watches Darkness would hear no songs of healing. Young Hunter knew that Medicine Plant was right the night before when she spoke of that one.

"Now," she said to Young Hunter, "we must hunt him."

53 回 PLANS

Red Hawk was the first to come down from the great tree. Although he had not liked the idea, Blue Hawk stayed in the high branches keeping watch. He would have preferred to climb down at the same time as his brother, but he had finally agreed. It was strange to be separated from him, even by so small a distance as from the top of the tree to the earth beneath it. Yet he felt, he had to admit this to himself, a certain warmth within himself as he sat there with Morning Sky also keeping watch from behind him, her hands resting on his shoulders.

"My sister's idea is a good one," Morning Sky said, kneading his shoulders with her hands as she spoke. "She knows that you have the best vision of all of us. You are the one who first saw the great snake last night. Surely you will see anything before it comes close enough to be dangerous."

Blue Hawk said nothing. It did not seem right to talk without his brother close by. But he no longer felt so ill at ease. He was beginning to understand why it was that Young Hunter and Willow Woman would sometimes go off alone when the two brothers traveled with them. He tried not to think of that. It was important to keep his eyes focused on the place where the great snake had been stretched across the trail, that place where the water of the river was very deep as it entered the lake. In the bright light of the early morning he could see deep into the river and deep into the lake that the river emptied into.

He saw schools of fish moving in the lake, a family of otters swimming and playing along the opposite shore of the river. Those creatures of the water would not be moving about so freely if the great snake was close. Now Red Hawk and Evening Sky came into sight. They look as small as little many-legged creatures. Red Hawk looked up and waved. Blue Hawk made a circle with his hand in front of himself and then swung his open hand out from his chest. All was clear. Red Hawk turned and continued with Evening Sky along the trail.

Blue Hawk kept watching them, but he was no longer worried. He knew what his brother and Evening Sky would tell them.

"The great snake has gone back into the lake," Morning Sky said softly into his ear. It was as if she was reading his thoughts.

It was true, Blue Hawk thought. The trail was clear. They could continue on toward the Village Among the Red Stones as soon as Red Hawk and Evening Sky returned. A day's journey and they would be there. They would start on their way as soon as his brother and Evening Star returned. But he hoped that they would not return too quickly.

Bear Talker drew the shape on the back of a fresh-stripped piece of elm bark with a sharp stick. He took care as he did so, making certain that he indicated the landmarks along the shore in great detail. Young Hunter found himself wondering how Bear Talker could see the lake so clearly, see its whole shape at once. Even looking at it from the top of a very tall tree only part of the lake could be seen at any one viewing. Only a high flying bird—or one who could some- how look down from that same height—could see all of the Waters Between as one.

Young Hunter looked over at the basswood bag, which lay empty next to the big hollow log. He had placed the bag there so that Black Friend could come out and hunt. He was certain that there would be food of some kind for the long black snake to find in such a place. If not there, then among the piled stones of the hillside behind that log. Black Friend had slipped out of the bag without a backward look and disappeared into the log. He would be back. Young Hunter was sure of that, but it felt strange to see the bag empty and stranger still to not feel the weight of the bag against his chest or slung across his back.

"Your long friend will be back," Bear Talker growled. "He knows that he must help you. Here, look here. Do not sleep. This is the place where you will find the boat. And this bay here, above the Red Stone Village, between the two tall hills, this is where you must call the greatest one who swims. Here you must face him." Bear Talker tapped the bark with his stick, indicating the first hill at the very edge of the pictured lake. "And here, this is where we will bring that great one. To this place so that we may speak with him. We will be waiting."

Young Hunter wiped away the sweat that had formed on his forehead. Bear Talker sat within the shade of the big fallen log, but Young Hunter sat in front of him in the full heat of midday. He understood and did not understand this plan. But Medicine Plant and Bear Talker both seemed certain of what it was that he must do. Not one, but both of them had seen in their dreams what it was that should be done. And though he did not understand his own dreams as well as those two who were his teachers, Young Hunter had also seen the same thing, though less clearly. The voice of his own dream had told him that it was now time for him to return to the Waters Between. It had begun there. There it would end. There he would see Padoskoks, the bigger-than-big snake, once again.

Their plan would be carried out in two nights, when the face of the Night Traveler was full and the night waters of Petonbowk were almost as bright as day. Medicine Plant had already gone ahead, taking with her a dozen other women, including Willow Woman and Sweetgrass Woman. All of them were needed to carry the rope that those women had helped his grandmother and his wife make during the days he was gone. Bear Talker and Young Hunter would catch up with them and they would make camp together before their paths diverged.

"Here," Bear Talker slapped the ground with his palm and growled. "Look here. Here you will meet friends. They will help you."

Young Hunter nodded. The shape that Bear Talker had drawn was clear in his own mind. He would not need to carry the piece of bark with him. He could see that picture of the Waters Between easily, held in his inside sight. Young Hunter looked at Bear Talker.

"Ask your question," Bear Talker said.

"The deep-seer who hunted us, that one with the twisted spirit who watches from the darkness," Young Hunter said. "Medicine Plant said that we must hunt him. How can we do so if we all go now to the Waters Between?"

"We will hunt him by going away from him," Bear Talker said. "That one is clever. He is good at hiding and will not come out in the light of day. If we look for him, we will not find him. So we must run away from him. Then he will follow us." Bear Talker laughed. "That is not right. He will not follow us. He will follow you. He thinks that you are young and brave enough to be foolish. He does not know how many friends you will have to help you. He thinks that he will be able to come upon you without being seen. But you will see him." Bear Talker reached out and thumped Young Hunter hard on his chest. "If all goes as we have planned, all of those who meet there will see him, too."

As he soared along the shore of the lake, his quick eyes took in everything below. The great one that moved beneath the water was not far away. He saw a deep shadow in the depths of the lake, but it was moving away from the place that his flight would take him. It was moving toward the bay between the two high hills. That was good.

The weight of the fish that he carried was too much for him to fly much further, but he was close now. The red stones reflecting the bright light of midmorning were just ahead of him now. Talk Talk lowered one of his wings and began to circle down toward the place where he was needed.

The wolves had not hunted today. They were full and resting and even though he had danced in front of them and spoken to them, they had simply ignored him or rolled onto their backs inviting him to play. So he had gone hunting on his own. They might not be hungry, but he needed to find food. It had been good when he saw the otter. It was far up on shore with the big fish it had just caught. Talk Talk had swooped down behind it and squawked in the otter's ear, taking it by surprise. The otter had fled toward the water, its body humping up and down as it ran. When it turned and saw the big crow that was picking up its catch, the otter squealed and chattered in protest. But it was too late. Talk Talk had already taken flight with the fat fish dangling from his strong black beak.

Talk Talk fluttered his wings to slow his flight. He landed next to the large red stones that seemed to have recently fallen together downslope in a small avalanche from the base of the hill near an elm tree still blackened by a recent strike of lightning. He hopped over to a small opening near the base of that pile of stones and dropped the fish there. Then he waited, watching that opening. He could see the glint of water from the small pool made in a depression in the stones just inside that cave. But nothing moved. Nothing happened. Talk Talk tapped four times on the stone with his beak.

"Nidoba, nidoba, nidoba, nidoba," Talk Talk squawked. "Friend, friend, friend, friend."

Slowly, a hand appeared from further back in the crevice. It worked its way out from within the pile of stones. That hand opened and closed like the mouth of a little one whose feathers have not yet grown dark, a little one begging for food. Talk Talk watched that hand find the fat fish, grasp it, and drag it back inside.

"Wliwini, nidoba," said a weak human voice from beneath the piled red stones.

None of his tricks had worked. He had tried each of them the night before. He called to them, imitating voices that he knew they would recognize. They did not even look up. He made sounds of distress, the cries that a child in danger calling for help, the pleading voice of an old woman who has fallen. They stayed together close to the lean-to they made. Even their dogs did not move.

Then he made sounds to frighten them. The roaring of a great bear, the whistle of a storm wind, terrible cries from creatures that have no names except in dreams. They did not act afraid. Worse yet, the two old women with gray hair began to laugh. The darkness was his time. But he had been able to do nothing that night. Watches Darkness was deeply disturbed.

They had not been unaware of him. He had been able to sense that. Though he kept his thoughts silent, he felt the minds of the deep-seeing ones in that small camp seeking his mind. It was not easy to hide from them, but he did so. He had learned much in his years of hunting. Although they did not have the power to seek out his mind, the others in that camp were armed. They held spears or kept them leaning close by. Once, and only once, Watches Darkness tried to sneak up to the camp, his sharp stone knife held in his teeth. But before he was close enough, the young man with the broad shoulders who was sitting with his back to the fire, the one who was a deep-seer but still unsure of his vision, that one suddenly stood. There was a throwing dart already hafted in his atlatl. He swept his arm forward and the spear came whipping through the night, straight at the place where Watches Darkness had made a sound so small that even an owl should not have heard it. The spear barely missed him, burying itself deeply in the base of the hollow stump he ducked behind. Watches Darkness crawled backward on his belly like a worm away from their camp. He did not try again to creep close to them.

As he lay in his hiding place, away from the hateful light in the sky, Watches Darkness tried to think of how he might attack them, how he might destroy them. If he still had the One Who Walks Like a Man with him, he could have used him to attack them. To come at them from two directions at once. But he could no longer do that. The great pale bear was gone, destroyed, he was certain, by these enemies. Now he was alone.

Watches Darkness thought of one plan after another. But only one seemed right. There were too many of them, too close together. He could not hunt them all. He would take them one by one. Yes, yes! He would wait until they were separated. When the darkness came again, he would watch and wait, watch and wait. He would hold back. He would let them think he had given up. He knew where they were headed. They were going to the big lake. He would go there ahead of them. There was a place he had seen where he could hide near the base of the tall hill near the bay. That was the place where they would go. There he would watch and wait. Yes, yes! And the first one he would hunt, the one whose heart he would eat that night, was that broad-shouldered young man who dared to throw the spear at him.

The two dogs beside him, Young Hunter was the first to reach the top of the pass between the mountains. Putting his hands above his eyes to shield them from the brilliant light of midday, he breathed in the wind that came to him from the land where the Day Walker rests. The wide floodplain spread below him toward the Waters Between. For a heartbeat he felt the way an eagle feels just before it takes flight. He narrowed his eyes and let his arms spread out, fingers open like an eagle's long wing feathers reaching to grasp the wind. For the first time, he knew that all he had to do was let go of his hold on his body and he would be able to lift up and float over the land.

Agwedjiman nudged at his hip. Young Hunter dropped his hands back down. "Do not worry, my friend," he said in a soft voice. "I will not travel without you."

Young Hunter placed his hand on the head of Agwedjiman. He shifted the bag with Black Friend in it to his other shoulder. It would have been good to just stand there through the rest of that day. But he knew that it could not be that way. He could already hear someone coming up the slope, rocks rolling under his feet as he climbed, his breath loud. Bear Talker.

The deep-seeing man said nothing when he reached them, but he was not silent. His breath rattled and wheezed and he was coughing from the effort. He sat down so heavily that the stone he put his weight upon rocked free from its resting place. Had Young Hunter not grabbed his arm, Bear Talker would have rolled down into the valley below with the round stone, which bounced and cracked against the rock ledges until it disappeared among the small twisted trees.

Bear Talker grabbed hold of one of the small trees, which was rooted deeply into the creviced ledge, and pulled himself up off his belly into a sitting position. No one said anything. At last the deep-seeing man regained his breath.

"There are better ways to travel," he growled.

Willow Woman leaned on her spear, holding it with both hands. It was the first time she and the other women had stopped since that day's dawn, and the bruises from her battle in the cave two nights be-fore had made her feel stiff and sore when she woke that morning. Now, though, her whole body felt as if it was glowing and she could not keep from smiling, even though she knew that there were still dangerous things to do.

She hooked her elbow around her spear and placed her hand on her stomach, which was growing rounder now every day. Even though they had not stopped, she had been eating as they walked and ran. Her own pouch of dried meat pounded together with maple sugar and dried berries was empty. Both Sweetgrass Woman and Medicine Plant had kept giving food to her as they traveled, not only food they had brought with them, but berries they gathered, certain roots and other parts of special plants, things that were meant to be eaten by a woman whose yet unborn child needs those things. The little one within her moved, a ripple against her palm. Willow Woman nodded.

"You have helped your mother," she whispered. "You have been giving me strength as we travel together."

She turned and looked back. By now, she thought, Bear Talker and Young Hunter will be in the high pass. When he arrives here, everything will be ready for him. She looked over at the women still coming down the slope toward the bay. The twelve of them were linked together by the long rope, each of them carrying over her shoulder a coil longer than a long spear cast. Sweetgrass Woman and

Medicine Plant, her little son on her hip, were walking beside the women, ready to take their place should one of them tire.

Willow Woman turned her eyes back toward the water. From the ridge where she stood she could look down into the clear water all the way to its bottom where green plants danced. It was her job to keep watch, to be certain that the biggest one who swam was not too close. Both Medicine Plant and Bear Talker had been certain that the great swimmer would not come to this place until the Night Traveler was walking high in the skyland. But they had still thought it wise for the person with the sharpest eyes to act as a lookout when the women did their work close to the water.

Willow Woman looked around. This was a place where she had not come before. It was usually the people of the Red Stone Village who fished here, and it was just at this time when they would normally be arriving here. But today there were no wigwams being set up near the water, no fires burning near racks erected on which to dry fish, no children playing or dogs barking. Like the other villages that would make their camps near the Waters Between during the season of long days, the Red Stone people had been warned to stay away from Petonbowk.

Willow Woman imagined what it would be like to camp here by this bay with a hill on either side. It was a good place. She imagined herself sitting on the large flat stone that jutted out into the water there, enjoying the warmth of the sun or the cool breeze that would come off the water as the Day Traveler went to his rest. A very large beech tree grew close to that flat stone, one of its heavy branches stretching out over it. That tree was so old that it had a great hollow in it close to the ground. The place inside the old beech tree, Willow Woman thought, must be large enough to hold a whole family of bears. She wondered what it looked like inside. Perhaps she could walk over and look into it. As she thought of that, a cold feeling came over her. She felt as if something with many legs had landed on the nape of her neck.

Willow Woman turned her eyes back to the water. She would not look into that hollow tree. It would not be pleasant inside that tree.

Perhaps something had crawled into there and died and it would be bad smelling. It was her duty to stay here and keep watch. That was what she would do.

As they came across a little meadow, he saw them. He had not moved from the place where he stood, leaning back among a group of birch trees. The dogs were behind and slightly below him, on their bellies in the swale so that they could not be seen, while Bear Talker was still making his slow way up the winding trail toward this small elevation before they came to the place where the red stones were piled on the beach.

At first, Young Hunter's eyes had been on the sky, for the one that flew low overhead with a fish in its black beak looked very familiar. But just as he had been about to call out, he had seen the flash of light that came from further across the meadow. Light reflecting from something. He kept silent and watched. Soon a young woman appeared. The light was reflecting from the necklace of bright stones hung around her neck. There was something familiar about her, even though Young Hunter knew he had never seen her before. Then the one she had turned to speak to came into sight. Young Hunter opened his mouth. Could it be? Ah-ahhh!

As they came closer he had no doubt. It was Red Hawk. But that young woman who walked with him, that long-haired young woman who was just as tall and strong-looking as Young Hunter's friend, who was she? And where was Blue Hawk? Young Hunter stared intently at the woman who was familiar and yet new to him. She walked with the same long, confident stride as Red Hawk. Her features, though softer, were almost the same.

Young Hunter turned and looked down at his dogs. "My friends," he said softly, "something strange has happened. I think one of my human friends has transformed himself into a woman."

He looked back and his mouth opened wider still. Another couple had appeared around the corner in the trail that intersected with the trail Young Hunter had been following. It was yet another tall young woman and with her was Blue Hawk. Twins. And twins who looked so much like the two brothers that they might have been carved from one piece of wood.

The first couple was now less than a spear's cast away. Young Hunter stepped out from the shelter of the trees and raised a hand in greeting. As quick as a mink, the young woman who walked with Red Hawk crouched and raised the spear that she held in one hand. Red Hawk placed his hand on her arm.

""Evening Sky," he said, "wait . . ."

From behind him, the voice of Blue Hawk came, ". . . this is our great friend, Young Hunter."

"Unh-hunh," said the two young women, speaking as one. "We see."

Even their voices were similar to those of the twin brothers. More musical, perhaps, but as alike as the calls of mated birds. Young Hunter tried to find words, but he could not. He could stand it no longer. He sat down on the ground and began to laugh.

"What . . ."Red Hawk said, his voice indignant.

". . . is so funny?" Blue Hawk continued.

"Tell us!" Evening Sky and Morning Sky demanded as one.

Young Hunter shook his head and just kept laughing and laughing.

There had been much for them to talk about. Young Hunter had told them of the great bear and the deep-seeing man whose mind was so twisted that he hunted other human beings. He had told him of the plan to be carried out that night and how they could help. Red Hawk and Blue Hawk, in turn, told him of what they had seen and done since they had parted many days before. They told of Gray Otter and the village in the swamps. Then Evening Sky and Morning Sky told of how Red Hawk and Blue Hawk had played ball against the young men of their village—and won that game because the young men did not *really* try their best. But as the sisters said that, Young Hunter heard the pride in their voices at how well his friends had done.

Together, the four of them told of their travels from Gray Otter's village. They told of seeing the biggest one who swims from the top of the big tree. They told of visiting the Village of Red Stone and warning its people—who were already afraid and uncertain because of things some of them had seen and because their deep-seer had left them and never returned. Sometimes, all four of them had spoken the same words at once.

Young Hunter had finally stopped laughing, but he found it hard to keep a smile from his face as he listened to his two friends —and their two friends—tell of their adventures and he noticed how often Red Hawk and Evening Sky looked at each other. But the eyes of Blue Hawk and Morning Sky met each other just as often. Perhaps, Young Hunter found himself thinking, after they marry, they will have twins and their children will have twins. Soon the Dawn Land will be filled with nothing but twins, all speaking together at once.

Young Hunter turned his face aside and coughed hard, trying to control the laughter that he felt coming over him again. It was hard to do, but he managed to compose himself and keep listening to his friends without their noticing his amusement. But perhaps that part of it was not that hard to do—conceal his amusement from them. At moments it seemed as if the twins could see and hear nothing but those young women who seemed as like them as two spearpoints chipped from the same slab of flint.

It happened like that when he was telling them about Carries Snakes and introducing Black Friend to them. The long black snake had come out of its bag and bobbed its head in front of each of the four young people, who looked at it with great respect. They had held out their hands to stroke its head as Young Hunter told them to do and Black Friend had rubbed its head against their hands like a dog being caressed. But Red Hawk's hand had brushed against Evening Sky's hand as they petted Black Friend and the two of them had looked at each other. Even after Black Friend had slipped back into his bag—with, Young Hunter was certain, a glint of amusement in his bright black eyes—Red Hawk and Evening Sky had stood there, their hands still touching.

A great tree might fall behind us, Young Hunter thought, and they would just keep on looking at each other.

He smiled. He already felt as if he had known the two young women for a long time. They would be good friends and he imagined the delight with which Willow Woman would greet them. As he thought of his wife and felt the warmth that such thoughts always gave him, he understood what their new friends meant to Red Hawk and Blue Hawk. His heart was glad for his friends. Everyone else had known for a long time how lonely the two young men actually were, despite their companionship with each other, how shy they had been around the young women of their age.

Once before, his grandmother Sweetgrass Woman told him, in the time of her childhood there had been two old men like Red

Hawk and Blue Hawk. Their names were Green Frog and Other Green Frog. They were twins who looked exactly alike without even tattoos to tell them apart. They lived together. They had never married. Both of them had taken a deep liking to the same young woman, but she had not wanted to have two husbands. At last she told the two men which of them she wanted to marry. Green Frog always said that she wanted Other Green Frog. Other Green Frog always said that it was the other way around. So neither one of them married her. They were kind men, good hunters and generous, like uncles to everybody in the village. But they always seemed a little sad, for they had no children or grandchildren of their own and their lodge of birchbark was set apart from the others in their village. One day, when they were very old, they walked together into the forest on a winter hunt. They never returned. Some feared that it would be that way with Red Hawk and Blue Hawk. Now, it seemed, their lives would finally be complete.

And from the way Evening Sky and Morning Sky teased the twins, it was clear that their fondness for them was based on a surprisingly deep understanding of who the young men truly were. It was a teasing that was never hurtful but always filled with insight. It was fun to listen to that teasing and though they protested, Red Hawk and Blue Hawk were delighted by the attention their new friends—partners, Young Hunter thought, partners—gave them. It lightened his heart.

Young Hunter saw, too, with that other part of himself who sometimes stepped aside and watched from a small distance, why it was that he was so ready to laugh about his friends' good luck. Such laughter eased his uncertainty. He was deeply worried because he knew that the night would be filled with great risk. Bear Talker and Medicine Plant had told him clearly what he should do, but there was no certainty that he would succeed in doing it. When a spear is thrown at you, you might have the ability to avoid being struck by that spear. But if your foot slips as you start to dodge, that spear may still strike you. It was that way with seeing how one might behave to face something that is unseen, something that only your deeper eyes can see approaching. Seeing is one thing. Doing well what must be done is another.

Day Traveler had long since passed the center of this trail through the sky land. They were not far now from the two hills and the bay. They were only a look away. They had been walking for some time along the ridge above the lake, looking down at its shore. The red stones of this part of the lake's edge glowed with the light from the Day Traveler like coals from a giant's fire. They could see far up the lake to the seven islands where the Thunder brothers lived. The lake was calm, but the five young people all knew what swam somewhere in the deep waters. Despite their interest in each other, Red Hawk and Evening Sky, Blue Hawk and Morning Sky had grown noticeably more vigilant as they came closer to the lake. They remembered what they had seen from the safety of that great tree's highest branches. That was a relief to Young Hunter, for he had feared that he and the dogs might have to keep watch over the two sets of twins.

A flutter of wings came from overhead and a large black bird landed on a hemlock branch next to Young Hunter. The branch bounced up and down from the bird's weight as it cocked its head to look at him with one intelligent eye.

"Talk Talk," Young Hunter said.

"Friend, friend, friend, friend," the big crow squawked. "Come help, come help, come help, come help." He bounced again on the branch and flapped up into the air, circling overhead and looking down at them. "Come," he called, "come help." Then he flew down toward the red stones near the edge of the Waters Between.

As they went down the slope, Young Hunter saw the blackened trunk of a dead tree that had been struck by lightning and the place where stones and earth had slid down to make a large mound of stones piled almost like a big wigwam. Talk Talk landed in front of that pile of red stones and looked back at Young Hunter.

"Friend Here, friend here, friend here, friend here," the big crow squawked.

Young Hunter looked toward the nearby waters of the big lake. They were two spearcasts away from him. Far enough for some safety, he thought. He went down on one knee and looked into the crevice that was the width of a man's arm.

"I would ask you to come into my lodge," said a weak voice from within. "But my door is too small."

Walks-in-a-Hole filled his hands again with the dried meat that Morning Sky shook out of her pouch.

"Food," he said, "that is raw is good." He smiled up at Talk Talk, who was perched on Young Hunter's shoulder. "Raw deer meat is good. Raw fish is good. But I am very happy to eat *this* food." He held up a piece of the dried meat, which had been pounded together with maple sugar. Talk Talk leaned forward and carefully took it from the hands of the short deep-seeing man. Walks-in-a-Hole was no longer as round as he had been some days before and his legs were weak from disuse. But he was otherwise unharmed.

"Bedagi saved me first," he said. "The biggest one that swims was about to swallow me when Bedagi threw his spear of lightning. It struck so close that I could see and hear nothing. When I woke up, I was here inside this stone lodge. Bedagi had thrown me into the place of safety."

Walks-in-a-Hole looked out toward the seven islands in the Waters Between.

"Bedagiak, Thunder Brothers, hear me. I am Walks-in-a-Hole, foolish little Walks-in-a-Hole, and I thank you. I give you great thanks."

Walks-in-a-Hole held out his hands toward Evening Sky, who poured the contents of her pouch—sweet dried berries—into the small hands of the little deep-seeing man.

"Umpphhh, these are also very good. So, Bedagi saved me. His lightning spear threw down those heavy stones over the door. Those stones that you moved aside to bring me out. So the biggest one who swims could not reach in to get me. But I could not get out."

Walks-in-a-Hole smiled up at Talk Talk.

"Then my new friend came to me. Great thanks to you, my black-winged friend. He fed me all those days. There was water inside my little lodge and room enough to turn around and a hole in the back that I could use to take care of my other needs. So I was able to eat and drink, wait and dream."

Talk Talk ruffled up his feathers and preened them with his beak. "Good big crow, good big crow," he said.

Walks-in-a-Hole looked around at the five faces. "You look as you looked in my dream, my young friends."

He stopped and stared up at Young Hunter. Then Walks-in-a-Hole slapped him on the chest with such surprising power that Young Hunter took a step backward. Black Friend lifted his head out of the woven bag and peered at Walks-in-a-Hole, nodded as if to say he agreed, and then slid back out of sight.

Young Hunter looked at Walks-in-a-Hole. He had heard of the little round deep-seer, a man who was little but possessed a great strength and an even greater sense of humor. It was no wonder that the people of the Red Stone Village loved and respected him.

"Only you are a little shorter than I thought." Walks-in-a-Hole laughed. "Come my friends, let us start walking. Now that you have helped me, it is my turn to help you."

The Night Traveler glowed like a grandmother's face leaning down to look at her little ones. From his hiding place, Watches Darkness looked out but did not look up at the sky. The one he hunted had been close, but there had been too many nearby. Now there were not only the two old ones who were deep-seers, but another one had joined them. Watches Darkness had sensed them and kept his thoughts as small as those of the little many-legged one who gnaws the rotted wood inside a hollow tree. They had passed him by without noticing him. Now the one he was after was out on the waters of the lake, the deep waters. Watches Darkness shuddered at the thought of the cold deep water. But he would return, return close by the place where Watches Darkness waited. And when he was close enough—Watches Darkness ran his finger along the sharp edge of the dark spear blade—then, then, then. Yes, yes!

The dugout was well made and had been hollowed out so thin that it floated higher in the water and moved more lightly than any other boat that Young Hunter had ever used before. It was the dugout made by Walks-in-a-Hole himself, a boat designed to move across the water like froth blown by the wind. It was big enough for four people, but Young Hunter rowed alone. Aside from the bag that rested in front of him in the prow of the dugout, he was alone. Yet he knew he was not alone. He felt the eyes that watched him. Dark eyes watched him from the shore. Deep eyes watched him from beneath the glittering ripples of the old lake's surface.

As he paddled slowly, he brought the song up deep from within himself. Walks-in-a-Hole had been certain the song would work. It had worked all too well for him.

> Biggest one who swims
> Come to me now
> Biggest one who swims
> Come take what I give to you.

Young Hunter felt the tug of the line that was fastened tightly to the stern of the dugout. He reached back and placed his hand on the taut line. When he stopped paddling it made the dugout drift backward. He was as far out as he could go. Resting his paddle, he looked around. In the night it seemed as if he was very far from the shore. In the light of the Day Traveler, he would not seem so far away from the safety of the dry land. He could see the rounded tops of the hills to either side of the bay. He stopped singing to listen. At first he could hear nothing, then he thought he heard a small splash further out. He began to sing again.

> Biggest one who swims
> Come to me now
> Biggest one who swims
> Come take what I give to you

Once again he heard that splash and then the sound of something breathing. It breathed hard, like a moose breathes when it lifts its head above the water after grazing on the water plants which grow on the bottom. Then one can also hear the water dripping from the moose's great horns. Plip. Plip. Plip. Plip.

The hair rose on the back of Young Hunter's neck. He was hearing the sound of water dripping. It came not from in front of him, but from the side. Very slowly, moving only his eyes, Young Hunter looked to the side . . . and then began to shift his eyes up as he saw what at first looked like the glistening trunk of a beech tree rising up

from the water. Higher he looked, higher still. Then his eyes met the
great eyes that looked down into his. Those calm eyes held within
them twin reflections of Night Traveler's face. Those eyes were as
deep as the depths of Petonbowk. Padoskoks. Bigger-than-big snake.
Biggest one who swims.

Young Hunter turned his head as slowly as he had turned his eyes,
looking up at the one who was so close that it could come down on
him with one easy strike. He found that he was not afraid. He knew
that he was in great danger, yet there was no fear in his heart and he
breathed easily as he looked. The great one's head, from which water
still dripped in slow drops, was as large as a bear, not the head of a
bear, but the whole animal. Its mouth, though closed, could easily
swallow a bear in one gulp. Two small horns, like the first horns of a
buck deer, grew up from the top of the giant snake's head. The patterns of scales about its eyes and around its broad forehead looked familiar to Young Hunter. Then he realized where he had seen them
before and why the great one did not seem strange to him in any way.
Padoskoks looked like the great boulder on which Carries Snakes
once sat. The tattoos upon the face of the tall old deep-seeing man
had been in the same patterns as the scales on the face of the giant
snake.

"Old One," Young Hunter said, "I know you."

The great being lifted up higher from the water. Now Young
Hunter saw the two legs below where the neck of the great being
widened into a broad chest. Was it lifting up higher to strike at him
or to turn away and dive back into the depths? Young Hunter never
knew, for it was then that Black Friend lifted up from the woven
basswood bag and hissed so loudly that the giant one who looked
down turned its eyes toward the eyes of the long black snake.

Padoskoks slid down in the water, closer to the boat. Only its head
was out of the water and it was only four arm lengths away. Its eyes
were now almost level with those of the black snake that still stood in
the prow of the dugout. Young Hunter could not hear what Black
Friend said, if indeed he spoke with whatever words it is that a snake
knows. But he felt as if a message was being given, a message that

Carries Snakes had longed to give to this great one. The death of the tall old deep-seer had not prevented that message from being given. Young Hunter took a deep breath. It was time for him to continue singing.

> Biggest one who swims
> Come to me now
> Biggest one who swims
> Come take what I give to you

He did not turn around or turn his eyes away, but he pulled four times on the line that was attached to the boat. Those hidden up on the shore felt that signal and they pulled. The dugout began moving back toward the shore, back past the rock that thrust out into the water at the base of the great hollow beech tree. And as the boat moved, the biggest one who swims followed.

As the others pulled, three people walked down to stand with their feet in the water. They looked out across the glittering bay toward the small dark shape that was Young Hunter's dugout. They had seen something large beside that boat, but then it was gone. Yet, though they could not see it, they could feel it. They knew that the biggest one who swims was there.

Bear Talker and Medicine Plant stood with Walks-in-a-Hole between them. Walks-in-a-Hole shook his rattle and Bear Talker began to beat his drum. Then, following the deep powerful rhythms of rattle and drum, they sang. It was a song without words that could be easily said. They could best be sung, for they held as many meanings within them as the soft throb of the heartbeat of the endless rush of wind and waves. They sang to the great one who was there in the waters of Petonbowk. They asked, in their song, that he show mercy to the small human people and not hunt them. They, in turn, would always respect him and not trouble him. They would not call him or speak his name, but they would always remember that the deepest waters belonged to him.

As she sang, Medicine Plant felt a tug at the hem of her doeskin dress. She did not stop singing, but she looked down. Her son, Old Eyes, stood there, one hand holding her skirt. He had slipped away from Sweetgrass Woman, who stood a little ways from them, her arms still held out. But Old Eyes did not look back at her. He did not look up at his mother, but out toward the Waters Between. His mouth open, he was singing with them, making the song even stronger.

* * *

The boat was almost close enough. Watches Darkness lay on his stomach on top of the flat rock that jutted out into the lake. He saw nothing but the one whose back was turned to him and the boat drifting toward the rock. It was good that his back was turned. It would be easy that way. He only had to decide where to strike him. Should he strike to kill or just to wound him so that he could look into the eyes of Watches Darkness before dying? Yes, yes, that would be better, much better. Watches Darkness would have to jump into the boat, but it would not be into the water, not into the deep water. It would be fine. It was almost close enough. Now!

Watches Darkness leaped into the boat, landing on his feet just behind the one whose heart he would soon eat. His spear raised, he found his footing and was about to strike. Then he froze, unable to move as a huge head lifted up from the water in front of the boat. Higher and higher, lifting above him. Then in a way that was both slow and swift at the same time, that long neck came toward him, snaking around the broad-shouldered young man. The mouth opened and grasped him and Watches Darkness was lifted up. Watches Darkness could not move. He could not speak. The great being held him as firmly in its jaws as a fisher holds a squirrel. His spear fell from his hand, its point sticking in the bottom of the boat, its shaft sticking up like an arm pointing to the sky.

Young Hunter had felt the eyes of the one whose mind was twisted long before that one leaped into the boat. He had been ready to turn and dodge the spear of Watches Darkness. Then he saw something in the eyes of the great being whose head was still level with the prow of the dugout. He had trusted what he saw and had not moved. Now, as Watches Darkness was lifted up into the air, Young Hunter still did not move. There was nothing he could do now but watch.

Padoskoks lifted its head high above the water and it turned away from shore. It began to swim away, so swiftly that it seemed to be growing smaller. Then, still holding Watches Darkness in its mouth,

it dove down, down toward the deepest water. Ripples spread across
the bright surface and then the lake became calm, so calm that the
reflections of the branches of the trees that hung out over the lake did
not move. Padoskoks was gone and so, too, was Watches Darkness.
Black Friend slid back down into the basswood bag.

"There is a world under this world," Bear Talker growled.

Young Hunter turned around. His dugout was almost at the
shore. Those who had pulled it in were waiting there. Willow
Woman, Sweetgrass Woman, Red Hawk, Blue Hawk, Evening Sky,
and Morning Sky looked toward him, waiting for him. But Bear
Talker had not waited. He had walked into the water to grasp the
stern of the boat. Medicine Plant stood beside him, her hands holding the other side of the dugout. Walks-in-a-Hole, his hand now
holding the hand of Old Eyes, stood behind them on the shore.

The words his two teachers were speaking were for Young Hunter
alone.

"In that world, everything is the opposite of this one," Medicine
Plant said. "When it is cold here, there it is warm. We sometimes see
that other world reflected in Petonbowk. It is there under the deepest
waters. The one whose name we will not speak now, that greatest one
who swims, has taken the one who watched the darkness down
there. Maybe, in those deepest waters, his spirit will learn to see the
light."

It had been a long walk. He had walked alone, accompanied by only the one he carried with him. His dogs had not come with him, for the place he was going was not a place to bring them. He had not run, for he knew that his journey should be taken slowly and with care. He would run when he returned. There was much that he would be returning to. Not only would he be going back to his wife and their soon-to-be-born child, to his teachers, and to the welcome peace of the double lodge he and Willow Woman shared with his grandparents, he would also be going back to a wedding. All of them would travel to the village of Evening Sky and Morning Sky. In that village, those two young strong women would join their lives with their new husbands, Red Hawk and Blue Hawk. They would build two lodges in that village—one to either side of Gray Otter's lodge.

Young Hunter looked forward to those dawns ahead, but he had felt some sorrow as he made his long walk. There would be a parting when that walk was done.

When he saw the lake, he took a deep breath. It was a place that seemed aglow. A light seemed to come out of the lake itself and he knew that the springs that fed it were strong medicine. The small island in the center of the lake appeared to ripple, almost as if it was a part of that world under this world, which could be glimpsed in reflection.

Young Hunter sat down on a stone by the side of the lake. A birch tree with one low broken branch hung over that stone. He ran his hands along the smooth bark, marked with the powerful wings of thunder beings. He cupped some of its waters in his hand and washed his face.

"Wliwini," he said. "Thank you."

Then he took the basswood bag from his shoulder and hung it over the broken branch.

"Black Friend," he said, "I have done as Carries Snakes asked me to do. I have brought you home."

The black snake poked its head out of the bag, looked at Young Hunter and then pulled back in again. It was so much like a child playing the game of I-see-you-but-you-do-not-see-me! that it made him chuckle. He shook his head.

"I see you, my friend," he said, patting the bag with his hand. "It is all right. I know that you want to return to your own people.

Black Friend came sliding out of the bag and reared up. He placed his head on Young Hunter's shoulder and slid about his neck, making himself into a circle as he had that day when he linked together the tall old deep-seeing man who was his best friend and this young broad-shouldered man whose heart was good for all the people. Black Friend hung there for a few heartbeats before he slid down onto the ground and into the water. His dark body seemed to become a part of the water as he swam with graceful sinuous motions like waves turned into flesh. Further and further out he went, straight toward the small island as Young Hunter watched, one hand raised in farewell. The bright water rippled once, as if lightning had flashed from deep under the surface. The long black snake was gone.

Young Hunter sat for a long time, looking at the quiet waters between them.

The Waters Between is the third in a trilogy of novels that take place in ancient times in the area now known as Vermont. My Abenaki ancestors,
however, have always seen that land called Vermont as "Ndakinna," a place
unbounded by maps drawn on paper. Although my own home was and remains the little Adirondack foothills town of Greenfield Center, New York
(in the same house where my grandparents raised me), the Green Mountains can be seen from our hill. Vermont is no more than a look away. Some
of my earliest memories are of the times my grandfather, Jesse Bowman,
would load my grandmother and me into the old blue Plymouth and drive
us over to Vermont to "see the deer over to home," as he put it. Our family
remains deeply connected to Vermont, through our involvement with the
Abenaki nation and through decades of doing poetry and storytelling in the
schools. It has even drawn my younger son, Jesse Bowman Bruchac, to follow his namesake great-grandfather "back home" to live in St. Albans. A
part of my vision and my imagination were shaped by and will always be
connected to Vermont, a place I keep returning to, a place my family's heart
never left behind.